M000251268

Becoming Madam Secretary

Becoming Madam Secretary

Stephanie Dray

BERKLEY
New York

BERKLEY
An imprint of Penguin Random House LLC
penguinrandomhouse.com

Copyright © 2024 by Stephanie Dray
Penguin Random House supports copyright. Copyright fuels creativity,
encourages diverse voices, promotes free speech, and creates a vibrant culture.
Thank you for buying an authorized edition of this book and for complying
with copyright laws by not reproducing, scanning, or distributing any part
of it in any form without permission. You are supporting writers and allowing
Penguin Random House to continue to publish books for every reader.

BERKLEY and the BERKLEY & B colophon are
registered trademarks of Penguin Random House LLC.

Library of Congress Cataloging-in-Publication Data

Names: Dray, Stephanie, author.
Title: Becoming Madam Secretary / Stephanie Dray.
Description: New York: Berkley, 2024.
Identifiers: LCCN 2023028913 (print) | LCCN 2023028914 (ebook) |
ISBN 9780593437056 (hardcover) | ISBN 9780593437063 (ebook)
Subjects: LCSH: Perkins, Frances, 1880–1965—Fiction. | Women—Political
activity—United States—Fiction. | Women cabinet officers—United
States—Fiction. | LCGFT: Biographical fiction. | Historical fiction. | Novels.
Classification: LCC PS3604.R39 B43 2024 (print) |
LCC PS3604.R39 (ebook) | DDC 813/.6—dc23/eng/20230629
LC record available at https://lccn.loc.gov/2023028913
LC ebook record available at https://lccn.loc.gov/2023028914

Printed in the United States of America
1st Printing

Book design by Ashley Tucker

This book is a work of fiction. The author's use of names of historical or real figures,
places, or events is not intended to change the entirely fictional character of the work.
Some words, phrases, and conversations are loosely based on documented historical
incidents and correspondence, and are used fictitiously. In all other respects, any
resemblance to persons living or dead is entirely coincidental.

To Butters—the cat who proved that sometimes the best people have whiskers. Like FDR, he was a sunny-tempered optimist. His courageous paw prints are hidden in every chapter, and though this was the last book we worked on together, his indomitable spirit lives beyond the final page.

HISTORICAL NOTE

Dear Reader,

Frances Perkins left behind her public papers, an influential biography of the president in whose cabinet she served, and an extensive oral history of her long, storied professional life. What she did not leave behind was a record of her personal life, which I pieced together from surviving correspondence, accounts of those who knew her, and other circumstantial clues.

To preserve her voice, I adopted her own language whenever possible. Perkins spoke respectfully in the polite vernacular of her time, but some terms she used are inappropriate today, so I've used those only when necessary. And for purposes of clarity, I generally refer to locations and government programs by the name that is most familiar to us today. Other choices and changes are explained in the Author's Note at the end of the book, which I hope you will enjoy after reading this story.

Prologue

New York City
February 1933

T HE AMERICAN EXPERIMENT WAS OVER, THEY said. The republic, ruined. Democracy, done. It lay in broken, cracked-open pieces like the drought-afflicted farmland in the heart of the country. Trampled under the sole-worn shoes of thirteen million jobless in the breadlines. Crushed under the weight of the economic depression and buried under collapsing banks.

Some cried out for a dictator like that swaggering bully Mussolini in Italy. But my countrymen elected Franklin Delano Roosevelt—a man who couldn't walk, much less swagger.

They summoned him to save America, and in turn, he summoned me . . .

Now, braced against the cold in a fur-trimmed coat and my trademark tricorn hat, I warily approached the snowy stoop of Roosevelt's house on Sixty-Fifth Street, both comforted and unnerved by the sight of pistol-brandishing Secret Service agents positioned at the entrance.

"You've been cleared to go in, Miss Perkins," one said, motioning me inside.

Having arrived early for my eight o'clock appointment with the president-elect, I hesitated, my nervous breath puffing into the icy night air. I'd walked through the door of Roosevelt's home many times before, but this time I feared it might open upon a new world. Somehow, I squared my shoulders and found the courage to cross the threshold, nearly tripping over a filthy rolled-up rug in the hall.

I didn't expect the place to be tidy—the Roosevelts liked things to have that pleasantly *lived-in* appearance—but I was greeted by an absolute mess. Snow-dusted hats and dripping overcoats hung on all the chairs. Folders of papers spilled out atop every table. Boots, umbrellas, and overflowing ashtrays cluttered every corner. This was the telltale detritus of a successful political campaign, and since the election, Roosevelt's house had become a camp for reporters, politicians, and his protective detail.

I was grateful for the latter, given the assassination attempt just days before in Miami. In the face of death, the president-elect hadn't flinched, and the bullet had somehow missed him. Tragically, a mayor in his entourage was now fighting for his life with a very poor prognosis for survival—a chilling reminder that public service was dangerous in every possible way.

Personally, I couldn't count all the times that I'd campaigned beside FDR, in the line of fire, literally and figuratively. I used to enjoy the thrill of it, but those days were over. I was now almost fifty-three years old with heavy responsibilities at home. I couldn't risk it anymore, and that's precisely what I intended to tell him.

"Miss Perkins, he'll be with you shortly," said Roosevelt's ever-present secretary. "How are you this evening?"

"Just fine," I lied. We were on friendly terms, but I was too nervous for small talk. So I quietly took my seat outside his study, clutching my sensible black handbag, reminded of just how much time I'd spent waiting in this little room these past few years, working with the cagey, polio-stricken man who had just been elected to lead our country.

By the time the door opened, my knuckles had gone white around the handle of my pocketbook. Then FDR pushed his wheelchair out from behind his desk to greet me, an ivory cigarette holder angled at a debonair tilt from the corner of his smile. "Good evening, Frances."

In spite of my apprehensions, I felt an instant rush of pleasure to see him. Churchill once said that meeting Franklin Roosevelt was like opening your first bottle of champagne, and that knowing him was like drinking it.

That wasn't far off the mark.

Others said FDR's true political gift was his larger-than-life presence, his ability to wheel into a room and command the attention of every person standing. Still others said it was his charming wit, his buoyant sense of optimism, or the resolute sound of his boarding school lockjaw as it crackled over the radio during troubled times.

I say his true political gift was that he liked people . . . and he made them feel liked. He certainly knew how to make *me* feel as if I were his closest friend and confidant. And for one or two moments of his life, that might have even been true . . .

Now he flashed me his most winning grin. "Have a seat, Frances. Have a seat."

I lowered into the chair in front of his desk, and he got straight to the point. "Well, I guess you know what I want you for. I think you'd be a good secretary of labor, and I'd like you to come along with me to Washington."

It was exactly what I feared, and my mouth went dry. "I—I am, of course, honored and terribly surprised—"

"Oh, come on now, Frances, don't say *surprised*. You're no fool. What did you think I wanted to see you for?"

"I hoped you might want to say goodbye."

He hooted, merriment shining in those otherwise inscrutable blue-gray eyes. "Oh, don't be clever. You've been reading the papers, haven't you? I floated your name."

"Yes, but if I've learned anything, it's that one shouldn't believe the papers." We had another light laugh, and I finally admitted, "Well, you're right. The newspapers did force me to give offhand consideration to the idea of serving in your cabinet. Which is why I've come to convince you that you must not offer me the position."

Twenty minutes later, we were still arguing about it, and he finally snapped. "*Frances*, surely you're sensible of the fact that I'm trying to make you the first woman in the country's history to ever serve in a presidential cabinet—so what is it that you need to hear?"

We had already debated the public reasons I shouldn't serve.

People won't like a woman in the cabinet—

I don't care.

Unions want one of their own—

I care even less about that.

The Department of Labor is broken, filled with corrupt thugs—

You're just the one to fix it.

Of course I felt a flash of pride that he should have such faith in me, but I couldn't let pride sway me. I couldn't possibly take this job and leave my fragile family now when they needed me most. This appointment would subject my husband and child to untold humiliations and danger.

It might even break us completely.

Roosevelt knew about my precarious personal situation, but just as I opened my mouth to plead mercy in light of the magnitude of the sacrifice he was asking of me, Roosevelt shifted in his wheelchair, and I heard the scrape of his metal leg brace on wood.

That stilled my tongue as I tried to push away the knowledge that FDR was a man who sometimes dragged himself up the stairs using nothing but the power of his forearms. A man who put himself through punishing campaigns, risking all the humiliations of his personal frailties. A man whose own family—complicated as it was—would be thrust into the unforgiving world of presidential politics during the worst catastrophe in our nation's history.

Considering that, how, precisely, was I to plead that private disasters should exempt *me*?

Fortunately, I had a better, more articulable reason to decline. And on this, I intended to be perfectly firm. I had taken the past twenty-four hours to sketch out very unreasonable terms, and now I pressed the list into his hands.

"What's this?" Roosevelt asked.

"This is what I'd want to do—what I would *try* to do—if I were your secretary of labor. You shouldn't even consider me for the job unless you want me to do these things for the country."

He folded the page. "That's fine."

"You didn't read it," I scolded.

Only slightly abashed, he cleared his throat, pushing his spectacles up the bridge of his nose. Reading aloud, he mumbled, "*Get rid of child labor, limit working hours, create a minimum wage . . .*"

"All perfectly permissible for a state government," I pointed out. "But of unknown constitutionality at the federal level. I'm not sure some of these things will get past the courts."

With a wink, he said, "Let's find out."

As always, his hubris only fueled my own. "Keep reading. You've promised people a New Deal. If you mean to make good on that promise, we'll need unemployment relief and public works to get people back on the job."

"Well, I agree." His lips curled with amusement. "Of course, I don't know how you'll do it, but you're the economist. You'll have to invent the way to do these things and not expect too much help from me."

He was a shameless political animal, happy to let his underlings execute plans, take credit for them if they succeeded, or pretend he had nothing to do with them if they flopped. "So, you're proposing to let me run wild?"

He returned his gaze to the list. "Well, except for this social insurance plan. Now, *that* is crazy, Frances. Just crazy!"

At last, I thought. *We've come to an impasse.*

Didn't he know that the aged, disabled, blind, deaf, widowed, and orphaned were among the worst victims of this deep economic depression? The elderly especially, having lost their life savings, were cast aside like so much refuse, many of them freezing to death this winter in ramshackle shelters the people were calling Hoovervilles.

I didn't see the point in allowing myself to be enlisted to serve unless he was willing to let me help them. Almost everything else on my list was just patchwork to hold together the crumbling foundations of our country. Unless he was willing to make lasting and *revolutionary* repairs, from the bricks to the mortar, I didn't want the job.

I meant to tell him that. I'd even practiced my refusal in the shower that morning. But now I found myself asking, "Can't I at least get a committee going and make some studies to convince you?"

"Well, you can study it," he allowed, handing back my list. "Is that all right?"

He meant to ask if I'd now agree to be his secretary of labor. And I swallowed, glancing down at the list of things he *had* agreed to—an expansive agenda that had never been tried before in the United States. "Are you *sure* you want these things done? Because you won't want me for secretary of labor if you don't. I'd be an embarrassment to you, because when I start on a thing, I round up cohorts. I whip up public demand. You wouldn't want *me* if you didn't want that."

It was a promise and a threat, so I expected a scowl. But FDR only grinned his spider's grin, knowing he'd caught me in his web.

He'd let me twirl myself up in my own hopes and ambitions. Now that I was stuck, he leaned in for the kill. "Frances, I said I'll back you. And I consider that you have a *duty* to say yes."

Oh, that was low, for he knew patriotic duty was bred into my very bones.

Panicked, I tugged at the only loose thread. "You've got to give me a day to consider. My husband is—well—I cannot let him read in the paper that I've been appointed to something without consulting him."

"That's okay," FDR said, pretending at patience. "But you've got to go out and see him tomorrow, then let me know tomorrow night. The inauguration is little more than a week away."

A week away. Could I really upend my life so quickly? My mind was a fog of indecision, but Roosevelt's secretary broke in to remind us both that he had other appointments, so I thanked him, said farewell, and started for the door.

That's when Roosevelt called after me. "Frances, I suppose you'll nag me about this social insurance plan of yours forever . . ."

He said it lightly. Teasing. But I knew him too well to think it was only that. *He wants me to be his conscience*, I thought. It was, after all, a role I had played for years. But I wasn't FDR's priest or wife or mistress; and though he was the North Star by which everyone around him guided their course, my life didn't begin or end with Franklin Delano Roosevelt.

PART I

Chapter One

★ ★ ★

New York City
Summer 1909

M Y FAMILY BUILT THIS COUNTRY WITH muddy hands and a spark of madness. On my grandfather's side, we were brickmakers, shoveling clay out of pits along the Damariscotta River in Maine. On my grandmother's side, we were rebels, writing pamphlets against taxation without representation and taking up muskets against the redcoats.

Alas, just like some bricks break in the kiln, so, too, did some of my kin crack in the fire of the American Revolution. Madness runs in families, they say. Courage too. And I wasn't entirely sure which of those inheritable traits was most responsible for my decision as a young woman to move to New York City, where I'd be living in Hell's Kitchen, one of the most notoriously violent tenement slums.

The neighborhood—insofar as one could call it that—was so much under the thumb of gang leaders that policemen couldn't enter without fear of being pelted with stones by lookouts who then escaped down the drainpipes into a maze of rat-infested back alleys.

Yet here *I* was—with my lace parasol in one hand, traveling valise in the other—jostling past shabby storefronts with soot-stained awnings, noisy saloons selling three-cent whiskey, and a rogue's gallery of ruffians brandishing penknives, looking to separate me from my valuables.

Fortunately, I hadn't any valuables on my person unless one were to count my fashionably ornamented hat and the few pennies I hid in my lace-up boot.

No doubt, I made a curious sight in the tenements, where strangers stood out. I also had an unfortunate moon face with dimples that gave the impression of doe-eyed youth even though I was twenty-nine years of age. And because my previous employment at the Philadelphia Research and Protective Association hadn't afforded a salary generous enough to pay for more than the occasional banana sandwich, I was thin enough to sometimes be confused with a teen-aged girl.

But I wasn't a lost little naïf. I had learned from hard-won experience that in places such as this—where the foul odors from the docks mixed with the smell of horse dung and unwashed humanity in the streets—it was best to stride with a purposeful gait, keeping fixed upon my face an expression that said, *Ill-intended gentlemen will very much regret trifling with me.*

I'm convinced that stride and expression are all that account for how I arrived unmolested at the tall wrought iron stairway entrance of the brick settlement house on West Forty-Sixth Street.

Amid surrounding squalor, the settlement house was surprisingly well kept, its front stoop graced with pots of scarlet chrysanthemums. This place was meant to be a sanctuary for the poor where they could bathe, seek nursing care, or attend classes. And no sooner had I approached that sanctuary than did the curious, cold, and calculating looks I got on the street melt into something a little more civilized.

When I rang the bell, the supervisor was waiting for me. She introduced herself as Miss Mathews and ushered me inside while scrutinizing my fashionably narrow skirt with a whiff of disdain.

The dour-faced Miss Mathews was herself dressed all in black like social agitators of the older generation, adhering to the S-shaped corset. And I noticed her manner was just as constrained when she sniffed and said, very stiffly, "Welcome to Hartley House, Miss Perkins."

"Thank you," I chirped cheerfully, taking in the lovely foyer, then following her into a little office, where I sat at the edge of my seat, gloves folded in my lap, the heels of my lace-up boots lined up primly as she reviewed my file. "I'm very much looking forward to my time here at Hartley House."

"You come to us highly recommended," she said, as if she couldn't possibly imagine why. "And I see you have a fine education. Mount Holyoke College. Wharton Business School. And now New York's School of Philanthropy. Our understanding is that you're here on a fellowship from the Russell Sage Foundation."

"Yes," I said. "I've been given the opportunity to pursue a master's degree in economics, and I intend to make a survey of child malnutrition for my thesis."

Her eyes narrowed over the top of the file. "Not many women go to college, much less graduate school. Unless they are quite wealthy. Are you an heiress to a family fortune, Miss Perkins?"

In what I hoped was a crisply professional manner, I replied, "No, but my father owns a stationery store on Main Street in Worcester, Massachusetts, if you've ever been. Perkins & Butler Paper and Twine."

"I haven't had the pleasure."

Of course she hadn't. And it wouldn't have mattered if she had. Because my family's brickmaking business dwindled before I was born, forcing my father to stray from the family homestead in Maine in pursuit of middle-class mercantile respectability. But we still had the land and the legends . . .

Before my beloved grandmother passed, she regaled me with tales of our family's fiery revolutionaries and abolitionists. James Otis. Mercy Otis Warren. Oliver Otis Howard. With such relations, was it any wonder I had set forth like a vagabond patriot bent on improving the world?

Clearing my throat, I explained, "I sought an education because it's a point of family pride to have learned women. You see, we are kin to the first female scholar in Revolutionary America."

Did I imagine that Miss Mathews was at least a little impressed? "Well, then, it seems you are a young lady of good breeding, but young ladies of good breeding pass through every day. They come for idle curiosity about the poor. Or to rebel against their parents. Or to mark time before marriage, after which we never see them again."

"I assure you that I am not marking time before marriage."

Miss Mathews closed my file. "Why not? Aren't your parents expecting you to marry respectably?"

My parents had, in fact, expected me to do just that, and despite my protestations, my mother continually pressed suitors upon me. But I chuckled and said, "Fortunately, my younger sister has fulfilled family expectations by becoming betrothed to a dentist in Worcester, so I consider myself off the hook and decidedly on the shelf."

Miss Mathews now seemed vaguely amused. "Aren't you interested in finding love, Miss Perkins? In marrying and starting a family of your own? You seem to be a pleasant enough young woman with the sort of dimples that might attract beaus."

I decided to ignore both my own frustrated desires and the slight mockery in her tone. "I'm not as young as I look. What's more, I believe God has called me to better the lives of my countrymen. I could never allow romantic love to obliterate my responsibility to love mankind."

Her lips remained pursed but twitched at one corner as if to fight off an approving smile. "Well, I do not doubt that you're a good Christian on a mission from the Lord with a fine patriot pedigree, Miss Perkins. Or that your intellectual interest is genuine, or that your motives for social work are pure. But I suspect you will find it difficult to live and work in a neighborhood like this."

"I don't see why," I protested. "I've worked in neighborhoods like this before. You know that I volunteered at Hull House in Chicago with Jane Addams, and most recently, of course, I worked in Philadelphia's rougher neighborhoods."

"Where I understand that you fell afoul of the criminal element."

Ah, so this was the reason for my chilly reception . . .

"I like to think that *they* fell afoul of *me*," I said. After all, my job in Philadelphia had been to defend impoverished young women—especially white and black girls coming off trains from the South—against the pimps, procurers, drug dealers, and fraudulent employment agencies in the city. "As it happens, the criminal element didn't appreciate my creative efforts to combat and expose them."

"I'm told you were attacked."

"I assure you that it was a nearly comical incident in retrospect." I waved a dismissive hand as if to laugh off the incident, though I had been really frightened at the time. A notorious pimp and one of his thugs accosted me on a rainy night when I was returning to my apartment, but I ran them off with my trusty parasol. After that, I persuaded the police to put him out of business, so now I said, "All is well that ends well."

Miss Mathews crossed her arms over her bosom. "We don't approve of courting mischief here at Hartley House. We don't mix with gangsters, politicians, and other criminals in this neighborhood. And we certainly don't confront them. Ever. Is that understood?"

I felt rather like a schoolchild having my knuckles rapped with a ruler, which made me slightly indignant. After all, the Philadelphia Research and Protective Association may have been a bit of a tin-pot operation with a laughable budget, but as executive secretary, I had gotten into the habit of making my own rules.

Now I had to remind myself that I'd left all that behind. So I nodded and smiled. "Understood. I'm only here at Hartley House to study starving babies. How much mischief could I *possibly* court doing that?"

She made a sound at the back of her throat, but my answer seemed to satisfy her. "Very good, Miss Perkins."

Assuming our interview was at an end, I began to rise with the expectation I'd be shown to my quarters, where I could finally put down my bag, take off my boots, and clean off the dust of my travels. But she stopped me by asking, "One more thing. Why in God's name would a woman want to study *economics*?"

It wasn't so absurd a question, for in those days, the field of economics had been largely centered on finance, attracting business-minded fellows, aspiring tycoons, and the occasional wild-eyed Socialist. It was, in short, a field dominated by men. And at Wharton, my classmates often whispered behind my back, making no secret that I was unwelcome.

Check out Miss Dimples—
—never heard of a lady economist—
What's the world coming to?

But I had persevered, doing well enough to earn the admiration of my professor, who recommended me for a fellowship. Now here I was, contending with a social reformer who viewed my course of study as a puzzling, if not vulgar, fascination.

"Why economics?" I echoed gamely. "Because many people in America believe poverty is a moral problem having to do with sloth or some other sin we can blame on individuals. But I believe poverty in America is an economic problem that can be solved . . . and I intend to solve it."

Chapter Two

★ ★ ★

Hell's Kitchen
Summer 1909

Dear Mother,
What do you mean that you don't know what I am doing in New
York? I have written you about it in detail two or three times.
While it would be very nice to be with you all this summer, I
simply can't afford to let this opportunity go by.
Love to all,
~Fanny
PS I'll try to come to Maine for July Fourth.

I settled into my small but tidy quarters at Hartley House, with a spare bed and desk against the wall. The rest of my luggage was due to arrive—just a hatbox and small trunk with books and clothing. For now, I pulled from my traveling valise a framed picture to set by my bedside.

It wasn't a portrait of family or a sweetheart. It was a landscape of the Perkins family homestead in Maine—a saltwater farm with an old brick house graced by lilac bushes near the door. A hundred acres of the most beautiful land in the country, where my white-haired, wire-thin, wise old granny had presided as matriarch until the age of ninety-eight, pickling fiddlehead ferns with Yankee frugality, and baking pies with nary a complaint about her shaky, arthritic hands.

As a child, I spent every summer with her playing in the

meadows, swimming in the river, or helping her with the pump faucet in the summer kitchen. Those were idyllic days—my sanctuary and escape from my father's house in Worcester, where I spent my lonely adolescence buried in a book to escape my younger sister's violent tantrums and the resulting arguments between my parents over what to do about her.

Of course, my parents found other things to argue about, too, and their difficult and distant relationship certainly did not recommend the institution of marriage. Thankfully, my grandmother made me think other paths were possible for a woman. She supported my decision to leave home. And when I grew restless in my teaching job in Chicago, seeking solace in volunteering and writing, her pride and encouragement were worth far more to me than the pin money I earned selling short stories to a magazine.

Unfortunately, I hadn't been able to make my creative pen flow since her death, but I knew she'd have approved of my coming here to New York City on a fellowship for more serious study. After all, my grandmother believed I could make something of myself and do something good in the world. She even flattered me to think it might be something important . . .

If somebody opens a door of opportunity for you, it's the Lord's will, she always said. *So walk right in and do the best you can.*

Which was precisely what I meant to do.

I WAS AWAKE early at Hartley House the next morning, pinning my long brown hair up in the style of the day and fastening an apron over my dress. I felt a yearning to explore Hell's Kitchen and buy fruit for my breakfast from one of the urchins on the street corners, but Miss Mathews insisted I take some hearty porridge in the kitchens before giving me a tour of the facility.

Reciting from the annual report, she said, "Hartley House was founded on the premise that if the homes of the poor can be made more attractive and comfortable, there will be less cause for family dissension and disillusion, less seeking of the saloons by the men, less misery and wretchedness for the women, more happiness in the tenement districts, and less evil in the community. So we created a small housekeeping school where poor girls can be taught how to keep a home neat and tidy and attractive."

I did not believe, of course, that poor people lived in misery and squalor because they did not know how to keep a neat, tidy, and attractive home; I believed they could not *afford* to keep a neat and tidy home and did not have time to do so when working seventy-four hours a week without respite. This was to say nothing of my objection to the idea that a lack of women's housekeeping was the source of evil in any community.

Nevertheless, I managed to hold my tongue.

And Miss Mathews continued, "When we first started this settlement house, there were only three bathtubs in the surrounding blocks. One for every four hundred and fifty people."

"It sounds as if Hartley House was greatly needed," I said cheerfully. And I was determined to remain cheerful, because I felt as if Miss Mathews was testing me—which was all right by me, as I had always done very well on tests when I wanted to.

Miss Mathews cleared her throat. "In addition to baths, we offer a kindergarten, nursing care, a playground, a gymnasium on the roof, cooking classes for adults, and a sewing school to train young women for a profession." I thought it an impressive array of services even before she added, "We also operate a station for the Penny Provident Bank, so child factory workers have somewhere safe to deposit their funds before they're robbed by gang members."

Child factory workers.

I winced at the phrase. I'd become accustomed to the harsh realities of tenement life over the course of my work. I was no longer shocked by blind women begging on the street, or youths stealing from fruit stands. I no longer furled my nose at the scent of vomit outside the saloons, deposited by men so worn down they had fallen into the bottle. Truth be told, I no longer even blushed at the carnal acts I sometimes witnessed in alleyways.

But I had never, and *would* never, get used to watching little children march off each morning to spend their day rag picking or threading needles or toiling over dangerous machines for a few coins, cruel overseers barking at them without a care for the butchery that might result. And I was haunted by the memory of one particular girl whose blood I could still scent in my nostrils and whose screams woke me in the middle of the night . . .

Realizing that Miss Mathews was eying me suspiciously, I shook the memory away.

"Miss Perkins, you've gone pale," she said. "Are you quite all right?"

I forced a smile. "Perfectly. Please, carry on."

Miss Mathews eyed me another long moment before showing me the reading room, which boasted more than a thousand books. I traced the spine of a leather volume appreciatively. "How wonderful that neighborhood residents can come to a library and educate themselves at no cost."

Miss Mathews hastened to correct me. "Oh, we always charge a small fee. The poor only appreciate things they pay for. Which brings me to another rule, Miss Perkins. Hartley House never gives money to the poor under any circumstances. You may gift our visitors with flowers or candies occasionally, but only as an act of friendship. We're not public almoners. If financial relief is required, we refer the matter to the New York Charity Organization Society."

"I see."

Finally, she led me to the nurse's office, where mothers lined up with sick babes. The little ones barked out loud wet coughs or hiccupped with sobs. Some were so pale their lips were tinged with blue. These babies could be sick with anything. Tuberculosis, whooping cough, cholera, typhus . . . contagions had a way of racing up the stairs of crowded tenement buildings, ravaging the inhabitants. And these contagions worsened with malnutrition, which I was to study.

I'd be weighing these children, taking measurements, and asking questions about their diets. My eagerness to begin my work must've been apparent, for Miss Mathews said, "Now, I understand you'll be busy with your studies, Miss Perkins, but that will not excuse you from helping to keep Hartley House tidy. I've left a list of chores on your bed upstairs."

Never one to shirk my duties, I flashed another smile. "Splendid! I'll start straightaway."

AN HOUR LATER, I'd just finished mopping the floor by the entryway when I was approached by the loveliest woman I've ever seen in my life—a dark-haired, sloe-eyed beauty with a pale, graceful neck.

"Welcome to Hell's Kitchen," she said. And I assumed the beauty was a volunteer here at Hartley House, because she asked, "How are you settling in?"

"Quite well." I stopped to wring the mop and smile at her. "I'm terribly sorry—I didn't catch your name, though I daresay you look familiar. Have we met before?"

"No, I don't think so." She laughed, stooping to help me with the bucket. "You'd have easily remembered me. I'm Miss Harriman."

I startled. Could this be *Mary* Harriman, daughter of the railroad baron? The society pages dubbed her "the American Diana" because she was an avid sportswoman—part of the pony and polo set—with admirers ranging from American industrialists to Parisian designers and Russian princes. But she wasn't *all* parties and pearls. As a debutante, she'd founded the charitable Junior League, and recruited her gaggle of mink-wearing friends to support settlement houses, including this one.

Finally finding my voice, I said, "How nice to meet you, Miss Harriman. I am—"

"Oh, I know who you are, Miss Perkins! Your reputation precedes you. I heard all about how you stabbed a pimp with an umbrella in Philadelphia."

Her evident glee was a bit unsettling. "Well, I didn't precisely *stab* him. It was more that he skewered himself when he came chasing after me in the dark, never expecting me to stand my ground."

"A technicality. You used his own momentum against him."

"I suppose I did, like the jujitsu that Theodore Roosevelt practices."

I regretted these words the moment they left my mouth because I remembered her father had been in a very public quarrel with the former president, who believed men like E. H. Harriman were partly to blame for the terrible conditions in places like Hell's Kitchen. Yet here his daughter was, volunteering to help.

Perhaps Miss Harriman thought I was needling her, because she asked, "Did you draw blood?"

"Pardon?"

"With your umbrella. Did you draw blood?"

"Oh, it was a dark and rainy night, and I didn't think to check. But I assume I left the villain with a nasty bruise."

"Serves him right," she said, sloshing a little water on the floor as she carried the bucket to the door. "I've considered taking up some form of martial art myself. Something from the Orient. After all, I speak Japanese."

"Do you really?"

"Fluently. But I never learned jujitsu. My suffragist friends are all learning their own version to defend themselves, but I don't know what it's called."

"*Suffrajitsu*," I teased.

She laughed without breaking stride, and I followed her, my curiosity getting the better of me. "Your father doesn't mind your dedication to charity work in neighborhoods like this one?"

"He didn't approve at first," she explained. "But I drew up a balance sheet, adding up all the hours we've spent arguing, to prove to him that it simply isn't profitable to manage me when he has a railroad to run."

I laughed approvingly because it sounded like something I would do. "I find that numbers can be very persuasive . . ."

She grinned. "Yes, and I believe my father has finally come round to the idea that I am too expensive to control and that he ought to let me have my way, even in choosing my own husband."

"How enlightened," I said, only a little sarcastically. "Do you have a groom in mind?"

She opened the door to throw out the wash water. "I have my eye on Mr. Rumsey, a talented artist and dashing polo player. We share a passion for art and horses."

"Well, I wish you every—"

"Eleanor!" Mary called out to a willowy woman on the street who wore her fair auburn hair up in a tower of Gibson girl glory. "There you are. I told you we should've come together."

"Then we'd both have been late," said the tall Eleanor, approaching the stoop with a bit of apprehension. "For my mother-in-law is being rather difficult this afternoon and put all manner of obstacles in my way."

"Oh, dear. Well, I'm glad to see you escaped," Mary said. Then she turned to me. "Miss Perkins, my friend here, who I've been trying to drag out of the shadows since our days as debutantes, is Eleanor Roosevelt. She normally teaches dancing at Rivington Street, but as members of the Junior League, we both wanted to give you a personal welcome to New York's settlement house movement."

I knew the Roosevelts were one of the finest families in New York. But theirs was a sprawling family tree, so I felt safe in jesting with Eleanor, "So nice to meet you. I don't suppose you have any close relation to the former president . . ."

"He's my uncle," she said.

And I wanted to die on the spot.

For of course, in those days, the younger generation was under Theodore Roosevelt's spell, and I was not immune. Upon hearing his inauguration speech in 1905, which called on the descendants of our founders to save the country from the new horrors of industrialization, I'd prayed to God to make me an instrument in that mission.

Be careful what you wish for, my dearly departed grandmother had said. After having lived through nearly a century of tumultuous years, she viewed the world with a raised eyebrow and strong suspicion that the Lord was a trickster.

And when I think back on my life, I can't help but see a sly winking pattern to it. A web of strange coincidences, lucky decisions, and chance meetings with people whose destiny it was to shape the modern world. Eleanor Roosevelt was certainly one of those people, though I couldn't have guessed it when I met her. All I knew then was that I was grateful for new potential friends, as well as a lighthearted start to the decidedly heavyhearted work I was to undertake here in Hell's Kitchen.

Chapter Three

New York City
October 1909

T HIS BABY IS STARVING TO DEATH," I SAID, gently pressing my lips to the soft brow of the trembling infant.

I'd been holding the little cherub for the better part of an hour, trying to coax her to take a feeding bottle, to no avail. And now the nurse admitted, "One of the worst cases I've seen. And in Hell's Kitchen, that's no mean feat."

It certainly wasn't. Every morning for months now, I'd cared for skinny little children referred to us by the board of health doctor. I measured them, weighed them, made notes about their stunted growth, their visible ribs, and their bellies swollen with hunger.

What I learned in my graduate lectures was amply demonstrated here at Hartley House—that industrialization, which ought to have modernized and elevated the lot of mankind, was instead plunging people into impoverishment.

This was what I'd come to study, but I could no longer bear only to *study* such suffering. "Where is this child's mother?"

"Waiting outside," the nurse replied. "Nearly as bad off."

I saw that was the plain truth of it when I went to find the baby's mother—a shambling scarecrow of a woman who stood waiting on one of Hartley House's three wrought iron staircases with another half-starved daughter on her hip, this one about five years old.

Upon seeing me, the mother immediately burst into tears. "Please don't take my baby, miss. You may think me just an Irish slattern and a bad mum, but I give me girls every last crumb I have . . ."

"Oh, you mustn't cry," I told the mother, still cradling her infant. "I'm not in the business of snatching children. In fact, I've found some milk for your baby. I only want to help you and your girls . . ."

I brought the little family inside, found a quiet corner to sit, and, when I was sure the ever-seeing Miss Mathews wasn't looking, I gave the mother my own lunch—a sandwich and an apple.

The mother tried to give it all to her child of chewing age, but I said, "You need nourishment, too, or you'll faint dead away, and then what good will you be to your little ones?"

Still, she refused until I finally got her baby to take the bottle. Only then could she be coaxed to eat a crust. "You're good with the babe, Miss Perkins," the mother said, watching me carefully. "You must be a mum with wee ones of your own at home."

"No children of my own," I said with a pang, for it was impossible to work with infants every day without feeling a painful yearning. "I'm only going by instinct."

Nibbling the sandwich end, the mother finally confided, "Me husband died in a factory accident. Left us in terrible straits. But me lad—at least me lad kept us fed at first."

"What happened to your son?" I asked gently. "Did he run off?"

She reddened, lowering her head, and the crust of bread seemed to stick in her craw. Then she murmured something that sounded like *he's in his tomb*. And my heart ached. "Oh, you have my deepest sympathy for your loss. I—"

"He's not died." She hung her head in what I now realized was shame. "He's in *the Tombs*."

She meant he was awaiting trial in the run-down, disease-ridden city jail. "Oh, dear. Of what does he stand accused?"

"He threw a brick at a policeman who was chasing him and some other boys on the rooftops . . ."

That meant he was running with the gangs, and Miss Mathews might toss this woman out if she knew. In this neighborhood, where hardened gang members sometimes blew up shops with gunpowder, the police only managed to nab hooligans and brick-throwing boys for show.

The real law, so to speak, was *The* McManus—the Irish boss who ruled the neighborhood as part of Tammany Hall's political machine. His enemies called him the Devil's Deputy from Hell's Kitchen, and I'd been repeatedly instructed not to mix with his brass-knuckled young toughs, to stay out of politics, to steer clear of gang members and boys in trouble with the law. Our focus at Hartley House was to uplift the downtrodden mothers, drunken fathers, and exploited children. But how could we do that when it was all so interwoven?

"Me boy's a good lad at heart," said the mother. "Really, he is. Givin' up his childhood to work in a factory just to feed his mum and sisters. Doesn't have a father to teach him to be a man, and his imprisonment will be the end of us. As a woman, I can't make enough wage even if I worked sixteen hours a day, seven days a week. And who would watch me girls if I did? I don't know what to do. We'll starve for sure."

She dropped her head into her hands and began to sob, which wrenched my heart.

I thought about another mother I once knew who sobbed over her own screaming bloodied child. She had no idea what to do either and had looked to me for help I couldn't give. Well, I was older and wiser now, so I took *this* mother's hand and vowed, "Whatever I have to do, I won't let you starve."

A FEW WEEKS later, I returned from class to find my supervisor waiting for me with her hands on her hips. "Miss Perkins, I believe I was quite clear when explaining the rules of Hartley House. We do not give money to the poor."

Miss Mathews had indeed been clear about the rules. And I had been flagrant in breaking them.

I'd been supporting two starving children and their mother on what little money I had and the extra I scraped together from other volunteers. When that dwindled, I'd pawned my pocket watch. I'd even started writing again—scribbling a new short story in the hopes of selling it for a few dollars to keep the little family afloat.

In the meantime, someone must've alerted Miss Mathews to my transgressions, so now I blustered, "Well, I haven't so much *given* money to the poor as invested it."

Miss Mathews folded her arms. "At what rate of return?"

"Why, at the rate of return of living in a more compassionate world without the inconvenience of stumbling over dead babies in the streets."

I smiled brightly, trying to brazen it out, but Miss Mathews was impervious to my charms. "What do you suppose will happen when others find out what you've done? We'll have beggars on our doorstep night and day. Who will give them alms? Not you."

No, certainly not me, for my pockets were already empty. After graduation, my fellowship funds would run dry, and if I didn't find a new job, I'd be forced to return home to my disapproving parents, hat in hand. Still, I tried to defend myself. "I need only find a patron for this little family. I tried appealing to Mary Harriman, but she's out of the country just now, so I'm going to pen a note to Eleanor Roosevelt tonight in case she might be of help."

"*Absolutely* not," Miss Mathews said. "I forbid it. We cannot go about begging wealthy socialites to help each little case; it will drive charitable benefactors away from the settlement house movement. This case has already been submitted to the Charity Organization Society of New York City, and we will simply have to wait."

Unfortunately, I was never good at waiting, so the next afternoon, I set out to speed things along.

I found the mustachioed Mr. Edward T. Devine enthroned behind his desk at the Charity Organization Society, looking very much the same as when, straight out of college, I asked him for a job only to have him send me away with a pat on the head. Now he said, "Miss Perkins, how delightful to see you again after all these years!"

"I was rather hoping you wouldn't remember me," I said, a little bashful at the memory of how I'd once pestered my way into his office, all bright-eyed and bushy-tailed.

Mr. Devine tugged at his tie. "How could I forget? I recall that we had a very interesting discussion."

"Yes, we did, didn't we?" Back then, he'd asked me what I'd do, as a social worker, if I entered the premises of an indigent family and found a mother who had been beaten by a drunken father.

I said that I'd call the police at once.

He hadn't liked that answer, patiently explaining that government had no role in domestic disputes, and that it'd be better to sober the man up and get him to work.

What good will that do for his wife's black eye? I'd asked, thinking he was very wrong.

In fact, I still thought he was wrong, but that was a discussion for another day. Fearing I'd be late for class, I hastened to say, "I've stopped by to ask about the disposition of the case my supervisor instructed me to bring to your organization."

"Of course." He rifled through his desk for his notes. "About the mother of the boy in jail, and her two little girls?"

"Yes. They're in dire need of relief. We've been giving them what we can, but our pockets are empty."

I felt a sinking sensation when he grimaced. "Yes, well, I'm glad you stopped by, because I want to explain to you personally. You see, our investigators have learned unsavory things about this family."

"Surely you won't hold the boy's crimes against his innocent mother and sisters."

"The mother certainly isn't innocent. To begin with, she's been known, on occasion, to drink whiskey."

"Well, that is *shocking*," I said dryly.

Everyone in Hell's Kitchen drank whiskey because they were hungry and whiskey was cheaper than a tin of tomatoes. I thought Mr. Devine ought to be embarrassed for bringing it up, but then he added, "I don't know how to put this delicately, but I suppose after your work in Philadelphia you might've guessed the youngest child is illegitimate. So, we won't be able to provide relief."

I blinked with a flash of dismay. "If you could see the littlest child, sir. Her belly so bloated, her little ribs visible; she'll never survive without help."

"There are thousands like her, Miss Perkins."

"Maybe so, but I held this one in my arms."

"We have to choose the cases we think are most deserving."

My dismay turned to anger, and I shot up from my seat. "Tell me, what child isn't deserving? You'd condemn this baby to death because you dislike her mother's character?"

"My dear Miss Perkins, it's the tragic reality of the world that condemns them, not I. And you will exhaust yourself of this work quickly if you burn with personal outrage at every case."

I sputtered. "The idea that anyone shouldn't burn with personal outrage against child starvation is poppycock!"

With that, I grabbed my hat and my coat, abandoning all hope of attending class. As I swept out of the office, Mr. Devine called after me. "I don't know where you imagine you're going to find respectable people willing to help that sort of woman . . ."

I didn't know either, but to feed those little girls, I was willing to make a deal with the devil himself.

OUTSIDE TAMMANY HEADQUARTERS on Ninth Street, a knot of toughs spit tobacco and cracked their knuckles. Some said Tammany was turning a new leaf, and that from now on, women and children in the district would be invited for picnics, and otherwise welcome. So I decided to test that premise, approaching the door, bold as you please. "I'd like to speak to The McManus."

"Sure, lady, sure." One of the young toughs laughed. "The boss'll see you."

I pretended he meant it. "Thank you."

With that, I pushed open the door and went in, nearly blinded by the cloud of thick cigar smoke in the room. "Mr. McManus," I said, my feminine voice loud enough to silence the room.

Of course, I began to regret the brazenness of my actions when the smoky haze cleared enough to reveal hard faces of men I think I'd seen on wanted posters at the train station, like Stumpy Malarkey, Owney "the Killer" Madden, and One Lung Curran. (You didn't want to know how he lost the lung . . .)

Now all eyes pinned me in place, and there was nothing left to do but carry on. "I've come to see Mr. McManus about an important matter."

Through the crowd, Thomas J. McManus emerged, turning his big ginger head my way.

Then we took each other in, head to toe.

The so-called Devil's Deputy from Hell's Kitchen stood out from the rest of these hardened men because he was so tall an Irishman, and snappily dressed, with a twirly mustache and fiendish goatee. He must've noticed that I was a small young woman armed with nothing but a parasol, and, apparently deciding I was harmless, he indulged me. "What's the trouble, me gal?"

I thought to tell him about the desperate mother and her starving girls, but I was afraid he might just toss them a few dollars in charity, and that would be no solution. So I said, "It's actually a boy in trouble."

Someone shouted, "Aren't they all?"

And the whole room had a laugh.

Chuckling, McManus said, "Does the lad live in my district?"

When I nodded, the political boss set down his mug of beer, waving me closer. "Do *you* live in my district, Miss—"

"Perkins. Frances Perkins. And yes, I do."

I gave the address without mentioning it was a settlement house, but I think he knew, because his eyebrow lifted to a sharp point. No doubt he also knew the sort of prim, reformist ladies who lived at Hartley House, none of whom would be caught dead here talking to him. I shouldn't be talking to him either. Nevertheless, here I was. "You are my only hope, sir."

He raised the other eyebrow. And since I'd piqued his curiosity, I quickly explained about the boy throwing bricks at the policeman. I also told him about the situation in which I'd found the mother and sisters. I *wanted* to tell him that the charitable organizations wouldn't help, but that felt disloyal, so I left it at that.

Then, after what felt like an interminable silence, McManus finally grunted. "Tell me the lad's name and I'll see what I can do."

Thirty-six hours later, the boy was out of jail and back at work, supporting his family.

I didn't ask how because I didn't want to know. The McManus

probably threatened a policeman. Or he called in a favor from some lackey. Or he bribed a judge . . .

I couldn't condemn him for it, because I'd gone to McManus precisely because I thought he could get that boy out of jail, and I didn't much care how. The important thing was that the Devil's Deputy had helped me save people from starvation, which was more than all those upstanding charity-minded people were willing to do. Those pillars of rectitude wanted to feed only so-called *worthy* children, but a corrupt Irish boss helped when no one else would, and I wouldn't soon forget it.

Chapter Four

Worcester, Massachusetts
November 1909

I T'D BEEN A LONG TIME SINCE I'D BEEN BACK to Worcester, where the tree-lined streets bustled with horse-drawn carriages making their way to the reception hall.

My sister's wedding was a rather lavish affair for the daughter of a Congregationalist shopkeeper. But my parents had been catering to Ethel's whims since she was a child who screamed and beat her fists against doors. Ethel and I had never been close, and we held no common interests, but I admired her for having overcome those mad fits of her youth. And I wouldn't dream of missing her nuptials, even if it *did* bring me back into the clutches of our overbearing mother.

"Oh, Fanny," my mother hissed in my ear at the reception hall. "I wish you'd worn a different hat to the wedding. I've told you many times, with a moon face like yours, you must always wear a tricorn or something like it for counterbalance, lest you look ridiculous."

"Well, fortunately, no one is looking at me," I said, now enormously self-conscious about the broad-brimmed, feather-bedecked hat atop my head. Unable to do anything about my hat, I ladled myself a glass of wedding punch. "All eyes are on the bride, as it should be."

My mother sighed wistfully. "Your sister *does* look lovely, doesn't she?"

I nodded, and we both gave a fond little wave across the reception hall to Ethel, who smiled back, clutching the arm of her groom, and swishing her wedding dress in delight, while my father stooped to kiss her cheek.

Then my mother spoiled the tender family moment by saying, "Your father and I can finally breathe easy now that at least *one* of our daughters might give us grandchildren."

I gulped my wedding punch, wishing it were something stronger for this conversation. "Mother, should I be monopolizing all your attention? I don't want to keep you from mingling with the guests."

"Well, I see you less frequently than our wedding guests. And you *never* write."

"I write every week," I protested.

She sniffed and took a cookie from the table. "You were late last week. Just tell me you've met someone interesting in New York."

By *someone*, I knew she meant an eligible bachelor, so I was tempted to tell her that I'd met the Tammany Hall boss of Hell's Kitchen in a smoke-filled gentlemen's club frequented by gun-toting gang leaders. As far as I knew, the Irish politician was romantically unattached. But, not wishing to give my mother a case of the vapors, I pretended to misunderstand her question. "Oh, yes! I've met the most revolutionary economic thinkers in my graduate program. And did I mention I met Theodore Roosevelt's niece and the daughter of E. H. Harriman?"

At the mention of these names, my mother looked suitably impressed until I began to describe our volunteer work at Hartley House. Then she said, "Well, that sort of thing is all well and good for the likes of Eleanor Roosevelt and Mary Harriman; they're wealthy ladies with time to spare. But there isn't any future for *you* in this so-called *social work*. How will you support yourself? You're already so thin; you're positively wasting away."

I sighed, realizing that in the few hours I'd returned to the bosom of my family, I'd scarcely finished my wedding punch before being stripped of my confidence in my appearance, the pride of my vocation, and the unqualified joy of seeing my sister married off to her respectable dentist. Was it any wonder I'd flown the nest at my very first opportunity?

Now my mother twisted the knife, adding, "You were paid much more as a teacher at that academy in Chicago."

Yes, but those affluent girls at Ferry Hall didn't need me, I wanted to say. *Not like the girls in Hell's Kitchen. Certainly not like one particular girl in Worcester whose screams I'll never forget . . .*

Of course, if I said that, it'd draw us too near the forbidden subject of our most serious falling-out. Over the years, the wound had scabbed over, and, not wishing to rip it open again, I adopted a breezy tone. "Not to worry! After I graduate, I'm sure Miss Mathews will give me a glowing recommendation for a paid position."

This was, of course, a bald lie.

And I knew it was a lie even before I took the train back to New York, where my conversation with McManus was now common knowledge in Hell's Kitchen. No sooner had I crossed the threshold of Hartley House with my traveling case than did Miss Mathews inform me that she wanted me gone at the soonest opportunity.

Thankfully, my professors intervened to persuade her to let me stay just until I finished my survey. But after that, I would be quite on my own . . .

THAT WINTER, MEASURING children's bellies by day, and studying by night under the baleful eye of Miss Mathews, I lived what I imagined to be a relatively harried existence. It was a forty-minute walk from the door of Hartley House to the New York School of Philanthropy—a cold and dangerous journey by foot. So my afternoons were always a rush to finish chores in time to catch the streetcar, which would carry me away from the occasional sound of gunfire of Hell's Kitchen to the peaceful winter wonderland of Gramercy Park.

My stomach was often growling by the time classes let out, but I couldn't afford the eateries in that part of town, so I made it a habit never to turn down a free meal when offered. Which is how I ended up representing Hartley House at the fourth annual Present Problems dinner, where various organizations discussed urban housing, congestion, and rapid transit.

Because I hadn't had a proper meal all week, I piled my plate at the buffet. But now I was too nervous to take a bite, because I'd somehow found myself seated beside the black-lace-clad Florence Kelley—one of the women I admired most in the world . . .

Florence Kelley was a legendary reformer who trained at Hull House with Jane Addams and had earned a law degree. Having once been appointed as a public inspector in Illinois, she was also a moving spirit behind the recent founding of the National Association for the Advancement of Colored People. She'd also translated Friedrich Engels's work into English. In short, she was an extraordinarily learned woman—a suffragist and a true pioneer for equality and other causes I cared about.

So after babbling incoherently in admiration, I startled when Mrs. Kelley said, "You're hired, Miss Perkins."

"Oh, I wasn't asking for a job. I was only trying to express my deepest gratitude." Unable to disguise my awe, I added, "You won't remember this, of course, but you gave a lecture at Mount Holyoke when I was a student. Meeting you was a tremendous honor and inspiration."

"Well, you're right, Miss Perkins, I don't remember. Yet I made certain to have you seated beside me tonight because I wanted to speak to you. People in social work circles have been talking, and I've heard tell of your exploits."

Mortified, I said, "I assure you, I was only defending myself with my parasol, and I'm not in the habit of stabbing—"

"Of course," she said, merriment in her eyes. "But that isn't what I'm referring to."

"Oh. Well, I can also assure you that I don't normally consort with Tammany Hall political bosses; it's only that—"

"Not to worry, my dear," she said, patting my hand. "Jane Addams has vouched for you. She says that *you're one of us* and just the kind of enterprising young lady I need."

I felt my eyes widen. "Should I be honored, alarmed, or bewildered that you've been asking after me?"

She only grinned. "Do you know what we've accomplished at the Consumers' League?"

"I know you've exposed horrendous working conditions and the evils of child labor."

She lifted her chin with pride. "Recently, we also won a battle at the Supreme Court to limit factory working hours for women in Oregon. We'd like to do the same for women here in New York."

"That is wonderful," I said. "Though . . ."

She arched a brow. "You don't approve?"

"I very much approve. It's simply that I'm curious why you aren't trying to limit working hours for *everyone*. The hungry children I see have fathers who are forced to work night and day without even a break to observe the Sabbath. That's no sort of life. These men never get to see their children. Why not help them too?"

"Oh, we intend to," said Mrs. Kelley. "Yet, given the specific legal rationale that convinced the Supreme Court, we must start with women and children. And by *we*, I mean *you* and me. Come work for me."

I actually pinched myself under the table to be sure I was awake. "Why, this is most flattering—truly—but I'm currently working at Hartley House to complete a survey toward my master's degree."

I didn't tell her that Miss Mathews was counting the days until she could give me the boot. But perhaps Florence Kelley already knew, because she said, "We can accommodate your schedule until you graduate. Besides, the most important work won't start until next winter."

Now I was intrigued. "For the sake of curiosity, might I ask what you'd like me to *do*?"

"I'd like you to help run New York's Consumers' League."

I've seldom been struck speechless in my life, but I was then. The Consumers' League was no tin-pot operation like the one I'd run in Philadelphia. This was the sort of job I'd only *dreamed* of. And now Mrs. Kelley explained, "We'll want you to lobby the state legislature to pass a bill limiting the workweek for women to fifty-four hours."

A sudden trickle of sweat pooled at my nape. "But I haven't any experience with lobbying. Why would you want me for the job?"

"Because I'm told you have a certain dauntless quality, Miss Perkins. One that borders on reckless bravado. That you're willing to go where no one else will go and do what no one else will do. Well, the job is to *investigate*, *agitate*, and *legislate*. You've already proved you know how to do the first two. And we'll pay you a thousand dollars a year to do the third."

A thousand dollars a year . . .

Not a large income, but I could survive on it without having to pawn my watch whenever cash was tight. "Goodness," I said, with a jolt of pride and joy. "This is a serious offer?"

"It is," said Mrs. Kelley.

I tested the ground under my feet. "What if I asked for twelve hundred a year?"

"I'd tell you that we can only offer a thousand, but I'll get you a stenographer and you'll be working with the Goldmark sisters." That was even more enticing because I knew that Pauline and Josephine Goldmark were both formidable researchers, writers, and legal reformers. "Would you like some time to think about it?"

"Yes, thank you," I said, then changed my mind. "Actually, no. I shall accept at once."

Mrs. Kelley laughed. "Ah, *there's* the dauntless woman I've heard about. I was beginning to worry. Very good. We'll want you to start right away. I'm expecting great things from you, Miss Perkins."

Chapter Five

New York City
Spring 1910

Dear Mother,
Well, I'm late again this week in my letter, but it's only because I
am kept very busy. You're right to say I haven't been able to save
a cent this year, but don't worry about me. Because while I'm not
so well-off financially as I would have been in teaching, I'm much
happier, and finally on the track of work that will amount to
something in the end.
~Love to all, Fanny

My new office was in the United Charities Building on East Twenty-
Second Street near Gramercy Park, where I sat down before an oak
desk, whirling around in my wooden swivel chair in celebration.

Unfortunately, I was caught out mid-spin by Mary Harriman,
who stopped by the office on her way to some function, dressed in a
snappy riding habit. "Oh, don't stop celebrating on my account," she
said, offering me a congratulatory bouquet. "Twirl away! I'm delighted for you. And I know you must be happy to escape the restrictions of Hartley House."

Since I had collected enough information to write my master's
thesis, Miss Mathews and I had both agreed that I need not darken
the doorstep of Hartley House again anytime soon. I was now living
at a more agreeable settlement house in Greenwich, so I laughed and

said, "I think Miss Mathews is even happier to have me gone, though I daresay she views my rise in the profession with bemusement."

"It isn't a puzzle," Mary protested. "I am a proud member of the Consumers' League, and I think you are *just* the right woman for the job."

I gratefully accepted the bouquet she offered. "Thank you, that is so kind of you to say. And these flowers are lovely; such a bright and vivid crimson!"

"Do you like them? They're cut from my garden. I bred them for that color. I've had a passionate interest in genetics since college."

"You have quite varied talents and passions," I observed.

"I like to keep life interesting. And I suspect there is more to *you* than meets the eye. Are you a sportswoman, Miss Perkins?"

"No, but I enjoy paddling a canoe and the occasional game of golf or tennis."

"What else do you do for fun outside of work?"

I had to think about it. "Well, I like to travel and see shows; I've dabbled in painting, but I wasn't any good at it . . . I scribble a little. Short stories, mostly. The occasional poem."

"Oh, that's wonderful! I know quite a few brilliant writers and editors in Greenwich Village. I'll make introductions." Then she startled me by kissing my cheeks in the European fashion. "Now I must be off—wedding planning, you see—but I just wanted to say that I think you're one of the few people alive who might be able to manage under Florence Kelley. Beware, Miss Perkins. You're not working for a gentle saint."

I TOOK MARY Harriman's warning to heart, and in the months that followed, I learned that my new employer was, indeed, a force to be reckoned with.

To begin with, Florence Kelley was no stuffy, old-fashioned reformer. In fact, she was considered radical. As the only child of an abolitionist congressman, she'd grown up in a family that would not eat sugar or wear cotton because they were the fruits of slavery. Now she refused to wear clothing made from the labor of children, and she wouldn't eat anything cooked by overworked women in unsanitary commercial kitchens.

She was passionate about her causes, and working with her was like standing beside a smoking volcano that at any moment could burst into flames. Her temper was hot and explosive. And one morning, after a particularly contentious argument with a state inspector who refused to shut down an unlicensed shop to which Mrs. Kelley had traced spreading cases of leprosy, she launched a heavy book across the office. I failed to duck in time and the corner struck my shoulder, bruising it. But I never uttered so much as a whimper, because Florence Kelley was my *idol*.

Fortunately, when she wasn't erupting with righteous rage, she had a playful sense of humor. Shortly after I settled into my office, Mrs. Kelley stopped by to offer me a slice of sponge cake. "Do you like pastries, Miss Perkins?"

"Doesn't everyone?" I asked, taking a big bite.

She waited until I was almost done chewing before asking, "What if I told you that it contained rat droppings?"

Instantly, my stomach roiled as I looked for somewhere to spit.

She cackled at my predicament. "Don't worry. I baked it myself. But if I'd purchased this cake in any bakery in this city, there'd be a better than even chance it contained rat droppings or worse."

"What could be worse than rat droppings?" Then, fearing I might gag, I added, "Never mind. Please don't answer that."

"Ah, but *you* are going to answer that, my dear. While we're waiting for the legislative session to open, you're going to investigate bakeries."

I decided that this was going to be the best of jobs and the worst of jobs. On the one hand, I had an entirely legitimate excuse to sample cookies, cakes, and loaves at a different bakery every day, all while sipping coffee and finishing my master's thesis. On the other hand, during my investigations—in which I posed as a harebrained customer who wandered into the kitchens—I witnessed so many nauseating things that some days I wasn't sure I could ever eat another loaf of bread without retching.

I saw cats birthing kittens in baking pans that went unwashed right into the oven. Lice-riddled child laborers mixing flour with their dirty hands. Feverish tubercular bakers coughing blood into the dough . . . For the rest of my life in New York, I'd only ever buy baked goods on the East Side or from the German bakeries that had formed a guild to keep up sanitary standards.

And I warned all my new friends to do the same—friends I'd made living in Greenwich Village like many other educated young women eager to make a mark in a man's world. We spent our weekends on soapboxes on street corners giving speeches about women's suffrage. We attended lectures and concerts and racy bohemian parties. We rubbed elbows with penniless writers, struggling artists, and eccentric millionaires.

Mary Harriman—who had recently married Charles Cary Rumsey—was among the latter. And, returning from her honeymoon, she befriended me with zeal.

When she learned of my plan to celebrate my graduation with a bit of mischief, she clapped her hands. "Oh, *do* let me come. We'll all have a lovely celebratory lunch together."

Mary would insist on paying, because she was exceedingly generous—but the staunchest of our suffragist friends protested, "You can't come with us, Mary. You'll ruin Frances's fun. If we're with you, the coppers would never dare arrest us for smoking in a hotel lobby."

Mary twisted her pearls on one elegant finger. "Perhaps I misunderstood this protest. Surely you don't all *want* to be arrested for smoking, do you?"

"No, but it's the principle of the matter," another young lady explained. "We want the policemen to let us smoke because women should have the same legal rights as men. Not because you're the daughter of a railroad tycoon with more money than God."

With a laugh, Mary asked, "What do you think, Frances? It's your celebration, after all . . ."

Personally, I thought Mary was so pretty that no policeman would've arrested her even if she were *penniless*. In any case, most of us didn't even smoke, so the effort was likely to be more comedic than not. The main thing was that something about Mary made it impossible to refuse her. "Well, of course you should come. If it all goes wrong and the bluecoats *do* arrest us, we'll need you to bail us out!"

Chapter Six

* * *

New York City
June 1910

I DIDN'T THINK MUCH OF FRANKLIN DELANO Roosevelt when I first met him. But in my defense, almost *no one* who met him in those days would've dreamed he'd amount to much.

He wasn't born a great man, and I'm not even sure he was a good one. Goodness and greatness came later.

When I met him, he was still an insufferable popinjay . . .

My new job required mixing with the city's *upper crust*, people with old names or new money who could use their influence to support our causes. So I was grateful to procure an invitation to a late afternoon society tea dance in Gramercy Park, where—after my long-standing habit of surviving on nothing but coffee and the occasional banana sandwich—I was inhaling cakes and asparagus wrapped in puff pastry like I'd never get another meal.

That's when I overheard the beginnings of a rather spirited argument between a group of old walrus-mustached high-hats and a clean-shaven young dandy wearing a starched collar that seemed to prevent him from dipping his pointy chin low enough to look upon the little people.

"Now, now, Frank," one of the old men said. "Don't get worked up about your uncle Ted. We know you have to side with your kin."

"I'm not kin to Theodore Roosevelt except by marriage," the popinjay protested, throwing his head back and sneering down his nose in the most supercilious gesture I'd ever witnessed in my life.

But it wasn't the gesture that got my attention. It was the name. *Theodore Roosevelt*.

Thus, despite the popinjay's starched collar and supercilious gestures, my interest was piqued. Mary knew everyone at the party, of course. In fact, she knew everyone who was anyone. So, pointing discreetly with my asparagus, I asked, "Who is that?"

"Franklin Roosevelt?" she asked. "Eleanor's husband."

Though I was forming a true friendship with the gregarious Mary Harriman Rumsey, I had only a passing acquaintance with the tall, shy Eleanor Roosevelt through our mutual work. And now I was confused. "Did he take *Eleanor's* name upon marriage? That would be quite modern . . ."

Mary grinned. "No, no, Franklin and Eleanor are distant cousins. And nothing alike. As you know, Eleanor is a very hardworking, earnest, and reserved person, whereas Franklin . . . well . . . let it suffice to say that at their wedding, I had to scold him for brooding every time someone congratulated him on his good luck in winning Eleanor's hand. His vanity was so pricked that he's made it a habit at every society wedding since to tell the bride *she* is lucky to have nabbed the groom."

I laughed. "So he's a rake or a boor?"

"Worse." Mary let out a tinkling little laugh. "He's a lawyer."

I laughed too. "Is he someone I should know?"

"Probably not, but I'll make an introduction anyway."

I let her present me to Eleanor's husband, who flashed me a practiced, dapper smile. "A pleasure to meet you, Miss Perkins. I'm Franklin Roosevelt. Of the Hyde Park Roosevelts."

He paused as if waiting for me to show special recognition, which left me wondering if I should say I was Miss Perkins of the *East Newcastle Perkinses* . . .

Before I could, he added, "You must be new to New York."

At exactly the same time, I said *no* and Mary said *yes*, because she knew that to old Knickerbocker families like the Roosevelts, I'd *always* be a newcomer. And she hastened to explain, "Miss Perkins comes to us from New England, of old Revolutionary-era pedigree. She's the new executive secretary for the Consumers' League."

"You must be good at taking notes," he said in a way that made it difficult to know if he was teasing.

"Oh, Franklin," Mary said with a roll of her eyes. "The *executive* secretary runs the operation!"

He scratched his very prominent chin, mischief behind his grin. "The Consumers' League, eh? Isn't that one of the causes my missus has taken up? Mary, I can scarcely keep track of the trouble you get Eleanor into. Something about white labels and not buying anything silky from Bloomingdale's."

"Bloomingdale's treats their workers abominably," I explained. "They keep them on their feet for more than twelve hours without even a break to use the lavatory, working for poor pay."

Mary continued, "Socially responsible consumers look for a league-approved white label to know whether a garment has been sewn in humane conditions."

I admired high society women like Mary Rumsey and Eleanor Roosevelt who made good on threats to cancel accounts if fashionable stores wouldn't stop exploiting their workers. But Franklin Roosevelt mockingly squinted at us from behind his pince-nez spectacles. "Aha! So, Miss Perkins, *you're to blame* for Eleanor's scratchy cotton undergarments!"

It was cheeky and indelicate to talk about undergarments to ladies, but I considered myself modern and allowed myself to be amused. "Consider the adversity of a cotton undergarment as a training of the conscience."

"And never fear," Mary broke in. "Miss Perkins is going to be lobbying the state legislature to pass a fifty-four-hour workweek bill so that we can all enjoy silk underthings again."

Franklin Roosevelt honked a laugh. "Well, thank heavens! A lady lobbyist . . . that'll be a sight. How did you qualify for a job like that?"

Mary answered for me. "Miss Perkins just earned her master's degree."

"Well, isn't that something," he said.

I usually had a fine instinct for the mood of a conversation, but Franklin Roosevelt was rather inscrutable. He was also *strikingly* good-looking, with winsome eyes of an unusual blue-gray color, like a stormy sky over the ocean. Unfortunately, he somehow gave the impression that he knew precisely how good-looking he was, which made me feel positively self-conscious in my high-necked lace tea gown, which was at least a season out of date.

"What did you study, Miss Perkins? English literature?" he guessed.

"Economics and sociology," I replied.

"Sounds dreadfully dull," he murmured over his tea.

I prickled, while Mary said, "Not at all!"

Then, recovering myself, I insisted, "Surely these are subjects all citizens in a self-governing society should study if they're to make wise decisions at the ballot box."

Roosevelt's head jerked up. "Oh, hell's bells, Miss Perkins! You're not one of those stone-throwing suffragettes like the ones in Britain, are you?"

"No, but only a somewhat antiquated reverence for plate glass windows keeps me from being the stone-throwing kind."

Roosevelt honked another laugh.

On the defensive now, knowing it was unseemly in some circles for a woman to want the vote, I said, "Do you remember those lady garment workers who went on strike—what did it get them? They hadn't the protection of a vote, or even the protection of gallantry. The policemen beat them with batons and left them bleeding in the streets. All because they wanted safer working conditions."

"Terrible," Roosevelt said.

But that's *all* he had to say about it. I suppose he saw me as a bristly bluestocking—an impression I probably furthered by explaining, "We helped care for some of those girls in the aftermath at Hartley House."

Still, Roosevelt's expression gave nothing away, and Mary reminded him, "It's a settlement house, like the one on Rivington Street where Eleanor teaches dance."

"Ah, yes. When we were courting, Eleanor took me to see her settlement house and introduced me to her students—poor little immigrant girls who smelled like cabbage. Why do you suppose these Irish Catholics eat so much cabbage?"

It's what they can afford, I thought.

"I am more concerned with milk," I said, because men who disapproved of uppity women were usually mollified by this; females were supposed to concern ourselves with mothering and children, after all. "My master's thesis was on child malnutrition. Do you know how many bottle-fed babies die in this city because of contaminated milk?"

Roosevelt's toothy smile faltered, and I gathered he considered me to be an irredeemable killjoy. He even looked down at his goldfiligreed pocket watch as if he were late for some important event.

Unusually boorish behavior in a man of his upbringing . . .

But the dancing was starting up, and I didn't wish to ruin his fun by talking about anything important. Heaven forfend! "Well, in any case, Mr. Roosevelt, I just wanted to meet you so I could compliment your defense of your wife's uncle earlier. Theodore Roosevelt was a historic president and is a great man."

"Yes, yes," Franklin said with a distracted nod. Then he blurted, "You know, I'm thinking of going into politics myself."

"*Really?*" Mary blinked. "How wonderful!"

The way she chirped that last word made it impossible to know if she meant it really *was* wonderful or the worst idea she'd ever heard.

"Yes, I'm thinking of running for the state legislature," Roosevelt continued.

As someone whose job it was to persuade the state legislature to pass the fifty-four-hour bill, I was now keenly interested. "Why?"

"It's a good starting place for a career," he replied.

"I meant . . . is there some special wrong you'd be running for office to remedy?"

"Well, I'm not beholden to anyone, you see." That wasn't an answer, but he rambled on. "Once I'm elected, I'll campaign for a presidential candidate, then get myself appointed to something in the Navy like Eleanor's uncle Ted did. Then I'll run for governor, and once you're elected governor of New York, if you do well enough in that job, you have a good show to be president."

Now I was the one blinking. Because if I didn't blink, I'd have laughed in his face.

I've never minded ambition—and though I didn't know it yet, it'd be my strange fortune to be on intimate terms with several men of serious presidential ambition—but this admission was too bald and calculating to sound like anything but the most entitled dreams of a trust fund dilettante.

Worse, he just kept going on and on. "I'll rent a big flashy touring motorcar that everyone can see coming a mile away, and drive all over my district shaking hands and railing against *bossism*. I've watched Eleanor's uncle long enough to know that's all there is to politics."

Dear God, what a buffoon, I thought. *And they let him vote, but not me?*

Now desperate to exit the conversation, I said a silent prayer of thanks when the band struck up a tune. Since Roosevelt was eager to hit the dance floor inside, he made polite excuses and left Mary and me tittering over our tea. "God help me if that's the sort who gets elected to Albany," I said.

"Oh, Franklin can't win an election," Mary insisted. "Not even the Roosevelts take him seriously. Eleanor is devoted to him, but others in the family call him Feather Duster Roosevelt."

I stifled a laugh. *Feather Duster Roosevelt.* I couldn't imagine a more apt nickname. At hearing it, I immediately dismissed him as a lightweight.

Certainly, I never guessed I'd just met the man to whom my fate would be forever tied.

Chapter Seven

New York City
August 1910

I DIDN'T GIVE FRANKLIN ROOSEVELT ANOTHER thought that summer. As it happens, I had more pressing things to think about. Namely that I was falling in love with New York City.

Though my father insisted it was a "den of iniquity," I thought it had such energy, history, and potential! From the Statue of Liberty to the Lower East Side to Wall Street and Broadway, people came here from all over the world in search of new ideas and a better life. And I was now searching for mine in the narrow streets of Greenwich Village.

Earlier that summer, Mary Harriman Rumsey had introduced me to Mr. Will Irwin, the editor of *Collier's* magazine, and I'd joined his coffeehouse writers' group. That is where I met Sinclair Lewis, a cloddish cub reporter with flaming hair and a chip on his shoulder a mile wide.

We called him Red in honor of that hair, his perpetually flushed cheeks, and his occasionally radical associations. He looked like a picked chicken and wore cheap, ready-made suits of dark blue that never fit him. Despite these and other failings—mostly having to do with boyish overeagerness and rampant alcoholism—Sinclair Lewis was a *brilliant* writer. And once I'd told him how much I admired his work, he took to me like a lovesick mooncalf.

Now I couldn't shake him.

His persistence ought to have annoyed me—certainly, his constant declarations of love annoyed my friends. He was a terrible pest, but he made me laugh, so I tolerated all manner of shenanigans. And now, sitting in our writing circle, Red waggled his pale eyebrows at me. "Sweets, when are you going to get your own place and let me move in so we'll both save a few pennies on rent?"

Primly setting down my cup of coffee on our scribbled manuscripts, I said, "I assume that's another marriage proposal, and not a scandalous offer to live with you in sin."

He grinned, nearly toppling the table as he adjusted his chair. "Of course it's another marriage proposal. When are you going to make an honest man of me?"

I smirked. "Is that even possible, Mr. Lewis?"

He smirked back. "I'll keep asking until you say yes."

"I'm not going to say yes."

He pretended not to believe me. "You're playing hard to get. An excellent actress, I might add. You should try for the stage."

"I'm not pretty enough to play the ingenues," I replied.

"Who told you that?" Balling his fists as if ready to do battle, he said, "You have the most lively brown eyes. Besides, I've never had any use for ingenues."

Trying not to blush, I looked around the circle at our impatient writer friends. "Oh, hush, will you . . . Whose story is next?"

"*Yours*," Mr. Irwin said, thumbing my pages with a frown. "When are you going to write something serious, Miss Perkins?"

My stories were always about true love. An innocent girl who went out to work for the railroad, in the restaurant. She was a good little girl from southern Missouri or some other place out west. And she always came out all right. No one ever said my stories were terrible, but on this day, my editor friend groused, "I'll never understand how you study dreadful tenements, then write trite stories with happy endings."

I knew he thought my fiction was puerile. Perhaps I didn't have any business writing love stories when, just blocks away, children were being worked half to death in sweatshops. We were always aware of that in Greenwich Village, where a mix of poets, malcontents, and idealists lived alongside immigrants in soot-stained brick buildings ornamented by zigzagging, laundry-strewn iron fire escapes.

From the doorway of Greenwich House, where I now lived, we always heard a mix of accents and languages echo from the streets. On hot nights, we'd throw open the window and listen to arguments about everything from women's suffrage and family limitation to the tyranny of the Russian tzar.

On good days, we caught a whiff of coffee from the trendy cafés, or an aromatic tomato sauce boiling on the stove of an Italian eatery. On bad days, we curled our noses against the smell of smoke, sweat, and horse dung from the streets. All in all, it was an exhilarating neighborhood, filled with youthful energy, but also what I now know to be outrageous *pretension*. We were drunk on art and intellectualism. We were also ardent and insufferable reformers. Which is probably why Mr. Irwin argued, "Miss Perkins, stop writing happy endings and start writing stories that change the world."

Stung, I countered, "I can't imagine why *anyone* would try to change the world unless they believed in happy endings."

The immigrants in those tenements believed in happy endings, after all; it's why they came to America in the first place. And I needed to believe in happy endings too. My work would be too depressing without hope.

After our writers' circle broke up for the afternoon, I nursed my bruised ego. Red's merciless margin notes didn't help.

For the love of God, Frances, there are no seals in the Great Lakes!
—couldn't pay a Midwesterner to eat that—
Try looking at a map.

But now he tried to cheer me up. "Looks like you're in need of a little consoling, courtesy of the Lewis Comforting Corporation, Ltd."

Caught brooding, I brushed it off. "Your services aren't required."

"But for you, they're free of charge. If you want to know the truth, I enjoy your romantic cowboy tales, even if it's clear you've never stepped one foot on the prairie." I smiled in spite of myself, and he said, "There, you see? It's working already. Let me take you to a picture show. My treat."

"You can't afford to treat me."

"True. I'm out of scratch, so let's just sidewalk stroll like sweethearts."

"We're not sweethearts, Red."

He batted his eyelashes. "Says you!"

"Do you know what *would* cheer me up? My suffragist friends are going to picnic on the beach this afternoon. I'm going to join them; why don't you come along?"

He smirked. "Your suffragist friends don't like me."

Now it was my turn to smirk. "*None* of my friends like you."

"Yet you keep inviting me places! Which is how I know you're sweet on me."

"Maybe I just think you spend too much time locked in your room, writing and writing."

"See? You're already looking after my welfare like a good wife. Let's get hitched this afternoon."

"No."

"How about tomorrow?"

"No."

He leaned in with a mischievous grin and whispered, "How about a little canoodling under a blanket by the beach bonfire tonight?"

I gave an indelicate snort. "Fat chance."

He laughed. "I'll take those odds!"

SOUTH BEACH WASN'T as idyllic as the Damariscotta River, where I spent the summers of my youth canoeing in Maine. But it was the most natural countryside New York City had to offer.

After a picnic lunch of sandwiches and a bit of walnut fudge, my friends and I all went into the water. In those days, women wore the kinds of bathing suits that made it impossible to swim. Mine was black-and-white-striped taffeta with matching silk stockings and lace-up slippers, the weight of which was sure to drag me under. So I held fast to the rope from the dock and jumped through the waves with Mary Harriman Rumsey.

Mary probably *owned* a beach or two, but she never lorded her money over us. Meanwhile, Red stayed submerged neck-deep, clowning around with the occasional splash. I knew he was self-conscious about the way his one-piece striped bathing suit exposed his pale skin and the gauntness of his frame. I never teased him about it and I didn't let my friends tease him either, but I did make sure he ate another sandwich, because Red brought out a motherly feeling in me.

Of course, that wasn't the feeling he hoped for . . .

When our friends were collecting driftwood for a bonfire, Red gulped down the last bite of curried egg sandwich, somehow managing to spray crumbs all around him. He usually jumped up when he was finished eating, causing a great plume of sand that rained down on fellow picnickers. But this time he stayed put and said, "Marry me."

I brushed crumbs off my arms. "You say that to all the girls."

"Yes, but they've all given me the mitten." He inched closer on my towel. "C'mon, sweets. Don't be aloof. We've got a lot in common. For one thing, we're both restless and dissatisfied with this cruel world."

"The difference is you don't think there's a way to fix it."

"Not true! Maybe a little true. But I promise that if you find a way, I'll write about you."

"Oh, well, in that case, fixing the world will be worth all the effort."

He furrowed his brow. "Be serious. Don't you ever think about getting hitched? I might be a tall, ugly, thin redhead, but I'm not, methinks, especially stupid."

"You're not ugly and you have a fine mind," I insisted. He was strange-looking, but my affections for him were such that I imagined I could see his inner beauty like an aura around him. I was still young enough to imagine mystical things like that, like one of the romantic heroines in my short stories . . .

"Then why not marry me?" Red asked.

"Because I've gone to a great deal of trouble in getting an education, and now I need to do something with it. Mrs. Kelley is entrusting me with convincing the state to adopt a fifty-four-hour workweek for women and children, and I cannot do it if I must also care for a husband and a home."

"Doesn't Mrs. Kelley have a husband and a home?"

"Not anymore," I confided, lowering my voice because it was still a scandal. "Her husband was a cruel louse and she divorced him. Yet another reminder of why I should be wary of marriage and concentrate on convincing the legislature to adopt my bill."

"What will happen if you can't convince the legislature?"

I swallowed hard, because a bill like ours had already been struck down by the courts. But Mrs. Kelley was counting on my youthful energy and new ideas. "Well, if I cannot get it passed, Mrs. Kelley is likely to fire me, and then maybe I will be forced to give this work up and get married after all."

Red grinned. "Then I'm rooting against you!"

I had been teasing before, but now I was serious. "You don't dare if we're to remain friends."

He gauged me and said, "Oh, all right, don't have a conniption. But haven't you ever been in love with a man?"

Reluctantly, I admitted, "Yes, once . . ."

"Did you break his heart?"

Wiggling my toes in the sand, I decided to confess, "He broke mine."

Red sobered. "Who was he?"

"Just a classmate at Wharton."

"The villain enters stage right," Red quipped. "Was he bookish and bespectacled or devilishly handsome?"

"Both. And terribly persuasive. He talked me into supporting the Socialist Party because it's the only party that champions women's suffrage."

"So where did the romance go sour?"

"Well, he came to believe I wasn't a good Socialist. He accused me of looking for ways to make the existing system better for the proletariat instead of upending the entire class structure, to all of which I pled guilty. And that was the end of love."

Red tried to make sympathetic noises.

Really, he did.

But in the end, he burst into laughter. "Only *you* would get your heart broken over an economic theory. But don't worry, I'll stay sweet on you even if you become a dirty capitalist and make a million dollars."

ON THE FERRY home, Red and I stood at the rail, the brackish-scented wind buffeting us as we passed by the Statue of Liberty, who held her torch aloft in the harbor.

We liked to people watch on the ferry because Red had a

marvelous sense of mimicry. He could imitate a twitchy accountant checking his watch, as if late for his wife's chafing dish party. He could take on the plastic expression of one of the Wall Street types, burying his nose in a newspaper.

Together we'd imagine entire life stories for these strangers.

On this day, Red motioned to a young lady, sitting alone, shy and demure. "Now there's an ingenue . . ."

"She *does* look new to the city," I said, observing her scuffed shoes. "Perhaps a country girl from Minnesota come to earn a living as a teacher?"

"Too cliché," Red said. "I'm sure she's more like you. She's studied sociology and wants to live in a cell in a settlement house, like a nun without the bother of a black robe, and be kind, and enormously improve a horde of grateful poor."

"You're mocking me," I scolded, with a sidelong glance.

"It's a line for my novel."

Which is what he always said when he was being cutting. "All right, then, tell me her story."

Red pressed his shoulder to mine and began to spin his yarn for the book he was currently calling *The Village Virus*. "She's a college girl. As for talents, she writes stories, enthuses on any number of topics, and desperately wants to help the world. So much so that every time her sweetheart proposes marriage, she turns him down flat."

That was probably another line he was trying out for his novel, but he was still poking fun at me, so I poked back. "Her sweetheart must not be the right fellow for her."

Red's grin turned feral. "Funny, that's not what *she* said. She said she had an education and ought to do something with it."

I was about to tell him that I didn't want to play this game anymore, when he noticed a young man in a newsboy cap and brown suit approach our ingenue. "A suitor enters stage left . . ."

"Not a good one," I observed. "His approach is wrong. She looks *bewildered* by his proposal."

"Nevertheless, he got her to smile."

My lips thinned. "Oh, we all smile at men when we don't know what else to say."

Red laughed, and I was tempted to laugh, too, but "the Suitor" was now forcing his way onto the bench next to the girl. When he slipped his arm around her, she pulled in her shoulders as if to escape, and my grip tightened on the handle of our empty picnic basket. "He's pressing unwanted attentions."

"Oh, I don't know," Red replied.

I kept watching, distinctly suspicious. My suspicion grew to alarm when the ferry docked and the Suitor took the girl's hand to lead her off the boat.

I elbowed Red. "We need to follow. Because here's a story. Probably the true story. She's a young naive girl, come to the city, friendless and short on funds. She meets a charming man who promises that he can lead her to a boardinghouse. He knows the proprietor and can get her a low rate. Except once he gets her to that boardinghouse—which is actually a bordello—he debauches her and sells her into sexual slavery."

"Your vivid imagination is getting carried away, sweets."

"That man is a procurer," I insisted. "I used to expose pimps and bawds in Philadelphia, so I know his type!"

I'm not sure he believed me, but Red was always up for a caper, so he let me tug him along. We trailed the couple outside the ferry station. At one point, they nearly disappeared into the subway, but Red coughed up a token so we could follow. "What are we going to do if we catch them?"

"I don't know," I said. "But we have to do *something.*"

I wasn't familiar with this part of town, and when the couple finally slowed in front of an apartment building, Red tired of the game. "Come now, Frances. He's just taking her home to his apartment."

"That isn't much better!"

Red reached for my hands. "We've had our fun. Now come home with me, and we'll drink a lot and maybe do whatever it is this couple is going to do together."

Appalled at his lack of gallantry, I said, "If you're not going to do something about this, I am. That lovely girl is not going to have her life spoiled."

"Oh, *hell*," Red said with resignation, letting go of my hands to fling open the door to the apartment building. "You there! Unhand that girl at once."

The Suitor turned, startled. "Just who are you?"

Red puffed his scrawny chest. "Someone who wants to know your intentions toward that young lady."

Up until now, the young lady in question had seemed soft and imperiled. Now her cheeks burned with offense. "What business is it of yours?"

Red gulped. "Well—it's . . ." He glanced at me, and when I nudged him in the ribs, he announced, "It's the business of anyone who doesn't want to see you ruined."

To bolster him, I added, "We saw this man approach you on the ferry and press unwanted attentions."

"How dare you," snapped the Suitor. "We're a respectably married couple."

"A likely story," I said. I knew how pimps worked. "I don't see any wedding rings. And I'd like to speak to the superintendent of this building."

He wouldn't want his landlord to learn about his planned seduction of an innocent. He'd likely now storm away, leaving the girl behind, bewildered, embarrassed, and upset. Anticipating this, I moved closer to her so that she might have a shoulder to cry on. But the Suitor didn't storm away; instead, he walked over to the superintendent's door and hammered on it.

"What's all this about?" groused the superintendent, opening the door while pulling his suspenders over a half-buttoned shirt.

The Suitor pointed to Red and me. "These lunatics followed us from the Staten Island Ferry, and now they're demanding to know if we're married."

"They're married," the super said.

I squinted. "Married?"

The super nodded. "A nice, respectable couple."

"*Respectable?*" I asked, still dubious.

Then a passing neighbor waved. "Good evening, Mr. and Mrs. Abernathy. How are you doing tonight?"

A slow dawning horror came over me that I'd misjudged the situation.

The Suitor—who must've been Mr. Abernathy—frowned. "We've just had our evening spoiled by some busybodies. I don't know if they're drunk or crazy, but either way I'm thinking of calling the authorities and having them thrown into the Tombs."

I began to sputter, offering apologies faster than I could think of words. "Oh dear me, I'm so dreadfully sorry." I tried to explain that my social work led me to be suspicious, but in the end, all I could say for myself was, "I've made a terrible assumption!"

Then my cheeks must've glowed with humiliation, because when Red's apologies stumbled over mine, the superintendent laughed so hard his suspenders snapped.

All at once, Red grabbed my hand and gave me a sharp tug. We burst out of the building and *ran*, all while Mr. Abernathy shouted after us, "God save us from Greenwich reformers!"

Back in the village that night, we laughed ourselves into a stupor.

I didn't want to be known as a hapless, overstepping goody-goody, but I've always been able to laugh at myself, and it was too funny not to share the story with our friends. In any case, I learned an important lesson not to attack before I was sure of my ground. A lesson that would prove indispensable in Albany.

Chapter Eight

New York City
December 1910

INVESTIGATE, AGITATE, LEGISLATE. THAT WAS Mrs. Kelley's motto at the Consumers' League.

She'd piled up research from all over the country about the harms of working overlong hours. The stacks of papers on my sturdy oak desk stood at least two feet high, but before I could even move the candlestick telephone and appointment book out of the way, one of the Goldmark sisters would pile on some newspaper articles.

To read it all, I put in many late nights. And on one of those evenings, Mrs. Kelley peeked into the office and asked, "What on earth are you doing here at this hour?"

"Trying to commit this to memory," I said. "If the legislators ask a question, I want to have the answers at my fingertips."

"You've quite an admirable work ethic, my dear."

I smiled. "I got it from my grandmother."

She patted my shoulder with maternal concern. "Be that as it may, I'm not a plantation overseer or a greedy industrialist. Go home to bed, my dear. You won't be any good to us in Albany if you're not rested."

Sheepishly, I admitted, "I believe I may have missed the curfew at Greenwich House."

"Well, then come home with me tonight and let me fix you some warm milk and settle you to sleep on my chaise longue so you can get back at it in the morning. And I won't accept no for an answer, so don't quarrel."

I wouldn't have dreamed of it, if only because it seemed as if no one *ever* won a quarrel with Florence Kelley. Besides, I not only admired her, but I was also coming to have great affection for her, which made me even more frightened to disappoint her on the job.

"DON'T YOU DARE put one more piece of paper on my desk," I said the next morning when Mary Rumsey waltzed into the office with a list of influential community leaders who would support our bill. "There isn't any more space—not even a cubbyhole."

My favorite railroad heiress only laughed. "Very well. I'll keep it and pester you later. In the meantime, I've arranged a chaperone for you in Albany."

"I can look after myself. I've been fending off pimps and pickpockets for years."

"Politicians are different sorts of villains," Mary insisted. "Albany is a seedy little boys' club, teeming with boastful men who will ignore you because you're a lady. What you need is a well-connected gentleman to introduce you around, and I know just the one. Someone with brains and finesse."

Her tone made me suspicious. "Are you trying to make me a match?"

With an exasperated little laugh that was not a denial, she said, "Frances, surely you don't want to be a dried-up spinster without a family of your own . . . and time is of the essence."

I was tempted to step on her toes for saying a thing like that; she sounded like my mother. I knew that the longer I waited to marry, the more difficult it might be to have children. And I did dream of having children of my own one day. But oh, I hated to be managed!

To fend her off, I said, "I'm perfectly happy as a spinster, but in any case, I'm already being courted."

"Red Lewis doesn't count."

"Why not?"

She smiled indulgently. "Do you want me to tell you the real reason or the nice reason?"

"The nice reason," I said.

Mary took me gently by the arms. "Because Sinclair Lewis is a struggling writer who can never support you comfortably enough that you can continue the work that means so much to you, and which you do so well."

It was still the prevailing belief that if a woman wanted to work for the betterment of society, she needed a private fortune. Certainly, that's how it was for Mary, but I didn't want it to be true for me. "So you're trying to match me with some stodgy old high-hat with a fat wallet? What must you think of me!"

Mary's eyes flashed with soft amusement. "Paul Caldwell Wilson is neither stodgy nor old."

At hearing that particular name, I wavered in my indignation, for I knew of Mr. Wilson by reputation. He was a financial investigator who had been exposing the corruption of Tammany Hall. He was a tireless watchdog with a reputation for genius. And now I murmured, "I had no idea Mr. Wilson came from *money* . . ."

"Marshall Field's money, to be exact," she said. "But he doesn't advertise it. You have a great deal in common. And as a bonus, he's very attractive. Trust me, you're going to adore him."

ALBANY WAS AS unappealing a place for a state capital as I could imagine, with noxious industrial waste polluting the run-down riverfront. The hilly streets boasted seedy saloons and flophouses. And the capitol building itself—a Romanesque mishmash of architectural styles with red rooftops—was rather badly maintained.

I was already choking on cigar smoke as I took my first step onto the tobacco-spit-stained carpet, under a dusty chandelier. As I noticed that each of the chamber lobbies was sectioned off with a brass rail, someone behind me said, "That's where you stand, Miss Perkins. In the lobby with me and the lobbyists."

Startled, I turned to see a man I didn't recognize, wearing perfectly polished shoes and a paisley pocket square. He looked to be in his thirties, fit, fashionable, and well barbered. "Oh, thank you, Mr.—"

"Paul Wilson," he said with a dazzling smile. "Mrs. Rumsey asked me to look after you."

"So nice to meet you." I offered my hand, which he shook in a firm and frank manner. "How did you know me on sight, sir?"

He smiled wryly. "There aren't many lady lobbyists in Albany. Besides, I've seen you before."

I doubted that. Surely if we'd met before, I'd have remembered that thick dark hair and the way his sapphire blue eyes crinkled when he smiled. "You're certain?"

Mr. Wilson nodded. "In Greenwich Village. You were atop a soapbox with your suffrage banner, giving a speech."

"Oh, dear. Was I dreadful?"

He grinned. "I thought you and your speech were *splendid.* Especially when a heckler pelted you with a tomato. You caught it, thanked him for the tip, made a joke about saving it for a sandwich, and got the crowd laughing at the heckler instead of you."

Not *precisely* the detail I wanted people to remember, but he plainly meant it as a compliment. "Being pelted with fruit seems to be a professional hazard of suffragists these days. Ought I to expect the same here in the halls of the capitol?"

"Not to worry," he said. "Tammany Democrats are too lazy to throw fruit."

"I take it you're a Republican?"

"A progressive Republican," Mr. Wilson replied. "I believe in good government, public accountability, and Theodore Roosevelt."

"I like him too," I said.

"I wouldn't confess it to anyone else around here if I were you. Not with Tammany in control."

I supposed the fact that the chamber was almost empty on the opening day of the session didn't speak well for their industriousness. Still, I said, "They can't all be bad, can they?"

Mr. Wilson squinted. "My dear lady, Tammany boys are the scum of the earth! You'd be astonished by the corruption I've discovered working at the Bureau of Municipal Research."

He was underestimating what might astonish me, but I liked that he was a serious man, with serious concerns, doing serious work. In truth, he had the air of a young but stern professor about whom one might harbor forbidden thoughts. So I let him play the schoolmaster.

"Do you see that man?" he asked, motioning with his chin toward a bulky Irishman chewing the fat with reporters across the room. "That's Big Tim Sullivan, the King of the Bowery—the so-called spider at the center of the web of vice and criminality in this town."

I tilted my head, dubious. "He looks like a genial uncle who buys circus tickets for the kiddos, but I suppose looks can be deceiving."

"There's a more obvious villain," Mr. Wilson said, discreetly pointing out the tall well-dressed man with a diabolical goatee. "That is *The* McManus."

"Yes, I know him," I said, relishing the way Mr. Wilson startled. "The Devil's Deputy from Hell's Kitchen."

"You *know* him?"

I nodded. "I used to live in Hell's Kitchen."

Mr. Wilson's eyes went wide. "Well, then you must know he has at least a dozen young toughs working for him, breaking kneecaps."

I bit my lower lip, trying not to laugh. "I assure you, it's more than a dozen."

Looking around the chamber, I pointed out one studious young assemblyman reading over his beak of a Roman nose. "What about that one in the bow tie? What's his moniker?"

Mr. Wilson started to answer, then snapped his mouth shut and tried again, deflated. "Well, if there's an honest Tammany man, you've found him. That's Al Smith."

Just then, someone leaned across the rail and cried, "Hey, Al!"

Al Smith looked up, gave a wave, then ambled over, puffing his cigar, and began chatting with everyone. Even me. "Perkins? I remember you! You're that slip of a gal who barged into the club to bother McManus about some truant boy."

I smiled sheepishly as Mr. Wilson gawped. But the cigar-smoking Mr. Smith beamed. "I like a gal with gumption. Which is why I'm going to give it to you straight. I'm on the committee, and your fifty-four-hour bill ain't movin', so you better ask for a hearing."

"Why isn't it moving?" I asked.

"Everything's stalled thanks to Frank Roosevelt."

Mary had insisted that Feather Duster Roosevelt couldn't win an election, but he'd pulled off a surprise upset. Just as he predicted, he'd rented a flashy red touring car and drove it all over Dutchess County, winning over voters with his big matinee idol smile.

As for any political positions he might have held . . . well, he'd stayed largely mum about that, relying on the Roosevelt name while railing against Tammany Hall Democrats. Now the feather duster had taken his seat alongside them in the state capitol and was apparently causing mayhem.

"He's gummin' up the works," Mr. Smith explained, adjusting his bow tie. "Fightin' the boss. Makin' it so bills like yours can't get to the floor."

Franklin Roosevelt.

Of all the people to get in my way! In the coming days, as I filled my engagement book with meetings, I was inclined to share the frustrations of legislators, who were all hopping mad about that young Roosevelt.

Just who does he think he is?

—making an ass of himself, staring down his nose at us—

Stuck-up prig doesn't know how politics work.

The only thing *I* knew about politics was that I needed votes, and Frank Roosevelt was making it impossible to do my job. But I reasoned that if he fancied himself to be a reformer, well, then he should support my bill. So I caught him just as he was emerging from a committee room.

Upon his improbable election, he'd apparently abandoned his dapper smile for a silver spoon expression of artificial sobriety, which, paired with his unfortunate habit of throwing back his head, made one feel the subject of his perpetual disdain. Now he sneered at a colleague. "No, no, I won't hear of it!"

I had no idea what they were arguing about, but as Roosevelt stormed away, I called after him, barely able to keep up with his long athletic stride. "Mr. Roosevelt! I hoped we might have a word. We met at a tea dance this summer. I'm Miss Perkins."

He started to smile at me, then smothered it, as if he thought state senators weren't allowed to smile. He was walking faster now, so I had to run next to him on the toes of my lace-up boots to keep up. "I'd like to speak to you about the fifty-four-hour bill, which—"

"Unconstitutional."

Realizing that he was headed for the gentlemen's-only assembly lunchroom, where I dared not follow, I hastened to say, "We've drafted a new bill that should pass muster this time. I'm sure that your wife, as a member of the Consumers' League, must have told you that overlong work hours at unsafe and unsanitary sweatshops have a dreadfully harmful impact on workers. Especially women and children, and—"

"I'm late for a lunch meeting, Miss Perkins," Roosevelt said. "Then I'll be busy *routing* corruption."

"That is laudable, sir, but you could be such a great help in this cause—"

"No, no. I've got more important things to do. More important things. Can't do it now. Can't do it now. Much more important things."

Was it possible he'd become an even more ridiculously pompous peacock since being elected to office? Certainly, he was less charming. Without a backward glance, he disappeared inside the lunchroom, leaving me standing there alone.

I was almost gratified when, later, I peeked into the lunchroom to see *him* alone. He'd already made so many enemies in Albany that most of his fellow legislators avoided him, grabbing their coffee and sandwiches to take back to their desks.

And I didn't blame them one bit.

"YOU MUST BE famished," said Mr. Wilson, who, after several weeks of the legislative session, was still taking seriously his duties as chaperone.

I'd found lodgings with the family of an old college friend in Albany, but amid the bustle of the legislative session, meals were harder to come by. Now, Mr. Wilson handed me a corned beef sandwich he'd purchased from the gentlemen's lunchroom, and I was grateful.

In between bites on a bench in the hall, I confessed my frustrations. "Imagine trading on the name Roosevelt—putting yourself out there as a champion of good, honest progressive government—and refusing to talk about a bill that would mean so much to working people!"

"Well, Franklin isn't the only Roosevelt," Mr. Wilson said, taking a bite of his own sandwich. "Perhaps you ought to write to the *better* one."

I gave a little roll of my eyes. "Theodore Roosevelt won't answer a letter from me. The former president must receive hundreds of letters from people he *knows*; he'd think I was a presumptuous stranger to ask his help."

"Or he might admire your gumption," Mr. Wilson replied.

It'd be more an act of desperation than gumption. A lark. A long shot. But Mr. Wilson asked, "What do you have to lose?"

"My dignity," I said.

"No chance of that. He'll see the letterhead of the Consumers' League and answer you within the week. In fact, I'd like to make a bet on it."

I peered at him sidelong. "What are we wagering?"

"Let's make it interesting. If you're right, and the former president doesn't answer your letter within the week, I'll give you fifty dollars."

I nearly choked to think he could throw around such a large sum. "Outrageous, sir. I don't make enough money to put up such stakes."

"I wouldn't ask you to," he said. "If you lose the bet, then you must allow me to take you to dinner. And I warn you, I'm a tiresome dining companion. I intend to bore you with talk about the city government's malfeasance and frighten you half to death with a barrage of numbers."

"Numbers don't frighten me," I said, smothering a smile. "I am an economist."

"Then why not accept my wager?"

"My parents taught me gambling is a sin." Not that I listened to them about much . . .

"Are you going to go tattling?"

"I shouldn't think so. They're good people, but the vein of New England puritanism runs deep."

"Even in you?"

"I definitely have my moments," I said, careful to dab the mustard from the corner of my lips with a napkin. "But this isn't one of them. I need a hearing for my bill, and maybe Theodore Roosevelt can get me one. So, Mr. Wilson, you've persuaded me to roll the dice."

Chapter Nine

Albany, New York
January 1911

My dear Miss Perkins,
I wish I could be present at the meeting of the Consumers' League
to which you have invited me. The organization does admirable
work, but much remains for it to do. I support your bill. And
with twenty percent of the nation's workforce composed of chil-
dren under sixteen, I believe child labor should be prohibited
altogether. You may circulate this letter, along with the lengthy
reasoning I have enclosed, to those who may like to hear my
opinion.
~ Wishing you good luck, Theodore Roosevelt, 30 E. Forty-Second
St., New York City

My hands had started trembling the moment I caught sight of the
former president's letterhead. They were still shaking when I picked
up the telephone and asked to be connected with Paul Caldwell Wilson. Now, hugging the letter against my chest, I very uncharacteristically squeaked, "Theodore Roosevelt called me *My dear Miss Perkins!*"

Mr. Wilson laughed at my exuberance. And once I'd read him
the letter, he said, "That should get you your hearing in Albany. Even
with Tammany in charge. Now, I have won the bet, so shall we dine
at Sherry's or Delmonico's?"

"How about Fraunces Tavern? I like to think of myself as a revolutionary woman, after all."

AT OUR PRIVATE table beneath a wall sconce and velvet curtains, where I could squint and pretend I saw George Washington saying farewell to his colonial troops, waiters bustled about in powdered wigs, buckled shoes, and knee breeches.

Paul ordered for us—turtle soup, to be followed by lobster Newburg, with French pastries and brandied peaches for dessert. The best of everything! I felt rather spoiled, and teased, "Quite a heavy price you're exacting from me for the loss of a bet, Mr. Wilson."

"I intend to make you pay dearly."

Sipping fancy filtered water, I asked, "In what currency?"

"Information." He grinned. "Before I bore you with my accounting work at the Bureau of Municipal Research, I will begin with a little light interrogation."

"Should I have brought a lawyer?"

He motioned to our fellow diners, most of them buttoned-up swells. "Lawyers are a dime a dozen around these parts if you want to hire one."

Smirking, I said, "I'll chance going it alone."

"There, you see? You're a natural-born gambler."

Mr. Wilson asked after my family, my education, my background, and finally my name. "How did Fanny become Frances?"

"I stopped going by Fanny after I left home and landed in Chicago," I said. "Not even I could ever remember if it was to be spelled with a *y* or an *ie*. And I wanted to be taken seriously. I wanted a fresh start."

"I grew up in Chicago, you know," said the dashing, blue-eyed Mr. Wilson. "Of all the places to get a fresh start, what drew you to the Windy City?"

"Oh, the first stable job I could find. I was offered a position teaching science at an expensive academy for girls whose parents feared for them to become intellectuals."

He stopped drinking mid-sip. "You don't mean Ferry Hall, do you?"

As it turned out, he knew the principal, and, as we chatted over the first course, we discovered many friends in common. But our conversation didn't become terribly personal until he asked, "You've lived quite an unorthodox life for a young woman when you could've settled down with a husband in Worcester. What made you want to leave your father's home in the first place?"

I could've told him that I'd left for financial independence, which was at least partially true. I could've told him it was a desire to see the world outside my father's stationery store. Which was also partially true. But, half-drunk on wine and delicious food and the pleasure of his company, I confessed, "It was because of a girl."

Perhaps noticing my downcast eyes, he leaned forward, concerned. "I'm terribly sorry; I didn't mean to pry into any matter that upsets you."

I tried to shrug as if it were no matter. "After college, I roped my sister into volunteering with me at a mission in Worcester; we were supposed to be teaching the Bible to girls who worked in the local candy factory. These were young girls, you understand. Some of them only ten or twelve, none of them older than fourteen. They weren't in school; they had to work to keep their families going. And on the rare moments they had for recreation, they didn't want religion. They were just children, really. They wanted fun!"

He nodded. "Yes, I should imagine so."

"Well, anyway, my sister led them in a choir, and I found some old peach baskets and fitted them up as basketball hoops. You can't *imagine* how much those girls loved to play basketball. They'd race from the factory—their hair still crusted with sugar, their skirts stained with chocolate, all of them burned and bandaged a little here or there from where they'd been spattered by molten caramel. Then they'd strip down to their bloomers and play like the devil himself was chasing them."

Mr. Wilson smiled a little, listening.

"The best player was a girl named Mary Hogan," I said, closing my eyes a moment to remember her face. "She was about thirteen or fourteen years of age, and what an athlete she was! The only time she ever missed a basket was when she was distracted by thoughts of a boy in the neighborhood who had been making eyes at her."

Perhaps sensing the story was about to take a dark turn, Mr. Wilson put down his napkin.

Trying to keep my voice from quavering, I continued, "Well, one day Mary didn't show up for the game. And all the other girls, just off their shift, were silent. I had to shake the truth out of them that Mary had been working the honey dipper in the factory, and it cut her hand clean off."

I stopped for a breath, my horror as fresh as if I were hearing it for the first time, and Mr. Wilson's expression was nearly equally pained. "That is *terrible*."

"Worse than you imagine," I said. "I raced to Mary's crowded little tenement apartment, only to slip on coagulating blood trailing up the stairs. There was *so much blood* because the factory owner hadn't called a doctor. No. He'd just sent this child away, forcing her to stumble home with a spurting stump wrapped in a makeshift bandage she'd torn from her skirt. How she made it home without collapsing, I'll never know. I found her mother cradling her, *shrieking* for help."

I paused in the story, pushing my plate away, remembering the iron scent of blood in my nostrils, which elicited a shudder from the very core of my being. "Mary's mother couldn't afford a doctor. I sent for one, though, and I felt the factory owner should pay for his services. Not that the old *rotter* cared. When I confronted the factory owner, he told me little Mary Hogan was lucky he didn't make her pay for the candy he'd thrown in the trash with her dismembered hand, because she'd ruined the whole batch with her blood."

"*No*," Mr. Wilson said, visibly shocked. "That's too cruel to say. Too monstrous to be true."

"I assure you, it's true. And not knowing what else to do, I went to my father for help. He took me to see his attorney to learn whether some suit might be filed. Of course, the attorney told us nothing could be done. My parents promised to put out a collection at church to pay the girl's doctor bills, but they thought that must be the end of it."

By now, Mr. Wilson was rubbing his cheek. "You didn't agree?"

"I could never accept it," I said with a shake of my head. "It didn't seem moral that a factory owner could make children use dangerous equipment and then blame them for getting hurt. And how was little Mary Hogan to work without a hand? What sort of future did she have? I decided I must do *something*, so I found out the name of the factory owner's minister and asked him to put the fear of God into his parishioner."

Mr. Wilson looked impressed. "Did it work?"

I nodded grimly. "We got a little money out of him. A hundred dollars for Mary Hogan and a terrible quarrel for me, with my parents, who believed I'd gone too far. The factory owner was an influential citizen in Worcester, and we had a stationery shop to run. *Didn't I worry how my actions might reflect upon our family?* Oh, it was a terrible row."

"I imagine so . . ."

I wet my lips and confessed the rest. "In the course of that argument, my mother let slip that she believed poor people brought their misfortune upon themselves and forbade me from doing anything else like I'd done for Mary Hogan. It was only the heat of argument;

looking back now, I'm sure she didn't mean it. My parents are good, fine, respectable Christians who always give generously to charity. And I love them dearly. But I was young and insufferably righteous, and decided then and there that if I couldn't help people while living under my father's roof, then I'd leave at the soonest opportunity."

"I'm so sorry," Mr. Wilson said, eyes soft with sympathy.

"I am too. Because I believe the factory owner retaliated against Mary Hogan's family—they moved away without a word, and I have never been able to find them or learn of Mary's fate. I made quite a mess of things."

It was unlike me to talk about this. In fact, I belatedly realized that this was a story I hadn't told anyone outside my own family before. Sharing it with Paul Wilson had been painful, but it had also seemed natural. Even more strangely, telling him seemed to drain some of the poison out of it.

I still had nightmares after that about Mary Hogan and her bloody stump. I'd continue to have them the rest of my life. But those nightmares came much less frequently after telling Paul Wilson. As if the act of finally having shared the pain had halved it.

Chapter Ten

New York City
February 14, 1911

Y OU SHOULDN'T HAVE," I TOLD RED WHEN he showed up at my office with half-melted chocolates wrapped in wax paper. "You *really* shouldn't have."

"Why not?" Red shambled to a chair. "It's Valentine's Day."

I glanced over my shoulder, hoping my colleagues were still at lunch. And despite my earlier conversation with Mary, I now said, "I don't want people to get the impression that we're courting."

"We *are* courting," Red insisted. "At least, I'm courting *you*, though I hear I have competition."

"Don't be silly."

"It's my nature," he said, throwing his feet up onto my desk like a rube.

"Be that as it may, you're going to be a serious writer one day." I pulled some of his chapters from a drawer. "You should start acting like it. Your latest chapters are brilliant."

"Yet I see you've marked them up with wild abandon."

"Yes, well, unfortunately, it is *my* nature to try to improve everything."

"Are you going to see him again?" Red grimaced. "That dapper chap with the fancy hair and properly polished oxfords."

"Mr. Wilson is just a colleague."

Despite our dinner at Fraunces Tavern and several winter walks afterward, I wouldn't dream of considering Mr. Wilson as a suitor.

Especially as I couldn't fathom that anyone as worldly as Paul Caldwell Wilson might ever entertain romantic interest in me.

It isn't that I thought myself unattractive. I certainly wasn't a beauty, but I wasn't *bad* looking. I'd occasionally been called pretty, perky, and pleasing to the eye. I knew how to make a favorable impression in the latest mode—with high heels worn under a gown with a high waistline and fashionably tapered skirt.

The trouble was that I was nearing thirty-one years of age, and ambitious gentlemen like Paul Wilson settled down with women a decade younger. Anyone who cared about his future would've told him to court a beautiful young society girl. One who could give him half a dozen children and dedicate her days to managing his household and her nights to adorning his arm like a diamond cuff link.

I did not sparkle—at least not in that way. So I was entirely surprised to find, upon returning to my new Waverly Place apartment, an elaborate display of orchids in shades from pink to purple, ensconced in a decorative porcelain vase—all accompanied by a simple card that read,

Will you be my valentine? – Paul Caldwell Wilson

Mary was positively gleeful when I told her. "Oh, Frances, doesn't he have fine taste? Orchids are difficult to find this time of year."

"But what could he mean by it?" I was still unwilling to believe Paul Wilson had serious designs. Perhaps he intended only a scandalous affair . . .

Love affairs were common enough in Greenwich Village, after all, where unconventional relationships flourished. Mary and I both knew women who loved other women. Men who loved men. Some who loved one of each. People with promiscuous attachments and living arrangements who indulged in drunken or drug-infused orgies. In Greenwich Village, one greeted this without judgment—or at least I greeted it with as much indulgence as my puritanical upbringing would allow. But now, for just a moment, caressing the soft petals of Mr. Wilson's orchids, I noticed a certain eroticism to their shape, and a flash of possibility heated my blood.

Ever so briefly, I allowed myself to imagine tangling my fingers through Paul Wilson's thick dark hair . . .

My more radical friends would argue that if I wanted him, and he wanted me, we should have each other without apology. But I was simply not modern enough to think of myself as some man's mistress . . .

"Well?" Mary asked, sensing my hesitation. "Will you be his valentine?"

"I'm too busy for whatever that might mean."

"He's a very good catch." As a happy young wife—now heavily pregnant—Mary seemed more eager than ever to play cupid. Stroking her swollen belly—eliciting a secret pang of envy from me—she insisted, "One should never be too busy for love."

"One can, however, be too busy for romantic adventurism, and I am. You know tomorrow is the hearing for my bill!"

Theodore Roosevelt's support had made all the difference in Albany, and I needed to make the most of the opportunity. Which was why Mary had come to pick out what I should wear. Now she adjusted a pillow behind her back and propped up her ankles on my bed while I piled garments on a nearby chair.

"*Too young,*" Mary said, dismissing my powder blue satin.

"*Too old,*" Mary said, flinging my black taffeta.

"*Too innocent,*" Mary said, thumbing my white lace.

Mary didn't even have words to describe her disdain for my gray wool. "Please let me help you."

Like a proverbial fairy godmother, she all but snapped her fingers and I was soon surrounded by a seamstress and two apprentices, being sewn into a closely tailored red-checkered coat with matching skirt and, at my special request, a very feminine tricorn hat. "After all, I feel as if I am being outfitted for war."

Mary jested like the Spartan women of old, "Well, then you'd better come home from Albany with your shield or on it!"

ON THE DAY of the hearing, I greeted women I'd recruited to come testify about difficult working conditions—these were poorer, working women, including representatives of the hat trimmers, the seamstresses, and the shirtwaist makers at the Triangle company, who'd recently gone on strike to protest unsafe conditions. But my feminine cohort and I were all vastly outnumbered by businessmen, several of whom made sport for themselves by pretending to brush past us in the smoke-filled hall while pinching our bottoms as they passed.

When one tried this with me, I stomped so hard on his foot with the heel of my boot that he let out a yelp, then scurried away with a limp.

"A needle or hatpin works too," murmured a gap-toothed seamstress as we took our places.

I felt an enormous sense of camaraderie with her and all these women. Most had tried, for years, to better their own conditions. The literate ones had written pamphlets explaining how they worked dusk to dawn without so much as a chair to sit on. But when they'd gone on strike, the police sided with their employers. They were left with no option but to petition the government for redress, and I had encouraged them to come and do so.

I didn't count it as a bad thing that the senate committee was chaired by *The* McManus.

He might be "the scum of the earth," as Mr. Wilson insisted all

Tammany men were, but the Devil's Deputy had helped me before. I didn't see why he wouldn't do it again. Now, stroking his fiendish goatee, McManus called factory owners to testify first so they could get back to their businesses before lunch.

"That might be a stroke of luck," I whispered to reassure the ladies. "It means we'll get the last word."

So we sat patiently as cigar-chomping industrialists, one by one, lumbered up to the podium to make tired arguments before the committee.

Think of the chaos if women and children only work nine hours a day—

—how will our factories compete?—

Commerce would come to a standstill!

"Besides," one factory owner said. "Women don't *want* to work fewer hours. They know idle hands imperil their souls."

From my bench, a chorus of feminine outrage finally broke out, and McManus gaveled us to order. "Don't make me throw ye gals out on yer pretty rumps!"

When we settled again, he called the cannery owners to testify. They were against us too.

Our season is too short for regulations—

—food will rot and people will starve—

Do you want to cause anarchy?

Well, that was balderdash, but I feared the committee was swallowing it hook, line, and sinker. I wanted to jump to my feet and ask why they couldn't hire *more* workers to meet the demands of a short season. The answer, of course, was that they'd have to employ able-bodied men, who commanded higher wages than little girls.

Not wishing to be expelled, however, I managed to sit on my hands and wait my turn.

Sometime in late afternoon, the opposition was finally finished.

Now the legislators would at last hear our arguments. Or so I thought . . .

I watched, perplexed, as the committee followed the businessmen out. "Are we taking our lunch break?" I asked.

McManus shook his head, motioning me forward. "Have yer say."

I glanced at empty chairs. "But you're the only lawmaker here."

"So I am."

I felt my nostrils flare. "We've been waiting all day, sir. It's supposed to be a hearing about our bill, but the legislators aren't present."

McManus cracked his knuckles. "My ear's not good enough, Miss Perkins?"

Angry murmurs erupted behind me. The women threatened to walk out. I was ready to go with them until I saw Paul Wilson at the back of the room. He'd persuaded me to use Theodore Roosevelt's name to wedge the door open; I couldn't imagine that he—or the old Rough Rider himself—would approve of my abandoning the opportunity to win even one lawmaker over.

So I took a deep breath and made my case.

"IT WAS ALL a sham," I told Mr. Wilson on the ferry back to Manhattan, digging my hands into my ermine muff, feeling as glum as the gray winter around us. "Every bit of it a sham."

"Yes," he admitted. "Probably."

I'd set out with a reformer's zeal, certain that my pluck alone could accomplish what so many experienced people before me had already tried and failed. I'd recruited those women to show up to the hearing and be counted. Their employers would probably hold it against them. I'd been naive and arrogant or both.

Mr. Wilson tried to comfort me. "It's hard to learn that some things are beyond your control."

"That's not a very good motto for a reformer, Mr. Wilson."

He chuckled. "No, I suppose not. Won't you call me Paul?"

I pressed my lips together, pondering. "It's dangerous to be on a first-name basis."

"Because I sent you orchids?"

"Yes. Thank you. They were beautiful. But yes."

"You never said if you'd be my valentine."

"Since it's after Valentine's Day, I didn't think you expected an answer. I don't even know what you mean by it."

He leaned against the rail with a devil-may-care smile. "What would you like for me to mean by it?"

I felt something hopeful stir in my heart, but a blooming headache crushed it back down again. "I'm afraid what I'd like is an aspirin tablet. Is there any chance you might ask again when I'm not feeling so terribly awful and angry at myself, Mr. Wilson?"

"Of course," he said. "You mustn't blame yourself for what happened in the hearing today. The plain fact is that you don't have the money to bribe Tammany Democrats, so they're going to bury your bill."

"I didn't get support from your Republicans either. What's their price?"

"Probably the same, which is why they aren't *my* Republicans. I know there's corruption in both parties. Thankfully, Theodore Roosevelt may be forming his own party to run for the presidency again. Don't you think it a marvelous idea?"

As Mr. Wilson told me about it, he removed his hat, letting the winter wind whip at his gloriously dark mane. And I saw a spark of passion in his dazzling blue eyes that I found quite appealing.

I found *him* quite appealing.

As for the rest, I confessed, "Party politics are just so depressing and exasperating that I don't want any part of them."

"Then you're in the wrong business."

Was I? I was a good social worker; I didn't want to scheme and to threaten or bribe politicians. I wanted to work for the betterment of the downtrodden. And in my sullen state, I grumbled, "Perhaps I'd have been better off becoming a nun."

"That, my dear Miss Perkins, would be an utter *tragedy*."

Chapter Eleven

New York City
March 25, 1911

I 'M TERRIBLY DISILLUSIONED," I ADMITTED OVER tea with Mary Rumsey and friends.

Every time I saw reformers make any kind of improvement, it never stuck. Even the smallest restrictions on child labor had resulted in factory owners sending mothers home with piecework to turn their kitchen tables into sweatshops. After all the abuses I'd witnessed in tenement slums, I was finding it difficult to hold on to my faith in humanity. And the sham of a hearing had felt like the last straw.

"Maybe you *should* consider taking a step back, my dear," said our hostess, who often sponsored suffrage parties here in her stylish townhome in Washington Square.

"Nonsense," Mary said. "What Miss Perkins needs is a well-earned vacation. I've been urging her to join me in Europe this summer. It'll be good to get away and see a new perspective."

"Oh, I don't know." I badly wanted to go but could scarcely afford it.

"Is there something that might be keeping you here in New York, Miss Perkins?" our hostess asked. "Or some*one*? There's gossip that you have an ardent suitor."

"Oh. Sinclair Lewis simply likes to pretend he's in love with me. He's a cutting satirist, and I think we'll all be reading his novels one day, but it's nothing serious."

The hostess laughed. "No, the rumor is that you've caught the eye of one of our city's most eligible bachelors, Paul Caldwell Wilson."

I glared across the table at Mary, who wore an expression of innocence that might have been sincere. She could be a gossipy party girl in certain company, but Mary would hesitate to share something she knew would make me as uncomfortable as this. Perhaps it had been the flower delivery boy who brought me the orchids. That little gossip. In any case, I squirmed. "Oh, well, yes, I, well . . ."

"Paul Caldwell Wilson is a man on the rise," our hostess assured me. "His financial exposés made a splash in Albany; he has certain corrupt officials on the defensive. I've no doubt that he'll be serving in office himself one day."

I briefly allowed myself to imagine a life with a man like that. Would it be such a sacrifice to tend hearth and home while he did battle in the capital? Certainly, if I was married with children, I *ought* to give up my job . . .

"Miss Perkins," someone said, and I snapped to attention, heat scorching my cheeks. Goodness, one bouquet of orchids and I was already imagining myself married to the man and having his children.

"There's no shame in having a life of your own," our hostess was saying. "Many of our most outstanding women leaders take a little break to find their purpose or to get married and have families and—"

"Abandon the movement," someone else accused.

"Not true!" Mary insisted. "I haven't abandoned anything in my life, except this tea party, I'm afraid. It's nearly four thirty, and something I've eaten is disagreeing with the baby."

We encouraged Mary to go home and rest; she was, after all, very close to her time. After she left, the conversation mercifully moved on to other topics, including the opening of the Barnum & Bailey Circus at Madison Square Garden. We were all laughing in anticipation of the trained geese when our hostess interrupted to ask, "Does anyone else smell smoke?"

I caught the faintest whiff—thinking perhaps it was scorched toast from the kitchen. Then someone started shouting outside, and we heard the clip-clop of a horse-drawn fire wagon with its bell ringing.

We hurried to the front windows to see what was going on, and then I flung open the front door. Someone had pulled the fire lever in the square. And I could guess, even before looking, which building would be on fire.

Hoisting my skirts to rush down the steps, I said, "It must be the shirtwaist factory!"

Heading that direction, I saw orange flames pouring out of the upper-story windows, and my breath caught when, to my dawning horror, I spotted the silhouettes of girls in those burning windows. Some of the same girls, no doubt, who had come to my hearing in Albany to try to convince legislators of the dangers they faced . . .

Now the poor things were struggling to get out onto the ledge and away from the flames.

I broke into a run, reaching the iron gates just in time to see a girl fall from the window. *Down, down, down* she went, arms flailing until she hit a plate glass awning, which shattered under the impact and broke her to bits.

As shards of glass skittered under my feet, I opened my mouth in a silent scream that tore through my disbelieving mind. Then I looked up to see scores of young women desperately fighting for a place to gasp for air at the windows on the eighth and ninth floors while the growing crowd below shouted, "Don't jump!"

My hand went to my throat in helpless dismay as I realized these panic-stricken girls had nowhere else to go. To escape the flames, they clung to the narrow terra-cotta ledges with their fingertips. But they couldn't hold on forever . . .

What could I do to help?

I ran in the direction of the firemen, who were struggling to get their equipment into place. But the firemen shouted at us to stay back as more young women began to fall, crashing onto the pavement, where firefighters were forced to scramble over their corpses to get their ladders up.

It was *raining* bodies now—each like a fiery comet streaking down to the pavement with a most horrific thud. And this terrified the horses, who reared up and whinnied and nearly toppled the fire wagons.

What a state of macabre chaos and confusion!

Up until now, my friends and I had said not a word to one another. But as the firemen extended a ladder to a window where five girls clung to one another, I groaned. "The ladders won't go high enough."

The fire was on the upper floors. The firefighters could never reach the girls they were trying to save. I wasn't the only one to realize it. Knowing they were doomed, the knot of girls made the decision to jump—seemingly as one. Flames trailed from their hair and billowing dresses as they twirled together in a final embrace, then broke through the sidewalk into the basement cavity below.

It was a sickening sight, and an indescribably sickening sound. This was *unbearable*. This was hell.

"There might be another entrance," I said, deciding to run toward the other side of the building and see if there was something— *anything*—that I could do. I was only halfway there when I froze at the sight of one man in the fire who could be seen helping girls out the window and dropping them to their deaths as if to do them a gallant kindness.

The last of the girls he held actually kissed him. Then they both jumped to their deaths.

The crowd in the square was screaming now—some of them fainting, some strong men pushing forward to help the firemen spread out nets to catch the girls.

On the ledge above, one little slip of a thing shouted as if up at God before throwing money out of her handbag onto the ground below with utter contempt. Then, following the coins, she tumbled head over feet into the net, and my heart leapt to think she'd been saved.

At least one! At least one is saved!

But before I could cheer, four more bodies crashed down on top of her, breaking through the net.

They all died. The ladders were useless. The nets were useless. The frantic efforts of the firemen, *useless*.

One of the girls in the windows waved her handkerchief at the crowd, and even from the distance, I recognized her. She was the seamstress who had whispered to me at the hearing when I stomped on a man's foot to keep him from pinching my behind.

A needle or hatpin works too, she'd said with her gap-toothed smile. Now she leapt to what she must've hoped would be a mercifully quick death. Instead, her flame-licked clothing caught on a wire, and she swung upside down like a circus acrobat, shrieking until her clothes finally burned away and the fall silenced her forever.

Now I was silent too. Silent, still, and numb with sorrow at the senseless horror of it all as billows of dark smoke rose against the sky. The crowd moaned and cried, most every other sound drowned out by the spray of fire hoses, which began to smother the fire. Too late.

It had all happened so quickly . . .

A half hour, no more.

With the greatest bitterness, I noticed that the *building* was fireproof. Nary a brick of it damaged. I was still standing in the shadow of that building hours later, damp and cold, helping to hand out blankets to make into stretchers for the piles of dead bodies on the sidewalk so that we could line them up for identification.

Special lights were dragged out so authorities could search for survivors, while the crowd swelled with grief-stricken mourners attempting to identify loved ones by blood-spattered clothing—for the flesh was too broken to be recognizable. I had never felt so sick and sad in my life as when I saw Maria—a little freckle-kissed fruit seller of thirteen years old—from whom I bought an apple each morning. She'd come running when she heard of the fire, and recognized her sister's boots.

"No!" Maria cried out, falling to her knees, spilling her basket of fruit into the gutter, which ran red with her sister's blood. Maria wept inconsolably, and in her shocked grief, she fixated upon her conviction that her sister would never have jumped.

"We're good Catholics, *signorina*," she insisted as I knelt beside her, trying to offer comfort as she wailed that her sister would never have made the sinful choice to take her own life.

"It was no sin," I whispered, trying to smooth her hair. "It was no choice." What kind of choice could it be? To jump or burn alive was no choice at all! "She fell. Your sister didn't jump. She fell."

I didn't know if it was true, and I didn't care. Sometimes a lie was a mercy. And I was outraged by the knowledge that if the fire had waited another month, when Maria turned fourteen, she'd have been in that factory too. Soon, she would be. If not this sweatshop, then another one, where she, too, could become a human torch unless someone did something about it.

I TOOK MARIA to her mother's apartment—another scene of grief—then wandered home in the dark, where Red waited on the stoop. Having come into the lingering crowd in his shirtsleeves, he said, "Wish I had a coat to wrap around you against the night air, sweets, but I can rub your arms."

"The cold doesn't bother me." I was a New Englander, after all, and my tears were dammed up by ice-cold fury in my heart.

"I think you might be in shock," Red said. "Do you want me to come up? I'll sleep on the couch. No funny business."

I shook my head and sat down next to him. When he started to light a cigarette, I flinched at the sight of the flame, and he snapped the lighter shut apologetically. "Sorry."

"It's just that the scent . . ."

I trailed off. What I was going to say was that the scent of the fire lingered, and it was ghastly, the air filled with ash that might have been . . . well, I didn't want to guess. My face and arms were streaked with it, and I wondered how many baths it would take to wash off.

Red took out a flask of whiskey and handed it to me. I took several gulps. Then I passed the flask back to him, and him to me, until we'd finished every drop. Only then, slightly drunk, was I able to give Red a farewell hug and go upstairs alone.

Of course, I couldn't sleep that night. When I closed my eyes, I saw the burning girls. The ones who jumped, the ones who fell. And I saw Maria's apples floating like flotsam on fire hose water and blood.

By morning, the community came together to try to see what could be done for the survivors. We'd raise funds, we'd find homes for the orphans as if it had been a tornado that had passed through— some terrible act of God over which no mortal had any control.

Well, I knew better.

The door to the exit had been locked, trapping women inside the burning building. The owner escaped without handing over the key, leaving his employees to die. More incriminating information leaked by the hour. And only one public official seemed to give a damn.

I can tell you right now that it wasn't Franklin Delano Roosevelt. No, it was Al Smith, Tammany's man.

The bow-tied, cigar-chomping Mr. Smith was there in Greenwich Village that morning, wearing his heart on his sleeve. He'd been to the morgue already and had a list of those identified so far, and now he went door to door, paying respects to the immigrant mothers and fathers, husbands and wives, brothers and sisters of the dead.

I saw him come out of a doorway, his collar wet with some poor woman's tears, and our eyes met. He tipped his hat. I nodded, and then he murmured, "My dear sainted mother worked in a factory like that when she was a girl, Miss Perkins. Could've happened to her . . ."

Later, I saw him again at the public meeting at Carnegie Hall, and then again at the one at the Metropolitan Opera, which was peopled with working-class girls in the gallery and their well-meaning social betters in the boxes. It was there that a redheaded girl named Rose Schneiderman took to the podium to say, "I would be a traitor to these poor burned bodies if I came here to talk good fellowship. We have tried you good people of the public and we have found you wanting. This is not the first time girls have been burned alive in the city. Every week, I must learn of the untimely death of one of my sister workers. Every year, thousands of us are maimed . . . because the life of men and women is so cheap, and *property* is so *sacred*."

A wave of collective shame passed over us as she said the public would give a few dollars and then turn away, and the law would *always* be on the side of those who let girls burn alive. She didn't think that would ever change.

Well, I meant to change it.

I'd breathed in the embers of that wicked fire, and now they melted my inner ice away. A hot new rage smoldered inside me, fueled by moral indignation. To think I'd felt *disillusioned*. To think I'd considered resigning, quitting, taking a step back from my work . . .

Well, any thought of that burned away in that fire. I had to ask myself why I'd been at a tea party in that square on that day, on that hour. Why had God put me there in that very spot to bear witness? There could be only one answer. God had called me to *do* something about these injustices.

And I would answer that call or die trying.

Chapter Twelve

* * *

RAIN POURED DOWN ON A HUNDRED THOU-
sand people marching up Fifth Avenue in protest. It was a
funeral procession for the bodies that could not be buried
or identified. Some protestors came to march with banners the authorities banned as too controversial. So they marched in a silence
more eloquent than any slogan.

The factory owners in the city threatened to dock the pay of
workers who marched, but that did not stop them. And thousands
more of us watched from the sidewalks and from windows draped in
black mourning bunting.

We weren't going to shrug off these deaths as *the cost of doing
business.*

Red told his reporter friends that the only organization in the city
that kept statistics on fire and safety hazards in New York City's
sweatshops was mine. Which was true. Now I made good use of
what I'd learned. At my office, I told a group of reporters, "There are
hundreds of other factories in this state, and probably in this city,
where conditions for the workers are just as bad. In fact, there are
other factories where it's worse. And this horrific tragedy can and *will*
happen again if we don't do something about it."

After these remarks were printed, the infuriated building inspector and fire commissioner were banging on my office door.
"You've made us look like fools," they blustered. "Like we're not

doing our jobs. You can't say what you did in the papers, Miss Perkins!"

I stood my ground. "I can say it and I did say it. Your own fire chief warned against this kind of disaster."

That's when the commissioner snarled, "If you don't shut your trap, you're gonna lose your job."

My reply was acid. "I suppose that's how the factory owners threatened those poor burned girls. Girls too desperate for a job to quit, and now they're silent ashes on the wind. Well, I'm not that desperate, and I won't be silenced."

What was the worst that could happen to me? If I were fired—even if I were driven from New York City in shame and destitution—I could return to Worcester to tend the cash register at my father's stationery store. Or I could go back to the family homestead in Maine and grow vegetables. I had options, but those girls had none.

So I did not bend.

Both men reddened, as if they had never, in their whole lives, had a woman speak to them with such firmness. Then the commissioner thundered, "We'll see what your employer has to say about that, Miss Perkins!"

Coolly, I picked up the receiver of the candlestick telephone on my desk and handed it over. "Give Mrs. Kelley my regards."

Their bluff having been called, the officials blustered out of my office the same way they'd blustered in, but that wasn't the end of it. They went to the board, and I gather they said something like, *You cannot let this woman say these things; it's dangerous to public morale. It's going to frighten people.*

When Mrs. Kelley called the next morning, I asked, "Should I pack my desk?"

"No. We said the Consumers' League stands behind you . . . but, Frances, you had *better* be able to prove what you say."

What she meant was that I needed evidence the public would accept. Not just observations of women investigators like me, whose words were so easily discounted.

"I might be able to help you," Paul Wilson said later that week, offering me some peanuts as we walked together next to the circus pen for performing geese.

He had hoped that a visit to the circus would cheer me, but I felt as if nothing ever would. "I'm happy to accept help. What do you suggest?"

"I know a fire prevention engineer from Chicago. You should meet him. Mr. Porter is considered a bit of an old crank because people don't like what he has to say. But he's the best at what he does and knows more than anyone alive about fire prevention."

"How did you come to know him?"

"He convinced my father to advocate for a fire wall in the Marshall Field's stores."

I didn't yet know what a fire wall was. But I did know that Paul Caldwell Wilson had a keen eye for the best of everything—from suits to restaurants—so if he said Mr. Porter was the best in the business, I believed him. And not long afterward, I received a visit from Mr. H. F. J. Porter himself, a middle-sized man with spectacles and a Vandyke beard. He dressed very meticulously, as people did in those days if they were persons of professional standing. Striped trousers topped by a nice black chesterfield.

"Miss Perkins," Mr. Porter said. "Your organization is the only one that has said anything about the atrociously dangerous fire hazards in the factories, and you didn't say nearly enough."

"I don't know enough to say more."

"Then I'll teach you."

Thus, my formal education in fire safety began. Mr. Porter taught me about fire walls. He taught me about the need for a horizontal exit too. He taught me about measured occupancy. And he taught me the three-minute rule. "You must be able to evacuate a floor in three minutes. *Three minutes*, Miss Perkins. Any longer and people will die."

"But how can anyone get people out of a building so fast?" I asked.

"I can show you how it was done in the Marshall Field's store," he said. "But you'll have to come to Chicago."

"I'll buy tickets in the morning," I said, but I could not very well set out for Chicago with a strange man by myself without courting gossip, so Mr. Wilson again played chaperone, accompanying us on the train.

Which is how I came to learn that Paul Wilson did not sleep. Though he'd booked a sleeper car, he walked the train late into the night, jotting down his racing thoughts into a notebook, annoying all the conductors.

"There's no help for it," he told me. "I can't sleep when my mind is filled with ideas on how to cut waste and get rid of police corruption and break up the gangs. Fortunately, I only need a few winks each night."

"A fortunate trait indeed, Mr. Wilson," I said.

"Aren't you ever going to call me Paul?"

"If I start calling you Paul, you'll call me Frances, and where would that lead?"

He lifted a brow. "Where would you like it to lead?"

"You have a shifty habit of answering questions with another question."

"Do I?"

I smirked. Perhaps I was being ridiculous. "All right. You can call me Frances, and I'll call you Paul."

He smiled as if liking the sound of his name on my tongue. And, truthfully, I liked the sound of it too.

IN CHICAGO, I inspected the Marshall Field's store and saw how doors opened *out* into safety. These doors would make work life safer if companies could be persuaded to adopt them—or forced to adopt them by the law, if need be.

"Have you ever climbed out a fire escape?" Mr. Porter asked when we visited another building. "You should try it."

I hesitated. After what I'd seen at the Triangle shirtwaist factory, I'd never like to be high above the ground. But Paul's strong hand encouraged me over the ledge. Precariously balanced in my high heels as I looked down at the dangerous pavement below, I said, "If there was a fire, it'd take a long time to climb down this fire escape to the sidewalk."

The expert shouted over the wind, "If this building was on fire, Miss Perkins, you'd never get that far. Tongues of flame would shoot out these windows and roast you to death where you stand."

"That's not a pleasant thought," I said, scrambling back inside, where Paul lifted me back over the sill. And I couldn't decide whether that was gallant or impertinent or both.

Fortunately, I didn't have time to decide, because the fire expert said, "That's why buildings need fireproof windows."

I made a note of that. In fact, I'd return home to New York armed with page after page of information to add to the evidence Mr. Porter had provided me with. On the train, I was already writing an article for the newspaper. And when my pencil broke, I asked Paul to lend me one of his.

He obliged, saying, "All in all, it was an eye-opening visit, wasn't it? I'm only sorry that we weren't here long enough for me to take you to meet my friends and relations."

"That would've been lovely," I said. "Perhaps another time?"

"I'd like very much for there to be another time," he said, his blue eyes pinning me with a meaningful stare. "You might remember that, before the fire, I sent you flowers. You asked what I meant by it. Well, now it's springtime and we've never had a chance to discuss it further. The timing was never right."

The way he was looking at me should've made my heart flutter. And it did, a little. But the rest of me was still consumed by the tragedy of the fire. "I'm afraid the timing isn't quite right now either."

Paul bowed his head. "It's only that I feel we're beginning to form some manner of attachment. Am I mistaken?"

"You're not mistaken, but at the moment . . ." I tapped my list about fire prevention reform. "This has to come first."

Chapter Thirteen

Dear Ethel,

It was lovely to meet my baby niece on our July Fourth weekend in Maine. And of course I don't mind that you named her after our grandmother. I am glad to know we'll have another Cynthia in the family. You mustn't let Mother give you a conniption fit with her insinuations. I left so soon only because I'm overwhelmed with work and probably shouldn't have taken a holiday weekend in the first place.

~Love to all, Fanny

In the wake of the Triangle shirtwaist factory fire, Assemblyman Al Smith had promised me there would be a Factory Investigating Committee. That autumn, he made good on his promise.

Everything would be on the table: fire prevention, working conditions, working hours, and safety regulations. But I was dismayed to learn the committee wanted to start by investigating bakeries instead of fires. "*Why?*"

Al Smith chomped his cigar with a grin. "Because if we learned anything from Upton Sinclair's book, it's that the best way to get people's attention is through their stomachs. A lot of voters can't imagine themselves trapped in a factory blaze. But everybody's gotta *eat.*"

I didn't mention that I knew Upton Sinclair from my days in

Chicago, and that *The Jungle* scarcely scraped the surface. "Are people really so self-centered?"

"Oh, don't judge 'em harshly, Miss Perkins," Al said. "Empathy takes imagination, and most people ain't got any. We'll get to fire safety reform. But first we need to give the public a little razzle-dazzle."

He decided that he'd call me as the first witness, knowing that a woman expert would be a curiosity. Perhaps a draw. And I felt a little case of nerves as the audience filed in for the first hearing.

I went onstage and took my place, but just as I finished stating my name and address for the record, a man came barging down the aisle.

"What right has she to speak about anything?" the man shouted. "She's no expert!"

Al Smith thumped a meaty fist on the table. "Order!"

The man ignored him. "I demand to know, Miss Perkins. Have you ever been a baker?"

"No," I admitted. In fact, I was a rather bad cook altogether, but I kept that to myself.

"Have you ever sold bread?" he asked.

"No."

The heckler puffed his chest. "Are you a doctor with a degree to practice medicine?"

"No, I am not."

"Then why are you here to testify?"

Al Smith waved his cigar in irritation. "Because we asked her to."

"She's a totally ignorant and incompetent person," the man roared. "A mere *girl*. I protest against her being allowed to speak before this commission."

Smith actually growled and stubbed out his cigar. "Now it's my turn. Lemme ask a few questions, Miss Perkins. Have you ever visited a cellar bakery?"

"Yes, Mr. Smith."

"How many bakeries? A hundred?"

"Four hundred and fifty-two, Mr. Smith."

"Do you take notes?"

Did I take notes? "Always."

"Have you found unsanitary conditions?"

"Many! Dead rodents in baking pans. Cockroaches in flour bins. Muddy shoes on baking boards—"

"Have you photographs of these things?"

Mr. Smith's questions went on like this, until the man who objected to me was red in the face. Then Al Smith calmly declared, "It seems to me you're an expert on the matter, Miss Perkins, and that your testimony will be invaluable." Then he winked. "Give 'em the best you've got."

"YOU DID GREAT, kiddo!" Al cried, helping the janitor to put away the now-empty chairs. "It's time for us to skiddoo, but you must be starvin'. Why don't you take the ferry back with me and let my wife fix you something for dinner?"

"Oh, I couldn't impose."

"Poppycock! I've told Mrs. Smith all about our lady lobbyist. Dinner won't be fancy, but she'll be thrilled to make you a plate."

I agreed to go along, never expecting to be utterly charmed by the experience.

Unlike many of his Tammany colleagues, Al Smith hadn't been enriched by public service. He still lived in a simple brick row house that he leased from the nearby church, with lace curtains in the window and a crucifix in the entryway. And as soon as we entered his humble abode, he cried out, "Katie, I'm home!"

His buxom wife shuffled out in her apron, and he grabbed her in his arms, dipped her, and gave her a lingering kiss on the mouth.

My inner puritan positively squirmed at the sight. My own parents would have *died* before they let anyone see them kiss like that. But I could tell this was a common occurrence in the Smith household, because Mrs. Smith only pretended to fend her husband off with a dish towel, all while blushing with pleasure.

And he didn't look chastened in the slightest.

He loves her, I realized. A realization I was to have again over a dinner of cold meat and potatoes that we shared with all his children, a heartwarming family tableau.

I secretly longed for a child and a family like this for myself, and it made me wonder if it was truly possible for a woman to have a public career and still have a happy homelife, or if that was a blessing reserved only for men.

After dinner, we sang songs round the piano, and before heading home, I sat with Mr. Smith on the front stoop, eating a lemon ice, feeling grateful to have been included. "Miss Perkins," he said. "I think you and me see the world the same. I think we're goin' in the same direction, so we might as well do it together."

I smiled. "What direction is that?"

"Up."

Chapter Fourteen

Albany, New York
January 1912

I WAS AT THE RAIL IN ALBANY BRIGHT AND early the day the new legislative session began, ready to do battle for the fifty-four-hour bill again. And this time I was chasing—literally—every vote. Hot on the heels of State Senator Franklin Roosevelt, I said, "I beg you to hear me out, sir. These women are on their feet in firetrap factories twelve hours a day, seven days a week, hunched over machines without so much as a chair to lean against."

He had the temerity to laugh. "Oh, I don't think a little physical exertion ever did a healthy young woman harm. Why, I've been running up and down these halls for hours, and I'm none the worse for wear."

My cool New England blood boiled. "How dare you *laugh*, sir?"

Roosevelt startled at my tone, but I didn't care. I should've been conciliatory to this man. I should've tried to sweeten his disposition. But his laughter infuriated me. "You know nothing whatsoever about the conditions under which women work, Mr. Roosevelt. You don't seem to know that some of them aren't young and able-bodied; some of them suffer from health ailments. Some are elderly, stooped, and in terrible pain—"

"Now, Miss Perkins," he tried to interrupt.

I wouldn't let him. "Mr. Roosevelt, if your comment was sincere, it would appear that you don't even know the elementary difference between running and standing still to perform a repetitive motion. What's worse, you don't seem to *want* to know, even though it is your job as a legislator and your duty as a Christian to care about what ails your fellow human beings."

His expression fell and, like a scolded schoolboy, he pulled at his lower lip. Feeling that I had him on the ropes, I said, "You simply must help these women. People look up to you, just as they look up to Theodore Roosevelt. So you must support a fifty-four-hour workweek."

Unable to meet my eye, Frank murmured, "I do support it, of course, but I have other priorities—"

"Is reelection one of them?" I broke in. "Because I assure you that every progressive considers this bill a test, and it will come up in your next campaign."

I was getting more comfortable making threats. But in response, Roosevelt only ducked into the men's lavatory, leaving me sputtering in the hall.

Coward, I wanted to shout. What business did he have strutting about with the Roosevelt name—and all the goodwill that came with it—while doing nothing to live up to the reputation?

After my efforts dragged on week after week, I complained to Paul, "I should've known I couldn't get support from upright grandstanders."

Paul glanced at me warily. "So you'll scrounge votes from the dregs of Tammany Hall?"

"Don't look at me that way, Mr. Wilson. I am impervious to those disapproving blue eyes of yours. I'll scrounge for votes wherever I can find them—even if I must get them from the devil himself."

Or, at least, the Devil's Deputy . . .

When McManus found me camped outside his door, he raised both his wicked brows. "Ye already have my support, gal. But we've only two days left in the session."

"Two days are enough to vote," I argued.

He shook his head. "These blokes will leave early for the weekend."

This was terrible news. "But I have the votes *now*; please bring it to the floor. I'm begging."

McManus gave me a fond, almost paternal look. "I don't have any hopes for it, but ye managed to get the votes without me having to bash heads, so I'll let ye have a go."

At long last, the fifty-four-hour bill was up for a vote. And much to the surprise of my righteous reformer friends, most of the thieving Tammany Hall ward bosses were for it. It was the supposedly good legislators who were against us, arguing that they had such "bright and airy" factories upstate that women would *rather* work in them all day instead of their own dingy hovels.

At that, Tim Sullivan, the King of the Bowery, could stand no more. "Oh, yes, it's a fine sight to see them women and girls working in those bright, airy spaces the senator has so eloquently described. A far finer sight, at noontime, to see the big upstanding men who tend their dingy hovels and nurse the babes and bring their women their lunch pails."

His biting humor elicited a roar of laughter in the chamber. We all knew that with women and children working in the factories from dusk to dawn, nobody was home nursing babies or making lunch pails. The fabric of civilized life was unraveling, and someone had to do something about it.

My bill passed in the upper chamber with a vote of 32–15. Now it only had to pass the other chamber, where I was even more sure of support. Elated, I took a late lunch break, rewarding myself with a rhubarb tart and custard. And I'd just finished wiping the crumbs from my lips when Al Smith stopped by to break the bad news. "An amendment has been slipped in to exempt the canneries."

"You can't mean it," I said. "The canning factories are the worst offenders! The Consumers' League can never support a bill exempting them."

"Which is why they put it in," Al said. "Now the two bills don't match and there's no time to reconcile them."

Someone had double-crossed me. Someone who pledged to support my bill had killed it instead. I was going to fail *again*. Panicked, I found a telephone to call Mrs. Kelley but couldn't reach her. I could only get hold of our lawyer for the Consumers' League, who reiterated that we could never accept an exemption for the canneries. "After all, what would the point of the bill be if the worst offenders didn't have to abide by it?"

The lawyer was sending the Goldmark sisters over on the next boat to help make a last-minute rally, but the clock was ticking, and I knew the legislators just wanted to go home. All I could do was scurry from office to office pleading with them to stay, and my heart sank to find Big Tim Sullivan with his overcoat already over his arm. "Oh, Mr. Sullivan, tell me you're not leaving early. Tell me it isn't over."

The King of the Bowery gave me a kindly smile. "Me gal, I know ye worked hard on this, so I can't fib. Ye'd be onto me before the worruds be out o' me mouth. So I tell ye, the big boss at Tammany don't mean to put it through. Ye don't have the support ye think ye do."

"Then why is everyone lying to me about it?"

He shrugged. "Because it's an election year."

How naive I'd been to threaten Frank Roosevelt's reelection. He could've just *pretended* to support me like everyone else. Members in both parties would now claim they'd *tried* to pass the popular bill, but time simply ran out. That'd be fine publicity for politicians, but what good would it do the girls in these factories?

Big Tim gave me a sympathetic pat on the shoulder. "Maybe next year."

I was inconsolable. "We have the sympathy of the public *this* year because of the Triangle fire. By next year, maybe the memory of burning girls will have faded, and we'll have done nothing to make working conditions better."

Big Tim just shook his head. "I'll stay a little longer for ye. But don't hang yer hopes on it."

"Thank you!" I cried, dashing to the phones to plead with my contacts.

But it was all to no avail. And at a loss as to what else to do, I found myself ringing up Paul Caldwell Wilson. I don't know why I called Paul. I should've been conferring with colleagues or berating legislators or drinking myself to oblivion with Red, who always had top-shelf liquor. Given my black mood, perhaps I shouldn't have called anyone. But I called Paul, and now there was nothing for it but to pour my woes into his sympathetic ear.

Always a man for numbers, Paul asked, "How many women work in canneries?"

"Ten thousand, give or take."

"How many work in other kinds of factories?"

Glumly, I replied, "Four hundred thousand."

"Then it seems to me a rather straightforward calculation. If I were you, Frances, I'd do what I could for the four hundred thousand."

It wasn't as simple as mathematics. Still, his words echoed in my mind, and after we ended the call, I went out into the hallway and began to pace. Could I call the bluff of the dirty double-crossers who amended my bill? Could I use the momentum to get them to vote for it anyway?

Even if I could, *should* I?

I'd be going against my explicit instructions. But I was tired of having clean hands when someone was doing me dirty. I wasn't going to be chased off; I was going to stand my ground and let them skewer themselves on the tip of their own dirty dealing.

Suffrajitsu, I thought. And with sudden conviction, I burst out of the corridor in search of McManus. "Please accept the version of the bill that exempts the canneries."

McManus raised his hands in confusion. "But the Consumers' League has said—"

"We want the bill, and I have the votes!"

To make sure of it, I lifted my skirts and *ran* back to the chamber to see if my supporters were still there. A quick count showed that four were missing—including Franklin Delano Roosevelt, who'd finally given his tepid support only to abandon me.

Damn Franklin Roosevelt, I thought. That popinjay was no doubt already sipping a cocktail with one pinkie in the air while patting himself on the back with the other hand for a job well done. Worse, Big Tim Sullivan and his lieutenants were headed out the door. "Oh, please, Mr. Sullivan, just a little longer."

"Me gal, if we stay any longer, we'll miss the night boat. And anyhow, it won't matter. They're goin' to pull a rules trick on ye."

"What's a rules trick?"

He patted me again, this time low on the hip. "Ye don't know much about this parliamentary stuff, do ye?"

I shook my head.

"Well, ye need a rule to go forward," he explained. "Now, *ooooooordinarily*, Senator Wagner chairs the Rules Committee. He be the one to give ye the rule. But Wagner now presides as temporary president of the senate."

I shook my head. "I don't understand."

"He can't fill both roles; so he'll *claim* he's helpless to give ye the rule. No rule, no vote. That's the plan."

The skullduggery of it was crushing. "Oh, Mr. Sullivan!"

I must've looked as dismayed as I felt, because the man reached for a kerchief in his pocket and held it at the ready as if he feared I might cry. "Did ye know me sister went out to work when she was just a wee thing? I feel sorry for them poor gals." He sighed. "I'd like to do 'em a good turn, so it might be that I have me an idea . . ."

I took his kerchief. "What idea?"

He brightened. "Leave it to me. They forgot who the ranking member of the Rules Committee is. The man who can give a rule if Wagner can't."

"Who is the ranking member?"

"Me."

In the end, it all happened the way Big Tim Sullivan said. Senator Wagner pretended to be helpless. Then Big Tim burst into the chamber. "I am the acting chairman of the Rules Committee. I demand a vote!"

Absolute mayhem erupted, legislators shouting at one another, everyone crowding around the brass rail to ask if they should vote for the bill or against it. Big Tim voted for my bill, tipped his hat, and then left to catch his boat. In the meantime, I assured supporters, "Yes, yes, we're for the bill. I've authorized it. We want it!"

Of course, I hadn't informed my stunned colleagues from the Consumers' League. Pauline Goldmark shouted, "No, no, you mustn't vote for a bill that exempts the canneries. Miss Perkins, you must not—"

"This is my responsibility," I said. "I'll do it and hang for it."

If these politicians were going to force me to compromise, well, I was going to compromise them too. Many had supported the bill when they supposed the fix was in and the bill would never pass. Now they'd *really* have to stand and be counted and some scurried away like rats. By eight o'clock, I was short two votes. But by now, McManus was enjoying the chaos, shouting, "I demand a recount! A recount!"

"A recount?" I shouted from the rail. "But Mr. Sullivan is already gone! I—I'll have to call him back from the boat."

While I ran for the telephone, McManus rose to his full height to whip up votes, and I heard him shout at some hapless legislator behind me, "If ye don't change your vote back, boyo, we'll make you eat crow at the ballot box, we will!"

A few minutes later, I got a call through to the ferry. "Please don't let the boat leave, or if it has, turn it around! Tell Mr. Sullivan I've sent a taxi to fetch him."

Someone was eavesdropping and raced back to demand a *closed call*, which meant the chamber doors would be locked. Oh, this was political *warfare* now. Even if I could get Big Tim back from the boat, he wouldn't be able to get in the chambers if the doors were locked.

"We'll buy time," McManus reassured me, invoking a rule that would allow every senator to talk for five minutes. Then he rose and spoke pure gibberish. Someone followed him reading a children's book. Someone else told dirty limericks. Such was the dignity of the New York legislature . . .

While the clock ticked, I looked out the windows to see if Big Tim and the others were coming. While I was gone, someone helped stall by talking about birds. When time was nearly up, the guards prepared to lock the doors—but at the very last *second*, Big Tim Sullivan burst in, huffing and puffing, and my heart soared.

Having missed the taxi, he'd hoofed it. And now, red-faced and perspiring buckets, he roared, "Record me in the *affirmative!*"

I nearly swooned, grasping the sleeve of his coat in excitement, and Big Tim laughed all the way from his round belly. "It's all right, me gal. We is with you. The big bosses forgot about Tim Sullivan."

The bill passed. It passed! Wild applause echoed around the chamber. Some in celebration of the bill, more in appreciation of the sheer brinksmanship of it all. And I let myself get swept up in the applause and congratulations.

Al Smith ambled over, cigar clamped between his teeth, and shook my hand. "You pulled a smart one, Miss Perkins."

Beaming, I confessed, "I thought it better to take half a loaf and try for more later."

But now I had to face the music. The Goldmark sisters were furious. As we made our way out into the dark night, they barely spoke to me. And before we parted at the ferry terminal, Pauline said, "This is on your head, Miss Perkins. You had better pack up your desk."

Chapter Fifteen

★ ★ ★

**New York City
January 1912**

MRS. KELLEY BURST INTO THE OFFICE, PA-
pers scattering in her wake. I was braced for her temper,
volcanic as it could be. And I nearly ducked out of the
way when her arms shot out at me, fearing she might strangle me on
the spot.

Instead, she wrapped her arms around my neck and wept. "Glory
be to God! Oh, Frances, this is a victory! So many lives will be improved. You beat them at their own game."

"I didn't beat them. It was a compromise . . ."

"Despise not the day of small things," said Mrs. Kelley. "If they
voted to limit working hours once, they'll do it again. We'll make the
canneries an election issue."

"We'll cram it down their throats," I vowed. It wasn't a ladylike
thing to say, but I hadn't gotten far being ladylike. I'd made progress
only when, like my brickmaking forebears, I'd been willing to put
my hands in the mud and get them dirty. That was another lesson I
wouldn't soon forget.

And it emboldened me to press harder on absolutely everything
that mattered to me.

"You complained to their *rabbi*?" Red asked as a group of my friends
sat around a big round teakwood table at a restaurant in Chinatown on
Mott Street devouring porcelain bowlfuls of savory chow mein.

We were celebrating the fact that Red's first book, *Hike and the*

Airplane, was going to be published under a pseudonym. We'd praised him lavishly, and he'd been self-deprecating, saying he was nothing but a "famooser."

Then the conversation turned to how I was driving the owners of Bloomingdale's to distraction, haranguing them to improve conditions and fire safety for their workers. In defense of myself, I said, "Well, the Industrial Commission in this state is in bed with every factory owner, so *someone* with moral authority needed to whisper in their ears. Why not their rabbi?"

Everyone at the table thought it was funny what I'd done and teased me. Between clacking chopsticks, Mary Rumsey, having left her baby boy in the care of his nanny for the evening, vividly imagined department store owners ducking out of churches and synagogues and going into hiding behind their top hats to avoid me.

"Good!" Paul Wilson said, dipping his egg foo yong in soy sauce. "Frances shouldn't be sorry."

"I'm not sorry in the least," I replied, glad to have Paul's approval. What shame could there be, after all, in haranguing factory and store owners to stop killing their workers? And if there *was* shame, well, someone needed to be shameless. Especially now that the owners of the Triangle Waist Company had just been acquitted of manslaughter charges.

The jury felt prosecutors hadn't proved the owners *knew* the factory door was locked when they fled, leaving girls to die. Given the insurance money, the shirtwaist kings would actually profit from the fire. The law, as it stood, incentivized men to work girls to exhaustion and even burn them alive. Which was why I intended to topple the law as it stood . . .

"I HAVE TO let you go after all, Frances," Mrs. Kelley said later that spring.

And I stood so abruptly that I dropped a book to the floor. "Why? What have I done now?"

Of course, I'd irritated so many important people that I couldn't count them. But which one had finally gotten me fired? A factory owner, an industrial commissioner, a legislator, or the Bloomingdales and their rabbi?

It sounded like a bad joke, and I was just waiting for the nasty punch line . . .

Then Mrs. Kelley grabbed my hand and gripped it hard. "What you've done, my dear girl, is impress Theodore Roosevelt, who is running for president again."

"I'm as delighted that he's running as I am embittered that I'm not allowed to vote for him, but I don't know what this has to do with my getting fired."

TR, as we now called him affectionately, was promising *a square deal* for all Americans. He said he wanted to give ordinary working people a chance. To do it, he was challenging Taft, the sitting president of his own party. It was a seismic shift in the political world. *Which*, Mrs. Kelley explained, meant his influence was highly sought-after by reformist groups—including the Committee on Safety, formed in the wake of the Triangle shirtwaist factory fire.

"The committee asked for Theodore Roosevelt's support in getting regulations passed. And the former president told them they'd have his support if they make *you* executive director."

I was sure I'd misheard. My knees wobbled. I sat back down. "He said what?"

Mrs. Kelley laughed, giving me an affectionate hug, then holding me out at arm's length again to look me up and down with pride as if I were one of her own children. "Frances, you're not getting fired. You're getting a new job. TR chose the committee's new chairman, treasurer, and secretary. He says with you as director, they can't fail."

I could scarcely believe it; I'd corresponded with Theodore Roosevelt only a few times—mostly by way of extending invitations to meetings and committees, which he always declined. His polite replies were among my most valuable possessions, but I hadn't thought he'd taken any notice of *me*. Certainly not enough to personally recommend me for a new job, much less insist I have it . . .

Now Mrs. Kelley solemnly intoned, "You must accept this new position, Frances. You've already done what I hired you to do, and now you'll serve as de facto chief investigator for the legislature. You'll show Al Smith and others what needs to be fixed. They'll trust you. You've made friends in Albany."

"A few enemies too!"

Mrs. Kelley patted my cheek with the motherly affection I'd craved all my life. "My dear girl, making a few enemies is how you know you're doing things right."

My new work was to be revolutionary—so I bought myself a new tricorn hat, which would, soon after, become my trademark.

My instinct as an economist was to begin with a litany of facts and figures. But Al Smith told me to stuff my notes in a drawer. Legislators needed to see, hear, smell, touch, and maybe even *taste* problems for themselves.

So I began my new job by saying, "Gentlemen, I'd like to take you on a tour."

We began by touring a candy factory, which seemed only fitting, after all. I warned legislators not to wear anything that they'd mind getting ruined. I myself donned an old ill-fitting overcoat with sturdy boots, because I knew how filthy these factories were. And of course we spotted hazards before we even got in the door. The rickety wooden stairway had no handrail. The metal stairs inside the factory itself were even worse, rusty and cluttered with mops and brooms. Stepping over a bucket, Al Smith said, "This can't be good."

"No, Mr. Smith, it is not," I said. "If ever there were a fire in this factory, hundreds of workers would never be able to get down the stairs in a rush without being pushed, tripping, or falling."

It'd fail the three-minute rule.

"Is that what you call *an obstructed exit?*" Smith asked, and when I nodded, he beamed like my star student.

Meanwhile, Senator Wagner, who was of recent German immigrant stock, mopped his brow as copper cauldrons hissed steam into the air and spattered chocolate like lava, which sometimes spilled over the sides and caught fire. "*Mein Gott.* What happens if the girls get their hair or clothes too close to the flames? Is there something to protect them from getting burned?"

The bewildered factory manager shook his head no.

Beyond the danger to the workers was, of course, the disgusting product itself. Would any consumer take a bite if they saw how flies swarmed the sticky syrup?

Now it was time to show these gentlemen what passed for a fire escape. It took several tries to get the window open, as it was sealed closed with sugar dust. Then, wondering if any would be brave enough, I asked, "Why doesn't one of you gentlemen try to climb out?"

Al Smith volunteered. He had to climb over steam pipes, and once he reached the fire escape, he called back, "Well, now I can't get down. Where's the ladder?"

"We got rid of the ladder," the manager admitted. "To prevent theft."

This was the Triangle shirtwaist factory fire waiting to happen all over again, and it made the legislators of both parties so agitated that they took over the questioning at the next factory.

How many people can escape through that door—

—do you have a sprinkler system—

What about fireproof staircases?

My only worry was that seeing too many factories in these conditions might convince legislators that there wasn't any alternative. So I brought them next to a state-of-the-art button factory, where much happier workers in protective uniforms traversed unobstructed aisles and fireproof stairways as a powerful ventilating system sucked up the harmful shell dust. Showing off the buttons, I said, "They make a beautiful product *and* a handsome profit besides." Then, satisfied that these visits made a tremendous impression, I concluded with, "Well, gentlemen, I'm grateful for the time you've been willing to spend—"

"We aren't finished, are we?" Smith asked.

Having seen a few factories, now the legislators wanted to see more. So I took them to pea-canning factories, where we discovered children as young as five years working. Some of these exhausted little cherubs fell asleep right on the factory floor in the slurry of discarded and rotting vegetables. And Al Smith finally exploded. "You can't have that!"

I put a hand on his arm, but he continued to yell at the supervisor. "You can't treat children this way."

"They're helping their mothers," the manager offered in feeble justification.

Which made Al shout even louder. "Day after day, hour after hour, without even a day of rest?"

"Food is perishable," the supervisor sputtered. "It'll go to waste if they stop. You can't ask that of canners."

"I'm a good Christian," Al replied hotly. "I've read the commandments. It says, 'Remember the Sabbath day, to keep it holy.' It doesn't say, '*Except in the canneries.*'"

Chapter Sixteen

New York City
Summer 1912

M Y FRIENDS AND I GATHERED FOR A BAC-
chanalia ball at Webster Hall, where the anarchist Emma
Goldman was handing out pamphlets on family limitation while Red made an ironic toast. "To cheating, fraud, and
backstabbing. The American way."

Though Theodore Roosevelt had been victorious in almost every
Republican primary election, the party bosses gave the nomination
to Taft. Only Paul Wilson seemed undisturbed by this turn of events,
lighting up his pipe as the orchestra played. "It's for the better, because now TR can form his own party."

What would come to be known as the Bull Moose Party represented a complete reordering of the landscape in which my work
must now take place. And I hadn't anticipated any of it.

"Well, we're with the proletariat anyway, aren't we, France?" Red
hailed the waiter. "Let's order another round. Another bourbon
for you?"

France was his new nickname for me, since I'd told him that
sweets was obnoxious.

Because I had the feeling Paul was just about to ask me to dance,
I said, "No thank you, Red. I think I've had enough to drink."

"C'mon, don't make me drink alone," Red insisted, loving the
atmosphere of revelry as dancers twirled around us. To the waiter, he
said, "Bourbon and branch water for the lady."

"She said no," Paul interjected.

"It's all right," I said, hoping to prevent a quarrel. "I'm a little thirsty after all."

I felt as if I had to say it because Paul, Mary, and the rest of my friends found Red to be terribly annoying and were always trying to ditch him. I understood why—at least on an intellectual level. Red was an odd duck, swimming in a sea of swans. But I truly adored Sinclair Lewis, and not only because he was a brilliant writer. He always cracked the surface of my New England reserve with his clever humor. And because I had always felt a little lonely in the world—a square peg trying to fit in the round hole of expectations—I felt as if we were kindred spirits.

Anyway, I was the one who'd invited Red along to this party, so now I tried to break the awkwardness by dragging the conversation back to politics. "With the Republicans splintered and such a mess, the Democratic convention ought to be quite interesting this year. I wish I could go."

Paul blew a ring of smoke. "Why can't you? I'm going."

"But you're a Republican."

"*Was*," he said. "The progressive movement is breaking both parties apart, and I want to egg it on. Why not come along?"

Red puffed up with effrontery on my behalf. "Hey, now, just what are you suggesting?"

Paul chuckled. "Nothing untoward. I promise to treat Frances with the strictest Victorian propriety."

"I'm tempted," I admitted. "But I have a mountain of work."

"She's too busy," Red echoed, sloshing a little of his drink into my lap. "France is always *very busy*."

Paul ignored him, producing a linen napkin to help wipe the spill. "Well, if you change your mind, Frances, let me know, and I'll get you a ticket."

LATER THAT NIGHT, I was awakened by a shout under my bedroom window. *"I love you, Frances Perkins!"*

It was a hot summer evening, so, like everyone else in New York, I'd left the window open for a cross breeze. Now, in my shift and bare feet, I stumbled to the window to see Red standing under the streetlamp.

"Frances!" he shouted. *"Fraaaaaaances, I love you! Fanny, Franny, France, I love you no matter what your name is."*

He was waking up the neighborhood, so I hissed down at him, "Red, what the devil are you doing?"

"I'm proposing marriage," he shouted into the night air. "We can live here in New York, or we can settle on your family farm in Connecticut or Vermont that you're always talking about."

"It's *Maine*, you numbskull."

"Marry me, Frances!"

"Stop it, Red. You're drunk."

"Let me come up and sleep it off."

I primly clutched the collar of my nightgown. "I most certainly will not."

On the sidewalk, Red staggered one way, then the other, and I began to worry he might fall off the curb. "But I love you, Frances. Marry me!"

From somewhere else on the street, a man shouted, *"Hey, lady, just say yes to shut him up so we can sleep!"*

How perfectly humiliating.

I hated undue attention and hated even more for people to know my private business. Now Red was shouting it all over the street. I called down, "If you really loved me, you'd go home this instant."

"It's not fair." Red held his arms up theatrically for our growing audience. "I may not have his wavy hair, or his engraved cards, or his money and paisley pocket squares, or a perfect tennis swing, but I love you, Frances Perkins."

Dear God, was this about Paul Wilson? Remembering the Valentine's Day chocolates and other sweet things Red had done to woo me—including accompanying me on suffrage marches—I felt a pang of sympathy. Certainly, some part of me was flattered that he might ever be lovesick over me. It was the natural human condition to want companionship. To be loved. To start a family. It was only that I'd closed myself off to the possibility . . .

Maybe I should let Red come up. I'd get him some strong coffee to sober him, and a wet cloth for his face. Some aspirin if I could find it. Then I'd try to figure out how to explain this to the neighbors. It was the decent thing to do. So I reached for my robe, and that's when he shouted, "I saw you first, Frances. *Finders keepers!*"

I froze hearing those words. Quite possibly the *worst* words he could have paired with a declaration of love. Did he think I was a possession—a lucky penny he'd found on the sidewalk and now claimed for his own?

If that was what he thought of women, I began to wonder if he'd ever been a believer in suffrage. Maybe he'd just gone along to win my affections. And now he proposed marriage—which gave a man such power over his wife. Power he was plainly not responsible enough to wield. "*Mr. Lewis*," I snapped. "You're behaving badly, showing me the gravest disrespect. If you don't go home, I'm going to ring up the authorities."

With that, I slammed the window closed.

Though it was muffled, I heard Red call my name a few more

times, until someone threw old tin cans at him and he finally staggered away.

Unfortunately, now I couldn't sleep. I lay in bed, stiff and angry. Feeling uncharacteristically spiteful too. So much so that when the sun finally came up, I rang Paul Wilson. "As it happens, I'd very much like to go with you to the Democratic convention."

Chapter Seventeen

Baltimore, Maryland
Summer 1912

P
AUL TAUGHT ME TO PLAY CARDS ON THE train, and he was very good at it, owing to his head for numbers and probabilities. He was also a shameless gambler. By the time we arrived in Baltimore, he'd won every penny off me, which he laughingly returned to my possession.

At the station, he insisted on taking my luggage, arranging for the porter to have it sent to the nearby hotel. We'd have separate rooms, of course, but I didn't wish to cause gossip, so I hung back to purchase a Coca-Cola and some Cracker Jack from a concession stand.

That's where I ran into Franklin Delano Roosevelt, his hat emblazoned with a slogan on its band that read *Win with Wilson*.

"Why, Miss Perkins," Frank said with a flash of Roosevelt teeth. "Fancy meeting you here."

"Fancy that," I said stiffly. I was still awfully sore at him for how useless he'd been during the struggle for the fifty-four-hour bill, and how he'd promised his support, only to disappear when it came time to vote.

"I'm here for the convention," he said. He wasn't a delegate or even an alternate, but Frank was throwing his featherweight behind Woodrow Wilson. He was at the train station, with a few stalwarts he'd apparently rounded up off the streets, to post manifestos and wave pennants for his candidate.

Offering me a flyer, Frank asked, "Have you considered supporting Woodrow Wilson for the nomination?"

I sputtered a laugh. "Me? I'm not a delegate. Or a Democrat. Or even a voter, for that matter."

"Ah, but you're a suffragette with *sway*, Miss Perkins. And after what we pulled off in Albany this year with the fifty-four-hour bill, don't you think reformers like us ought to have some say about who is president?"

Reformers like us . . .

Was he claiming credit for my bill? Taking umbrage, I challenged him. "After what *we* pulled—"

"That was a hoot, wasn't it?" he interrupted with the winsome grin of a natural-born salesman. "The way we turned that vote around at the last minute. Most fun I've had in ages."

"You weren't even *there*," I protested. "You left early. You disappeared. Abandoned the cause!"

He grinned wider. "Oh, I was there. You must not have seen me."

Exasperated by this bald-faced lie, I insisted, "I took a head count. I know precisely who voted for it."

"You miscounted." He had the audacity to wink.

Oh, the popinjay was daring me to contradict him. "You are maddeningly dishonest, sir."

Those were fighting words. Men had dueled over less. But Roosevelt only laughed. And the more he laughed, the angrier I got. "You are truly infuriating, Mr. Roosevelt! You were not present. I know you were not present, and *you* know you were not present, and—"

"Hello, Mr. Roosevelt," Paul interrupted before I could stop ranting.

Roosevelt tipped his boater hat. "Good to see you again, Mr. Wilson. *Say*, you're not related to the candidate, are you?"

"To Woodrow Wilson?" Paul shook his head. "No relation. Wilson's a common surname."

Frank frowned. "Too bad. If you were related, I'd have invited you up to the good seats!" Then, without missing a beat, he pressed a flyer into Paul's hand. "Tell your friends to throw their support to Woodrow Wilson. Be a Wilson for Wilson!"

With that, Roosevelt disappeared into a crowd of boosters, and I grumbled, "*Dear God*, if his candidate wins the nomination, he'll be even more insufferable."

"YOU HAVE TO give the devil his due," Paul said as chants for Woodrow Wilson went up in the armory hall, which was done up for the festivities with star-spangled bunting. "Frank Roosevelt knows how to get people to sing, cheer, and throw up their hats."

I was feeling less generous. "Yes, well, the one thing Frank knows how to do well is make a lot of noise."

Paul laughed, and as I desperately fanned myself against the sweltering heat, I realized that he never looked the slightest bit rumpled—much less overheated. Thankfully, he took pity on me. "Let me take you somewhere cool before you melt."

We went to Riverview Park, where we watched the roller coaster while cracking Maryland crabs at a picnic table—which Paul somehow managed to do without getting a speck on his white shirt and tie. Then we got ice cream cones and sat under a private copse of shade trees. It was there that Paul confessed, "Frances, that night when Sinclair Lewis was sloshing his drink on you, he told me you were his ladylove."

"Oh, dear," I said, embarrassed. "He was very drunk that night."

"Nevertheless, I believe he was sincere. And I'm wondering if you might be so kind as to let me know if you share his feelings. I'd rather not continue to harbor hopes if your affections have already been won by another."

I flushed, pretending to pay great attention to the way my ice cream dripped at the edge of my cone. I hadn't been sure whether Paul had been harboring hopes, but now I found an answering hope inside me. "I'm very fond of Red—even if I'm not speaking to him at the moment. *Very* fond. But if I ever shared his romantic feelings, I don't anymore. And, given his lack of maturity, I don't think it possible I ever could."

Paul nodded, his countenance serious. "Do you think it possible you might ever return mine?"

I was too tongue-tangled to answer as my heart began to hammer in my chest. Thankfully, Paul went on to say, "You're a remarkable person, Frances. Intelligent, interesting, and determined. You're a force of nature, and I'm curious about everything having to do with you. In short, I'm *smitten*. I have been for quite some time."

"I share those same sentiments about you," I admitted, blushing furiously. "It's only that I have an old-fashioned streak, and I cannot be as free with my affections as some in our crowd."

He nodded, voice softening. "I think I understand what you're driving at. Let me be clear. I'm a bachelor of thirty-six years. I've sown my wild oats. I'm after your *heart*, Frances."

I took a moment to absorb this, putting my hand over my chest as if to guard the object of his affections. "I've had my heart broken before."

"I suspected as much," he said.

"Not just by a man, but also by mankind. By the fire. It broke something in me." He nodded, patient, understanding. And that patience gave me the strength to admit, "But some people say a broken bone will heal stronger than it was before. Maybe the heart is like that."

He nodded. "Yes, I think so."

"I'm stronger now." I peeked up at him from under my lashes. "Strong enough to dare the possibility of love . . ."

He smiled down at his ice cream. "You make love sound like a risky proposition."

Now I smiled too. "It certainly is, for a woman of thirty-two who is accustomed to independence."

"I'm an enlightened man. What have you to fear in accepting my love?"

"So very much. Because to be loved, really loved, one must be *known*, and I find that terrifying. In truth, I think it takes courage— real spiritual daring—to allow oneself to be known."

"Don't you think it can be thrilling too? Like a roller coaster. Some moments a slow and arduous climb, others spent in weightless euphoria, some spent in free fall. Then, just when you feel you are plunging to your doom, you're saved by love, flung in an exciting new direction, and lifted to new heights."

"An apt metaphor," I said, for I felt, in that moment, very much at the edge of a precipice.

He took the liberty of reaching for my hand, and I let him hold it, his thumb gently brushing my knuckles. "Well, then, Frances, would you like to take a roller-coaster ride with me?"

Though I didn't pull my hand away, I still felt apprehensive. "Is this still a metaphor, or do you mean to invite me for an actual amusement ride? Because if you mean the latter, I must refuse."

"Haven't you ridden a roller coaster before?"

"Oh, yes. When I was young and foolish. Before I became a safety investigator. Now I can only think of the nuts and bolts and rigging, and all the ways the contraption could kill someone. That takes the fun out of it!"

Paul chuckled and leaned close. "What if I kissed you instead?"

Feeling the warmth of his breath, I shyly nodded my assent. Then he lifted my chin with his thumb and pressed a kiss to my lips. His were cool from the ice cream, but I melted under them in wonderment. He was right, this *was* thrilling. And though this kiss did not come with nuts and bolts and rigging, it felt strong and secure, like something that would endure.

Chapter Eighteen

★ ★ ★

New York City
July 1912

Dear one,
Every caress I give you and every loving word I speak is more than
momentary in its message. Dear sweet tender lad, you are most
precious to me.
~ Your F

Paul and I were terribly in love.

When he went on a trip to Europe late that summer, he wrote most every day, providing his exact nautical position. And I traced his journey on a map, wishing we were making it together.

Most of my life, I'd craved independence and even demanded it. Now, I seldom went a day or even an hour without wanting to ask Paul a question, or to tell him about something I'd seen or done. I penned a letter to him every day. Sometimes twice! And, shamed by my neediness, I scribbled on one note, *To think I write you like this . . .*

Darling Frances, he replied. *I, too, am longing. I think of nothing but how I want to caress your dear face and kiss your beloved lips.*

Love made a new woman of me. Someone less guarded. Someone who scribbled poems in notebooks on a whim. Someone less apt to keep everything inside. Love even made me a little more forgiving . . .

I accepted a groveling apology from Red over a game of dominoes at the Cafe Lafayette, which he finished by announcing, "Well, as it happens, I'm in love with someone else now too."

"*Really.*"

"Yes, *really*. A beauty editor at *Vogue*. I had been lunching at the tearooms she frequents just for a glimpse at her. And she's agreed to go out to dinner with me."

"Brave girl," I said, thumbing a domino.

My lack of jealousy seemed to annoy Red, but if we were to remain friends, he'd have to get used to it. I'd given my heart to Paul Wilson. And, realizing it, Red sighed. "You can't really be happy with a glorified accountant."

"He's a reformer. Like Theodore Roosevelt."

Red snorted. "I doubt Paul could take a shot to the chest like the old Bull Moose and keep right on going with his speech."

Red was referring to the recent assassination attempt against TR, and I didn't find it at all amusing. Not how close we had come to losing the former president, nor at the thought of someone taking a shot at Paul. So I warned, "I'm happy, Red. Truly happy, and you shouldn't want to spoil it for me."

"Well, all right, France. I'm sorry. I won't spoil it for you." But Sinclair Lewis could never help himself. "After all, happiness like that can't last."

WHEN I NEXT encountered Franklin Roosevelt in Albany that winter, I said, "Congratulations, Mr. Roosevelt. It seems you backed the right horse."

In that presidential election, the Socialist candidate, Eugene Debs, won six percent of the vote. Meanwhile, the split between the Republicans and the breakaway Bull Moose Party proved fatal to both. Now incoming Democratic president Woodrow Wilson had rewarded Frank for his support by offering him the post of assistant secretary of the Navy.

Naturally, Frank was taking a postelection victory lap just to rub it in our faces. *Go, Franklin, go,* all his fellow legislators in Albany advised, because they wanted him gone.

I knew he didn't need any convincing. His career was progressing exactly the way he said it would two years ago when we met at that tea dance. In fact, I was beginning to think that when it came to politics, Frank was some kind of idiot savant.

Beaming with success, he said, "Miss Perkins, we've done all right for ourselves, haven't we? To think we both started in Albany at the same time . . ."

"Yes, we did, and there's a lot to take pride in," I said diplomatically. After all, it was time to mend fences. If Frank Roosevelt was going to be an insider in the new administration, he might be useful to my work. Still, I was painfully curious about something. "May I ask you a question, Mr. Roosevelt? When we met, you were defending your wife's uncle. You said many fine things about Theodore Roosevelt, expressing your deepest admiration. And you said it wasn't only because of the familial connection."

"Yes, yes, that's true."

"So how could you campaign against TR?"

"Because we're from different parties," he said. "I campaigned for Wilson because he is a Democrat and so am I."

"But *why* are you a Democrat?"

His bushy eyebrows furled as if he found my confusion confusing. "Because my father was a Democrat."

Was that really all there was to it? "Well, my father is a Congregationalist. But I became an Episcopalian soon after I left home. Surely it's easier to change parties than religions."

Frank broke into a big smile, threw his head back, and hooted.

"Don't say that too loud! Around these parts, party politics *is* religion."

I allowed myself to chuckle, admitting he had a point. "But you've spent most of your career running *against* Tammany Democrats from inside the party, when you could have just gone Bull Moose."

He tugged his earlobe. "I imagine that would have made family dinners more pleasant than they have been as of late." Then he laughed. "You should understand it perfectly well, Miss Perkins. When you first arrived in Albany, you had nothing whatsoever in common with Tammany boys. But they were the only ones who could give you an opening."

And it was Democrats who gave *him* an opening. He must've supposed he couldn't get ahead as a Republican, always in Theodore Roosevelt's shadow, his every advancement vulnerable to the charge of nepotism or dynasty.

I began to see that running as a Democrat let him turn the Roosevelt name to his advantage while being regarded as his own man. I could respect that. At least a little.

Since I was accustomed to his dashing off and leaving me high and dry, I said, "Well, I don't mean to keep you. I know you're busy."

"Yes, yes. Well, in any case, thank you, Miss Perkins. I've enjoyed working on important reforms with you. I hope we get to do it again in the future."

I bit back my desire to remind him that he hadn't championed *any* of my efforts. "I hope so too."

We shook hands, and he started to walk away, then stopped. "You know, Miss Perkins, I was wrong about you. I mistook you for one of those Bible-thumping harpies or prissy little silk-stocking reformers. Now I've seen you smoke and drink and make the boys around here laugh. You make them think you're one of them. That you like them."

"I *do* like them," I insisted. "Most of them, anyway. If I didn't like people, Mr. Roosevelt, I wouldn't do any of the things I do."

He grinned. "You remind me of my mother."

I arched an offended brow. "Surely you and I are about the same age."

"I mean that you're strong-willed, like she is. Persistent too. You try one thing, and if it doesn't work, you try something else. You never let yourself get too dispirited. If you fall down, you get back up, dust yourself off, and start over. In truth, I've learned an awful lot from you."

It was such a lovely thing for him to say that I wasn't at all certain he was sincere. But I found that I *was* sincere when I said, "Good luck in Washington, Mr. Roosevelt. I wish you success."

THAT SAME WINTER, Paul and I had a wonderful time strolling what some called the *Freak Art* exhibit in New York City. And we were entertained as much by the reactions of the crowd as we were by the work of avant-garde painters like Matisse and Duchamp.

"I can't understand how this is tolerated," some woman in the crowd screeched. "This artist ought to be pilloried! It makes me fear for the world."

Many people felt the same. No lesser authority than Theodore Roosevelt had declared that what he'd seen here was not, in fact, art.

But for once, I disagreed with the old Bull Moose. "I've decided things needn't be conventional to be beautiful."

Staring at me instead of the artwork, Paul said, "I couldn't agree more."

We paused to take in the cubist-inspired *Nude Descending a Staircase*, which fascinated me with its sense of motion and modernity.

And when I told Paul, he said, "I'm not surprised. You're a very modern woman."

"You're mocking me."

"No. I embrace change and shall soon prove it."

I assumed Paul was speaking about his recent decision to back the mayoral aspirations of John Purroy Mitchel, one of his closest friends. I didn't think the young and eager Mitchel had a chance but didn't want to be discouraging. As it happened, Paul had something quite different in mind when it came to embracing change. He led me to a quiet bench in the fir-bedecked exhibition hall, where I was happy to rest my feet. There I noticed that Paul—who never perspired—was sweating profusely. "Dear God, are you ill?"

"A little lovesick, yes."

All at once, Paul went down on one knee with a wobbly smile, and my eyes widened. "What *are* you doing?"

"Proposing marriage," he whispered. Glancing over his shoulder to make certain that he had attracted no one's notice but mine, he continued, very earnestly, "Frances, you're more revolutionary than any artist. In fact, I think you are a work of art wrought in human form, and I hope you will do me the honor of agreeing to marry me."

Suddenly light-headed, I couldn't form words. Fortunately, he added, "Don't answer just now. I'd like you to take time to think."

I nodded, *thinking and thinking*. Even as my heart swelled with *feeling* . . .

I loved Paul. I loved him deeply and felt I always would. That made me want to throw my arms around his neck and say yes right away. But *thinking* about it made me wonder if love was enough reason for marriage. As a woman, wasn't my situation rather out of the ordinary?

I was now in correspondence with important people all over the country on matters of building regulations, fire regulations, and labor legislation. I'd gotten something of a good reputation, and ordinary citizens sometimes wrote me letters, asking for help.

Because of my work, new laws were being passed. New York State was getting better sanitary conditions and factory safety and enforcing laws against child labor. Could I give all this important work up for marriage?

As if he could read my racing thoughts, Paul said, "I wanted to propose *here* so you'll remember my vow to you now that ours will be a thoroughly *modern* marriage."

Well, he could say that. He could even mean it. And I was touched by his sincerity. But law, society, and even simple biology would test his promise. If we had children—and I *wanted* children—I'd have to quit my job. Could I really stop now when I was finally saving lives?

Chapter Nineteen

Newcastle, Maine
Summer 1913

Dear Paul,
Please don't blame yourself. I love spending time in Maine—for I think of it more as my home than any other place—but my mother can be horrid and disagreeable.
~F

In contemplating marriage, I'd invited Paul on my family's annual pilgrimage to Maine to meet my parents and enjoy a lovely week along the banks of the Damariscotta.

During the visit, Paul was his usual dapper and well-mannered self, smoking his pipe in the library with my father, showing an interest in my sister's little children, and even indulging my mother's constant complaints about everything from the bright sun to the quality of the oysters that year.

To charm my family, Paul brewed us a special coffee made with eggshells on a lazy Saturday in the summer kitchen where I used to help my grandmother dry her wooden spoons and rolling pins. And when my mother and sister quarreled about some trivial matter, Paul and I escaped to the canoe to paddle along the rocky shore, where old bricks still littered the ground like a crumbling monument to my family's gloried past.

"My grandmother taught me to swim right there," I said, pointing out the spot. "I always think about her when I'm here. I feel close to her here—almost as if I can hear her voice—even though she's passed on."

Dipping a paddle into the muddy water, Paul asked, "Would she have approved of me?"

"She'd have *adored* you," I insisted.

Paul seemed enormously glad to hear it. "I can see why you love it here. It is very much like you. Natural, unpretentious, mysterious below the surface."

"A little salty too," I teased.

"As I recall, your kisses are sweet," he replied in a way that made me want to sin. But Paul refused to do anything improper while visiting my family.

The scandal, as it happened, occurred upon his leave-taking.

Paul had to get back to the bureau, so my mother and I dropped him at the train station. There, Paul gave me a goodbye kiss, like any man in love might do. We waved farewell, but as soon as he disappeared onto the train, my mother pinched my arm. "How *could* you allow that? You behaved like a harlot."

Deeply offended, I snapped, "I'm a grown woman, all but betrothed."

"To allow yourself to be kissed in public! Your father and I already fear for what liberties you allow Mr. Wilson in New York . . ."

Furious, I did not stay long after that. The suspicions of my parents clarified matters. Until I married, I'd always be a child in their eyes—to be scolded and worried after. I'd also be a child in the eyes of society. That wasn't enough reason to get married, but it combined powerfully with my love for Paul and the way he made me feel as if we might face down the whole world together.

When I returned to New York, I invited Paul to breakfast at my apartment, where I burned bacon and eggs on the old iron stove and even managed to ruin the toast before he laughed and asked, "Will you give up and let me take you out?"

"New Englanders don't give up," I said, nibbling on a crust that was only a little charred. "And there's something important I want to discuss. Something private."

Paul waggled his eyebrows suggestively.

I ignored the flirtation. "*If* I agreed to marry you, Paul, would you mind terribly if I kept my own name?"

I had just a little bit of a reputation of being somebody whose ideas were good. I was very puffed up, I suppose, about the fact that I could sign a letter and my name meant something. So it was to my immense relief that Paul said, "You should use whatever name suits you."

I took a shaky but grateful breath, then screwed up my courage. "In that case, I gladly accept your proposal of marriage if the offer is still open."

Instantly, Paul rose from the table and grabbed me up into an embrace. "You've made me so happy, Frances!"

"Oh, put me down," I said, laughing with joy. "You're making a terrible fuss!"

"When should we get married?" Paul asked, setting me on my feet but raining down kisses on my cheeks, nose, and forehead. "And where? The lease on my apartment is almost up, and then there's the campaign."

I'd unwittingly fallen in love with a man who might have a political future, for if his friend won the mayor's race, Paul would be asked to serve in the new administration. In that case, my betrothed wouldn't have time for the social ceremony of a formal wedding his family might host in Chicago or that mine might host in dreary Worcester. When I felt the heat of his cheeks against my fingertips and the softness of his lips near my ear, I knew I didn't want to wait. "Why not marry here, straightaway?"

Paul eyed me suspiciously. "You wouldn't want to plan? I know you love to make lists."

"What you don't know is that very occasionally I'm also recklessly impulsive. Besides, if we elope, we can do it without any fuss."

"Ah." He chuckled. "*There* is my little puritan. A civil ceremony, then?"

That idea was in keeping with a modern marriage, but I still cherished at least one tradition. "I prefer a church, if we can find one on short notice."

"I'll find one," he vowed. And so he did.

Our wedding dawned on a fair September day, and I was steady-handed and completely at peace as I donned my best cotton day dress in suffragist white. There'd been no time to purchase a fancier dress, certainly no time to assemble a trousseau. I hadn't even told Mary Rumsey about the wedding because she would've insisted we shop for lacy underthings for the marital act. About which I *was* a bit nervous. I was going to have to find the courage to admit someone to all my inner places, and that terrified me. But I was too happy to let a little terror stop me.

I didn't have a veil or a bouquet, or a matron of honor to help fasten my grandmother's diamond pin on my dress or my pearls round my neck. Jewelry was certainly not designed for the independent woman, so I was struggling with the pearls when the telephone rang.

I fumbled to answer, thinking it must be Paul warning me of some change to our plans. But on the other end of the line, a woman whose voice I did not recognize broke into sobs. "Miss Perkins, I'm desperate to call you like this. I have nowhere else to turn."

I didn't want to be late for my wedding, but I couldn't end the call when someone was in such distress. "Whatever is the matter?"

With great emotion, she introduced herself as the wife of a factory owner who'd been convicted for criminal negligence thanks, in part, to my agitation for fire safety regulations. "He's being sentenced today and I'm begging you to recommend clemency to the judge."

I stiffened. "On what grounds?"

"On the grounds that my husband is a good man! He's learned his lesson. Tell the judge he meant no harm to those girls who died."

No, I thought. *I'd wager he didn't mean them harm.* But he couldn't be bothered to protect them if it cost him a penny. Those young women lost their lives. It was only plain justice that it should cost him something too. "I'm sorry, I can't argue for clemency."

"You must," she said. "Can you imagine what this will do to his mother? She wants to speak to you."

"No, that won't be—"

"Miss Perkins," cried the mother. "Please don't take my son from me. He's all I have!"

I would've been heartless for these pleas not to touch me. I *wasn't* heartless. It was a terrible thing for a man to go to prison. To lose his freedom. To be forced to leave behind his wife and children and elderly mother. A *terrible* thing. But not so terrible as being burned alive . . .

I gripped the phone. "Madam, if your son is as good a man as you say, then his friends should tell the judge he deserves lenience. Your son is a stranger to me. It isn't my place to plead for clemency."

The wife took the phone again. "Haven't you ever loved a man, Miss Perkins?"

What a question to ask on my wedding day!

I glanced at the clock. If I didn't hang up, I'd be late. Yet the woman insisted, "I've called your friend at the Consumers' League, and she said that she'd go to the judge if you go too. Please. I am at your mercy."

Oh, this was dreadful. I had no idea which "friend" she might have spoken to. I was all alone and had no one to ask for advice. Not Mrs. Kelley. Not the Goldmark sisters. Not Al Smith, Mary Rumsey, or even Red Lewis.

Of course, the person from whom I most wanted advice was Paul, but he was likely already at the church . . .

I pinched the bridge of my nose. If I recommended clemency, and the judge took it into account, that'd be on the judge's head, not mine. *He'd* been appointed to dispense justice, not me. I didn't wish ill upon anyone. So why not give in? My God was a merciful one, after all. Mercy was a high virtue. But what good were laws if they were enforced only upon those who had no one to plead for them?

All my life I'd been accused of being too softhearted to understand harsh realities. The truth was that I understood harsh realities better than most who made the rules. And I knew what kind of person rarely had to play by the rules like everyone else. Clutching my grandmother's pin like a talisman, I reminded myself of my purpose. "I'm sorry. I won't do it. I have a public duty to fix upon employers direct responsibility for the safety, health, and welfare of their workers. If I—*of all people*—ask the law to go easy on your husband, more girls will die."

I felt miserably cruel. I hated myself for refusing. Yet I knew it was the right decision.

I also knew I was too upset now to go forward with a wedding. The beautiful peace of my wedding morning had been shattered. Now my stomach roiled, a headache pounded behind my eyes, and I felt as if I might cry.

Everything was *ruined*.

I couldn't get married today. Still, I couldn't leave Paul waiting for me at the chapel. I'd have to tell him myself, face-to-face, so I hurried to Grace Church on Tenth and Broadway, where I expected to find him pacing nervously.

Instead, Paul was perfectly composed, chatting amiably with the reverend as if he had unshakable faith that I'd never abandon him. And the way he looked at me when I came through the doors—with such love and trust—felt like nothing short of *grace*.

It was the church's namesake. And I thought of how rare it was to find grace in this imperfect world. What a blessing to be given a companion for life. What a sin it would be to fling this gift back in God's teeth!

All aches, pains, distress, and thoughts of postponing the wedding fled in an instant. Then Paul's sparkling sapphire blue eyes met mine. "Frances, are you ready?"

"Yes," I whispered. "I am."

We took our vows, and they felt as sacred as they were meant to be. I pledged myself to him, and him to me, and when we kissed, we sealed our fates, one to another.

That night, my new husband carried me over the threshold. At first I'd demurred.

It's a ridiculous old-fashioned tradition. And I'm too heavy; you'll drop me!

But the moment I felt myself suspended in Paul's strong arms, dependent upon another person for maybe the first time in my adult life, my eyes welled with tears. "Do you know, Paul, that before you came into my life, I was cold and raw and trembling except on the outside? My life was a lonesome place."

He kissed my fingertips. "Now, my dearly beloved, neither of us will ever have to be lonely again from this day forth."

Chapter Twenty

Newcastle, Maine
September 1913

Dear Fanny,
I would've liked to have you married at home and had a wed-
ding, but if you thought it better to have it as you did, then I
suppose it is all right and I give my warmest blessing.
– Your loving father

Paul and I took an impromptu honeymoon in the wilds of Maine, existing on little more than love and glorious fall foliage. We promised ourselves a more proper honeymoon after the mayoral campaign, but for now, we had the trees and each other.

Feeding me blueberry preserves on a biscuit, Paul promised, "After the campaign, let's take an extended visit to Europe and travel in style."

"Can we afford an *extended* visit to Europe?"

Paul rose up on one elbow in the meadow grass, slightly affronted. "Frances, I'm not as rich as Mary Rumsey, but I have so comfortable an inheritance that you'll never have to eat another banana sandwich in your life."

I laughed, and when I did, he playfully smudged blueberry on my lip with his thumb. "You're beautiful . . ."

I winced, remembering how my mother told me I'd never be a beauty and that to wish for it was the sin of vanity. "Oh, stop—"

"It pains me you don't know it." I thought him blinded by love, but he explained, "Your eyes are stunning when they twinkle with mischief. Your lips are irresistible when they quirk into that sly smile. And you're exquisite when you laugh. You think yourself plain in photographs, but you're beautiful in motion."

"Like the painting no one liked?" I asked, remembering Duchamp's controversial work.

"Only fools didn't like it," Paul said. "You're more beautiful than that painting and even more likely to change the world."

AFTER THE HONEYMOON, it was time to announce our marriage. We'd already written to family, but it turned out to be considerably more difficult to break the news to colleagues. Pauline Goldmark groaned and covered her face as if I'd told her someone died. "Oh, Frances, why did you marry? You were such a *promising* person."

She apparently thought the person who died was *me*. And here I thought marriage would free me from judgments! If I told her how deeply I loved Paul, or how eager I was to have his child, she would've thought less of me, so I said, "I was always being challenged by somebody who thought it would be a good idea to marry me or who recommended that I should marry. I know Paul Wilson well. I like him. I've known him for a considerable time. I enjoy his company and I thought I might as well marry and get it off my mind."

It was better to answer that way. My grandmother had always taught me to remain tight-lipped when it came to that which was most dear to me. And this kind of answer kept people at a distance from a marriage over which I was now so protective.

Thankfully my former boss received the news better, but Florence Kelley saw right through my guarded explanation. "Oh, my dear, do you think I've never been in love? Of course, *I* was foolish enough to marry a violent man, whereas *you* are marrying a gentleman. But I can see how deep your feelings run; you can't hide it from me."

I blushed, embarrassed. But then she said, "I wish you the very best, but if I ever learn that Paul Caldwell Wilson treats you poorly, I may come after him with a broomstick."

Smiling warmly, I embraced her. "I don't doubt that for a moment."

Fortunately, Red also took the news better than I hoped, sending a note that read, *Dear old France, I am very happy to hear of your marriage, and darn it again, I wish I were not so broke—I'd send you a silver tea set, I would.*

As for me, I was no longer broke. Though it left me vulnerable to the charge of my more radical friends that I'd *gone over to the bourgeoisie*, Paul and I moved into a beautiful redbrick house on Washington Place West. I had never lived somewhere so grand, and it was a bit of a shock because I'd become accustomed to living in cramped little flats with shared bathroom facilities. Suddenly, I had servants, more furniture than I knew what to do with, and expectations that I'd play society hostess.

"You're going to love it," Mary Rumsey assured me, delighted by her successful matchmaking. She and her husband sent an outrageously expensive wedding gift, and now she was flitting about my parlor in a red dress with the latest scarf from Paris, helping to arrange the furniture. "You're a woman who was meant to have a staff at work *and* at home."

I wasn't sure about that, but there *was* something wonderful about being able to invite one's friends and co-workers to dinner and entertain them in high style. And while New England thriftiness came to me as second nature, Paul said there was no need to economize. "Spend whatever you please. Buy the season's latest fashions!"

I wasn't the sort to obsess over the latest modes from Paris, but new colors *were* coming into vogue—peach and marigold and plum . . .

Still, one thing gave me pause. "Do you think I'm getting plump?" I asked, catching my reflection in the mirror as we readied for bed.

"Of course not," he said, removing his tie without looking at me. "And even if you were, I would only find it pleasing."

I smirked, climbing under the sheet. "I used to be so thin, people thought I was a teenaged girl, but the funniest thing happened to me the other day . . ."

Paul settled into bed beside me. "Do tell."

"I was standing outside the elevator in Albany when I ran into one of the legislators."

"One of your gentlemen bandits from Tammany?" Paul asked wryly.

I ignored his ribbing. "The point is, he was terribly upset. When he saw me, he grabbed my hand, proceeding to pour his heart out."

"Come now, Frances. Tammany boys don't have hearts."

"Not true! Because of that crack, I'm not going to tell you *why* he was in tears. I'm just going to tell you he shared some political secrets with me he ought not have. Then, when he got hold of himself, he startled to realize what he'd done. That's when he blurted out that he couldn't help himself in crying on my shoulder because I was the only woman in Albany and *every man's got a mother, you know.*"

Laughing, Paul said, "I can't imagine that he meant you looked like *his* mother, Frances. He just meant that when in distress, a man can only be vulnerable to a kind and nurturing woman. I've never let anyone see me cry but my mother. It's the male mind."

"Oh, is it?" I asked, sliding closer under the covers. "I feel as if I should take notes on *the male mind.*"

"Take notes if you must." Paul gently tugged me against his chest. "But I don't approve of my bride making *too* close a study of other men."

"That doesn't sound like something a modern husband would say."

"Sadly, I retain some small streak of old-fashioned jealousy."

I laughed. "Well, I won't make too close a study of other men. Perhaps just of their minds and their mothers."

"Such stimulating bedroom talk," Paul said sarcastically, kissing my neck. "I can't get enough of it."

"Oh? Tell me, what is your first memory of your dear mama?"

Paul chuckled by my ear. "Stop."

Impishly, I asked, "Did she cut your sandwiches and say you were a well-behaved boy?"

"*Stop*," he said again, this time groaning as he fell back against the pillow. "If you ever want to *be* a mother, you must stop. Talking about one's *own* mother is an infallible method of contraception."

"Aha," I said, jabbing my finger against his chest. "That's useful information. Not here, at this moment, but in Albany. Perhaps I'd get further if I reminded men of their mothers." After all, I recalled the admiring way in which Frank Roosevelt had spoken about *his* mother. How silly I was not to make a connection before. "Men don't flirt with their mothers in smoke-filled political offices. Or try to pinch their mothers' bottoms in committee hearings, or make rude and lascivious propositions to them on the ferry back from Albany."

Paul now bristled, as if he had never conceived of these outrages. "I'd like you to name the men who try such things with you."

Having realized my otherwise mild-mannered new husband had a strong protective streak, I made light of it. "Why? Are you going to duel them at dawn? I've learned to handle myself!"

"You shouldn't have to."

"No, but I'm not going to buy that marigold suit Mary has picked out for me. For my next meeting of the Factory Investigating Committee, I'm going to buy something dark and somber and *motherly* and see how far it gets me."

Chapter Twenty-One

★ ★ ★

New York City
November 1913

PAUL AND I WERE THERE IN THE CRUSH AT Times Square, enjoying the reams of confetti the night John Purroy Mitchel won the mayoral election. Later, at home, shaking confetti from our shoulders, I put a hand to my hip and said, "Well, you've done it now."

Paul laughed, hanging my coat. "I did nothing."

"You won your very first political campaign! A long shot if ever there was one. I believe you are both a gambler and a phenom."

Paul tried not to preen. "It wasn't *my* campaign. It was Mitchel's. *He's* the wonder boy candidate. And the public is ready for third-party reform."

That was only partially true. Paul's friend had won the mayoral race mostly because Tammany's candidate had died. And because both former president Theodore Roosevelt and current president Woodrow Wilson backed him, one of the few things on which both men, of different parties, could agree. The so-called fusion ticket carried the votes of the Bull Moose Party, Republicans and Democrats alike. And now Paul pretended to grimace. "I have a feeling that working at city hall is going to cut into my time on the tennis court."

My husband's new job overseeing the city's budget for Mayor Mitchel would come with a bump in salary, and many responsibilities. But despite the fast new pace of our lives as newlyweds, those were happy, prosperous times. With me working for legislators and

Paul working at city hall, we were in the thick of things. In fact, Mayor Mitchel was such a charismatic reformer that some were already talking about his becoming president. His future was limitless, and because he depended on Paul, that meant my husband's future was limitless too.

I hadn't set out to marry a man in politics, much less one who rose to such public prominence, but I was immensely proud! Now every day, people stopped by our house to leave their cards with the butler on our little silver tray, offering their congratulations. How strange it was to feel as if people were *currying favor*. Soon our home became a beehive of political activity. Also a refuge for the young mayor, who suffered from debilitating migraines he didn't want anyone to know about.

One afternoon when the mayor came staggering to our door looking like death warmed over, I told him, "For goodness' sake, forget whatever you've come to discuss—just follow me, lie down, and let me get you a cool cloth for your head." I had transformed our little garden house into a place of respite for the mayor's staff in which to strategize. Now it was also somewhere for the mayor to rest where no one would know how sick he was.

One afternoon, a Hearst reporter and photographer loitered at our door. *They must have followed the mayor here*, I thought. So I didn't bother to send the butler but went out to shoo the reporters away myself.

Unfortunately, they hadn't come for the mayor. They'd come for me. "Miss Perkins! We hear you've married but you're keeping your maiden name. Won't you tell our readers why?"

"What in the *devil*?" Paul groused, coming up behind me. "How dare you accost my wife at our front door? If you don't leave at once, I'll set the dogs on you."

We didn't have any dogs—not yet, anyway—but Paul was so

angry at this intrusion that I feared his anger might itself become a news story. So I patted my husband's arm. "Now, Paul, these gentlemen are just doing their jobs. Would you mind terribly going upstairs to fetch the telephone book? I'd like to check this nice young reporter's credentials."

My new husband took the hint that I wanted to handle this myself. It was an early test of his respect for me, and he passed, even while grumbling all the way up the stairs. While I pretended to wait for Paul, I said to the reporter and his photographer, "Someone has given you boys the wrong steer. I'm taking my husband's name."

It wasn't a *brazen* lie, after all. I'd decided that in most social situations, I'd happily answer to Mrs. Paul Wilson. It was only in a professional capacity that I'd remain Miss Perkins. It was a great advantage in social work and professional life to be a Miss, whereas a Mrs. was understood to be awfully occupied in the house and with children . . .

I explained none of this to the bewildered reporter, who asked, "You're taking your husband's name?"

"Of course."

He squinted. "But when somebody from the office called your house to ask for Miss Perkins, you answered and said you were Miss Perkins."

"Oh, dear. One certainly can't get anything past you! Why, yes, naturally I said that I'm Miss Perkins. I've been Miss Perkins until just recently. I don't want a caller to think that I'm not the same person. If they have business with me, I won't conceal who I am and snub them."

The reporter rubbed his chin, conceding the point. "Well, then what do you say about these suffragettes who refuse to take their husband's names? Do you approve?"

"Why, I haven't given it the slightest thought," I said, playing dumb and blinking like a newborn fawn until the glum reporter finally gave up and trudged away.

When I told Paul and the mayor and our servants, we all laughed about it the rest of the night. But later, I asked Paul, "You're *certain* you won't mind if I use my maiden name? I know we're laughing about it, but it might cause a fuss."

Paul rubbed the back of his neck. "Frances, if you're out there somewhere in public using my name every time you make a wild speech about fire hazards or women's suffrage or family limitation, that might put me and the mayor in an awkward position. I'd honestly *prefer* it if you used your maiden name professionally."

I saw his point. I'd long been outspoken about controversial subjects. If I took a position as Miss Frances Perkins, few people would make a personal connection to my husband or the mayor. Thus it was decided. And I felt lucky to have married the most modern, civilized, and lovable of husbands.

A man who would, I was certain, be the most wonderful father to the baby I was now carrying.

Chapter Twenty-Two

★ ★ ★

New York City
April 1914

I AWAKENED TO FIND CRIMSON BLOOD STAIN-
ing my nightgown and the bed linen. I reached for Paul in the
light of dawn, but he'd already gone to work. In pain, I sank
from the bed to the floor, fearing that I was suffering a miscarriage.
Then I remained there on my knees in prayer, because I couldn't
get up.

Please, God, save my child . . .

When our housekeeper finally knocked with coffee and the morning paper, I managed a weak plea. "Won't you call for the doctor?"

Alas, I knew the truth long before the doctor made his appearance. In my soul, I already felt the stillness inside.

How was I to tell Paul about the miscarriage? We'd been so excited to learn of the pregnancy. Together we dreamed of a whole
brood of children with attending pets and pillow fights. Now that
dream flowed away in a bloody river of pain.

Once the sheets were stripped, I bathed and curled around myself
in the armchair, longing for the comfort of my grandmother, who
used to wrap me up in blankets and read to me. I even longed for my
mother, who could be tender once in a blue moon, but she was far
away. I was all alone, so I balled myself up tight until our housekeeper
knocked again and spoke in broken German-accented English. "I'm
sad with you, Mrs. Wilson. It happens to me also, many times."

I knew miscarriage was common, especially in this city. So

common, in fact, I thought I had no right to be as miserable as I felt. One must get on with things and go about one's day.

But I couldn't . . .

Eventually the housekeeper asked, "I should call Mr. Wilson?"

Like a wounded animal, I wanted to hide myself in a dark corner. I stared at my hands, at my wedding ring, feeling guilty, convinced that I must've done something wrong to lose Paul's baby. I'd taken the trolley to work the day before—what if its jerking had caused a miscarriage? "No, don't call Mr. Wilson. He'd only come home straightaway, and there's nothing he can do. I'll tell him tonight."

I reminded myself that Paul was so busy at city hall that he was always up before dawn to attend to the mayor. Then he worked late into the night with ideas about how to balance the budget and spur employment. My husband subsisted on only the fumes of sleep, and I often teased that he was going to work himself into a state of nervous exhaustion. But now I was the one who felt on the verge of a nervous break. And that would just not do.

I had to compose myself.

Curled up on that chair, I closed my eyes. I didn't rouse until I heard the phone ringing, and shouts from the street. I was surprised to see it was still daylight—in fact, a quick glance at the clock told me it wasn't yet two in the afternoon. Then my housekeeper called up from the foot of the stairs. "Someone shot the mayor!"

I must be having a nightmare, I thought, but it was the waking kind. Fear propelled me out of the chair and down the stairs despite the heaviness in my limbs and the pain that shot through my abdomen. I had scarcely gotten to the bottom landing when the front door flung open, and there stood my husband, spattered in blood.

"Paul!" I cried, horrified to think he'd been hurt.

I flew to him, and he caught me around the waist. "It's all right, Frances."

Paul explained that the blood wasn't his. The assassin's bullet had missed Mayor Mitchel and hit the lawyer standing nearby. "A flesh wound, but there was a lot of blood. A lone madman has been apprehended. Everything is all right, except for my shirt."

It was not all right. The mayor could've been killed. The lawyer could've been killed. And Paul—who'd been standing beside them both—could've been killed. Remembering when Theodore Roosevelt was shot while giving a speech, I thought, *Dear God, is this the price of political life?*

If so, I wanted no part of it.

LATER, PAUL STROKED my hair in the darkness of our room, and I thought, *I could've lost him too.* I'd lost my baby and nearly lost my husband in one day. The realization made me cold all over. Before I married, I'd only ever had to worry about myself. Thus, I'd never known true fear. Or true grief. Or that both needed to be shared . . .

Haltingly, I told Paul about the miscarriage, and, seemingly caught in a whirlwind of his own emotions, he whispered, "I'm sorry, Frances. I wish I knew the right words to comfort you."

No words could comfort me, so I resolved to put this pain away and never to speak of it again. It was the only way I knew. The New Englander way. The *Perkins* way of dealing with pain.

Get up. Dust yourself off. Try again.

We'd simply try again for a baby. And this time, I was determined to do everything right.

WHILE I PUT all my energy into making my body a fertile place to grow a child, Paul's career blossomed. Running New York City was, after all, a bigger job than running most American states. Alas, the workload and high public profile caused tremendous strain. Paul relied on me to ease things for him at home when he staggered in the door after another crushing workday. He desperately needed a vacation, but there wasn't time for our long-awaited official honeymoon. And even if we had time, it was no longer safe to cross the ocean because of the shooting of the archduke and the outbreak of war in Europe. The mood in usually buoyant New York was suddenly dark. And when I turned down an invitation to Webster Hall with our old crowd, Red groused, "You're no fun anymore, France."

Red had a new job, a new book out under his own name that had released to rave reviews, and he'd hounded that fashionable girl who worked for *Vogue* into marrying him. I was delighted for him and wished I could've gone out with the old crowd, but now I had other responsibilities. "I have to host a dinner party for the mayor."

A dinner party at which I would abstain from wine to improve our chances of being able to conceive.

"How many of these insipid political dinner parties do you have to host?" Red asked. "You're not the mayor's wife, after all."

No, but Mayor Mitchel's wife had no interest. She didn't cheer her husband's speeches, make small talk at political functions, or host dinners. That task fell to me. I couldn't blame Red for wondering how I'd somehow become the kind of woman who was dreadfully concerned about seating arrangements and whether the candles were lit and the leaves swept from our front steps. But, on the defense, I said, "These dinners are more important than you think."

Red sighed over his cigarette and blew out a long, dubious ribbon of smoke. "You're giving up *everything* for your husband's career and a brood of ankle biters. Do you even write your little romantic stories anymore?"

I frowned. "No. They were never very good anyway."

"They were better than you think," Red insisted. "You're a woman of many talents, sweets."

"The last time I submitted a story for publication, the magazine editor told me I ought to confine myself to writing academic surveys, factual reports, newspaper articles, and the like. So now I only scribble the occasional poem in a private notebook when the urge strikes me. I stick to the things that I'm good at."

"Like housekeeping and dinner parties?"

I frowned. "Among other things!" I had not, after all, given up *everything* for my husband's career. I was still working with Al Smith and the Factory Investigating Committee. Besides, thanks to my grandmother's example, I had turned out to be quite good at running a household. And with Mary's help, I was even better at entertaining.

It's true that neither activity nourished my soul, but it was a time of sacrifice. "Red, even if I *could* come out with you tonight, don't you think the mood of the world is a little grim for a bacchanalia ball? Look at the war in France."

"It's not *our* war," Red protested.

"Paul thinks it soon will be," I replied.

I knew this was a sore subject; I had nearly come to quarrel with Florence Kelley about it. As a committed pacifist, my mentor believed any talk about America getting involved in the war was akin to treason. So I was relieved when Red dropped the subject. "At least bring your mister to visit my new place on the shore next weekend. We'll have good food, drink some wine, and play some cards. I promise it won't be nearly as fun as a night with the old crowd at Webster Hall. You can even wear sackcloth and ashes."

"I prefer a hair shirt," I teased.

I accepted the invitation because I thought Paul really needed the rest. Of course, my husband grumbled the whole way there, but he enjoyed *mauling* Red over a game of cards. And in the end, we loved our weekend by the sea so much that it made me pine for my beloved Maine.

"Your family seat is terribly far for a regular commute," my husband said. "Why don't we buy a little place on the shore?"

I startled because I couldn't get used to having enough money to buy things on a whim. "Just like that? Buy a house because I miss the water?"

"What else is money good for?" Paul asked.

So we bought a summer cottage, our beloved little "shack" on the beach where we escaped the hustle and bustle of the city every weekend for the privacy and relaxing atmosphere in which we might conceive another child. To that end, we gave up smoking and drinking and went swimming often to get into the best condition so as to give the next generation a fair start. A few of our friends also had houses near ours on Long Island, the Rumseys and the Lewises among them. So Paul and I shared lovely weekends filled with socializing, bicycle rides, and moonlight kisses against stone walls.

But as the war in Europe dragged on, we had to cut these weekend jaunts, because Paul and the mayor both believed our harbor might fall victim to saboteurs or be attacked by German U-boats, and my husband was determined to be prepared. Personally, I hoped that if men were fighting and dying in trenches an ocean away, for reasons so complicated no one could adequately explain it, it *need* not involve America. I even let Mrs. Kelley convince me of that fact, with her passionate and persuasive arguments on behalf of the new Woman's Peace Party, made up largely of mothers who wanted to keep American sons from harm. But perhaps her arguments only appealed to me because I was again expecting a child and did not want to bring a baby into a world at war.

"YOU'RE NOT QUITTING, are you?" Al Smith asked, adjusting his bow tie.

"I must," I replied, for my work with the Factory Investigating Committee had resulted in more than thirty new laws, and our final report was nearly complete. I was also enormously pregnant and no longer fit for public view. When the baby was born, I planned to be a more traditional wife like Mary, who mothered children and did volunteer work. I reasoned that I got quite enough of public affairs through my husband's job with the mayor. "Haven't I earned a respite?"

Mr. Smith smiled fondly. "That you have, Miss Perkins. Congratulations, kiddo. I wish you every happiness."

I *was* happy. I'd already come to love the child in my womb and found myself whispering pet names to my belly. Oh, how I longed to meet my little bloom! So, with my resignation and the fondest farewell to Mr. Smith, I hurried home from Albany in anticipation of a much more restful new life.

What I did not anticipate was a mysterious vision problem. In the days that followed, I could scarcely read, and spectacles didn't much help. I was swollen, fatigued, and cranky. Then one day I dizzied on the stairs and found myself having to crawl. Fortunately, Paul found me and helped me to bed, his brow creased with worry. "Please humor me with a doctor's visit," Paul insisted.

I humored him because I didn't want to lose another child. Alas, I was in no way prepared for the doctor's grim diagnosis. "You're in a preeclamptic state. You'll need to stay in bed for the duration of your pregnancy, Mrs. Wilson."

I feared I'd go mad if I must *really* lie abed and do nothing, but still I said, "Yes, whatever is necessary for the well-being of my baby."

The doctor continued, "I must emphasize that this condition is dangerous to mother and child. There are many instances of sepsis and worse. When the time comes, Mrs. Wilson, you may have to deliver by cesarean section."

This news was even more sobering, for I knew all too well that such operations often killed mother, child, or both. Childbirth was less dangerous for women of means, but there were some things even money could not fix. Which meant that I had a different kind of war to prepare for . . .

Chapter Twenty-Three

* * *

New York City
May 1915

My dearest Paul,
Try harder than you have ever tried anything in life to under-
stand our baby as it grows up. You have so much to give a little
one—tenderness, care, and understanding, and the baby will
need it all. Put Perkins somewhere in the baby's name and in
remembrance eternal let there be sweet talk about me sometimes.
Let the baby know all the things that are good and strong about
me and draw a merciful veil on my weaknesses so I should still
give him something if it's only ideals.
~Frances

That I might die in childbirth was the reality that must be faced. Paul, however, could not bear to discuss it. Whenever I tried, he quite literally fled the room—sometimes with polite excuses, and other times without even the veneer of that.

He was frightened. I was too. But I already felt such an enormous sense of responsibility for our baby that I couldn't let fear prevent me from doing my duty. In the end, I wrote down my final wishes in a sealed letter that I left for him on the bedside.

Mary, who now had both a little boy and a little girl, reassured me, "The worst won't come to pass, Frances. Childbirth is a battle, but I've never known anyone to fight harder than you."

"Well, my little darling," I whispered to my belly, now resolute. "For *you*, I will put up the fight of my life."

Perhaps I did, but chloroform has erased everything from my mind but being whisked into a surgical room when I finally went into labor. Then I awakened burning with fever, a little surprised to be alive.

Gulping in air, I tried to sit up, but there was too much pain. Then I saw my husband staring out the hospital window and managed a smile anyway. "*Paul.*" I said his name with tenderness and joy, but when he turned, his complexion was so ashen that my smile fell away. "Where is the baby?"

He couldn't answer. He tried, but no words came. It was a nurse who said, "Mrs. Wilson . . ."

She need not have said another word, for the pity in her voice broke my heart.

"He was stillborn," Paul finally managed. "And you must be calm, because you have toxemia and are still in danger."

He was stillborn. It had been a little boy. Did my son die before even taking a breath? Gone even before they tore him from my body . . .

Despite my fever, I went cold inside at the thought. I simply froze over like a river in winter, blanketing all life below under the stillness of snow to keep the crushing pain of grief from reaching me. It was the only way to keep myself from cracking.

When I was finally brought home—still raw from being cut open—I asked the housekeeper to lock the door to the empty nursery. I didn't want to dwell on a loss that would overmatch me. I must rest and *forget*. But of course, the scar would always remind me . . .

One afternoon, I overheard the doctor talking to my husband in the hall. And Paul whispered, "She's still quite fragile. Is there medicine to make her well?"

"Only time," the doctor replied. "At her age, she likely won't survive another attempt at childbirth, so you must behave accordingly. Some women are not meant to be mothers."

Some women are not meant to be mothers . . .

Those words felt as if they tore open my still-bleeding wounds. They compounded my grief, threatening to break the thin ice holding me up. In the days that followed, the springtime sunshine gave me personal offense, contrasting so cruelly with the dark grief that was consuming me. It felt as if the only way I could cope was by pretending as if this tragedy had befallen someone else.

Mrs. Wilson.

She was the woman who was going to live here in this fine house and raise a brood of children, and plant bulbs in the garden, and host political dinners. *Mrs. Wilson* wanted that. But now she had no child, nor was she ever likely to have one. Neither did she have a vocation. She had given it up and now had no sense of herself at all.

Poor Mrs. Wilson.

I could only stumble around in her big empty house like a stranger. "I can't speak of it," I warned Paul when he tried to comfort me. "We must simply go on as if nothing has happened."

He said he understood, but thereafter he moved out of our bedroom and seemed to spend as much time as possible away from our home. As weeks passed, he'd call late to say, "I'm so sorry, darling, but the mayor needs me to vet candidates for the municipal court." Or Paul had to write a speech about the new official city flag. Or he had to find the funds for the Fourth of July celebration and the new courthouse. Or he had to attend the launching of a new ship in the Navy Yard.

I couldn't complain. It was his duty. He'd agreed to work for the people of New York City, and he owed them his tireless efforts. I knew his increasingly long work hours at city hall couldn't be helped.

But they now seemed like an indictment of our once happy marriage. And for the first time since we'd wed, I felt terribly alone.

I should've gone to Maine that summer. We'd planned the trip before the death of our son, anticipating the joy of introducing our newborn to my parents and his Perkins birthright. Now I couldn't face my family. I also couldn't keep rambling around this house feeling sorry for myself. I was suffocating, and not simply because of the summer heat. Screwing up my courage, I finally told Paul, "Mary has invited me for a visit. You won't mind if I go, would you?"

"Go," Paul said amiably. "It'll do you a world of good."

So off I went to Mary's Long Island estate, where the first few days were a welcome change of pace. Mary's Dutch colonial mansion had so much space that her husband scarcely noticed me. He let us frolic like schoolgirls at a slumber party, spending the night together on one of the sleeping porches to keep cool. And while the evening's ocean breeze swept over us with the stars overhead, Mary and I drifted to sleep gossiping about Sinclair Lewis's latest piece for the *Saturday Evening Post*.

The next morning, over a breakfast of fruit and pastries by the sea, Mary pulled up the brim of her sun hat to look me in the eye. "I never thought I'd say this, but I'm sorry Red is now too busy with his writing to spend time with us. He used to be able to cheer you up."

"Dear God, don't worry about me. People are dying in trenches in France. If anyone needs cheering, it's—"

"You're allowed to grieve, you know," Mary interrupted.

I stared at the ocean waves. "Not like this. I've never felt this way before, and I'd rather not talk about it."

"What are you afraid of?"

I'm afraid it will break me.

I'd miscarried once, then given birth to a dead child, and was now almost assuredly barren. Meanwhile my handsome vigorous husband—with his limitless political future—was tethered to me. I'd lose him. If not to a madman's bullet, then to some other woman eventually. And under the circumstances, wouldn't I be selfish to try to hold on to him?

Loving Paul had been my solace, but love was also a vulnerability. As a safety inspector, I should've realized that in love there are no safety precautions—there is nothing to do when you reach the edge but fall. Well, I had fallen and shattered and simply did not know how to put myself together again.

Chapter Twenty-Four

New York City
October 1915

Dear Paul,
It's been sweet and lovely between us, and I don't regret any of it,
but the fact remains that something has happened to me in these
years and I've lost something of myself . . . so if you understand at
all, just let me go.
~ Frances

Our marital separation didn't begin intentionally. It was simply that we were so often *apart.* I spent the rest of that summer with the Rumseys while Paul worked at city hall. Then, having stayed so long away from our house and its empty nursery, it seemed impossible to return.

Feeling as if our marriage had gone so adrift that we must formalize it, I wrote Paul a letter, but when I told Mary about it, she cried, "Frances, what on *earth* are you doing?"

"Marriage was a mistake," I told her. "I suppose it's to be expected that when two people experience all the pleasures and disillusions and simple little homely activities together that one's individuality might be lost. But I can't be my own garden unwatered. What shall it profit a woman if she shall gain the whole world and lose her soul?"

It was the sort of talk we heard every day from our feminist friends. The kind of talk that usually caused us to nod our heads in understanding, if not sympathy. But now Mary looked ready to dash water in my face. "Frances, you're having a nervous breakdown."

I felt almost as if she really *had* dashed water in my face. "I'm not the type of person to have a nervous breakdown."

"Any person can," Mary insisted. "Even you. You're sabotaging your life."

"Me, a saboteur!"

"Yes, that's what I said. You've suffered a terrible blow to your health, your heart, and even your faith. But instead of trying to repair the damage, you've left your husband. Your husband, who—"

"—is stifling me—"

"Frances Perkins cannot be stifled. Don't pretend he keeps you chained up just because you want to run away."

How dare you, I wanted to say. She was prying into private business. I was a woman of thirty-five and resented having my feelings dismissed. I wanted to get up and storm off, except then she'd say I was running from her too.

My voice quavered. "Don't you see that it's important I separate from Paul so I *don't* have a nervous breakdown?"

"It may not be in your control. You lost a baby and almost died, Frances; there are attendant animal factors—"

"If you're about to compare me with one of your horses who has lost a foal—"

"I'm saying there are biological forces at work," Mary interrupted, her words running over mine. "Your body still hasn't healed, so why do you expect your mind has?"

She was making me combative. Sarcastic too. "I suppose you recommend the *rest cure* from 'The Yellow Wallpaper.'"

It was a reference to a story written by a feminist driven mad by the insistence of her physician that she do absolutely nothing after childbirth. Of course, I immediately regretted mentioning this, because *madness runs in families*, they said. And I knew it ran in mine . . .

Perhaps because she knew it, too, Mary gentled her voice. "Just admit you're suffering."

"Many women suffer the loss of a child and bear up under it, while living in terrible conditions besides, in poverty and hopelessness. Whereas I've led such a charmed life that this is actually *the very worst thing* to ever happen to me."

"Exactly." Mary leaned forward to grasp my hand. "Which means you have no experience grappling with this kind of grief. You're not well, Frances."

"So what?" I asked, pulling my hand back. "To *get* well isn't the first consideration in life. To *do* well is the important thing. To do what you're supposed to, and do it well, and meet your destiny. You'll get well and be happy on the side."

I WORE MY wedding dress to march next to Florence Kelley at the Women's Suffrage Parade that autumn. I also wore white spats and a white tricorn hat, carrying a banner I'd written, which read, *Feminism Means Revolution and I'm a Revolutionist.*

Other states had already granted women the right to vote. New York ought to be next. To convince our fellow citizens, we'd arranged this absolute spectacle. Forty thousand of us marched the parade route, carrying flowers and flags, holding hands in solidarity, and lifting our voices to the heavens in song.

Mary Rumsey rode on horseback like the Amazon she was, and some frail old widows were pushed along in their wheelchairs, while lithe teenaged girls carried the floats.

It had long been argued that only one sort of woman wanted the vote—upper-class white businesswomen. Certainly, our ranks were swelled with them. Doctors and lawyers and teachers and other professionals. But we were joined, too, by scrubwomen and young homemakers with babes at the breast, and by members of the Colored Women's Suffrage Club of New York City, who marched in spite of their righteous resentment of segregationists within the movement.

I felt neither the bite of the chill wind on my cheeks nor the ache in my feet as we made the five-mile march—too buoyed to feel anything but elation at this splendid display. We carried flags, played instruments, and planned public meetings all over the city in anticipation of the legislature passing women's suffrage into law.

We had reason for optimism this time, for President Wilson had finally come out in favor of women's suffrage, and so had the mayor of New York. Mayor Mitchel was there in the reviewing stand, cheering us on, and Paul was by his side . . .

It was the first time I'd seen my husband in months, and my wave of euphoria crested, exposing the sharp edges of pain below. I hadn't spoken with Paul since sending that letter. Since his calm acceptance, and his promise not to thwart me if I wished for a separation. But after the march, Paul was waiting for me with hot coffee and my warmest coat—a coat that I'd left behind with the rest of my life.

"Come home, Frances," he said simply.

I didn't want to let go of the wonderful feeling of having been part of an army of women. Part of a *movement*. But I didn't want to hurt Paul either, and despite his gallant efforts to disguise it, he *was* hurting, which hurt me too. Now, at my silence, he asked, "Have I done something to destroy even our friendship?"

With a hurried shake of my head, I hastened to reassure him. "You've done nothing wrong. I don't mean to withdraw my friendship. The bond between us is too great to make that possible even if I wished it."

"Then let's be friends," Paul said. "Come home. And let us comfort each other."

He deserved to be comforted. I wasn't the only one who had lost a child, after all.

So why couldn't I go home with him?

What a wretched, blundering fool I'd been to think I might make this kindhearted man a splendid wife. I was nothing more than a cold block of ice. "There's a girl in your office, Paul. Her name is Rose."

He tilted his head. "Is she a friend of yours? I think she was here somewhere today—did she march?"

"She didn't," I replied. "She stood by *you*, near the reviewing stand. She's always standing by you, staring with adoring eyes. People have noticed."

Paul stood in obvious confusion.

"You're a brilliant man," I told him. "But oblivious at times, so you may not realize she's in love with you."

Now my husband's blue eyes flashed with a bit of anger. "Is that why you won't come home? This is about some girl in my stenography pool?"

"Of course not. It's only that I think you could be happy with a girl like that. She's young, and pretty, and probably quite fertile."

"*Frances*," he snapped, hissing steam into the night air. But I couldn't bear to stay to hear what else he might have to say.

MARY WAS RIGHT that I was running away. As autumn blew into winter, I met with Florence Kelley about the remaining agenda of the Consumers' League. I accompanied Al Smith on legislative trips. I went to Albany and visited my favorite Tammany Hall boys. I went to the shore to visit with friends. By Christmas, I'd finally run out of people to visit and places to go, and, not wishing to impose myself on anyone for the holiday, I finally went back to my husband's house, where I found Paul with a decanter of liquor, staring at the fire.

"I hope you don't mind," I said, putting down my bags. "As I mentioned on the telephone, it's a temporary situation. I'll try not to make a nuisance of myself."

Paul shook his head, and I realized he was going gray at the temples. I'd also heard, through close mutual friends, that he was spending time with the girl from his office, and I wondered if I'd ruined his holiday plans.

Then he whispered, "I've done a terrible thing, Frances."

"What terrible thing?"

He stared into the glass in his hand. "You were right about Rose."

I felt a little crack open in my icy facade, but I knew it would freeze over again soon enough. "I see. Well, if you've found happiness—"

"Do I look happy?" Paul asked as I took in the stubble on his chin and the dark circles under his eyes. "I don't love that girl, Frances. But I took up with her anyway. Do you understand?"

I understood even before he told me.

I wished he hadn't, but Paul was always honest. Some said to a fault. Still, it was one of the qualities I loved best about him, and I appreciated that honesty now, even as we stared at each other, taking in the wreckage of our marriage. "You've been lonely," I said to excuse the both of us.

"Yes, I've been lonely these five months since our son died. But that's not why I took up with Rose."

I stiffened. "I'd rather not know the details."

"I did it to see if you'd care. So, do you?"

Another crack inside me opened, this one making me unsteady on my feet. "Of course I care, but I couldn't blame you. I could never ask you to wait for me to feel like myself again, if that's even possible."

"Why not?" Paul asked. "Why don't you ask anything of me but to let you go?"

"Because you want children. Don't lie and say it doesn't matter, because it was our dream to make a family."

"We *are* a family. We took vows." He winced, for I gathered he'd broken at least one of them. "But I've done the unforgivable now, and there's no coming back from it."

"It isn't unforgivable."

The ease with which I said this seemed to make him even more upset. He turned away, walked to the door, and then returned. "I hate that you can stand there so calmly when I'm so guilt-ridden and *furious.*"

"When you're upset, it seems better that I remain calm and rational."

"Frances, there's nothing rational about what we've been through. And I love you. Doesn't that mean anything? If you love me, too, shouldn't it mean everything?"

To think I'd once thought his kiss was like a sturdy rigging. Love was the most dangerous ride in the world. And because of it, I felt as if I were in free fall.

I really am having a nervous breakdown, I thought. I had to hug myself to keep from shaking apart. "Paul, I'm going to say this only once because I can't bear to speak of it again. I can't carry another baby and come to love that child, and think of names and decorate a nursery, only to have that baby die. I'd gladly risk my life—it's only the heartbreak of losing another baby that I cannot risk. I fear it would be worse than dying."

I said all this in one breath, and now I was left both gasping and ashamed. How damaged, dramatic, and *deranged* I sounded. How overwrought!

I should never have spoken these words aloud, but now, these fears finally having been expressed, they seemed to lose their terrible hold on me.

As if realizing it, Paul came and wrapped his arms around me. I thawed at this simple human comfort and kindness.

It solved nothing, but still, we cleaved to each other. Then went together for Christmas mass. There, we lit candles for the two little angels we had lost. We prayed together. And God, in His infinite mercy, gave us *grace*.

For there in that church, I was reminded that marriage was for better, for worse, for richer, for poorer, in sickness and in health, to love and to cherish, till death do us part.

And we were both still very much alive.

Chapter Twenty-Five

★ ★ ★

Newcastle, Maine
February 1916

THE GRAVEDIGGERS HAD TO RESORT TO pickaxes to break through the frozen ground. But now the hole was dug, and on this blustery cold day, we gathered to lay my father to rest.

Though my mother had quarreled with my father all their marriage, she was left utterly bereft upon his passing. So much so that a migraine confined her to bed. And my sister—now a mother of two but always prone to strong emotions—had broken down at the funeral, sobbing so piteously that her husband had to escort her away from the grave.

Thus it fell to me to stand vigil as the dirt was shoveled over my father's casket, all the while remembering how he sat me upon his lap when I was a child and taught me to read the classics in the original Greek. I remembered, too, that he told a neighbor he thought I ought to be able to vote.

Though we'd been distant in recent years, I'd loved him deeply, and to lose my father now was a new grief to pile onto the old. My only comfort was Paul's hand on my shoulder at the grave.

You needn't make the trip, I'd said. After all, the war in Europe was ruining our economy in New York, and my husband was helping unemployed transients by putting them to work on public projects.

It was a great deal to manage, but Paul insisted on coming to the funeral in Maine, and I was unutterably grateful.

Now my husband told me, "I had a terrible time of it when my own father passed. He was a distant man, not very demonstrative. He could be quite hard on me. Especially when I dropped out of Dartmouth for a time. Still, his passing was like an earthquake under my feet. It was hard to get my bearings; I can only imagine how you must be feeling."

"I didn't know you dropped out of college," I said. In fact, I hadn't known there was anything troubled about Paul's relationship with his father at all.

I only knew that mine was gone. "I think we can never be prepared for the loss of our parents. We know, someday, we'll lose them. That we'll have to find some way of going on. We're taught to memorialize our parents and make meaning of their lives through our own. But no matter how old they get, or how ill they get, it still takes you by surprise."

"Yes," Paul agreed as the wind blew snowflakes across his brow. "I'm sorry you have to suffer this grief so soon upon the other . . ."

He was worried about me, but I no longer felt frozen inside. Nor did I feel as if I might shatter to pieces. Perhaps it was because I didn't want to dissolve as my mother and sister had done. Perhaps it was because I had Perkins soil under my boots now, and I knew that none of my proud Puritan ancestors would have countenanced my falling to pieces.

So I felt like a sadder but saner version of myself as I told Paul, "Since we're confessing things to each other we have never said before, I shall admit that I wish I could've seen our baby's face. I know he was gone, but I would've liked to hold him. They shouldn't have taken him before I awakened."

Paul stared at his feet. "I'm sorry. I should've insisted they let you hold him."

"I don't know if it would've helped. I just can't help thinking about it sometimes. Thankfully, it doesn't consume me the way it once did. I'm steadier now."

"You can lean on me when you don't feel so steady, Frances. We *are* a family."

Family, after all, was an important and sacred thing. I felt that strongly while standing near the graves of my father, my grandmother, my grandfather, and relations going further back than that. The headstones reminded me that I was a part of a legacy that stretched out behind me, and that I ought to be brave enough to see what could still stretch out before me. So if Paul was willing to try for another child, so was I.

"NO COFFEE, THANK you," Paul said from bed beside me one summer morning when the housekeeper brought up our breakfast. "I shall abstain in solidarity with Mrs. Wilson until she is delivered of child."

"Gallant, but foolish," I told Paul as I fluffed the pillows behind my back. "At least one of us should be functional."

The physician had left me a list of strict requirements for preserving my pregnancy.

Avoid coffee.

Avoid liquor.

Avoid sweets.

Avoid riding in trolley cars or motor vehicles.

Avoid walking in high heels.

Avoid walking altogether . . .

I was, in effect, to simply remain still as a potted plant.

Paul had adjusted his schedule so that he could tend to me personally, but that still meant early mornings at the mayor's office. So now my husband quickly swallowed one bite of toast followed by a bite of eggs before hopping out of our bed. "Off to city hall. You get some good rest today, darling."

"All I *do* is rest," I complained, but not too petulantly, because I'd do anything to bring this child into being. But oh, the bother of bed rest! I was going to miss the Independence Day parade, and I was quite sore about it. "Does the mayor want you so early because of the garment workers' strike?"

Paul nodded. "He's considering what position the city government should take. We don't want policemen bludgeoning girls in the street."

"Let me help," I said.

"My dear, you mustn't tax yourself."

With a sigh, I crossed my arms, desperate to be useful. "I can make phone calls from bed. I can—"

A sharp pain in my right side cut my words off, effectively ending further discussion about it. Not long after, I also found myself short of breath, my hands and face swelling—all symptoms that pre-eclampsia had returned. Then, in the wee hours of the night that summer, the clock stopped at eight minutes after two.

I remember that much, but I couldn't understand why I was on the floor . . .

The room was spinning, some shrill sound rang in my ears, and I was holding my belly protectively, trying to guard the child within.

"Frances?"

It was Paul's voice, but I shook my head, disoriented, unable to answer.

"Frances." He tried again, checking me for injuries. "Are you hurt?"

"I don't think so, but what's happened? An earthquake?"

Trying to help me to my feet, Paul grimly said, "An explosion, I think."

There was only one kind of explosion I could imagine in New York City. An industrial accident. There'd been several recently—a reminder that though we'd done much to improve industrial safety in the city, there was still more to be done. "I'm going to make sure there's hell to pay for whatever factory owner has shaken me and my baby out of bed."

A distant siren sounded, and Paul said, "The boom came from the direction of the harbor. I think it's the war."

I could scarcely believe that. "The Germans wouldn't *dare* bomb our harbor. The United States is neutral."

Seeing my anxiety, Paul immediately agreed. "You're right." He was suddenly all solicitation. "Of course you're right. Let's get you back into bed. You're sure you're not hurt?"

"I feel unhurt," I said. But I wondered, *What about you, little baby? Was I wrong to try to bring you into a world at war?*

By dawn, we learned that the explosion had taken place where munitions were being assembled to ship overseas, most of them having been purchased by France and Great Britain. The blast had even damaged the Statue of Liberty. An accident caused by a careless watchman, some said. Paul was convinced it was sabotage. Whatever the cause, it was a reminder that however far away the war might seem, it was not far enough.

FIVE DAYS AFTER Christmas, a nurse delivered my long-awaited baby into my arms. Oh, how I melted at the sight of my daughter's little face. Why, look at that button nose! Those little rosy lips. She had more hair than I'd have expected—wonderfully thick like Paul's, except flaxen.

When my husband was finally admitted, he gasped. "She has my eyes!"

"I think all babies have blue eyes," I said.

"But look how *fair* she is," Paul countered. "Our golden girl."

She was a Christmas miracle. And I'd never known such joy as when I inspected her little fingers, and all her little pink toes. She had such soft, warm skin, downy against my cheek. Pressing my lips to her hair to soothe her little hiccup, I scented something powdery that imprinted on my heart. And did I only imagine the intelligence already shining in those blue eyes?

She was perfect. And she was ours.

We agreed on the name Susanna, a family name for me, and one Paul found dignified enough for an economic policymaker's daughter. Watching him hold her—his eyes tearing over with an overabundance of love, his strong protective arms cradling her while her little pink fingers grasped his thumb—I, too, had to fight back tears of joy.

Later, at home in Susanna's nursery where afternoon sunlight filtered warmly through the window to capture us all in its glow, I was beset by a sudden spiritual certainty that there was something sacred about a father, mother, and child. And I felt compelled to scribble a few lines.

A holy trinity . . .
Separate but indivisible.
Being of one substance.
And what task, is this great trinity of mine, but love?

THE BIRTH OF Susanna opened a well of maternal warmth inside me that made me doubly sad when my milk never came in. Fortunately, I had help; the hired nurse and our household servants were eager to fuss over Susanna. But I was forever cradling her in my lap and cooing to her and bundling her up against the cold for walks in Central Park.

Embarrassingly, the first night that Paul and I had a social engagement at city hall, I found it almost *painful* to leave her, even for a few hours. I knew Paul also hated to leave the side of her cradle, because he hired a portraitist to photograph mother and child so that he could look at our picture in his office every day. And on the weekends, the proud father pushed our expensive satin-lined carriage—a gift from Mary Rumsey—down Fifth Avenue to shop for rattles and stuffed animals and mobiles to hang over the baby's crib.

I still worried at the way Paul shuffled papers through the night without sleep so that he could keep up with his work at city hall, but he somehow made me feel as if our little family had his undivided attention, and all was bliss. In short, the first months of our daughter's life were the happiest of mine, even though they were grave for my country.

Susanna was only three months old when Woodrow Wilson went before Congress and asked for a declaration of war to make the world safe for democracy. This took me by surprise, for the explosion in the harbor had been ruled an accident, and I had hoped against all reason that we might stay out of the European conflict. But Paul had been right all along. Now he and the mayor asked me to serve on a council to coordinate various women's war relief organizations.

"You aren't going to do it, are you?" Red asked when I saw him next.

Red and his pregnant wife had just returned to New York after a few years of bohemian wandering, in time for the publication of his forthcoming novel *The Job*, which was about the rights of working women, containing dialogue replete with chats we used to have.

In any case, after we caught up and I showed off my beautiful baby, our conversation drifted to current affairs, and Red said, "I just don't think we have any place in getting involved in the war."

"Mrs. Kelley and most of my friends feel the same way," I said. "But it's of no matter now. We *are* in the war, so we must win it."

Speaking before women's groups across the city, I said much the same thing. "If we are to take the war seriously, we can't stay in the bosoms of our homes, or just go to a few meetings. We must go out into the community and do real work with our hands."

Women responded to my call. We rolled bandages. We trained to drive ambulances. We helped care for young mothers whose husbands had been shipped out. New Yorkers were coming together for the war effort!

If only the mayor hadn't chosen now, of all times, to pick a different fight . . .

"Don't go after Catholics," my husband warned as the two men strategized at my dinner table.

"I'm not *going after Catholics*," the clean-shaven mayor argued in exasperation. "I'm going after the poor conditions in the church orphanages. I'm protecting the children." The mayor looked to me for support. "Tell him, Mrs. Wilson."

I might be a natural-born meddler, but I wasn't about to undermine my husband. "Mr. Wilson doesn't need me to tell him anything."

Paul smiled gratefully, and despite the late hour, he poured himself yet another cup of coffee, as if to make up for all the months he'd gone without it for my sake. And in frustration, he said, "John, it's the way you're going about it. Spying on nuns and tapping their phones. Plus, you're picking a fight with Catholics *in an election year*."

That was apparently the wrong thing to say, for the mayor thundered, "I should allow the abuse of children because of an election?"

Upstairs, in the nursery, my baby awakened at the mayor's shout, and I scowled at him. "Well, now it seems little Susanna has an opinion about this matter. Shall we bring her down and ask her thoughts?"

Abashed, the fiery mayor tempered himself. "Let's leave it for the night, Paul. I don't want to upset your wife and child."

After the mayor left, Paul drained the dregs of his coffee and shook his head. "Sometimes it seems as if that man is incapable of common sense or compromise."

I had to agree. It was often left to my husband to smooth over ruffled feathers when the high-handed mayor did things like refuse documentation to an official simply because he didn't like him. Now that the reelection campaign was in full swing, smoothing ruffled feathers had become almost Paul's entire job.

"The campaign is going to be brutal," Paul told me. "I'm not going to be able to get away. But this summer heat in the city can't be good for a baby. Why don't you take Susie to Maine without me?"

Though I was reluctant to leave my husband, I couldn't wait to return to Maine, so I said, "I suppose it's never too early to start her on a yearly pilgrimage."

HOW WONDERFUL IT was to show off Susanna to my mother and sister and all the Perkins family relations who had gathered—some of whom still seemed in a state of shock that I'd married and forged a happy family life.

But it was even more wonderful to bring my child to the place that connected us to my past and made me optimistic about the future. It was deeply satisfying to dip my baby's little toes into the Damariscotta River, to let her crawl in the meadow, and to fall asleep with her weight on my chest as the crickets sang their song each night.

I could already imagine her as a growing girl here, paddling in the canoes with her cousins, collecting old bricks, and playing in the old settler's garrison.

Then again, I ought not get ahead of myself. For if I blinked, I might miss her childhood for how fast she was growing! Susanna could already sit up and even point at toys she wanted to play with. Her gaze was easily captivated by the colors of the wildflowers, and anything bright and bold. In my grandmother's summer kitchen, when the afternoon sun cast spots on the floor, she'd giggle with delight, kicking her chubby legs, crawling to me as if to share her joy.

Of course, I had to watch my baby carefully, as she was constantly exploring with her little rosebud mouth, tasting everything she could get her hands on—even her own thumb, which she sucked when she slept. And I'd spend hours just gazing at her closed lids, with their golden lashes, thanking God for the miracle of her existence.

Chapter Twenty-Six

New York City
August 1917

My beloved Frances,
I am so happy and glad that you will soon be close beside me. In
my arms, in my eyes, seeing as I cannot do anything so well
without you . . . I adore you, admire you, and rely on you greatly.
- Your lover, Paul

While we were in Maine, my husband wrote us every day, asking to
know if "Susie" was eating solid foods yet, if she was getting too much
sun, and whether it was safe to take her into the water, as there was a
suspicion that swimming had some connection to infantile paralysis.

How charmed I was by his fretting and devotion. And I was eager
to return to New York at the end of summer, both to reunite with
Paul and to take part in the marvelous happenings back home, where
women were finally getting the vote in New York State. Once that
happened, there'd be no stopping women's suffrage throughout the
whole country. I was so overjoyed for myself and my daughter and
the future of this country that I nearly wept. I was terribly emotional
reflecting upon how many generations had fought for this victory,
which gave me immense pride and joy.

A joy blunted only by watching Mayor Mitchel's reelection go
down in flames.

As the vote tallies came in that November, we all took it hard.
None harder than the mayor himself. "It's over, Paul," Mitchel

groaned in my parlor, holding his head. "The progressive movement is dead."

I tried to comfort him. "You musn't say that. As Mrs. Kelley always reminds me, reform is very hard, and sometimes there are setbacks."

Progress was rarely linear. After all, more than a century earlier, some women in the United States had been allowed to vote, and we were only now winning that right back. But I dared not offer this as consolation to the despondent mayor, who said, "These corrupt machine bosses have destroyed my reputation and my future too."

Goodness, it's only one lost election, I thought. Still, there was no point in trying to tell him all defeats are not final. He was too upset to hear reason, and after he left, Paul said, "He's going to enlist."

I looked up from beside the bassinet where Susanna slept. "Isn't he too old to fight?"

"Yes, but he's going to ask for an exemption. He feels it's only right because he campaigned against pacifism. But I fear John isn't going to war for patriotism or politics—he's terribly fatalistic."

My husband worried about his friend, and I worried about him, because when I first met Paul, he didn't sleep like ordinary mortals. But since his boss lost the election, my husband took to bed early and didn't rise again the next day until dinner.

I knew it had been a grueling four years. At city hall, Paul had been responsible for everything from representing the mayor at public events, to managing the budget, to offering policy advice and preparing the municipal yearbooks. His life had been a nonstop blizzard of chicken dinners, ribbon cuttings, dull public hearings, and the occasional subpoena before a grand jury thrown in.

It was time for him to slow down—for both of us to rest and grow our family. After all, with Paul's inheritance, money was not a concern. But over breakfast, he said, "I feel terribly useless."

"I'm sure we can find work that appeals to you," I said, for one of our mutual friends had complained that my husband hadn't yet roused himself to pursue any of the lucrative opportunities in private business now being offered to him.

"I need to do something for the war," Paul said.

My husband was too old to be in uniform, but now I feared that he, too, might ask for an exemption. Most of our younger friends—including Mary Rumsey's husband—were joining up. Paul felt pressure to join them, and I couldn't blame him for wanting to serve, so I suggested, "I wonder if you could apply for a position with the War Shipping Board."

The country needed merchant marines—the war had decimated commercial shipping, and as a result, America was suffering shortages of everything from sugar to cars. We needed more ships. To get them, we'd have to construct an emergency fleet, which required a man with Paul's managerial mind.

My husband would be good at a job like that. The problem was that it meant moving to Washington. So when he got the job offer, he said, "It's only for the duration of the war. I don't see the sense in turning both our lives upside down. It'd probably be wiser for you to stay here."

With a new baby—and my hopes for another—I dreaded living apart. Still, I couldn't complain of this separation, because men all over the country were leaving their families to fight in the trenches. Keeping a stiff upper lip was the least I could do.

Fortunately, Paul's new job paid a decent salary and let him contribute to the war effort, even if he couldn't fight on the battlefield. He took lodgings with a friend in the capital and caught the train back to visit on weekends. And while he was away, I steeled myself to leave Susanna in the care of her nurse so that I could ramp up my volunteer work.

It still pained me to leave her, even for a little while, but everyone must do their part. Men who went off to war had a right to know that their families were being cared for by the community. I thought it a disgrace that America had the highest rate of infant mortality of any developed nation in the world. I knew, from painful personal experience, New York City was a dangerous place to give birth. Thus, as a tribute to the babies I'd lost, I volunteered to be the executive secretary for the Maternity Center Association, dedicated to combating the high rate of infant mortality in the city.

We made house calls to new mothers and delivered bottles of milk and baskets of clothing to the needy. We opened clinics—even one at Hartley House, where I'd studied child malnutrition in the first place. And now, given my rise in the world, Miss Mathews was decidedly more pleasant, allowing us to train midwives and obstetricians under her roof. We were saving little lives at a time when the war was chewing people up, and at long last, I again felt as if I were thriving, doing important work that made a real difference in the world.

A BLIZZARD OF red roses, white asters, and blue irises fell upon us like snow from the summer sky, dropped by military planes as part of the funeral service. For John Purroy Mitchel had died in a flight training exercise, falling from his plane five hundred feet to his death.

As in life, the former mayor had reached for the heavens, only to plummet back down to earth. And I tried not to imagine that, because I knew what the human body hitting the ground looked and sounded like.

Of course, my husband believed that just like those girls in the Triangle factory fire all those years ago, his friend had *jumped*.

"You can't be sure of that," I had said on the morning of the funeral.

"I'm as sure as anyone can be," Paul had replied, trying and failing to fasten his tie in the mirror. "The Air Force says he forgot to fasten his seat belt in the cockpit. I spent four years at the man's side almost every waking moment. He was careful. He'd never have forgotten."

"Maybe there's some other explanation," I murmured, because I *wanted* there to be another explanation. Maybe the seat belt had failed. Maybe he'd accidentally unfastened it. Maybe something went wrong with the plane that *forced* him to unfasten it . . .

Paul wasn't convinced, and, giving up on his tie, he sank down on our bed, letting his head fall into his hands. "It wasn't the seat belt that failed, it was me. I failed him as an advisor and as a friend."

"That's nonsense. When Mayor Mitchel got some notion into his head, there was no changing his mind. I watched you try to moderate his temper. You gave him the best advice you could. He lost reelection all by himself."

Paul's eyes watered. "We didn't deserve him. We broke his heart."

Well, now he had broken ours. If Mitchel really *did* jump, I didn't know what to think . . .

All I knew was that my husband was wrecked, his eyes glassy and red-rimmed. "I can't go to the funeral, Frances. I'm afraid I'll lose my composure."

"Oh, but you *must* go. I promise I'll be at your side every step of the way."

I kept my promise, sticking close to my husband in the massive crowds that lined the way for the funeral cortege. Thousands had turned out to pay tribute to the former mayor, including Theodore Roosevelt as honorary pallbearer. But when it was over, my husband fell into malaise.

Now, I knew from experience how grief could lay a person low. Still, I worried when Paul could barely rouse himself to catch the train back to Washington. And when he did finally go back to work at the War Shipping Board, I didn't hear from him all week. Then he'd return on the weekends only to spend every day in bed.

The man who never needed sleep now couldn't get enough of it . . .

"Well, don't wake Paul on my account," Mary said, having come to the house one afternoon for lunch before we headed out to do work for the Maternity Center Association. We'd opened sixteen clinics, hired almost thirty nurses, and were already lowering infant mortality rates throughout the state. But Mary sensed my worries were closer to home. "Have you called the doctor? He might have influenza."

A wave of what we were calling the Spanish flu was sweeping the world. We didn't yet think it was terribly serious, but some people were getting very sick. And Paul *had* been traveling back and forth a great deal. "It's possible. I'll call the doctor just in case, but I worry that Paul is terribly depressed."

This was difficult to confess, as I knew my husband wouldn't like my speculating. Still, I had to tell *someone*, and if I couldn't tell Mary, then whom could I tell?

She was immediately sympathetic. "He must think he's lost both his friend and political future."

I knew, of course, that if John Mitchel had gone on to higher political office—even to the White House—my husband would've gone with him. Paul had never expressed grand political ambitions; he was more interested in policy than power. But whatever future he'd envisioned at Mitchel's side was now, truly, over. And Mary advised, "Just give him time."

Unfortunately, I've always been too impatient. That night, I sat on the edge of Paul's bed and stroked his shoulder, asking, "What's wrong, darling?"

"I wish I knew," Paul admitted, rubbing at the stubble he'd allowed to grow on his cheek. He looked thin, too, as if he was forgetting to eat when we were apart. He also had the faraway stare of someone who was drunk or had taken ill. Perhaps it was influenza after all . . .

When I suggested it, Paul shook his head. "It's not a physical ailment. It's a darkness upon me, Frances. *Despair*. It's been more than twenty years since I felt this way."

Now I was alarmed. "You've felt like this before?"

"Once. In college. I couldn't study or think clearly. Everything seemed like a catastrophe beyond my capabilities. I couldn't even get out of bed and brush my hair."

I ran my fingers through that fine head of hair. "That certainly isn't like you . . ."

Paul managed a weak smile. "At first, we thought I'd come down with something. Then I attributed my low spirits to my strained relationship with my father and my fear I'd never measure up. But it was more than that, and that's why I was forced to drop out of school for a little while."

Surprised that he could keep such a painful thing from me all these years, I asked, "Why didn't you tell me?"

"I was too ashamed. Besides, it happened so long ago. I got past it. Which means I can get past it again. Just give me time, Frances."

"Of course," I said.

Mary was right, I thought when, not long after, Paul seemed like himself again. Maybe even an exaggerated version of himself. On the weekends, he was suddenly a flurry of activity. Tennis every morning. Bridge games every night. He wanted to go out for dinner and to parties, even though the influenza pandemic was spreading like wildfire, more deadly than ever. Because it preyed on young people most of all, I was terrified we might bring back a contagion and infect Susanna.

At the military hospitals and our clinics, we were encouraging the use of masks, but Paul hated wearing his. To burn energy, he went on a shopping spree, buying new dolls for Susanna, a new automobile for himself, the latest appliances for our housekeeper, and a diamond necklace for me.

Admiring it before a mirror, I said, "It's beautiful."

"You deserve it, my darling." He kissed the back of my neck as he fastened that sparkling thing. "I know I've been terribly hard to live with lately."

"You've only been *sad.*"

"I've been wallowing," he said. "Now I'm determined to embrace good cheer. We're going to enjoy the finer things in life."

I smiled appreciatively. "I do love the finer things, but we want to leave *some* inheritance for Susanna, don't we?"

"Not to worry! I've made some very shrewd investments that are about to pay off so well we might just be able to keep up with the Rumseys."

I knew about some of these investments, though I hadn't thought any of them likely to make us filthy rich. Fortunately, between the two of us, Paul was more expert with budgets, and I was happy to leave ours in his care.

Chapter Twenty-Seven

New York City
August 1918

Dear Frances,
I miss you, my love. I love you and the little girl who will per-
petuate all the sweet things in you, my darling heart.
~ Your loving Paul

There was a general feeling among women during the war that if you thought you had the right to say something about life, you should contribute as much public service as a man would contribute. Especially while our husbands were away. That is how I found myself at a picnic to promote war bonds on a hot summer day.

I'd just persuaded someone to keep up payments on a so-called liberty bond when I looked up from the table to see Al Smith grinning at me from beneath a straw boater while licking a lemon ice. "Well, hello, stranger."

"We could never be strangers, Mr. Smith."

"I haven't seen you in months, Miss Perkins!"

"I've been busy with motherhood and the war effort."

"Well, as someone running for governor, I think you ladies are doing the country proud, even if I've been half hounded to death by Mrs. William Astor Chanler about that new Lafayette charity."

The Broadway star turned socialite and war relief dynamo had started a charity, which, among other things, was employing sewing circles for soldiers and refugees. And though I had no particular talent with sewing, I was helping coordinate her efforts with other relief organizations. So Al Smith and I both had a bit of a laugh about Mrs. Chanler's persistence.

Then he thanked me for my own efforts. "You're a model citizen, Miss Perkins. Which is why I'd like to ask for your vote."

I blinked up at him from under my parasol. No one had ever asked me for my vote before. I realized, of course, that this upcoming election would be the first one in which I *could* vote. But it was still a powerful thing to be asked.

After a moment's consideration, I said, "Well, you shall have my vote. I cannot think of anyone who would make a better governor for New York State."

Smith's trademark smile grew wider as he ate his lemon ice. "I don't s'pose you'd be willing to tell other women that? I'd like you to help my campaign by giving speeches to women's groups. I know you're busy with a child at home and that I'm asking a big favor—"

"It'd be an honor," I said, and I meant that sincerely. "If you're sure you want me to do it. Because I've never been partisan, and my husband is—or was—a Republican."

"I'm sure," Mr. Smith said. "Here in the city, they don't mind that I'm Catholic, part Irish, and part Italian. They don't hold it against me that I grew up poor, dropped out of school, and worked as a fishmonger from the age of fourteen. In fact, they like me better for it. But upstate, they suspect I'm the most dreaded thing of all—a *city slicker*. I need people like you, with fine old pedigrees, to convince them I'm the real deal."

"Well, I'll certainly do my best," I promised.

Mr. Smith grinned. "Oh, I know you will."

"WE'VE GOT TO stop meeting at train stations, Miss Perkins," Frank Roosevelt said with a tip of his bowler hat. "Someone might accuse us of carrying on a romance."

I hadn't seen much of Frank Roosevelt since Woodrow Wilson had won the presidency and appointed him to be assistant secretary of the Navy. Now Frank wagged his prominent eyebrows as he hopped into the seat next to me, and I was taken off guard by his flirtatious good humor. I was also a little astonished at his polite apology for the way his long athletic legs crowded mine.

According to the newspapers, Roosevelt had returned home so sick from wartime duty in Europe that he had to be carried off his ship to his mother's house. He'd suffered a nasty bout of the Spanish flu, so if I saw something softer about old *Feather Duster Roosevelt*, I supposed that was to blame . . .

We were both on our way to give a speech for Al Smith's gubernatorial campaign, and I said, "It's nice to be on the same side for a change, Mr. Roosevelt. But I didn't think you approved of Tammany men."

Frank chuckled. "Oh, you know I had to make peace with Tammany in the end."

"Well, Mr. Smith isn't *really* Tammany, deep down, anyway. He's an honest man."

"By design," Frank replied, tapping a restless heel against the floor. "The bosses made a point to keep Al honest. They never let him get tangled up with any dirty deals. They kept him clean because they knew he was a capable fellow and that he could go far."

"How cynical you are," I mused. "As it happens, I know Al Smith and his family quite well. I can tell you that they're the salt of the earth. So, it might be true that Tammany never asked him to do anything dirty. Yet it's also true that he wouldn't have done it if they asked."

"You're a true believer."

"Why campaign for the man if you're not?"

Frank shrugged. "Because we're chummy these days. If Al wins, it'd be good to have a governor who owes me a favor."

I restrained the urge to roll my eyes at his naked opportunism. "Well, I'm making speeches for him because he really cares about people and the hard knocks they have taken. A lot more in Tammany are like that than you allowed for back in the day. Even Big Tim Sullivan made sure his poor constituents had a new pair of shoes every year."

"Well, I suppose you're right." Frank pulled at his long chin thoughtfully. "I was an awfully mean cuss when I first got into politics."

I was surprised to hear him admit it. Even more surprised when he continued, "Self-righteous too. I imagined that my own moral rectitude was hard-won, when the truth is that it's easy to do the right thing if you're never faced with temptation to do the wrong thing."

"That's a remarkable bit of introspection," I said warily. "Whatever has occasioned it?"

He fidgeted. "Well, I learned a great deal in Washington. You see, President Wilson didn't have time to take state committee members out to lunch. He used to ask me to take them off his hands. To listen to their suggestions. To pay attention to their problems, straighten it out, promise to do something, or tell them why I couldn't. And I realized that they aren't mean, bitter creatures. They just want to know they're being listened to."

I was deeply skeptical that a few lunches with state committee members had brought about character growth in a man like Franklin Roosevelt. But as we continued to chat, I couldn't deny there *was* something different about him. I suppose it might've been going overseas and seeing the bloodshed. Or maybe it was that so many young men he knew were dying in the war, including Theodore Roosevelt's son Quentin. Or maybe all this reflection had something to do with the rumor that was going round in Washington circles about a love affair and messy breakup between a certain married assistant secretary of the Navy and his pretty secretary . . .

Whatever the reason, Roosevelt was more emotionally exposed than he used to be, and, as if to cover it, he asked, "Did I hear you married Paul Wilson?"

I sputtered an incredulous laugh. "Yes, you know I did. Five *years* ago."

Frank grinned. "That's right, that's right. Smart fellow. Belated congratulations. I like to congratulate a bride when she's chosen well."

I smirked. "My husband also chose extremely well."

"That's the spirit, Mrs. Wilson."

He was taunting me, and I enjoyed throwing it back at him. "It's still *Miss Perkins* for the likes of you."

He grinned like a naughty schoolboy.

It was only after the train pulled out of the station that he sobered. "Too bad about Mayor Mitchel. He could've gone all the way to the White House, but I'm sure your husband will find a way to get back in the political game."

I wasn't so sure. Paul had taken his responsibilities at city hall seriously, and public criticism smote him to the heart. It hadn't been a game to him, and he didn't seem eager to hitch his wagon to a new horse. After all, my husband didn't have the colossal *ego* that sometimes seemed necessary to survive the rough-and-tumble of the political world.

I knew that wasn't a problem for Frank Roosevelt, so I asked, "What of your future plans?"

Frank threw his head back like he used to, but the old supercilious gesture was gentler now. Almost a little cheerful. "All in good time, my dear Miss Perkins. We have an unfortunate tendency to celebrate the early bird, without worrying about the misfortune of the early worm."

That struck me as funny. *Genuinely* funny. I couldn't help but laugh with him, and after that, things went much easier between us. You get to know people on a train in a way that you wouldn't otherwise. People relax a little together. They let down their guard. Even Franklin Roosevelt—and I don't think I've ever known a man quite so guarded.

One thing we had in common was an interest in Revolutionary history; Roosevelt was practically a walking encyclopedia, pointing out battle sites as we passed them and recounting anecdotes about where George Washington might have slept.

I learned that Frank's Revolutionary ancestor, Isaac Roosevelt, was an officer in the Continental Army, a friend of Alexander Hamilton, and an advocate for the Constitution of the United States with a Bill of Rights.

"I have Revolutionaries in my family line too," I said.

"Is that so? Let me guess, since you're from Boston, is it Sam Adams?"

"No one quite so famous," I said. "You might have heard of James Otis Jr. though—"

"I know of him! Otis was brilliant. *No Taxation without Representation* was a slogan of his invention, wasn't it? I often wonder, in fact, why he isn't mentioned by Americans with reverence, like Washington and Adams."

"Probably because a British tax collector bashed his skull, and he was never right in the head again."

Of course, some people said my illustrious kinsman was never right in the head to begin with, but that is nothing I would have admitted to Franklin Delano Roosevelt.

As the train chugged on, we talked about the American experiment and our mutual belief that our country was founded for a purpose and with a mission: to provide for liberty and the general welfare. And, of course, that America was still a work in progress. A theme we'd return to many times in our lives . . .

"Speaking of works in progress," Frank said at one point, thumbing a potboiler detective novel he'd brought with him to read on the trip. "How do you like marriage, anyway? I didn't figure you for the sort. You struck me as someone who liked her freedom."

"Yes, but unmarried women have less freedom than unmarried men do. And marriage has its compensations, as you well know."

Roosevelt nodded, but his bespectacled glance slid to the window. And I suspected things might be rocky with Eleanor when he said, "There's the children, of course."

Sensing that was a safer subject, I boasted, "I have a little girl of my own now. She's almost two years old."

"Do you have a picture?"

Surprised to be asked, I searched my handbag and produced a photograph of Susanna to show him. Then he produced a few of his own. It was all very polite and civilized, this talk about children.

He told me of how he liked to go camping and running and swimming with his.

"You obviously love them very much," I said, because it was something you said to fill the time.

But his expression took a serious turn. "*Very* much . . . Do you remember when we met, Miss Perkins? You were telling me about malnourished children. You mentioned babies dying from tainted milk. I had to look away."

I *did* remember that. I had a distinct memory of him looking down at his watch. I'd assumed he was bored or a boor or both. Yet now he explained, "Eleanor and I had just lost a baby, you see, and the wound was fresh."

"I'm so sorry," I said, unable to suppress an answering pang of grief. "I—I've lost children too."

It wasn't like me to volunteer something like that. And it certainly wasn't like Roosevelt to expose his underbelly. But we looked into each other's eyes and sat together in that sadness.

We shared it. An unexpected silent communion, during which I decided that Franklin Delano Roosevelt might be a more complex man than I had ever guessed.

Chapter Twenty-Eight

⋆ ✳ ⋆

New York City
November 1918

I ARRIVED HOME LATE FROM CAMPAIGNING FOR Al Smith to find my husband gone.

He must be out with friends, I thought, quite unalarmed. Then, changing for bed, I noticed that his suitcase was missing from the closet. Well, I supposed he must have returned to Washington for an emergency at the War Shipping Board. So I asked the housekeeper if he'd left a note, but she said she hadn't seen him leave. Neither had the butler.

That was strange. How had my husband slipped out of the house unnoticed, and without a word to anyone?

I didn't start to really worry until I noticed that Paul's desk—normally cluttered—was bare. By the next morning, we still hadn't heard from him, and when there was no answer at Paul's office, my worry became genuine fear.

My first thought was that he'd contracted the Spanish flu. Paul had always said that if he fell sick, he'd leave the house to keep from spreading the contagion to the rest of us. That meant he could be holed up by himself somewhere, terribly ill, with no one to care for him.

Fretting, I considered calling the authorities, but with so many people sick, they were overwhelmed.

I dialed up friends; no one had seen Paul. Then I drove myself to distraction trying to think of any place he might have gone. A hotel—or maybe he'd rented some house.

Of course, there was our cottage by the ocean . . .

I called there and someone answered in silence, then left the receiver off the hook so I couldn't ring back.

Now I was terrified.

I grabbed my coat, readying to head out in search of my missing husband, stopping only to kiss baby Susanna, who sleepily reached for me and warmly nestled under my chin before I entrusted her into the sturdy arms of the housekeeper.

When I got to the shore, I found Paul's motor parked in front of our beloved little shack. The front door was unlocked and slightly ajar, despite the chill. I called out my husband's name but heard no answer. So I stepped inside—finding that the place was extraordinarily tidy.

It looked as if Paul had spent *hours* organizing the books and papers. Quietly, I put the telephone receiver back on its hook, at least a little relieved not to find my husband on the floor burning with fever. Then I found a letter on the bed. My own letter from years ago—the one I'd left when I feared I'd die in childbirth.

Try harder than you have ever tried anything in life to understand our baby as it grows up. You have so much to give a little one . . .

Why was he reading this?

A cold and salty ocean breeze swept in through the open back door and carried with it to me a sense of overwhelming dread. I ran outside. "Paul?"

Frantically, I scanned the horizon. Then I took off at a run, stumbling toward the beach. When I reached the surf's edge, I saw my husband bobbing in water far too cold for a swim. There was no telling how long he'd been out there, and I waved my arms; I think he saw me, but he lingered, letting waves buffet him.

Was he drowning?

I started into the water after him, unfastening my clothes as I went. I had to remind myself that I could stand it, because cold weather was in my blood. Still, the water was so frigid that it *hurt*.

I was up to my neck before Paul was close enough for me to see his face. Water glistened on pale cheeks, and he was so dead-eyed, it was frightening to behold.

After some harrowing moments, I caught him by the arms. He trembled, weak with exhaustion. Together, we somehow dragged ourselves out of the water, panting and gasping from the effort, sand and grit scraping our skin.

It was several moments of shivering and teeth chattering before we could speak. Even then, we couldn't manage it without coughing or spitting water.

"*For heaven's sake*, Paul! What could you have been thinking to go out in that water?"

He didn't answer. Only then did I remember how we'd come to be here. How he'd slipped out of our home. How he'd taken the phone off the hook. How he'd tidied everything, leaving the front door ajar and an old letter for me to find. Dread swept over me anew . . .

Shivering violently, I insisted, "Let's get inside and into dry clothes, and we'll make some tea. Then you're going to explain this."

Inside, I found a dry pair of trousers for him, and I put on a shirt of his until my own clothing dried out. Then I lit a fire and put on the teakettle. Only once we were both bundled in blankets did I say, "You mustn't terrify me like this."

"I don't mean to terrify you," he murmured. "If I'd found the courage last night, it would've been all over by now and you'd have nothing left to fear."

I stared, uncomprehending. Or at least, I didn't want to comprehend. "Were you going to drown yourself?"

I asked it so bluntly that he cringed. "No. You and Susanna wouldn't get any insurance money if they found me with my pockets full of stones."

So he wasn't going to drown himself, but he'd put himself in a position where the ocean could do it for him. And he didn't leave a note of his own so that it might be ruled an accident . . .

"*My God, Paul.* I know this has been a dreadful year, absolutely dreadful, but only a few weeks ago, you said we were going to enjoy the finer things in life."

It was as if I hadn't spoken. My husband was in a world of his own, whispering, "You'd be better off without me. You and Susanna both."

Shaking with fear for him and anger for what he'd just put me through, I said, "What rot!"

"It's true." His voice was hoarse and anguished. "You realized it once and tried to leave me, but I convinced you to stay, and now look at what I've brought us to. There's no more money, Frances. I've lost it. All the money my father left me. All the money I saved over the past twenty years of my career. Our nest egg is gone."

I sat with the weight of this confession, absolutely reeling. "How?"

"I thought I was so smart with money. People entrusted me with the finances of the entire city, and I did well for them, didn't I? But when it came to *our* money, I was just another mark for a gold scam. I'll never be able to replace what we lost. Not if I worked another fifty years, and I don't think I'll live that long."

The pain in his eyes was worse, much worse, than the panic that flailed in my heart. I knew I had to think rationally. I couldn't fall into a pit of despair, because *he* was already there. I wanted to berate him. I wanted to yell, and throw things, and demand to know how he could've been so foolish and how he could've risked so much in one investment scheme. But mostly, I wanted to know how he could ever imagine that *money* would compensate for the loss of a beloved husband and father.

Remonstrations could come later when he wasn't so pale and shaky. Right now, I had to understand the facts. "Are we bankrupt?"

"Not yet. We aren't in debt. I still make a wage, and I suppose we can sell some things to get by."

Well, at least that was good news. We weren't starting behind. There was nothing to be done about the money we had lost. We would just have to make more . . .

I poured more hot tea in my husband's cup and encouraged him to sip it. "Paul, I didn't marry you for your fortune. You ought to know that. I was supporting myself for more than a decade before we ever met. And if we can afford help with the baby, there isn't any reason I can't go back to work."

"That isn't what I want for you or for Susie. At least not until she's older."

It wasn't what we'd planned, but I was already spending so much time volunteering that it felt as if I already had a job without the paycheck . . .

To soothe his pride, I said, "All right, then we'll sell some things until we figure the rest out. We'll manage." Seeing he didn't believe me, I hastened to add, "I'm not saying we won't miss the money, but worse things have happened to other people. We're both able-bodied and intelligent. As long as we can find work, our daughter won't lack for a roof over her head. Things may be very inconvenient for a very long time, but if we have one another, we can make it through this terrible accident."

Paul's fingers curled tight around his teacup, and he stared into it as if it had no bottom. "I want to believe that, but right now, all I know is that I'm not the man you married."

I pressed my forehead to his and whispered, "Well, I need that man back. I know you're shaken and feeling low. But I married you because you're the only person to make me feel as if I wasn't facing this world alone. So I'm not going to let you leave me, or Susanna, or this world either."

Paul broke down crying then. A big strong man, crying in my arms. But we vowed to face the future together and make it all right.

Chapter Twenty-Nine

Washington, DC
January 1919

THOUSANDS OF SOLDIERS WERE OUT OF work now that the armistice had been signed and a victorious United States was winding down its military presence in Europe. What that meant for Paul's job at the War Shipping Board was uncertain, so with little Susanna in tow, I made the trip to Washington to plan our next move. I found Paul in better spirits; he'd sought treatment for his depression in secret, and our financial situation was becoming clearer.

We'd already sold the automobile and the diamond necklace and given up the place on the beach. We couldn't afford to employ a butler and housekeeper anymore. And we certainly couldn't keep our big, beautiful house. Of course, if we moved to the nation's capital, we wouldn't have to explain why we were selling it, and that would soothe our pride. But now, it was our two-year-old daughter who needed soothing.

"There, there, Susie, don't cry," Paul said, trying to calm her on his hip.

Our toddler didn't like this unfamiliar place, so Paul sang a silly little song to her about everything in the room.

That's a mirror. That's a mirror. Peek!
That's a picture frame. Don't drop it. Eek!

Susanna settled until the telephone rang. I took her so Paul could answer, only to see a quizzical expression on my husband's face when he did. "It's actually for you, Frances."

"For *me*?" I had no idea who'd call me here.

"It's Governor Smith's office."

Al Smith had won the election, and he'd already sent me a lovely letter of thanks for the speeches I'd made on his behalf. I couldn't imagine what this might be about, but my husband and I again juggled Susanna between us until I could pick up the phone.

The man on the other end snapped, "We've had a devil of a time finding you, Miss Perkins. When were you planning on coming back to New York?"

"Sometime tomorrow, why?"

"The governor wants to see you in Albany right away. He'd like you to come up on the Empire State Express and be here around noon."

"All right." If Al Smith needed me, certainly I'd be there. "But what does he want, so I can prepare?"

"I'm not at liberty to tell you what the governor wants. Just be there."

I hung up, bewildered.

"He has a legislative agenda to get into place in a hurry," Paul said. "He probably wants your help."

"Well, that's a funny way of asking. Having someone else call to demand I take the next train home while I'm having a weekend with my husband."

Paul chuckled. "In my experience, politicians—particularly those newly elected—have a high sense of entitlement, and very little consideration for other people's private lives."

NEWLY ELECTED GOVERNOR Al Smith was waiting for me, singing a cheery little tune. With true pleasure, I said, "Congratulations on your election once again. I have some materials I thought you might like about the child labor bill."

"I've got something else to talk to you about."

I said, "All right."

"I was thinkin'. How would you like to be on the Industrial Commission of New York?"

Just like that, with no preliminaries, no dancing up to it.

"You can't mean it," I said, for an appointment to the state's industrial commission wasn't just some kind of job. He was offering to make me *a public officer*.

Hardly anyone had ever heard of a woman in public office. Women couldn't even vote in federal elections yet. But he said, "Of course I mean it."

At the realization of how important this was and what attention it would garner, I shot out of my chair. I walked to the window and stared out, hanging on to the blue velvet curtain for balance. "Do you know what you're offering? You ought to think it over."

He laughed a marvelous raspy laugh. "Don't you think I've thought about it? That's why I asked you."

Trying to keep my cool, I laughed with him. "Well, but what on earth makes you think it'd be a good idea to appoint me?"

"Because you have a male mind."

"No, sir," I contradicted. "I only have a good mind."

He chuckled. "All right. A good mind. I think the Industrial Commission is in terrible condition. Nobody's been louder about that than you. We got to reform it and turn it inside out. I know you're the person to do it."

I wanted to preen with pride at his faith in me, but this was a truly outrageous idea, and he must've seen that I still believed it to be an elaborate prank. "Miss Perkins, I've been thinkin' since the election. Women are gonna vote from now on in New York State and I oughtta show 'em some attention. Bring 'em into my administration. Naturally, I thought of you."

Though I was flattered, I said, "Surely there are other women with genuine political ambition, whereas I have none."

"Well, I know a lot of women. Mostly wives and sisters of political leaders. But I don't want to appoint somebody's sister or wife. That's kind of an insult to women, whereas you have experience, and I know that if you have something to say, I can rely on it. So will you let me appoint you or not?"

Still shaky, I said, "You have to give me time to think."

"Why? Have you got anything on your conscience that makes you feel it wouldn't be right for you to be a public officer?"

"Oh, no, Governor, there isn't anything wrong that I know of. It's only that I've spent my whole life poking at the system. Now you're asking me to be part of it."

"That's the only way to fix it, Miss Perkins."

My reformer friends certainly didn't agree. In fact, they thought politics was grubby. That anyone who got into government would inevitably be corrupted.

On the other hand, Governor Smith was part of the Tammany machine, but he was also above it. He'd never dirtied his hands with graft or anything else that might make him ashamed. And now he said, "You're a Christian woman, aren't you? You want to do good with your life, don't you?"

I couldn't argue with that. "Don't I have to be confirmed to this position? I've made a lot of enemies in Albany."

"You let me worry about that, Miss Perkins." Looking rather pleased with himself, he asked, "Anything else holding you back?"

"My family . . ."

"Oh, your husband won't object. I know Paul. He's interested in improving the state."

He was likely entirely right that Paul wouldn't object. But what about Susanna? "I am a mother of a small child."

"I know you'll need to hire a nanny," he said. "So you should know the job pays eight thousand dollars a year."

My jaw dropped in such an unladylike way that I had to snap it shut again. That kind of money would be a lifeline for my financially struggling family, and I wondered if he knew it. Even still, I hesitated. "I'd just like to talk to someone before I agree."

"Who?"

"My husband and Florence Kelley, to start with . . ."

Smith rolled his eyes. "Do you think Mrs. Kelley will say you ought to keep your hands out of vulgar politics? Here's something to think about. If you girls are going to get what you want through legislation, there better not be any separation between social workers and the government."

Leaving the governor's office, I called Paul, who was enthusiastic about the job. Then I hopped the first train back to Manhattan and flew into a coffee shop where Mrs. Kelley agreed to meet me.

The moment I told her about the appointment, she wept. "Glory be to God! To think someone I've trained, someone who cares about women, will have the chance to be an executive officer . . ."

"You think I should take it, then?" I asked as she dabbed her eyes with a kerchief. "There are going to be an awful lot of mistakes made. I'm sure I'll make some of them. There are things we both know need to get done that I might not be able to get done. Will I get hit over the head by reformers for that?"

"Not if you give it an honest try," she said.

I took a deep breath, found a telephone right there in the coffee shop, and asked to be connected to the governor. "Well?" Al asked impatiently. "I think you better do it. It's the right thing for you, and the right thing for women."

"All right. I'm scared to death, but I'll do it."

Thus began my career in government.

Chapter Thirty

★ ★ ★

New York City
February 1919

NOBODY HAD CRITICIZED NEW YORK'S IN-
dustrial Commission more than me. I'd said they were
useless, corrupt, and moribund. I'd once even signed a
petition demanding that the governor fire them all. Now I was to be
one of their colleagues . . .

Remembering the harsh language I'd used, I was nervous to face
them. When the time was right, I'd have to apologize for some of the
more inflammatory things that I'd said. In the meantime, I intended
to be as amiable as possible.

I wore a new dress on my first day—something not too pretty.
Something their mothers might have worn. I arrived at nine a.m. sharp
and was met by my new secretary—the surliest woman in existence.
When I introduced myself, she looked me up and down, fixing me
with a basilisk eye, utterly unimpressed. Then she grunted. "You can
call me Miss Jay."

"Jay! Well, that's a fine patriotic family name," I chirped, trying
to make a connection; it was best, after all, to be friendly with one's
secretary. "I don't suppose you're related to the founding father or his
descendants—there's a poet, I believe. John Jay Chapman . . ."

"Never heard of 'em," she said, a Brooklyn accent coming to the
fore. "The name is Frances Jurkowitz, but people around here
can't pronounce anything longer than two syllables, so I go by
Miss Jay."

"Well, Jurkowitz isn't so difficult to pronounce. I'd be happy to call you by your real name."

She stared, lips pursed as if she'd sucked a lemon. "Let's not make problems."

Well, then. Miss Jay it would be.

I was sworn in. And that was that.

Then Miss Jay pointed with her chin. "There's your desk, Commissioner Perkins."

Commissioner Perkins. It was so odd to hear my name with a title. Not just *Miss Perkins.* Or *Mrs. Wilson.* I now had an official title of public responsibility, and it meant more to me than I ever expected it might.

In my new position, I tried not to be a smarty or a show-off. At least until I witnessed for myself how this commission operated.

One of my first cases that year was a government-employed doctor who had been taking bribe money from insurance companies. There was no question about his guilt. The man needed to be dismissed immediately. Yet the men of the commission debated this case until late in the night, saying what a fine doctor he was. They admitted his corruption couldn't be tolerated, but they couldn't agree to get rid of him. The discussion went on and on until I was staring at the clock, thinking of little Susanna and how I ought to be home tucking her into bed.

Women like me had things to *do* at home. Dinner to cook. Children to help with their studies. Housekeeping, and party planning to help their husbands' careers. None of the women I'd ever worked with would've allowed this conversation to go around in circles.

The truth was that these commissioners were getting nothing done because they wanted to find a way of letting the criminal off easy—in fact, I'm convinced they'd have let him off with only a warning if I hadn't been there. That told me I wasn't an interloper in this position; in fact, I was needed. So at eleven o'clock at night, I finally said, "We all agree this man has been taking bribes. He must be gotten rid of, and it must be done *tonight*."

The governor had put me here to shake things up, and that's just what I planned to do. The commission needed to be reformed, and I was in a position to reform it, so I took it upon myself to institute monthly reports. I made sure that factory inspectors were swapped around the state to frustrate too-friendly relations with the business they were meant to regulate. And when workers went on strike, I made sure we took the mediating role we were charged with by state law. Which is how I found myself packing for a visit to Rome, New York, while Paul, in pajamas and slippers, fixed me a cup of his famed coffee with eggshells to keep me awake for the late-night trip.

My husband had moved back to New York City and taken a job with an insurance company. We'd been able to get a wonderful little apartment, and a full-time live-in nanny to take care of the baby during the day and to help tidy the house every evening.

But Paul was home often, and it bothered him a little that I wasn't. He insisted that he was quite proud of me; it was only that he relied on me to keep him of even temperament. And now he was uneasy. "How long will you be gone?"

"Unfortunately, there's no telling," I said, sipping the hot coffee. "It sounds like a very bad situation upstate. I can't persuade the other commissioners to go if I won't go myself."

"What's the emergency?" Paul asked.

"The factories in the town were taking advantage of cheap immigrant labor. The Italian workers went on strike, demanding an eight-hour workday. When the copper workers went to speak to their boss about it, he *literally* kicked them out of the office and threw them down the stairs."

"Charming," Paul said.

"You don't do such a thing to Italians; they have too much pride. In revenge, they overturned his car."

"He's lucky they didn't set it on fire."

I agreed with my husband. What I did not tell him was that things were feared to get worse. People were rioting now, and a negotiator needed to be sent in, so the governor was sending me. Thus, I took the overnight train, then settled into my berth with the evening paper and read about the riots all night long.

By daylight, as we approached the town, both the porter and the conductor warned me not to disembark. "A man was shot on the bridge yesterday, Miss Perkins. They got guns, they're shooting again today, and that bridge is the only way into town. We've been told not to let anybody off there."

"You have to let me off the train," I said. "I have official government business."

They didn't believe me.

We argued about it a good five minutes, and even when I told them they could call the governor himself, they still tried to convince me it was too dangerous. "Don't be crazy, lady. You're going to get yourself killed."

The conductor looked truly terrified for me. And ordinarily, that might not have given me pause. I'd always flung myself in harm's way. I'd earned a reputation, after all, as *a dauntless woman*. But that was before I became a mother . . .

Now I had a tiny daughter with little flaxen curls and eyes that looked up at me in adoration and need. I was less frightened for myself to be shot during a riot than to leave my child an orphan. The idea of it made my normally stiff knees go spongy.

But this was the job.

I'd known it when I took the oath of office with my hand on a Bible. I simply couldn't give in to the fear.

Florence Kelley often told me that to be rated as good as a man in a job, a woman must show herself to be better. She must be steadier, more trustworthy, and twice as skilled just to have the same chance. That meant I had to be at least as courageous as a man in my position. If I was too afraid to get off the train, then I wasn't the right woman for this job. And if I couldn't do the job, they might never offer a job like this to a woman again.

So I got off the train.

"I'll be careful," I promised the train conductor, and myself. "After all, I don't want to make a fuss for Governor Smith by getting myself killed."

I HIRED A car to take me over the bridge, and decided we'd better roll in with the convertible top down so the rioters could see me. I stood upon the back seat so that the workers could get an eyeful—in the hopes they might be less likely to shoot a lady.

I felt a little bit more confident when the taxicab driver explained that it hadn't been the mob who shot up the bridge. It had been *the factory owner* shooting at his own striking workers.

"Well, those workers might not have been armed last night," I said when we stopped the car in the middle of the bridge because it was blocked at the other end by a mob holding stones in their hands. I saw a few rifles too. "But I believe they are now."

When the mob charged forward, I shouted, "I'm Commissioner Perkins, and I've been sent by the governor to look into your problems."

Some of them clearly didn't speak English and scowled. Others smiled, and it was a relief to know those rocks weren't for me! Still, tensions remained high, and as I came into the town proper, I soon learned why.

I made my way to the nearby hotel to get breakfast and the lay of the land. That's where I learned state troopers were on the way, gathering at the edge of town. And the working people were frightened.

They'd been through too much to let state police start cracking heads without fighting back.

Then someone took me aside to say, "Commissioner, I've got to tell you something. You know these are mostly *Eyetalians*. Their blood is up. They have real dynamite. If the state police come in, they're going to blow things up."

I wasn't sure I believed him.

Nevertheless, he insisted, "You've got to call the governor and convince him not to send in the police. I'm going to promise all those people out there that you'll get him to call the police off. You've got to do it. Promise you'll do it."

"I promise I'll think about it."

I went into a little room by myself, pulled the chair out beside the telephone, and had a hard think. I wanted to solve this without violence. In fact, I wanted to prove that conflicts like this one *could* be solved without violence. I suppose the truth was that I wanted to prove that *I* could settle it without violence.

Which is why I finally called the governor. "Please believe me, sir. If you call off the state police, I can stop the rumpus."

I could almost see Al Smith chomping on his cigar in irritation on the other end of the line. "How?"

"I'll hold hearings. I'll get the whole commission up here."

"They'll never come."

"I'll make them come," I insisted. "I'll get at least three commissioners. I promise you that. We'll hold hearings in the courthouse and proceed in an orderly way and settle this. If the state police come through here, I think there will be mayhem. Somebody'll get shot. Somebody'll get hurt. Somebody'll get killed."

I said nothing about the dynamite. After all, I hadn't seen any dynamite with my own eyes. I told myself it would be irresponsible to share mere gossip. That wasn't the whole truth though. I knew bomb threats frightened people in power far more than shoot-outs. And if I told the governor about the dynamite, he'd feel he *had* to send in troops. So, I took the risk on myself and wrung my hands waiting for the governor's answer.

"All right," said Smith. "On your say-so, Commissioner Perkins, I'll tell the police to stand down. For now."

When the police withdrew, a cheer went up, and I walked to the town square, where everyone was gathered in the rising heat of that summer day. Men, women, and children waved their hands at me, shouting, "*Oh, la signora!*"

I wanted to give them the sense that things were going to be all right. I climbed on the bench and made a speech in what little Italian I'd learned in Hell's Kitchen all those years ago. "We're going to try to have law and order," I said. "I want everybody to cooperate. We'll hear everything you have to say."

I was able to get the gist of their concerns, despite the language barrier. They told me they were awful mad about the way they'd been kicked, beaten, and shot at, all for asking for safer working conditions and a higher wage.

I listened and listened and *listened* until things finally calmed down. By then, the sun was starting to set, so I asked to be taken to one of their houses, where I confided, privately, that I knew they might have explosives. "You must get rid of them now that it's dark. I promised the governor that if he pulled the police, you'd get rid of them."

This was a blatant lie. And I half expected them to protest that of course there wasn't any dynamite. Instead, I was horrified as word spread from house to house and people started coming out with suitcases, hatboxes, and even baby carriages filled with explosives. In amazement, I watched them dump sticks of dynamite in the canal, breathing a little easier to see them all sink in the water.

Chapter Thirty-One

Albany, New York
Autumn 1919

IT WASN'T UNTIL I'D SETTLED THE STRIKE IN Rome that I confessed about the dynamite to Al Smith. And when I told him, he threw his hat on the desk and shouted, "You've got some nerve to keep a thing like that from me!"

I winced, hoping the successful conclusion of the issue without scandal to his administration would earn me a little forgiveness. "I know it was very wrong not to have told you, but I was just doing what seemed best at the time. There aren't any rules for a situation like that."

"No rules? I'll tell you the rule. The rule is that you tell your boss when explosives are involved."

He was angry for many reasons, not least of which was that there'd been a rash of explosions in the country. A bomb had recently blasted Washington, DC, littering body parts on the doorstep of Frank Roosevelt. The public was at the start of a Red scare, on high alert, and politicians like Al Smith were jittery.

"If there'd been an explosion," he continued to rage, "people woulda been hurt. And I'd be known as the governor who pulled back troops instead of cracking down on anarchists and Bolsheviks."

I tried to defend myself. "I thought it best to get it to where it wouldn't explode. I thought it was the safest thing to do."

"Oh, no. What you thought is that you'd call the shots yourself. You're used to being in charge, but this is the *government*, and nobody elected you."

Well, I couldn't argue with that. I also began to realize that I was going to have to change my ways. So I stood there and hung my head in silence and let him chew me out until he was too tired to chew me out anymore.

Even after he vented his spleen, he continued to murmur, *"You have some nerve."*

It wasn't until he realized I was just going to stand there and take my medicine, and not break down in tears, that he finally admitted, "I'm not sayin' that you didn't do well, Commissioner Perkins. Even the factory owners were impressed with your energy and ingenuity. But I already know you're a phenom. I've known it for years. I sent you for a more important reason. I sent you because I *trusted* you."

The way he said *trusted* in past tense was a blow much worse than all the shouting.

It hurt.

I hadn't lied to him, except by omission, but he deserved better. I'd let him down. Now I felt just terrible about it. "Governor, I promise I'll work hard to earn back your trust."

Hearing that, he flung himself back in his chair. Crossed his arms over his chest. Glowered. Then finally said, "I know you will."

Things were a little stiff between us after that, so it was a relief when, a few weeks later, he finally called to say, "Come meet me at the Biltmore."

Governor Smith had a suite there for political business, and when I arrived, he was in shirtsleeves, with his vest open and one of his big cigars dangling from his lips. He motioned me into the bedroom, which was the only room that wasn't filled with secretaries and other politicians. Then he put a chair down in the middle of the room and told me to sit.

"Am I to be interrogated?" I asked.

"Don't tempt me . . ."

I sat gingerly because the room was a bit of a mess. Empty bottles were strewn across old newspapers and what I would come to recognize as the detritus of a political campaign. Then the governor opened our conversation by saying, "Somebody told me you wasn't a Democrat."

"Oh, really," I said with a startled little laugh. "I don't think I even know what a Democrat is."

"Don't be a wisenheimer," he said. "You've been around long enough to know."

"Yes, but I've never had the opportunity to vote until this last election; I never had to face the music about politics."

My tone was playful, but he wasn't amused. In fact, he began to grill me about *why* I wasn't a Democrat. I admitted that of course I'd noticed that when Democrats were in power, the reforms I cared about were passed. "But I wouldn't dream of enrolling in any party."

"Why wouldn't you?"

"Because partisanship ties your hands. Then you must be for the Democrats even though on some occasion there might be somebody else you'd be for."

He shook his head. "Now, that's the kind of mistake a lotta good people make. They think they got somethin' if they're independent. Your husband probably thought so when he worked for Mayor Mitchel."

Paul *had* thought that. The Mitchel administration at city hall had angered the stalwarts of both major parties by refusing to hand out political favors. My husband was proud of that, but they'd paid dearly for it at the ballot box. And now they were out of power, which is why Smith argued, "You don't get anythin' by being independent. Look what happened to Theodore Roosevelt and his Bull Moosers."

I stared down at my hands, still a little grief-stricken because TR had died at the start of the year. The old Bull Moose had died in his sleep, and those of us who admired him repeated the quip that if Theodore Roosevelt had been awake when death came, there'd have been a *fight*.

Now, all hopes of a progressive point of view in the Republican party were gone. So why hold out?

Smith continued to press me. "In our form of government, anybody can aspire to be elected. But does just anybody get votes? No, Commissioner, he doesn't get any votes unless he's got a crowd of people who are all bound together in some way. That's what a political party is—a group of people who stand by each other. They get a candidate. They promote him. Gradually a policy works itself out. If you don't have a two-party system, you'll have the kind of bedlam they have in France."

I argued with him about that. He argued back. I'm not sure I was ever entirely convinced of his logic, but in the end, I told him I'd do as he asked. It wasn't a sacrifice. Al Smith had never steered me wrong. He'd taken a giant risk in appointing me. Working with him, and for him, had been the most rewarding fun of my life. So, at the end of the day, if he needed me to be a Democrat, then I'd be a Democrat. That's the kind of loyalty Al Smith inspired in people. You wanted to go along with him even if you thought he might be wrong.

THE MAIN THING I remember about the Democratic convention in the summer of 1920 is that it was awash in shortened flapper hemlines and ladies making eyes at Franklin Delano Roosevelt.

Nobody who saw the assistant secretary of the Navy at that convention was likely to forget how handsome he looked that year.

Irritatingly handsome.

Frank had put on a little muscle, which filled him out and gave him even more of a film star appeal. And he was enjoying the attention. Thankfully Eleanor wasn't with him, because the whispers were shameless.

Where has that tall drink of Roosevelt been all my life?
—whatever Frank is running for, he has my vote—
Oh, I just want to watch him run.

Frank was a man on the rise, with a big toothy smile and a big booming voice, and, oh, he had lots to say. Someone had finally impressed upon him the notion that poverty is destructive, wasteful, demoralizing, and preventable. Which, of course, made it morally unacceptable to leave unaddressed in a democratic society.

And now he was an evangelist.

During one moment of chaos during the convention, he vaulted over several rows of seats to get to the podium. We all applauded this athletic feat, but even as I clapped, I thought, *He's going to let that applause go straight to his head . . .*

In the end, the Democratic presidential nomination went to the Ohio businessman James Cox at the top of the ticket and Franklin Roosevelt as his vice presidential candidate. And I was puzzled to find myself cheering Roosevelt as loudly as anyone else in the room. Oh, I was still *wary*. I knew Frank could be vain and insincere. I also knew he was still trying to follow in Theodore Roosevelt's oversized footsteps. He'd even started to *speak* like Theodore Roosevelt, sprinkling words like *bully* into his speeches. But at long last, even I was worn down by his charms, and I was beginning to really *like* Frank.

"WHAT A DISASTER," I said, looking over election returns with Paul at the breakfast table.

The Republicans had clobbered the Democrats in the elections and swept into office with coattails. Which meant Governor Al Smith was swept *out* of office, and I was suddenly out of a job.

Afraid for my family's future, I understood for the first time, *really understood*, how bad Paul must've felt when Mayor Mitchel went down in defeat. I regretted every moment I hadn't spent campaigning for the ticket, and I felt gloomy. Just terrible. So I never expected Al Smith to be the one to cheer me up. When I stopped by his office, he asked, "Have you seen these numbers? I did better than expected up-state! It was a Republican year, but I only lost by a few votes."

"Well, that's a fine attitude," I said, wishing I could share it.

He poured me a lemonade, grumbling about Prohibition. "You know what this means, Miss Perkins? It means that two years from now, I'll run again, and I'll win. Then we'll both get back to business."

If Al Smith said something like that, you could take it as gospel truth. Still, two years was a long time to wait; I'd have to find other work before then, and so would he. But I knew that in our hearts, we were only biding our time.

Franklin Roosevelt was too.

On the campaign trail, he'd been pilloried by one of his own relatives who said, *Franklin Delano Roosevelt is nine-tenths mush, and one-tenth Eleanor.*

I expected to find him brooding over his loss, but Frank was sanguine when I ran into him at Delmonico's. "Just wasn't a good year for us Democrats. We'll get 'em next time."

I smiled. "What will you do now?"

"I'm taking a job on Wall Street. I'll have time to go jogging with my children at the family cottage at Campobello Island. Come and see me sometime. We'll take icy swims to reinvigorate the blood. Get our beauty sleep. That sort of thing."

I laughed, not taking his invitation seriously. "Sounds wonderful."

"What about you, Miss Perkins? Have you got a new job lined up?"

I thought it kind of him to ask. "I've been offered a position with the Council on Immigrant Education."

"Well, that's bully. Just bully."

I wasn't so sure it was *bully*, but the work promised to be interesting. Woodrow Wilson may have won the war and advanced international morality, but he'd been a disaster when it came to racial equality at home. Much to my shame, he'd reintroduced segregation into the federal government, and with the rise of the Ku Klux Klan, black people and immigrants were more discriminated against than ever.

I was now sure to be locked in ugly battle with the Klan over immigrant rights, but I needed a salary. For when Paul and I had disagreements these days, it was almost always about money or politics.

Paul was, as the saying goes, *a general without buttons*. He had important ideas about how insurance might be used to help provide for people who were caught in the wheels of capitalism's excesses. He had a strong interest in public affairs and had spent four years at the center of the political scene at city hall, and then two more while I served as an industrial commissioner. But now we were both frozen out.

And he was taking it harder than I was . . .

Chapter Thirty-Two

New York City
September 1921

P AUL IS WRITING A WONDERFUL NEW AR-
ticle about the possible uses of insurance in solving social
ills," I said at a small dinner party we were hosting for friends.

My husband had been particularly withdrawn that night, and I
was trying to pull him into conversation, but Paul only stared at his
plate. One of our guests—the editor of an important publication—
rushed to fill the silence. "How interesting, Paul. I'd love to read it."

"It's not ready to be read," Paul said.

Gently, I prompted, "Oh, come now. You *do* like to wax poetic on
the brilliance of insurance and how it could help so many workers
who get hurt on the job. Why don't you explain the premise?"

"I'd rather not." With that, Paul shoved his plate away like an ill-
mannered toddler instead of the exquisitely mannered man I had married. I put my hand on his, giving it a gentle squeeze to warn him he was
ruining our dinner party. But he just sat there, his countenance blank as
if he were somewhere else entirely.

Not long after, our embarrassed guests hastily made their excuses.
After showing them out with apologies, I confronted my husband.
"What on earth is the matter? I've never seen you behave that way
before."

"Frances, I simply don't have the strength to pretend I want to be
here anymore . . ."

I stared at him. "You don't want to be here, in our house, with me and your daughter?"

His gaze fixed on some point in the distance. "I don't want to be in this *world*." Startled, I again reached for him, this time instinctively, to offer comfort, but his hand was lifeless. "I'm a burden to you, Frances. An embarrassment. I'm no good for you, and no good for Susie."

Not this again. I clenched my teeth. "Why would you say that?"

His eyelashes fluttered as he seemed to come back to me a moment. "The voice in my head tells me I'm no good. Most days, I can drown it out. Then, I walk into the kitchen to cut the crust off Susie's sandwich and find myself staring at the edge of the blade, thinking I'd do better by her if I cut open my wrists."

My mouth went dry at this utterance and the abject humiliation in his voice. He'd never wanted me to know he had thoughts like this. It was obviously taking all his emotional strength and courage to admit it now.

"That voice is lying to you," I insisted, bringing his knuckles to my lips to kiss in reassurance. "You must argue with this voice. You're very good at arguing a point when you want to."

"But it ambushes me when I least expect it. On my way to work, standing at the curb, I think, *Step out into the traffic. Step out and end it all.* When I go to a meeting in a tall office building, I look out the window and think—"

"Don't say it," I snapped. "I can't bear to hear you say you want to jump. I've seen people jump because they had no other choice."

He winced. Then I winced, too, because I hadn't intended to shame him. Now, shyly, he tried to explain, "Some days, I don't feel like I have any other choice either."

"But why, darling?" I was desperate to understand. "I know we don't have the fortune we used to, but we live in a lovely apartment, with a delightful child, in a fine city. We have good friends, food on the table, books to read, and all forms of entertainment from card games to parks to museums. Not to mention interesting work. We have the kind of life other people dream of—the kind of life other people sacrifice *everything* just to reach for."

He shrank into himself. "There isn't anything wrong with our life, Frances. It's *me*. I'm what's wrong. I can't explain it, except to say that I'm trying to hold on by my fingertips. The only thing that keeps me from letting go is the fear of what my death might do to you and Susie."

"It would *devastate* us." I forced him to look at me. "You must believe me when I say this, Paul. If you won't believe losing you would shatter me, can you imagine the feelings of a little girl to know that her father abandoned her that way?"

That brought tears to Paul's eyes. Trembling, he told me repeatedly how much he loved me and our daughter, and how much he hated himself for this weakness. How much he hated himself for putting us through this. And I knew this wasn't playacting.

My husband was besieged by some plague of the mind, for in the days that followed, he would lie awake remembering, in vivid detail, every mistake he'd ever made, every person he'd ever offended, and every sin he'd ever committed—his overactive imagination even inventing a few.

I think I might have bankrupted the city, he confided in me at one point, apparently having forgotten that he wasn't working in city hall anymore. Then he confessed other lapses that, upon investigation, also had no basis in fact. He feared he might've allowed a corrupt policeman to go unreported, and I had to remind him that he'd actually brought about that policeman's disciplinary action. Then Paul feared he hadn't paid some debts we owed, frantically poring over our records only to find that everything had been paid in full. It was maddening for both of us. Heartbreaking too. His sense of worthlessness defied all evidence and reason, but it was real to him—a powerful, unstoppable force. A vortex in his soul, sucking him down, down, down.

Slowly the frustration in my heart melted in loving sympathy as it became clear my husband's brain was very ill. I didn't understand the illness, but I knew it *was* an illness. One beyond my capability to cure.

PRESBYTERIAN HOSPITAL HAD a fine reputation for treating mental illness. Once Paul was admitted and given bromide so that he might rest, I sat next to his bedside, trying not to wring my hands waiting for the doctor's diagnosis.

Eventually, I felt as if I must do something other than *wait*, and, seizing upon the opportunity to stretch my legs and get a drink of water, I went out into the hall.

That's when I saw Eleanor Roosevelt.

Unfortunately, she saw me, too, and under the circumstances, I was desperate not to be seen. Given the delicacy of my husband's illness, I'd told no one—not even Mary Rumsey—that I'd taken Paul to the hospital. The last thing I wanted now was to run into someone I knew. But I had the strangest impression that Eleanor didn't want to be seen here either. We both froze in place—my eyes darting to the side as I wondered if I could simply keep walking and pretend I hadn't noticed her.

After all, to that point in our lives, Eleanor and I didn't know each other well—we were only connected socially through Mary and the various causes we held in common. But Eleanor had nearly bowled me over with that long awkward stride of hers, and now there was no way for either of us to escape without acknowledging the other.

Eleanor was first to speak, her shadowed expression pulling into a tight smile. "Why, Miss Perkins, whatever are you doing here at the hospital? I hope it is nothing to do with your little girl."

"No, Susanna is in good health, it's only . . ." I trailed off, simply unable to think of a lie. "And you? I hope your children are well."

Eleanor took a deep breath, then another, and I suddenly realized how stiffly she was holding herself. "Thank you for asking. My children are also in good health, but my husband has been ill, and we've just brought him for treatment."

I marveled at the coincidence. "I'm sorry to learn of it. I hadn't heard."

"We've kept it as quiet as we dared."

Yes, I thought. *There are illnesses that one keeps quiet . . .*

However, I couldn't imagine that sunny-tempered Frank Roosevelt might ever fall prey to the sadness that was consuming my husband.

"It's going to be in the papers in the morning," Eleanor said. "Franklin has contracted a case of polio."

Polio. A dreadful disease that maimed children every year. Apparently, it struck adults too. Too stunned to think of a more graceful reply, I said, "How terrible. You must extend to him my best wishes to get well."

Eleanor squared her shoulders. "We aren't entirely sure that he *can* get well. At least, we don't know if he will walk again, but we're trying to keep our spirits up."

Don't know if he will walk again . . .

I recoiled at the unnaturalness of those words as applied to a man like Franklin Delano Roosevelt, whose tall, athletic frame I could easily conjure in my mind's eye. "Dear God, when was he stricken?"

"Several weeks ago. He's been paralyzed and in terrible pain. I've spent hours massaging his poor legs while specialists were called."

I heard the slightest catch in her voice and felt terribly sorry for her. I also felt grateful. Paul was suffering a nervous break, but he still had his legs. He could get well again. And I had only to worry about Susanna, whereas Eleanor had many children for whom she must now be strong. "Oh, Mrs. Roosevelt, what you must be going through . . ."

Eleanor lowered her gaze. "Yes, well, my grandmother always told me never to cry where people are; cry by yourself."

"My grandmother told me the same. You must let me know if there's something I can do for you, or for Mr. Roosevelt, or for the family."

With what must surely have been false cheer, Eleanor said, "If you could write Franklin a jolly little note, or even look in on him and talk to him about your work, that would be wonderful. He needs amusement but also to keep informed. To feel as if he is still the same man, with a place in public affairs."

"I'll be happy to do that," I said, even though I found it difficult to believe he might want company at such a vulnerable time.

Eleanor answered my private doubts. "The smiling faces of friends and a positive outlook now might be the only thing that will keep him alive."

That comment struck too close to home. My smile faltered, and she mistook my reaction for confusion. "You see, I can't let Franklin fall into despair. I happen to know that people give up on life, Miss Perkins. I know it only too well. When I was just about ten years old, my father drank himself out of a window and made an orphan of me . . ."

This private confidence dismayed and disarmed me completely. I could only think how distressed she must be to share it. How distressed we *both* were, and for such similar reasons. I imagined Eleanor must've immediately regretted such an admission. And having no idea what to say—feeling guilty for guarding my own secrets while hers were so open and raw—I unburdened my heart. "My husband is here in the hospital as well, because I'm worried that he, too, will give up on life."

Eleanor's bony shoulders went slack, and her eyes melted with sympathy. They also held courage. Courage that bolstered me to face what lay ahead.

For in that dark winter, while Eleanor Roosevelt grappled with her husband's confinement to a wheelchair, I grappled with the diagnosis that my husband suffered from manic-depressive insanity.

While Eleanor paraded friends, family, and even casual acquaintances through her husband's hospital room to enliven and amuse him, I was advised to reorder our homelife to keep my husband well rested, out of the public eye, and undisturbed by any form of excitement.

While Eleanor insisted her husband exert himself every day in therapy, trying to wiggle his toes, or bend his knees, or move his legs, I brought my husband home and followed the doctor's orders in subjecting Paul to long baths and doses of hot milk and cod-liver oil.

While Eleanor made room for a live-in nurse, I moved into the guest room of our apartment, so I could catch up with my work without disturbing Paul as he slept in our bed.

In March, while Eleanor saw her husband fitted for metal leg braces, I saw mine lapse into paranoid auditory hallucinations, awakened by mocking laughter inside his head.

The following spring, when Eleanor had a rare emotional outburst of grief over her husband's paralysis, frightening her children with her tears, I raised my voice with my darling little five-year-old Susanna, who couldn't understand why her once fun-loving father rarely spoke, and when he did, only in a low, distant way.

And while Eleanor set out to supplement her husband's inheritance through articles and public appearances to pay some of their medical bills, I was responsible for all of ours, which lay in neat piles upon our kitchen table as I wondered how we would ever manage.

Chapter Thirty-Three

Buffalo, New York
Autumn 1922

W HISPERS SWIRLED WITH AUTUMN LEAVES at the gravesite, where I stood stiff as a sentinel under a veil of black Chantilly lace.

Terrible tragedy—
—so mangled they had to cremate him—
She will never recover.

I didn't know all the friends and family members who came out to pay their respects to Mary Rumsey in the wake of her husband's recent fatal automobile accident. But I did, of course, know Eleanor Roosevelt, who stood not far from me and whose worried gaze centered on the grieving widow.

Poor Mary. Her marriage had been happy. Now, she was bereft and beyond consolation. Before the burial, she had been dosed by physicians with a calming agent, and now her beautiful doe eyes glistened vacantly; the only thing holding her upright seemed to be the strong arm of her younger brother Averell.

When the service was done, Eleanor and I exchanged a glance of understanding that we ought to count our blessings. We were lucky. Because whatever we'd been through in the past year, at least our husbands were both *alive*.

A few weeks later, we both happened to visit Mary the same day, and Eleanor said, "Mary, your husband wouldn't want you to withdraw from the world."

"Your children need you," I said, echoing much the same sentiment.

"They have their governess," Mary murmured, still curled up in bed, her hair a rat's nest and her usual energy sapped by grief.

Eleanor took a different approach. "You should go riding. Your horses are poor dumb creatures who don't understand why they're being neglected, and you need the fresh air, sunshine, and exercise."

Later, Mary would tell us those horses saved her life. That long rides in the winter landscape helped her to reorder her mind, make sense of her grief, and become a better mother. But it was a long time before she was herself again, and it still did take some coaxing . . .

"You must come to the Democratic luncheon," I told Mary on another visit. "I know you're a Republican, and that your father was a Republican, and probably his father before him, but I nabbed you a ticket to hear Eleanor speak on behalf of Al Smith."

"She's *speaking*?" Mary asked, for we both knew of Eleanor's shy streak. "Well, I suppose she must. Since Franklin's illness, she's been trying to preserve his political future."

This surprised me, for in the year since he'd been struck by polio, everyone spoke of Frank with sorrowful shaking heads over the tragedy that had crippled a man in his prime. Nobody believed Roosevelt could possibly have a future in politics now. Nobody but Eleanor, apparently. "Is Frank getting any better?" I asked. "Is there hope he can walk?"

Mary gave a helpless shrug. "He's always on a boat somewhere with his secretary and his friends, sunning, fishing, and looking for miracle cures. But I hear there are days when it's noon before he can pull himself out of depression and greet guests with his lighthearted facade."

I cleared my throat, for I knew the ravages of depression all too well. "Well, I hope he *does* find a miracle cure, because the rigors of a campaign are often too much even for men with two perfectly good legs."

Fortunately for Frank, he still did have two perfectly good legs. *Eleanor's*. And it was Eleanor, as a literal stand-in for her husband, who led the convention in chants and cheers.

Al Smith for governor. Again!

As for me, campaigning for Smith wasn't only a matter of political loyalty, it was also a matter of financial survival. With Paul's medical bills mounting, I desperately needed my old job back.

Fortunately, we won big that autumn, and this time I was in Governor Smith's inner circle, along with his closest advisor—a very competent woman named Belle Moskowitz, whom I had introduced to him in the first place. I would again serve on the industrial board with a more generous salary and more responsibilities, but I didn't mind the extra work because I loved having the power to do things other reformers only talked about. The only drawback was that it left me with less time at home with my husband and child.

One night when I was brushing Susanna's hair into fat corkscrew curls, my six-year-old daughter asked, "Mommy, can I come to work with you tomorrow?"

"No, darling, you have school. And after that, your nanny is going to take you to play tennis with your father."

Paul's newest doctor believed sunshine, strenuous exercise, and a rigid schedule would keep mental illness at bay. So far it seemed to be working. My husband was well enough to return, at least part-time, to his job at the Equitable Life Assurance Society—a position that played to his strengths without overtaxing him. And whatever Paul's frailties or faults, he tried to be attentive to me and to his *Susie*.

Before bed, he'd read to her from her favorite storybook about Peter Pan. On weekends, they'd build pillow forts in the bedroom.

They invented secret games that delighted me, except insofar as they so often cast me in the role of spoilsport when it was time for bed.

Susanna was a daddy's girl, so my heart thrummed with appreciation when she now said, "I'd rather go to work with you than play tennis with Daddy."

"I'd love to have you!" I met her eyes in the mirror and smiled. "But workmen's compensation hearings aren't much fun for little girls."

To keep her from squirming while I tied her curls with cotton strips, I made up little stories about each one. This curl by her chin was Tinker Bell. This curl by her ear was Wendy. And so on. "Are you going to have sweet dreams of Neverland?"

Susanna shook her head. "Neverland is scary. There are pirates."

"There are pirates everywhere, darling. But you mustn't be afraid, because I'm very good at fighting them."

Susanna looked dubious. "Do you bite off their hands, like a crocodile?"

"No, I have other methods. But if they *do* lose a hand at work, Mommy decides who should pay for the hook."

Chapter Thirty-Four

New York City
Summer 1924

Dear Miss Perkins:

I have silicosis from rock tunnel work. The doctor has taken X-rays and says they cannot do anything. Must a fellow just wait to die? I am forty-seven years old, is there any compensation when the company busted up or quit operating but has holdings in other parts of state?

-JT

I felt quite settled into my role at the Industrial Commission, and ordinary citizens increasingly sought my help to make industry safer and keep company owners honest, writing heartrending letters that made my work *feel* every bit as important as I thought it was.

But my boss was looking to move up in the world. Now signs and banners with *Al Smith for President* covered almost every inch of Manhattan in anticipation of the forthcoming Democratic convention at Madison Square Garden, where Al was the odds-on favorite to win the nomination.

It was exciting to be in the thick of it.

The governor's advisors said we needed Franklin Roosevelt to make the nomination, but Al howled, "For God's sake, why? The poor man hasn't made a public appearance since he caught polio."

I agreed with him. It'd been four years since Roosevelt was forced into a wheelchair, and no one could think he'd recover after all this time. It was simply too much to ask. Still the political strategists insisted. "Governor, you need Frank to make the nomination, because you're a Bowery mick and he's a Protestant patrician, and he'll take some of the curse off you."

"He won't do it," Belle Moskowitz said. And I was sure she was right. The Roosevelt I knew was too vain to expose his disability to the entire country. Besides, even if he agreed, how were we going get a man in a wheelchair into the rowdy convention hall?

The political gunslingers just said, *We'll manage it.*

"Easy for them to say." Belle shook her head. "Can you call him after the governor does, Frances? I'm told you have a relationship."

Now, I hadn't seen Frank much in the past few years. Oh, I'd written him jolly notes and peeked in on him as his wife asked me to do. But not as often as I'd intended, and I felt guilty about it, so when I rang him up, I asked, "Are you *sure* you're up to a political convention?"

Roosevelt laughed an infectious laugh. "Wouldn't miss it. I've got a plan to make it work. But do me a favor. Tell Governor Smith to stop attacking Prohibition straight on. It's going to sink him in a national election."

"I'll tell him. Cross my heart." And I was as good as my word. Not that Al wanted to hear the advice. Despite the laws against liquor, it was everywhere. Gangsters kept it flowing, taking over every city in America, their violence fueled by bootleg money.

My boss thought Prohibition was to blame, and argued, "People just want a little wine with dinner, a little beer in the pub, and what's wrong with that? I've been known to enjoy the occasional Bermuda swizzle at a party when the sun gets hot."

Al Smith simply didn't want to equivocate the way Roosevelt said he should. "No, kiddo. I gotta be myself. Swallowtail coat, fat cigar, brassy New York accent and all."

I loved him for that, but I didn't know if he could *win* being himself. And we desperately needed to win that year, because the Ku Klux Klan was on the rise. It had infested both political parties, preaching bigotry against Negroes, Jews, Catholics, and immigrants in general. The so-called Imperial Wizard had already corrupted the Republican convention. Now they were at *our* convention to rally behind William McAdoo, and I said, "We absolutely can't let him win."

Al grinned. "Then you'd better trot that fine patriot pedigree of yours out there to convince lady voters that I'm the cat's pajamas."

As the governor's best strategist, Belle Moskowitz explained the mission to me. "They think Governor Smith is indelicate, ill-mannered, and that his wife is *lowborn*. Some harbor extreme prejudice against Irish and Italian Catholics. We hope you can dispel some of that, Miss Perkins. You're going to speak at a breakfast for women delegates and the wives of male delegates. You've *got* to win them over."

It was a tall order because the delegates were already horrified that the galleries of Madison Square Garden were filled with common people. Italians from Lower Manhattan who couldn't speak English. Irishmen from the Bowery who spit tobacco. Big ham-fisted Russians from Brooklyn who joked and pushed. These weren't refined people, but neither was our governor, and we loved him for it. So I made a very delicately worded speech explaining Governor Smith's best qualities, and how gentlemanly he could be. How his nobility came from the soul. "I think he'd make a wonderful president."

I believed this. And so did Tammany Hall. But I'd never encountered the *Dixiecrat* faction before, nor realized what a grip they had on the party.

Of course, Frank Roosevelt knew, which is why he'd warned us about Prohibition.

After weeks of practicing, Frank was ready to execute the plan for his entrance into Madison Square Garden. His car would pull up at the side doors, where his sixteen-year-old son would get him on his feet and lock his leg braces. Then, using a crutch on one side and his son's arm on the other, the former vice presidential candidate would somehow hobble into the hall.

On the night he was to give his speech, I was nervous as a cat watching him arrive. The crowd cheered as he made his way up the aisle. And, to my surprise, seeing Frank brought a lump into my throat. I honestly never thought Frank had it in him to make himself so vulnerable. I was also overcome with sympathy by how much polio had ravaged him. The Franklin Delano Roosevelt I knew was strong, muscular, handsome, and vigorous. Now he was pale, thin, and trembling.

Still, what a performance he put on!

Frank joked with his son, an amiable mask on his face as he dragged his feet forward, hitching his hips for momentum. But was I the only one to notice the sweat pouring off him? Just this short walk took enormous effort, and I suspected it caused him terrible pain. Every step a struggle. Every motion of his crutch a precarious balancing act. A force of pure willpower.

How long could he keep it up in front of this enormous crowd, and what would happen if he lost his balance? I shuddered to think of what it might do to his pride. And I found myself murmuring a little prayer when Frank reached the part of the stage where he'd have to close the distance between himself and the podium without his son's steadying arm.

Please, God, don't let him fall.

I wasn't alone in holding my breath. It seemed everyone in the auditorium was afraid to make a sound, lest it knock him down. But Roosevelt somehow got to that podium, gripping those crutches so tight that I didn't know how he was going to let go to wave to the crowd.

He didn't even try. Instead, he threw back his head in that trademark gesture of his, now genial and warm. And we roared!

We couldn't seem to stop shouting for his valiance. We cheered until I didn't think it would end. Until I thought the rafters might come tumbling down, all of us enormously moved.

And though he was so unsteady on his feet, Roosevelt's voice was stronger than ever, talking up progress, saying, "America has not lost her faith in ideals—idealism is of her very heart's blood."

I felt electrified by this line.

Roosevelt called Al Smith *the happy warrior of the political battlefield*, and his speech absolutely tore the place to pieces.

We went wild. People stamped, paraded with flags, and sang "The Sidewalks of New York."

We chanted from the galleries, cheering as much for Roosevelt as for Smith. And I was as swept up in the optimism of that speech as anyone. Still, from my seat in the front row, I seemed to be the only one to notice that Frank was now stranded. He'd have to get down from the podium somehow, and it had taken almost all his energy to get up there. He was holding on for dear life, his knuckles white as he desperately glanced about for help.

That's when our eyes locked.

I saw the panic flicker underneath that buoyant smile. He was exhausted. He needed his wheelchair, but he wouldn't want anyone to see him wheeled away. I had to help him somehow, so I jumped up, grabbing two of my lady friends, and dragged them onstage with me. With our hats and skirts, we made a virtual wall blocking Franklin Roosevelt from the view of the crowd so his son could help lower him into his wheelchair and whisk him away.

That wouldn't be the last time I did that for Roosevelt. In fact, I cannot count all the times in my life that I shielded him. Still, that was the first time, and I remember it well because he smiled at me in humble gratitude.

And I'd never seen him humble before . . .

The rest of the convention really *was* a political battlefield. The delegates fought, ballot after ballot, over an inclusive future or one that embraced bigotry and clutched its collective pearls at alcohol and racy books. I was particularly appalled when William Jennings Bryan, who had run three times under the party's banner, shouted up at the immigrants in the galleries, "You do not represent the future of America!"

After that, the fight in the convention hall raged so bitterly that extra police had to be called. No one had ever heard of a convention going more than a week, but we simply couldn't adjourn. We still didn't have a candidate!

It took fifteen days and *one hundred and three ballots* until, to my everlasting gratitude, McAdoo and his KKK supporters finally lost. But so did Al Smith, and with him went our hopes for the presidency.

Chapter Thirty-Five

* * *

I T'S THE HOLIDAY," PAUL ARGUED, WAVING HIS glass of bourbon-laced eggnog. "And it's just one drink."

It wasn't just one drink, or even one argument. Over the past few years, we'd become a tiresomely quarrelsome married couple. Now, on this wintry morning, I reminded him, "Even if it weren't for Prohibition, the doctor says drinking is dangerous for your condition."

"My condition?" Paul shrugged. "It's been five years since I was hospitalized, Frances. You can't keep treating me like an invalid."

It might've been five years, but he hadn't been *cured.* Unfortunately, Paul was in denial about his diagnosis, bristling when I reminded him that he must go to bed early every night—that any deviation from routine might plunge him back into a depressive state. He was even angrier when I monitored his drinking, and it frankly exhausted me to do so. *"I'm not a child, Frances."*

He was right, so I decided not to press the matter. After all, it *was* the holiday season, and I didn't want to spoil Susanna's tenth birthday with another quarrel.

Paul had insisted on the extravagance of an ice-skating party, and I didn't have the heart to say no. Susanna was too excited about the prospect, eager to be the center of attention and eat all the cake she desired. My daughter was my very own little Tinker Bell, and I wanted her to live in a fairy tale as long as possible.

Of course, I was beginning to learn fairy tales weren't just for children but also had a place in politics. Al Smith had become an even more popular governor of New York than when he'd run for the presidential nomination, and now he'd decided to throw his weight behind a mayoral candidate.

The problem? The candidate was leaving his wife for a mistress. I was there in the office with Belle Moskowitz and the other political gunslingers when Governor Smith called up Jimmy Walker and told him if he wanted to be mayor, he was going to have to go back to his wife and treat her right. "You know what this town is like, Jimmy. And you know Tammany Hall. Strict Catholic boys."

"My wife won't take me back," Jimmy said.

"I talked to her," Al replied, which was news to me. "She'll take you back. She's a good Tammany girl."

Sure enough, a few months later, the newspapers were running photos of Jimmy Walker and his wife at church on Easter Sunday. Because Mrs. Walker was what I'd come to call *a mothball wife.* The kind politicians treated like a fancy old hat, to be taken out of mothball storage for public functions.

It was an eye-opening revelation, and I was having many that year. As Al Smith's chairwoman of the New York State Industrial Board, I was professionally frustrated. For one thing, my efforts against child labor were being undermined by the Catholic Church. It seemed as if every time we took one step forward in reform, someone tried to push my efforts two steps back.

These laws violate the sanctity of the family, priests preached from the pulpit, because it was apparently a father's God-given right to send little Bobby down into a mine to get lung rot. Governor Smith was losing support over the issue and being pressured to compromise. "They say we're trying to keep children from doing the dinner dishes!"

I had a bitter laugh at that. It was so absurd. "Maybe you need to explain that child labor in industry isn't just a moral evil—it also depresses wages and ruins the tax base of the state."

"That's good," Smith said, writing it down.

Getting reforms through had always been, and would always be, a delicate political dance. But it wasn't one that reformers like Florence Kelley had any patience for. And I felt trapped between two of the most powerful forces in my life when my mentor came into the governor's office to accuse Al Smith of having allowed his Catholic sensibilities to influence his policy decisions.

"Oh, *Mrs. Kelley*," I groaned, trying to keep her temper—and a little prejudice—from getting the better of her. Especially since I could see Al Smith go red with fury while she lectured him.

"Governor," she seethed. "Tonight while we sleep, several thousand little girls will be working in textile mills, all the night through, in the deafening noise of the spindles and the looms spinning, and weaving cotton and wool, silks and ribbons for us to buy."

"You think I don't know it?" Al snapped.

Then he all but tossed her out of his office, and it was left to me to smooth things over, for he needed her support, and she needed his. I'm not sure I ever fully healed the breach, but I tried, because I idolized them both. And it was to be my first—but not my last—taste of being painfully politically torn, caught in the middle of a feud between people I admired.

AT THE ANNUAL family trip to Maine that summer, my mother and sister got into a terrible row.

I broke the bad news to Paul over breakfast. "I'm afraid my mother is going to have to come live with us."

The savings my father left had dwindled, and like most widows at the time, my mother depended almost entirely on family. She'd been living with my sister in Massachusetts, but now Ethel wanted me to take a turn, and I supposed it was only fair.

"Why can't your mother stay at the old Perkins place?" Paul asked, buttering Susanna's toast.

"She's too old to live alone in the Brick House, and even if she weren't, the winters in Maine are too harsh." My mother didn't have my grandmother's constitution, after all. "She can't manage on her own. You don't want me to throw her into the street, do you?"

Paul grumbled. "Of course not. But your mother has never liked me. Not since I kissed you at the train station all those years ago."

Our daughter looked up from her plate with dawning disgust. "*Ick*. Don't talk about kissing!"

"Why not?" Paul asked. "Kissing, among other things, is how we got *you*, Susie."

Susanna turned positively green, as if this were the most nauseating thought that had ever occurred to her in her young life. And to rescue my daughter from mortification, I said, "Would you like having your grandmother live with us?"

I thought it'd be good for Susanna to have family close by instead of only seeing them on summer trips when we could get away. On one of those trips, my mother had taught Susanna to paint watercolors, and I thought it might be a hobby they could share. Maybe, living with us, my mother would even come to appreciate the life we'd built here in New York City.

There was still a part of me, even as a grown woman of forty-seven, that wanted my mother's approval. To demonstrate that she had reason to be proud of me.

That was, unfortunately, wishful thinking. Almost as soon as we established my mother in the guest room, she complained, "I'll never sleep here. This wretched city is so noisy, day and night."

"A regular Gomorrah," Paul said dryly from behind his newspaper.

"And it's a dirty city," my mother nattered on. "I'm so convinced you *must* have cockroaches that I'm afraid to eat off your dishes."

"She says, after her third helping," Paul muttered.

I couldn't blame him for being sour. My mother criticized him as freely as she criticized me.

Don't you mind having a wife who works longer hours than you do?

—such a pity you gambled away your fortune—

Don't you know liquor is the tool of the devil?

She was impossible, and because Paul put up with her, I no longer tried to stop him from drinking. Some nights I even filled a glass for myself, thinking we might cope better if we were *all* plastered.

"My mother doesn't even like our puppy," I confided in Mary Rumsey when she stopped by.

Paul had recently brought home an adorable mutt that we'd named Balto, after the city in which we'd first admitted our romantic feelings. (Of course, our marriage could scarcely be called romantic now, but that wasn't the dog's fault.)

"How could anyone not love this stubby little tail and furry snout?" I asked, kissing the puppy before letting him jump down from my lap.

Mary, who was in her riding habit on her way to a horse show, bent and scratched the dog until his tail wagged him off his feet. "He's darling. I bet he's an Irish terrier. Or at least an Irish terrier mix who is putting on airs. As for your mother, maybe she just needs a good time. We could introduce her to some older lady friends or buy her a new party dress."

I sighed. "She says she's too old to make new friends, and she won't let me buy her clothes because she's upset that she's become a little stouter."

"Haven't we all?" Mary asked, though I saw no sign of it on her. She was still a sporty woman who loved to flaunt the latest styles from Paris, and men still avidly pursued her. Why wouldn't they? She was a beautiful wealthy widow. But Mary said she'd never marry again, and I didn't encourage her to, because for all its rewards, marriage was a very hard business . . .

"I think I'd better send Paul on a long vacation," I said, rubbing my temples. "My mother's complaints aren't good for his sanity, and they're doing nothing good for mine."

The next afternoon while I was at work, my daughter fell at the playground and cut herself badly enough to need stitches. *My poor baby!* I felt just terrible, but my mother made it worse. "You should've been here to look after her, Fanny."

"As if I have a choice but to be at work!" I snapped. We couldn't have afforded a decent apartment on Paul's part-time salary. We couldn't have sent Susanna to a nice school. And who else would support my mother? She was, like so many elderly persons, one step away from the gutter or the poorhouse, and given the condition of the latter, it'd be difficult to decide which was worse.

"Maybe you don't have a choice about going to the office," she countered. "But you do many things for Al Smith above and beyond what you're paid for. *Political* things. I think that's unseemly and by choice. You think what you're doing at work is more important than what's going on in your own home, but you're wrong."

"It isn't *more* important, but it *is* important to make a difference in the world," I said defensively.

"Are you entirely sure that you *are* making a difference?" my mother asked.

My mother had never understood—or wished to understand—safety regulations or labor negotiations. So I tried to dismiss her question. But, oh, how it got under my skin and festered!

The truth was, I'd been asking myself a similar question for quite some time.

Restless in middle age, I wanted to feel the thrill of *inspiration* I'd felt two years ago when Franklin Roosevelt spoke at the convention. Instead, I'd begun to fear that I'd spent my whole career putting bandages on a thousand societal cuts that'd never heal. There were, it seemed to me, just *so many* economic problems to be tackled. And in more than twenty years of sustained effort, had I even made a dent?

All the regulations we spearheaded, all the legislation we passed, all the steps forward seemed insignificant in a country where greedy industrialists, selfish society circles, the Ku Klux Klan, and other small-minded bigots held so much sway.

"Think hard about your priorities, Fanny," Mother insisted. "Remember the Bible. The poor will always be with us. Jesus said that."

"Don't misinterpret scripture. He didn't mean that remark as a justification for abandoning—"

"You'll never get back this time with family."

A point driven home to me most cruelly the night she began slurring her words . . .

At first, Paul and I exchanged an astonished look, assuming she'd finally succumbed to intemperance, having taken a nip from his brandy snifter. Then my mother slipped from her chair to the floor, and we knew something was terribly wrong.

At the hospital, the doctor gave us the bad news. "Your mother has suffered a stroke. She's lost vision in one eye, and her speech is still quite confused."

There was no telling when, or if, she might recover. Nothing to do but to take her home and keep her comfortable. Nothing to say but hollow words of sympathy at the slow deterioration of her mind, and the even slower deterioration of her bodily functions. I watched helplessly as my mother regressed, speaking like a frightened child one moment, shrieking with rage the next.

And that is how she died.

Chapter Thirty-Six

* * *

Newcastle, Maine
Summer 1928

DESPITE MY CONTENTIOUS RELATIONSHIP with my mother, or perhaps because of it, her death sent me into a tailspin of grief. Losing her unmoored me from my past and left me uncertain about my future. It also forced me to face my own mortality, demanding a reckoning with my life.

I never wanted Susanna to feel the guilt, remorse, and regret mixed with love that I felt for my mother now. Especially as she was no longer the little child in whose adoring eyes I could do no wrong. Susanna would be twelve by the year's end, and these were crucial years between a mother and a daughter.

Because I didn't want to miss them, I took myself out of the political game and retreated with my family to Maine that summer. My sister and I had inherited the old Perkins place, so while Balto ran barking wild in the meadows with Susanna giving chase, my husband and I replaced furniture, painted doors, and fixed loose floorboards.

At least I could see the fruit of my labors fixing up a house, or organizing the rakes and shovels, hanging them on their proper hooks. Life was simpler here, as steady as the flow of the river. As true as the colors of the blueberries we foraged from the bushes. As honest as the salty taste of clams we dug from the river and cooked over a fire.

On very hot days, I swam in the river to cool off. Then, on a whim, Paul bought Susanna a little pony and cart, which I warned looked unsafe. Still, he insisted on taking her out. I later learned that they overturned it in a ditch and were too afraid to tell me of their misadventure. But I didn't blame them, because I was a little bit awful to be around that summer, brooding that I'd spent most of my adult life championing children, while the elderly were just as fragile, and more often abandoned. And who was doing anything about it?

Not me.

Here in the wilds of Maine, where we breathed fresh air, knew and trusted our neighbors, and always had butter for the table even in hard times, it was easy to forget about people living in tenements far away. Yet, as a young woman, I hadn't been able to imagine that my storied ancestors wanted to bequeath me a country in which poverty and suffering were tolerated. Maybe I'd been wrong to think I could do anything meaningful about it. And now only hard, physical labor helped me block out intrusive thoughts.

One night that summer, having worked myself to heat exhaustion pulling weeds in the garden, I retreated to my grandmother's old bedroom. And I'd just drifted to sleep when I was roused by a voice through the trees.

Franklin Roosevelt's voice, in fact.

It was unmistakable. I sat up, worried I was delusional, only to realize one of my neighbors had hooked up his radio to a loudspeaker to broadcast the Democratic convention in Houston.

Could I not escape politics even here? Incredulous, I threw myself back on the bed, covering my ears with a pillow, but there was no way to drown him out.

I found myself listening—*really* listening—because it was the first time I ever heard Franklin Delano Roosevelt on the radio, and he was simply magnificent. His words shook me. He spoke against withdrawing from politics and how he thought such apathy was an actual danger to a nation that boasted of being a government both for the people and *by* the people.

And hearing that was like hearing the summons of God.

Here I was, abed while *Roosevelt* had managed to get himself and his wheelchair to Houston. And if a man who couldn't move his legs could keep mustering the energy to battle for a better country, then I had no business taking myself out of the fight. Certainly, my grandmother did not believe—and I would never believe—any interpretation of the Bible wherein the Lord meant us to simply accept *the poor will always be with you* as a justification to abandon them.

I'd been frustrated working on a patchwork quilt of regulations with spotty enforcement. What I really wanted was to repair the crumbling bricks of the whole system. In fact, I wanted to build a stronger foundation, and I had learned from Al Smith that I could only *ever* do that in the political arena.

FRANKLIN ROOSEVELT'S SPEECH had secured the presidential nomination for Al Smith in '28, and I returned to New York just in time to take part in a debate about who should replace my boss as governor when he won the presidency.

We were all very optimistic about Al's chances. He was the most popular governor New York had ever known. And the campaign advisors assured us all that where New York went, the country usually followed.

Not that they asked my advice.

I was a mere state official, and a woman to boot; the party bigwigs intended to take over the national campaign. But Al refused to let the women of his inner circle be pushed out. "When I win," Al said, pulling out a chair for me at the table, "I'll need somebody who can take my place as governor. Someone whose roots go deep. Somebody *Old Money* and *Old New York*. Somebody who can win votes upstate and help carry the ticket."

A few names were bandied about, but in the end, we coalesced around just one. *Roosevelt.* The only worry was whether voters could get behind a man in a wheelchair.

"He plays down the wheelchair," I pointed out, for by that time Frank had learned to lurch forward with the assistance of his son's strong arm and a cane, giving the impression he could walk. "Besides, there's nothing wrong with his mind."

Al nodded enthusiastically. "A governor doesn't have to be an acrobat. The work of the governorship is brainwork, and Frank is mentally as good as he ever was."

The only problem was that we couldn't get hold of him on the telephone. "They say Frank is taking a therapeutic swim for his legs and can't be disturbed," Smith growled.

Maybe Frank knew this was shaping up to be a tougher election year than we supposed, but I thought he owed Al Smith. When everybody else thought Frank's political career was dead, Al kept visiting him and lifting his spirits. And it was Al who had launched him back onto the public scene. Now I was fairly certain that Frank was ducking our calls because he didn't want to be reminded of that debt.

"We should try Eleanor," I suggested. "He won't duck *her* calls."

I cornered her at a campaign stop upstate, where she was shaking hands and wearing a sash that read *Al Smith for President.* And she brusquely informed me, "Miss Perkins, I simply don't care one way or another if Franklin runs for office. It's entirely his choice."

I was coming to understand that whatever the bonds of the Roosevelt marriage, there was a distance too. Frank spent most of his time now in Warm Springs, Georgia, where he'd founded a research and treatment facility for polio. Meanwhile, Eleanor lived with two lady friends at a little cottage estate called Val-Kill, where they made furniture.

I think Eleanor Roosevelt really meant it when she said she didn't care if her husband ran for governor. But I also knew she wouldn't approve of his childish refusal to pick up the phone, so I pressed the point until she finally agreed to come back to Smith's headquarters. In the end, I was there in the hotel room when Eleanor rang up her husband in Georgia. After a brief conversation, she handed Al the phone.

The governor said, "I need you, Frank."

I could hear Roosevelt on the other end, saying he couldn't run for office. Couldn't abandon his polio foundation. He worried the rigors of a campaign would doom his prospects of recovering the ability to walk.

Puffing away on the last drags of his cigar, Al Smith promised, "We'll help you, Frank. We'll help you with all of it."

It was up to me to keep that promise. For Al assigned me to the ad hoc Roosevelt campaign and chucked me playfully under the chin. "Well, kiddo, go make Franklin Delano Roosevelt the next governor of New York."

Chapter Thirty-Seven

Buffalo, New York
Autumn 1928

J UST LIKE OLD TIMES, MISS PERKINS," SAID
Roosevelt as he was wheeled into the train car.

Of course, it wasn't like old times. He still looked so wan
and frail that I felt guilty for having pulled him into a campaign.
Everything was difficult for him. One of his legislative aides quipped
that he got more exercise just standing up than most other men got
in a week.

Sensible of his physical limitations, I reassured him, "The party
has only scheduled a few appearances for you. No more than six."

Frank looked over the schedule, then crumpled it and tossed it
away. "Don't give me this baloney," he said, channeling Al Smith. "If
I'm campaigning to become governor, let's campaign."

I put a hand to my hip. "Well, what do you feel like doing?"

What Roosevelt felt like doing, as it turned out, was ditching the
train altogether. After our first two stops, he insisted on going by
automobile—followed by a fleet of busses, carrying aides and reporters, so he could greet people at the side of the road, restaurant parking lots, and train stations, all without having to stand up from the
back seat.

I often rode with him in the car, briefing him about people he
was going to meet at a given stop. And I was astonished by the punishing schedule he cheerfully maintained.

Before polio, he'd been energetic.

After polio, he *had something to prove*. Namely, that a man with a disability was fit to hold higher office.

I felt terribly protective of him. I had, after all, played a part in dragging him into this and was only now becoming aware of the toll. The way his leg braces chafed every time he tried to walk. The way his back cramped if he didn't have a chance to shift in the seat. The way he'd wilt like a thirsty houseplant if we didn't keep him watered.

At the state fair, while Eleanor was charming voters with a visit to a stand where grape preserves were sold, the candidate drove around the track several times under the hot sun. Now he was parched.

"Mr. Roosevelt asked for orange juice," I reminded a campaign aide.

"Oh, that's all right," Roosevelt said, accepting the wrong beverage and waving the girl away.

I eyed him suspiciously. "What's wrong with you?"

"What do you mean?"

"You've turned out to be a remarkably good sport about everything, Frank. You don't complain when we're late to an event. You don't grouse at your aides or even give anybody the high hat."

He chuckled. "Oh, when you can't use your legs, you must become adaptable. When they bring you milk when you wanted orange juice, you just drink the milk and say *that's all right* and mean it. Otherwise, you'll be fighting a thousand petty indignities every day."

"You've become a philosopher," I said.

"I'm a Christian and a Democrat, that's all. Same as ever."

"Same as ever? Only in that you're still a shameless fibber. I can't believe how patiently you sat with that annoying union representative; you let him ramble. I remember a time I had to *chase* you down a hallway just to get a word. Even then, you ducked into a lavatory to escape me."

Roosevelt grinned at the memory, biting the tip of his cigarette holder so it shot up at a jaunty angle. "Well, I can't run away from anybody now. I can't even *walk* away if I'm bored, so I've learned not to be bored."

"That is quite a trick." I sipped my malted milkshake. "I suppose more of us ought to learn to indulge people's eccentricities."

"You should come with me to Warm Springs," he suggested. "It's a real education in humanity. In the waters there, I've held frail old people in my arms. Black people whose parents lived in bondage on plantations. White people so poor they didn't have shoes or running water. Uneducated backwoods people. Struggling farmers. All kinds of people, all struggling with polio. Didn't use to think I had anything to learn from folks like that, but they've taught me more than I learned in all the years before."

"What's the most important lesson?"

"That people want to feel heard. Everybody wants to have that sense of belonging, of being on the inside. No one wants to be left out. So it's not such a trial to indulge them."

I could see he meant it. Life had given him a big blow between the eyes. The man who'd been born with a silver spoon in his mouth had *suffered*, and that suffering made him empathetic. The plain truth was that polio had changed Roosevelt, and being with him was changing me.

To start with, campaigning with him made me feel more confident. I wasn't the most flowery orator, but at one stop, Roosevelt said, "You've got a good method going there when you give a speech. Be sincere, be brief, be seated."

"You don't think my approach is too scientific?"

"Not for you."

That wasn't *his* style, however. He was all garrulousness. Even if he was exhausted, having driven half the night, he'd somehow don his cheerful mask, tip his hat, and turn on the charm—by which he was teaching me that perseverance really was the absolute most necessary ingredient for success.

One night in the Yorkville district, I was horrified to find that a speech had been scheduled inside a crowded auditorium on an upper floor. There was no way for Roosevelt to get upstairs without being jostled or crushed. And certainly no way for me to shield his infirmity from public view, as I'd learned to do by standing in front of him with other ladies and adjusting my hat so that my coat would open up wide like a curtain. I couldn't shield him this time. I couldn't even get him into the building.

"I'll go up the fire escape," Roosevelt finally suggested.

"*Absolutely* not," I said, envisioning him falling over the rail.

He motioned to the strong men in his entourage. "They'll carry me."

I didn't like the idea. Not only because it might present the candidate as too frail to serve, but also because I feared for him to be hurt. But Frank insisted, leaving me to wait upstairs, worrying.

Looking about the crowded auditorium, which was filled past capacity, I noted that the windows weren't fireproof. I didn't see a sprinkler system either. And what idiot had closed the doors? As I stood backstage in the wings, fretting, an old voice echoed in my memory.

You must be able to evacuate a floor in three minutes. Three minutes, Miss Perkins. Any longer and people will die.

I glanced at my pocket watch, from habit.

One minute.

Two minutes.

Three minutes.

Then I went to the window and watched, hand on my throat, the slow progress of Roosevelt being carried up the fire escape like a child in another man's arms. It wasn't only perilous but looked painfully uncomfortable for him; worse, being carried onstage would be terribly embarrassing. But when he was finally carried over the ledge, set down on a chair so he could lock his braces, and then pulled upright again, it wasn't humiliation I saw on his visage.

It was *humility*.

One of the greatest virtues.

One I'd have least expected to find in Franklin Delano Roosevelt. He took that podium with more *stature* than he'd ever had before. And I was so moved that I don't even remember what he said.

By the time the event was over and we'd safely returned to the car, Roosevelt noticed I was rubbing my temples. "Didn't like my speech?"

"I didn't like the venue. That was a firetrap. I'm going to throttle someone if they ever send you somewhere like that again."

His smile fell away. "You know, Frances, the only thing that frightens me is fire."

He'd never used my first name before. I took it as a sign of our growing closeness, which allowed me to admit, "Me, too, Frank."

He rubbed his chin. "I prefer Franklin."

I was genuinely surprised to hear it. "Why, I had no idea! Everyone has called you Frank for years."

"Only political friends call me Frank. Someone like Al—he doesn't make any distinction between the kinds of friends he's got. I think you and I both do."

"Yes," I admitted.

"Well, you became more than a political friend four years ago when, in an arena filled with thousands of people, you were the only one who realized I was stuck at that podium . . . I never thanked you for shielding me so I could get back down."

"You never needed to thank me. It was common decency, and anyone else who realized you were in trouble would've come running."

"You're the one who did . . . which is all to say that I don't tell political friends I'm terrified of fire. Or that when I first realized I couldn't move my legs, I worried about fire all the time. I started dragging myself on my forearms to practice getting away in case I should ever be left alone and trapped by flames. Eleanor thought I'd cracked . . . but you see, I once saw my aunt catch fire. Terrible thing."

I nodded, leaning my head back against the seat of the automobile. "Sometimes I still dream about those girls at the Triangle factory fire falling like human torches from the sky."

We were silent a moment. Then he said, "I should've done more about that."

"Yes, you should have."

He frowned. "But I voted with you on fire safety regulations many times, didn't I?"

"Only when I twisted your arm."

He sighed with regret. Then sudden mischief passed over his features. "Well, at least we'll always have the fifty-four-hour bill."

"Not this again! You weren't there to vote for that bill. I know you weren't, and *you* know you weren't."

He gently poked my arm with his forefinger. "I not only voted for your bill, I helped you filibuster so Big Tim Sullivan could get back from the ferry on time."

I sputtered an exasperated laugh. "You did not. I suppose next you will tell me that you're the one who turned the ferry around—and that you did it by walking on water. Or like Moses, you parted the sea."

Roosevelt guffawed, still absolutely incorrigible!

I ENJOYED CAMPAIGNING with Roosevelt.

And I think he enjoyed campaigning with me. We probably enjoyed it *too* much, because Al Smith joked, "You can't keep her, Frank."

• 264 •

As his presidential campaign hit its fever pitch, Al needed me in front of women's groups.

My speeches went over well enough in New York, Boston, Philadelphia, and other cities. But I didn't feel as if our message was going over in the countryside, where farmers didn't know, or care, about what Smith had done to combat the side effects of unregulated industrialization.

"Rural citizens have never seen tenements," Mary Rumsey said when I grabbed a quick cup of coffee with her between campaign stops. "They only remember a time when everyone lived on the farms."

Thanks to men like her father, the edifice of American prosperity was now built on cheap immigrant labor. But many voters in the country didn't like that and were suspicious of Al Smith—who I believe had humbler beginnings than any presidential candidate since Lincoln.

I wanted them to know that Smith was a great governor and would make a great president, but when I was sent to speak in Maryland, I sensed the hostility toward him in every pore of my being. And the gossip was simply horrid.

Al Smith is a Papist mongrel—

—Irish, Eyetalian, or both—

I just can't abide that awful whiskey voice!

They went after his wife, too. The KKK had a strong hold on the Eastern Shore of Maryland, where women voters insisted Mrs. Smith was a drunken harlot.

"Why, that's simply not true!" I protested over a luncheon of softshell crabs. "I know Katie Smith well. She's a lovely woman. Absolutely lovely. I've been to dinner and listened to them singing at the piano together. I've never seen her drink a drop."

No matter what I said in her defense, the ladies of Maryland would only pat my hand and say, "Bless your heart, Miss Perkins. It's good of you to be so loyal, but we can't have Al Smith for president. He's going to bring the pope in over us."

I couldn't hide my astonishment. "He's going to do what?"

"There is a *plan*, Miss Perkins. Smith has already bought a palace for the pontifex, and he's going to give the pope control over the military and everything else."

There wasn't any reasoning with them, and I gather I committed a faux pas when, during conversation, I mentioned that I thought Robert E. Lee was not, in fact, the greatest man the country had ever produced.

Things got worse in Atlanta, where opponents tried to stop me from speaking. In Missouri, when opponents tried to scare my audience away, I began to worry that the campaign was in trouble. And in Oklahoma, when the KKK lined the railway entrance with burning crosses, I despaired that we had ever thought we could win.

On election night, as the results started sinking in, Democrats left the hall in tears, and it was hard for me to keep a stiff upper lip. Al Smith was a remarkable public servant, a genius at government administration. And I loved him deeply.

So it broke my heart when Al finally realized he'd not only lost the presidency but hadn't even carried his beloved New York State. Holding his head in his hands, he said, "I guess the time hasn't come when a man can say his beads in the White House."

He'd truly thought better of the American people. And the burning crosses had seared his soul . . .

Knowing what pain he was in when he conceded the race, my New England reserve melted and I wanted to cry. I felt just terrible for him. Terrible for the whole country. And terrible for myself. I'd expected Smith to win the presidency. I'd also expected Franklin Roosevelt to win the governorship. In short, I'd expected to keep my position.

Now that looked impossible.

I wasn't ready to go home and face my family, having plunged us back into financial insecurity again. So, long after Al and everyone else went home, I wandered over to the Roosevelt headquarters.

Democrats were getting slaughtered at the ballot box, and there was no reason to think Roosevelt would be any exception, so the candidate, his wife, and most of his people had gone home for the night, sure it was all over.

But not Sara Delano Roosevelt. The candidate's mother was determined to fret over the returns to the bitter end, so I sat in a hard-backed seat next to her and waited . . .

It wasn't until the wee hours that she roused me from a half sleep by handing me a slip of paper. "What do you think of these numbers, Miss Perkins?"

I glanced at it wearily, then sat up straighter. "I—I think Franklin might be winning."

It was only a few votes here and a few votes there, but it was adding up. How was it possible?

A few hours later, the number crunchers told us, "It's close. There might be a recount, but we believe Franklin Delano Roosevelt might be the only Democrat to beat the trend. He's going to win!"

His mother and I both let out uncharacteristic whoops of joy. Then she said, "I want to tell Franklin. Come with me, Miss Perkins. Let's make the call."

I listened in when she roused her son from his bed to tell him the good news. Then she hung up with a laugh. "I don't think he believes me. He says he's going back to sleep."

Well, I howled at that. Only Franklin Roosevelt could be so sanguine. "I suppose we ought to follow his example and get some sleep ourselves."

I could see where Franklin got his sense of mischief when she said, "Nonsense! We need to celebrate."

"But everything's closed."

Like a woman used to getting her way, she said, "Then let's wake up a hotel waiter and toast with a glass of milk."

I wasn't about to gainsay the elder Mrs. Roosevelt. Not with pride in her son radiating from her being. So together we made a victory toast with glasses of milk. Then we shared a taxicab home—where I watched her bound up the stairs like a woman half her age to tell her son he was going to be the next governor of New York. And I felt in my bones that everything was about to change.

Chapter Thirty-Eight

★ ✳ ★

Albany, New York
January 1, 1929

FOR THE OCCASION OF ROOSEVELT'S FIRST gubernatorial inauguration, Eleanor dressed in an elegant black velvet gown, and her magnificent hair was piled atop her head like a crown. As women reporters noted, "she could look rather dowdy in daytime clothes," but in an evening gown she was regal as a queen, carrying off wild jewelry—like her favorite enormous tiger-tooth necklace—with aplomb.

But Eleanor's carriage was tense on Inauguration Day, and I knew why. It wasn't only because she didn't want to fade into the domestic scene, as she'd be expected to do as the governor's wife. It was also because former governor Smith and his wife, Katie, had not yet moved out of the Executive Mansion.

Al felt that he had a duty to Roosevelt. He feared that the political pressures of the job really might compromise FDR's recovery from polio. I truly think that's why Al tried to keep his grasp on things long after he should have let go. "That poor afflicted man. What I've got him into! I promised we'd help Frank. I've got to keep that promise."

Now, of course, an outgoing governor is still in charge until Inauguration Day. He's got pardons to sign and unpleasant business he wouldn't want to leave for the new fellow. But right through Inauguration Day, Al Smith had been behaving as if he meant to stay in office with Franklin Roosevelt as figurehead.

After the oaths were sworn, we went back to the Executive Mansion for a reception, which should've been a joyous occasion for the Roosevelts, but the staff was dedicated to the Smiths and spent most of the event crying in the cloakroom.

It was all very unseemly.

Before I left to catch the ferry home, I stopped to say a fond farewell to the new governor. Waving me in, FDR said, "Al wants me to keep his secretary on. Belle Moskowitz. Do you know her?"

Of course I knew Belle Moskowitz, and also knew that she was more than a secretary. She had become for Al Smith more like a military *chief of staff.* "Oh, yes, she's a very able woman. Helpful and intelligent."

Franklin pulled at his lower lip thoughtfully. "My wife says she's a fine woman. Eleanor also says if I keep Mrs. Moskowitz, she'll run me and she'll run the state. That she'd do it gently. That she'd do it well. But Eleanor says I must decide whether Mrs. Moskowitz is to be governor, or I am."

A chill ran down my spine. I couldn't imagine a more ruthless way to cut off a woman's career. Sputtering in disbelief that Eleanor could be so politically merciless, I asked, "You're not going to ask me to advise you on this matter, are you?"

Roosevelt paused before letting me off the hook. "No. But I wanted to tell you they wrote an inauguration speech for me. Al and Mrs. Moskowitz. They had it all ready for me. Didn't want me to be troubled to have to write my own."

"That *was* rather presumptuous, but they only want to help; Al feels he got you into a terrible mess, after all."

I laughed, but FDR didn't crack a smile. "Frances, they don't think I can do the job."

"If so, it's only because *you* said that you couldn't do the job when we asked you to run. You said you didn't have the strength yet."

He stared down at his hands. "Well, nobody in the family liked the idea. Not Eleanor. Not Missy. Not my closest political advisors. None of them thought I was ready." Now he looked up at me from his chair, his eyes filled with stormy apprehension. "What do you think, Frances? Do you think I can do it?"

I didn't hesitate even a moment. "I'm *certain* you can. I wasn't sure until I saw you campaign your heart out from the back seat of a car. But now no one could convince me otherwise."

He smiled, rubbing his knees as if they pained him. "Well, then I had better not keep Mrs. Moskowitz on staff. The way I am now, I feel as if I mustn't allow myself to be bossed, or I might get into the habit. It'd be easy, because I'm *not* at my full strength yet, and if I let other people do everything for me, I might never be."

That should've been the end of the matter. The new governor should get to pick his own people, but Al Smith insisted on putting me in the middle. "You've got to convince him to keep Mrs. Moskowitz. She shouldn't be booted into the street. You've got to do this for me."

I felt as if I owed the man everything, so I said I'd try—by which I meant I'd ask FDR to try to find *some* place for Belle in his administration. She was enormously talented, she'd be good for the state, and it'd be fair play after her long years of faithful service. Besides, I loved Al too much to deny him anything.

Still, when next I saw Belle Moskowitz, I said, "You've got to get Al something to do. He needs to keep occupied. He's offering to come up to the Executive Mansion two or three times a week, but he's not governor anymore."

Belle took great umbrage. "He's trying to save the state. Franklin Roosevelt can never run that show. He's too weak and inexperienced. Somebody's got to help him."

I bristled but tried to be diplomatic. "He's stronger than you think. Besides, all new governors are inexperienced, and they do all right. Suppose Al had won the presidency. What would've happened? He'd have been running the country and far too busy to tell Roosevelt how to run New York."

Stubbornly, she said, "Roosevelt is going to be terrible."

I decided then and there that I would *not* recommend that Roosevelt find some role for Belle. "If you really think he's not capable, then why did we ask him to run?"

"Don't be naive, Frances," she said.

Had they asked him to run because they thought he was weak and malleable? If so, they didn't know him at all. I already knew he'd never be a figurehead. Franklin Delano Roosevelt had performed better in the election than almost any other Democrat in the country. He was wonderful with voters. Fun, funny, and boisterous.

He made each of them feel as if they were his friend. He wasn't a chameleon, but I'm quite certain there are no two people who saw the same thing in him. Nevertheless, they all liked him. The people of New York had elected Roosevelt, and if we lived in a democracy, they had a right to get *Roosevelt*.

Chapter Thirty-Nine

Hyde Park, New York
January 1929

"H OP IN, FRANCES," ROOSEVELT SAID, ONE arm resting casually on the steering wheel of the automobile he'd had specially fitted so he could drive with his hands alone.

He'd invited my family to his ancestral seat on a sunny winter day. Susanna was sledding with two of the Roosevelt boys while the governor's mother entertained my husband in the parlor. But FDR wanted to talk with me privately, so I got in the car. He drove all over the property, enthusiastically showing off his favorite trees, telling me his plans for planting more in the spring.

One might think paralysis would make him a cautious driver, but he drove so fast with the top down that the wind threatened to tear my hat from my head. And as I struggled with it, he teased, "Oh, the impropriety . . ."

With a laugh, I gave up, unpinned my hat, and let my hair go wild. And that's when he asked, "How'd you like a promotion? I want you to take charge of the state's labor department."

I took a moment to form a coherent sentence. "You cannot be serious."

He grinned, which sent that cigarette holder clamped between his teeth straight up in the air. "Your expression. I love it! Yes, I'm serious."

I wanted to make sure I understood. "You want me to oversee

thousands of workers—statisticians, factory inspectors, and workers' compensation boards?"

"Yes, and to be a member of the governor's cabinet. *My* cabinet."

I continued to eye him, incredulous.

Then, slyly, he added, "This is a good joke I think you'll enjoy. I asked Al whether I should offer you the job, and he told me no. He said you were wonderful, but that men wouldn't like to have you as a boss. That it would smart their pride to work for a woman. Isn't that funny?"

"He's right."

Roosevelt threw his head back. "Then let it smart their pride. You see, Al is a good progressive fellow, but I've got more nerve about women and their status in the world."

He was proud of himself, and I suppose he told me this to weaken my ties of loyalty to the former governor. I probably should've let him, but there were limits to what I'd tolerate. Playfully, I asked, "Do you *really* think you have more nerve than Al Smith? Remember that Al appointed me to a public post nearly a decade ago, when it was unheard of to appoint a woman to anything."

It had taken more courage then.

Which Roosevelt now unwittingly admitted by saying, "I think women voters will like it." It was a political calculation, but also maybe a personal one. "It's my belief that if you women had an equal share in making the laws, then the unspeakable conditions in tenements and the neglect of the poor would never have come about in the first place."

I remembered a time when he didn't seem to care about such things, but I believed he did now. And when he pulled to the side of the road and turned the engine off so he could face me, I realized this was an earnest job offer.

I didn't want to be churlish, but I felt certain I'd have to turn him down. There wouldn't be any flexibility in this position. If my daughter needed to come home sick from school, or if I needed to go with Paul to a doctor's appointment, I wouldn't be able to do it. And I certainly didn't want to move to Albany.

Roosevelt sensed these hesitations. "Frances, let me sweeten the pot. This will mean a raise of four thousand dollars over what you already make."

Dear God. I could send my daughter to college with money like that. It's true the economy was roaring, but it wouldn't roar forever. Did I have any business turning down such an opportunity?

On the other hand, this job would come with new scrutiny. If Paul's old illness were to be exposed in the newspapers, it'd prove an embarrassment to my family and to Roosevelt.

To my dismay, I felt he had a right to know. "Before this conversation goes any further, Governor Roosevelt, there's something I must tell you in confidence and good conscience. I cannot let you appoint me to something without knowing that my husband has a condition. It's managed for the time being, but—"

"I know all about it," Roosevelt said with a wave of his hand. "Eleanor explained. She said she ran into you at the hospital when I was there with polio. I'm awful sorry to hear about anybody suffering a dangerous case of the morbs."

Of course, Paul had suffered much more than a case of morbid melancholy, but perhaps the new governor didn't need to know the details.

Was I relieved or horrified that Eleanor had told him? Under the circumstances, it was probably her duty. Even so, I felt terribly vulnerable. And as if to comfort me, he said, "Every family has their difficulties, Frances. And every marriage has its struggles. Even mine."

"Marriage *is* complicated," I admitted.

"And sometimes lonely," he said, pulling down the brim of his hat to shield his eyes from the bright reflection of sun on snow.

Before that moment, I didn't think a man like FDR *could* be lonely. Especially since he was never alone. He was always surrounded by friends, children, relations, political advisors, and other hangers-on, most of them crowding his guest rooms and making mayhem at the dinner table. His life was very full at all hours of the night and day. But that didn't mean anything, did it?

When Paul was first ill, I had a social calendar filled to the brim. Yet I'd known excruciating moments of loneliness. I'd never have guessed that Franklin Roosevelt and I might have such a thing in common. That we might be kindred spirits. But perhaps we were . . .

"I'm honored and tempted by the offer," I said. "But have you talked to party leaders about appointing me? They might not like it."

"No, it was my own idea."

"Well, don't worry, I won't tell anyone about this conversation. So you don't need to regard this matter as sewn up. Talk to others, and if you decide to appoint someone else, that'll be fine with me. I'm quite happy doing what I'm doing now."

Roosevelt looked genuinely startled. "That's very decent of you, Frances . . . but I'm not going to change my mind."

I WAITED UNTIL after we'd taken the ferry back home to broach the subject with Paul. We were taking a winter's walk in Central Park with Susanna when I reassured him, "If anything about this job worries you in any way, I won't accept."

After all, my husband already endured gibes from friends, relations, and strangers about my career eclipsing his. I was always pleased at the way he ignored them with a wry smile, but the potential exposure of his medical history was something different. Quite a serious thing that he ought not be expected to brush off.

Thankfully, Paul tried to banish my fears. "This is your chance to prove that qualified women can, and *should*, take charge of things."

"You're not worried?"

"Not so much that it should stop you." He dug his hands down into his pockets as we walked. "I once told you that you're a remarkable person. Well, you keep proving me right." He stopped walking, reaching out to tug me a little closer with a suggestive glance. "A man likes to be proved right, you know . . ."

I feared he might kiss me in that moment, right out there in the open. Then he did, and instead of withdrawing, I kissed him back. This, of course, mortified our daughter, who was ahead of us on the path, making a game of sliding on the ice.

She pointedly turned her head away from the sight of parental affection, and I laughed. "Of course, Susanna isn't going to want to move to Albany."

"Albany *is* a dismal place for an artistic girl like Susie, isn't it?"

Nevertheless, that afternoon he put all his talents as a father behind convincing our daughter that my new job would be a wonderful thing. It helped that Susanna was a bit dazzled by Franklin Roosevelt and professed delight to think her mother might just be someone worth boasting about. But she suggested a new apartment in New York that would ease the commute, and I said we'd think about it.

It was cold and snowy, and I thought we ought to go home and get warm. But, feeling grateful for my little family, I reluctantly let them pull me into a snowball fight. Susanna and I ganged up on Paul, pelting him until he rolled her onto the ground. But she climbed atop Paul's strong shoulders, and her cheeks glowed pink with pleasure as she tried to stuff a snowball down his jacket. Then we were all on the ground laughing. It was all very unseemly, but with snowflakes and joy blotting out everything else, I wondered, *How did I ever get so lucky?*

Oh, Roosevelt was right to say that every family had its difficulties. Paul and I had more than our share. But in that moment, I felt loved and supported by my husband and daughter—sustained by the knowledge that we were still a sacred trinity.

NOT LONG AFTER, Florence Kelley threw me a little congratulatory luncheon, at which Mary Rumsey pretended to be put out. "You're making life very difficult on me as a Republican, Frances. How am I to continue with the party of my father when Eleanor's husband has so wisely elevated you to a position of real power?"

"Well, I *am* sorry to be such a bother," I teased. "Shall I call up FDR and turn down the job on your account?"

"Don't you dare!" she cried.

I was coming to the uncomfortable realization that other women felt a strong personal investment in my career. Even those who weren't my friends. Beyond any policy I might advance, they wanted to see *me* succeed. As if my rise validated their own ambitions and self-worth as women. It was both an honor and terribly humbling to hold such a mantle.

Chapter Forty

Albany, New York
Spring 1929

My dear girl,
There will be less death, misery, and poverty because you will be
at the helm in this state.
~Mrs. Florence Kelley

I went to Albany that spring with the support of my mentor, carrying the heavy weight of her hopes and expectations. And I was there with about a hundred officials to see newly elected governor Roosevelt first enter the Executive Chamber, with its red velvet upholstery and magnificent desk.

It wasn't until we all stood at attention that I realized the desk was in the center of the room. We should've moved it closer to the door! Now Roosevelt would have to cross that whole long chamber leaning on one man's arm and using a cane on the other side.

We all stood helplessly, watching every agonizing step of his slow and harrowing progress. I held my breath until he got halfway, stopped, and then waved his cane gaily. *"That's all right. I'll make it!"*

His confidence put everyone at ease; I should've known that my new boss couldn't be defeated by a little embarrassment.

Still, it was an adjustment to work for FDR. For one thing, he was more excitable than Al Smith—more prone to take rash action without all the facts. For another, it was basically useless to try to calm Roosevelt down over the telephone. If I wanted his full attention, I had to go to Albany and see him face-to-face—which I did, at least once every ten days.

Fortunately, we agreed on policy. I had a program in mind to get rid of child labor in the state for good—a fight I'd been waging ever since Mary Hogan had her hand chopped off working a honey dipper.

One Monday evening when I stayed for dinner at the Executive Mansion, Roosevelt said, "I want all the sweatshops in New York closed and the rest of the things on your list done, too, Frances. Go as far as you can. When you need help, come to me. I'm for the program—all of it. You do it, and I'll get the voters on our side."

He did have a marvelous way of rallying the public. He'd started giving fireside chats on the radio for New Yorkers every Sunday night, and the response was spectacular. Still, I wanted to make sure I *really* had the authority to do as I thought best. "I may need to fire some people . . ."

"You mean that ill-tempered secretary of yours?" FDR asked with a shudder. "She's like Cerberus guarding your door. I don't know how you've stood for it this long."

I laughed. "Oh, Miss Jay and I have learned to accommodate each other. I took her with me up the ladder because she's good at frightening people away when I need to concentrate."

He shrugged and admitted, "Sometimes it's good to have a bulldog. As for firing people, get rid of anyone you need to."

It was a far freer hand than I was used to, and I wasn't sure I could trust it. "Tell me, Governor, if ever I were to encounter a situation in which dynamite was involved, would you want to know?"

Roosevelt's gaze jerked up from his plate—he'd wanted scrambled eggs for supper, of all things. "Dynamite? What are you going on about, Frances?"

"Just making sure you're paying attention."

He started to scold me, but then one of his nephews or cousins or one of his son's school friends ran through the dining room with a dog, and behind them swept in a menagerie of the governor's entourage.

Whereas the Smiths had treated the Executive Mansion as if it were the property of the state of New York, the Roosevelts had moved in with their knickknacks, books piled on end tables, and photographs decorating the walls.

They kept the windows open for a pleasant river breeze, and we could always hear the shouting of his children outside playing sports, while Eleanor sat somewhere in white tennis shoes, her long legs crossed at the ankles while she knitted.

What I'd come to like about Eleanor is that she was very much a woman's woman. She talked with other women on the frankest, pleasantest terms. There wasn't any of this waiting for the men to come through after their coffee. What she had to say, she was delighted to say to you.

And spending this kind of time with the Roosevelts gave me insight into this most unusual couple. For example, one could certainly not call Eleanor *a mothball wife*. She wasn't an ornamental hat her husband took out of storage for public occasions. She was a real political partner who worked with him hand in glove. He trusted whatever she told him as the gospel truth and was always saying, "You know, Eleanor really does put it over. She's got great talent with people."

Still, they seemed to live two entirely separate lives. They didn't share a bedroom, and even in the same house, they kept their own schedules, enjoyed different hobbies, and socialized in two barely intersecting circles of friends.

A visitor to the governor's mansion might be forgiven for thinking that the ever-present and ever-loyal Missy LeHand was Roosevelt's wife instead of his secretary. After all, Missy was, far more often than Eleanor, the hostess of his fun and games with the big, riotous extended family of guests the Roosevelts gathered around them.

I was frequently one of these overnight guests because it saved me a midnight train back into Manhattan. And they insisted I stay even when every bed was full, which meant sharing a room with somebody— usually Eleanor, whom I had come to like and admire, even if I was wary of her.

For one thing, we were women of very different temperaments. Whereas I was apt to tell a joke to lighten the mood in a tense confrontation, Eleanor was more likely to push the boundaries. Whereas I had rejected most of the puritanism of my upbringing, Eleanor equated tasty food or a strong drink with moral vice.

She also had an uncanny knack for sharing personal details before establishing a true intimate connection, which I discovered one evening when, in our nightgowns, putting our hair up for the night, she asked, "You don't mind rooming with me, do you?"

"Not at all! I'm always honored to be welcomed into your home."

She gave a soft sigh. "Well, of course this isn't my home. I've never had a home of my own, you know. I lived with my grandmother when I was an orphan child. That was *her* home, and I had to be a very well-behaved girl there, or else I'd have nowhere else to go."

Genuinely pained on behalf of the little orphaned girl she once was, I said, "That must've been so terribly difficult, for you to be robbed of a happy childhood that way."

Eleanor nodded, continuing, "When I married, we lived with Franklin's mother at Hyde Park. That was *her* home. Even our house in New York City was a gift from his mother, and Franklin allowed her to choose all the furniture. I didn't even have a say when it came to the tea service."

She said this with surprising bitterness. And I couldn't blame her.

As much as I liked the governor's mother, I knew that Sara Delano Roosevelt was a formidable character. I probably wouldn't have enjoyed being her daughter-in-law. Still, I wasn't certain how to reply without insulting my new boss or his mother, so I only said, "Goodness."

Eleanor sighed again, this time more despondently. "Now here I am living in another house that isn't my own. Even the staff are civil servants. Nothing belongs to me except my maid."

Your maid doesn't belong to you either, I thought.

It seemed she was having a moment of feeling sorry for herself, and that was perfectly natural. We all had moments like that. And Eleanor's tragic childhood, marked by such painful losses, made me truly sympathetic. I could understand, too, the struggles of a difficult marriage. I understood them better than most. But I was constitutionally incapable of overindulging the notion that not having a home sufficiently fashioned to your personal tastes is a *travesty*. After all, despite Eleanor's legitimate complaints, she'd been raised in one of the most wealthy, privileged, and powerful families in America.

She may not have had a home she considered her own, but she split her time living in luxury and ease at Hyde Park, a vacation home on Campobello Island, her hobby cottage at Val-Kill, and the governor's mansion to boot.

It was hardly the kind of homelessness with which I was continually confronted at work, so I didn't reply except by way of a nod. My silence, however, proved to be a costly mistake. For Eleanor took it as encouragement and suddenly blurted, "I once offered Franklin a divorce, you know."

I froze, my grip tight on the hairbrush, but she didn't notice the tension, or ignored it if she did. "There was a girl about a decade ago . . ."

Oh, God. I did *not* want to tell her that all of New York and Washington, DC, had guessed about the girl. I didn't want to talk about the girl *at all.* I sensed this was something she didn't tell many people, and clearly she was confiding in me in an overture of friendship. Yet I simply could not imagine any situation in which it would be proper to discuss the marital infidelity of one's employer.

It's true that I'd known Eleanor longer than Franklin, and under different circumstances, such a discussion might have drawn us closer. But we weren't college girlfriends giggling at a sleepover; her husband was the governor, she was his First Lady, and I was a member of his cabinet. The position she put me in with this revelation was so exquisitely uncomfortable that I felt like a trapped animal, wondering if I could gnaw my own arm off to escape.

In the end, I made an inelegant excuse to use the powder room—and locked myself in there until I knew Eleanor had snuffed the lights. She probably thought me a terribly cold fish, and I worried that I'd handled the whole thing quite badly.

"It was awful," I told Mary. "I wanted to say all the comforting things that one might say, but she put me in the middle of a marital quarrel in which I decidedly do not belong."

"There isn't any marital quarrel between Franklin and Eleanor anymore," Mary said. "Sometimes she just resents their agreement to stay together. How can you blame her?"

"Because he's nothing but complimentary about her. Franklin praises her elegance. He speaks wistfully of her beautiful hair. He'd never let anyone criticize her, nor would he speak a word against her."

"He'd better not," Mary said. "She saved his life when he was struck with polio. What's more, he needs her."

"Doesn't she need him too?"

Mary laughed. "Oh, Frances. What you'll learn about Eleanor is that she is, above all else, a *survivor.*"

"LET'S GO FOR a drive," FDR said when things were getting too rowdy at the governor's mansion. It sometimes seemed as if we did most of our state business in his car. But sometimes our conversations in the car were decidedly personal.

One day he drove me down to Hyde Park for a walk in the rose garden and pointed out the place he wanted to be buried. Aghast, I said, "What a thing to think about! You're tempting fate."

He only laughed. "Everyone should make plans for the end. Or they'll do the *damnedest* things to you."

Later that summer, he pulled the car over and pointed at a field where two horses dipped their heads in the grasses by the fence line. "Frances, I don't know what I'm going to do."

He looked so grave that I worried. "What's happened?"

"It's my sons. How can I ever discipline those boys? The youngest two did something terrible, absolutely against all the rules. Eleanor and I decided they had to be punished in a way they'd remember, so we took away their pony for the summer. They were very down about it, and we thought we'd made some impression. Well, what do you think? Last week my mother buys these two horses for them. Two *horses*, not ponies. Now what am I going to do?"

I could only laugh at his predicament, though I was beginning to see more fully why Eleanor resented her mother-in-law.

"Do you have these kinds of troubles with Susie?" he asked.

"Oh, my daughter is a well-behaved girl, but these days I've become an embarrassment to her. She hates when I try to kiss her when her friends are watching."

"Kiss her anyway," he said, thumping his knee. "Eleanor says you spoil a child by rewarding unmannerly behavior with affection, and she's very wise about such things. But I just kiss the kids anyway and hope they'll be glad of it when I'm in my dotage."

I liked his approach. "There's only so much time to kiss them, after all, because they grow up too fast."

"They do. Bring Susie by for a visit, and I'll tell her she ought to be terribly proud of you. Doesn't she know you're saving the lives of girls who paint clocks?"

He was referring to young women who contracted radium poisoning while employed to paint luminous dials. The story of these girls had captured his imagination. And I'd learned that was the key. I couldn't take him to *see* the horrors of factory work as I'd done with Al Smith. FDR couldn't get into a factory with his wheelchair, and it'd be too dangerous to try. Thus, he relied on me to paint a picture for him in his mind.

And I learned to do it very well.

After all, the clock-painting girls weren't the only people we were trying to protect. The American dream was premised on the idea that every person should have an equal chance to make a good life. Some might do better than others, but everyone had opportunity. Yet most Americans couldn't weather a change in fortune; if a girl lost her hand in an accident, or if a child lost a father to an illness, or if a woman lived long enough to lose her senses, the catastrophe could rob an entire family of opportunity. Sometimes even an entire community. It was like knocking down one domino and watching it bring down the rest, until society itself crashed to its foundations.

And the dominoes were falling not just in the factories but also on the farms. A drought and falling food prices pushed young men into the cities to look for work, which was becoming increasingly scarce.

No one on Wall Street seemed the slightest bit concerned. They all told Governor Roosevelt, *The economy is roaring!*

Another governor, I think, would've been content with the

platitudes that everyone was repeating. But Roosevelt listened to me. And on July Fourth, he made a barn burner of a speech, saying that if Americans wanted to keep their freedom, they ought to don liberty caps like the Founding Fathers and resist the concentration of wealth into too few hands. Or we'd reap the economic whirlwind . . .

Chapter Forty-One

New York City
October 1929

PEOPLE WERE JUMPING TO THEIR DEATHS IN New York again. This time, it wasn't factory girls burning alive but an overworked brokerage firm clerk. The next was a now nearly bankrupt member of the New York Mercantile Exchange, who climbed out his lawyer's window and dove for the street below.

Despair over the market crash was spreading like contagion. A stockbroker in St. Louis swallowed poison. Another investor shot himself in Kansas. In Pennsylvania, one set himself on fire . . .

I tried to keep these reports away from my husband, for fear it might send him spiraling, but when Paul got hold of a newspaper, he waved it, shouting, "I predicted this!"

He *had* too.

When discussing whether to move to a new apartment on Madison Avenue, we'd talked about the silly prognostications that the market would never fall. I'd been a little worried that record profits weren't translating into jobs. But from the start, Paul had predicted the worst. "People are going to lose everything."

I shuddered to think of all the elderly whose investments were evaporating before their eyes, leaving them no way to ever make it back. At least we'd lost our money when we were young enough to start over . . .

Now I believed Paul that the stock market crash could be a

national calamity if its ripples through the economy were not acknowledged and aggressively managed. So I was furious when, in January, President Herbert Hoover said the economy was *improving*, that the economic depression was almost over, and that employment numbers were up, because I knew this to be categorically false.

I had the employment data from New York at my fingertips. Our numbers were *terrible*, and we were the commercial center of the country. Where New York employment numbers went, so went the nation's.

Fuming, I went straight to my office and said, "Someone has grossly misled the president of the United States."

I gathered my statisticians and had them call up the federal bureau to find out where the president's numbers were coming from. Then we went to work. We spent the whole day at it. And that's where we found the sleight of hand. One of my people explained, "They're just reporting seasonal Christmas employment, which always goes up every year."

"The president must know that," I said, reeling.

Hoover, after all, wasn't a foolish man. He also wasn't without heart. He had, in fact, made his name rescuing people from hunger in Europe during the war. But my conversations with federal officials made clear that President Hoover wasn't simply misinformed; he was lying. And I was appalled. This kind of dishonesty in such a dire crisis seemed to be an immoral abuse of power, and I felt my Revolutionary ancestors spinning in their graves.

Well, I wasn't going to stand for it.

I called a press conference that afternoon, where I told a room of stunned reporters, "The president of the United States has deceived people about employment. It is worse, not better. It's a cruel deceit because people will believe it. When Father comes home and says he can't get a job, Mother will be mad because the president is saying there are so many jobs to be had."

One of those stunned reporters said, "Miss Perkins, you have some nerve to call the president of the United States a liar."

Only then did it occur to me that I was going to cause a scandal. As telegrams flooded in, either congratulating me or berating me for attacking President Hoover, I realized I should've consulted my boss. Governor Roosevelt might not appreciate what I'd done. After all, I wasn't a mere social worker or activist or lobbyist.

I was part of his administration.

Remembering how Al Smith reacted when I took things into my own hands, I winced, picked up the phone, and rang up FDR. "I've done something you may think is very wrong. Are you feeling amiable?"

Roosevelt chuckled like a tolerant paterfamilias. "Yes, I'm feeling in a fine, amiable mood, Frances. Are you about to ruin it?"

I explained how I took President Hoover to task in front of the press, and my knees knocked when FDR shouted, "The hell you have!"

"Are you going to kill me or fire me?"

FDR sputtered, then started to laugh. "I think that was *bully*, just wonderful. How did you have the nerve? I'm just glad you didn't ask me, because I'd have probably told you not to do it. But the blood be on your hands." He said this with no small amount of glee. "If you're wrong, you'll get plenty of punishment from the country."

Unfortunately for the country, I was right. Factories shuttered, construction sites lay empty, beggars wandered the streets hawking apples. How callous did President Hoover's administration have to be to paint a rosy picture without helping these people?

"HEY, SWEETS," RED'S old familiar voice said on the end of the telephone line. "I hear you got yourself some important government job and are making a ruckus with it."

"And I heard you finally wrote a book people want to read," I teased.

Red could take the ribbing—he could easily afford to—because his smash hits had made him a millionaire. *Main Street, Babbitt, Arrowsmith, Elmer Gantry,* and *Dodsworth* were all bestsellers. And now he said, "Congratulations on giving Hoover a black eye."

"Well, thank you. I think . . ."

"Just remember the old lesson, though—never attack until you're sure of your ground, or it'll all end up like that time we followed a couple from the ferry."

I laughed, still chagrined by that memory. "This time, I have hard evidence."

Like a relentless harpy, I double-checked every figure that came out of the Hoover administration. It wasn't difficult to nitpick. Hoover's people weren't just sloppy, they were also cruelly dishonest, so I made no bones about this with the press. I even drove Hoover's chief statistician to resign in protest.

It got to the point that whenever Hoover put out new numbers, reporters called my office to confirm them.

Governor Roosevelt admired my fighting spirit, and when Congress called me to testify, he advised, "Don't say anything about politics. Just be an outraged scientist and social worker."

Which is, of course, what I thought I *was.* But I was now, for better or for worse, also a politician.

Chapter Forty-Two

Albany, New York
March 1930

Dear Miss Perkins,

Winters are terrible cold here, and it drives even good boys to bad acts. In January my mother's teeth were chattering so hard my older brother tried to nab a little coal from a passing train car. He got killed in the attempt and I miss him something awful. I'm only ten, but please tell me where I can get work to buy coal because there aren't any jobs to be had.

~Lorenzo Angelo, Rochester, New York

What had begun as a recession followed by a stock market crash was now a severe economic depression. Hoover said it would all be over in sixty days. With one million out of work—a figure growing every day—nobody else believed that. Some economists advised that we should simply let the system hit bottom no matter how long it took, "even if it means an entire generation dies out except for the best of the herd."

At hearing this, FDR exploded, "People aren't cattle, you know!" He told me, "We're not going to do *nothing*, Frances. Our nation began as an experiment in self-governance, and by God, in *my* state, I am determined to experiment."

We held meetings to hear people's ideas. Some enterprising New York companies were experimenting with unemployment insurance. Others experimented with reduced hours and alternating shifts.

Eastman Kodak was embracing a five-day workweek in Rochester, and it was working out, giving families an entire weekend together and helping the state economy besides.

Meanwhile, Paul and I dug out his old reports and ideas he'd had to solve the unemployment he'd faced near the end of the war when he worked at city hall.

I thought that modern state-run public works programs and employment offices to help find jobs were all well and good. But I wanted a *comprehensive* system of social insurance.

Roosevelt frowned when I told him about it. "It sounds radical. I've never heard of such a thing."

"Oh, I think you have," I said, sitting beside him in the car on the way to a public hearing. "Allow me to refresh your memory."

I handed him an index card with ideas Theodore Roosevelt had advanced while campaigning in 1912.

It is abnormal for industry to throw back upon the community the human wreckage due to its wear and tear. The hazards of sickness, accident, invalidism, involuntary unemployment, and old age should be provided for through the adoption of a system of social insurance adapted to American use.

FDR fiddled with the edge of the card, squinting at the words *social insurance.*

"It's common in Europe," I argued, but that only made him more suspicious, so I added, "It isn't a new idea in America either. Even Thomas Paine called for a fund in colonial America to defend against poverty."

"How would it work?" Roosevelt asked.

"Well, there are academics working on this who could explain it better, but let me try. Do you have a fire insurance policy on your home?"

"Yes," he said.

"*Why* do you have fire insurance?"

"So I can rebuild if the worst comes to pass."

I nodded. "Why not simply stash rebuilding money in a bank account in case there's a fire?"

He rubbed his chin. "Even if banks weren't crumbling, it'd be difficult to set that much aside, even for me."

"Right, and inefficient too. A real opportunity cost for you and for the economy at large. Especially since your house is unlikely to catch fire. Insurance pools risk, paying out only to the contributors whose homes have burned. Now, it would be much the same with social insurance. Not every worker is going to die on the job, leaving an impoverished wife and little orphaned children. Not every worker is going to be maimed. Not every worker is going to lose his job, and not every worker is going to live to old age and infirmity. But if they all paid into an insurance fund . . ."

Roosevelt was listening carefully now, leaning forward. "And you think it could work here in New York?"

"You said you wanted to experiment, Governor Roosevelt, and this is the most worthy experiment I can think of. It'd be the culmination of all the other reforms I've ever attempted my whole life long. A plan that really does have the potential to end poverty, at least as we know it."

"ROOSEVELT IS SENDING me overseas," I told Paul. "I'm to study British unemployment insurance to see if that system could work for us, but let's make it a sightseeing trip for the three of us."

My husband winced. "You know I hate the ocean."

I knew he'd been wary of the open sea since he'd nearly drowned in it. He'd avoided ocean travel ever since, but I hadn't realized it was now a phobia. "You don't think you can put up with it for a vacation?"

Paul hugged himself. "I'd spend the entire voyage there in agitation and be a nervous wreck anticipating the return trip."

"Well, it was just a thought," I said, trying not to sound as disappointed as I was.

He seemed disappointed, too, but then, all at once, he brightened. "Why don't you take Susie? She's nearly fifteen. Soon she'll be off to college and married. We have her to ourselves for only a short time longer. It'd be good for her to see the world."

He was right. Susanna was at a delicate age and was a sensitive girl. A little needier than most. And I wanted to give her a broad experience of life.

So, it was decided, then. Susanna and I went over on the *Rotterdam*, in a lovely stateroom. Once in London, we strolled by Big Ben. We watched the changing of the guard at Buckingham Palace. We took a river cruise on the Thames. And between these excursions, of course, I visited many officials and learned the complicated system by which the British provided relief; then I took Susie with me to a conference in Amsterdam, where we sipped hot chocolate from the lovely booths by the train station, which, unlike our train station at home, was not crowded with unemployed men begging for work.

While the economic depression was global, Europe wasn't suffering to the same extent America was. At least, not yet. I attributed that to their various systems of social insurance. I suppose I must've been lost in this thought while we polished off our pastries, because Susanna asked, "Mother, will you *always* be busy with work?"

"I like to be busy with work," I told her, brushing wisps of her honeyed hair out of her eyes.

Pulling away so I wouldn't embarrass her in public, she asked, "Do you know when I'll have my coming-out party?"

Dear God, were people still throwing *coming-out parties*? If her friends and their older sisters were having them, I supposed she must have one, too, but she was far too young. "Eventually, we'll plan one, but it's too soon, and I haven't the faintest notion where to begin."

Susanna sighed and rolled her eyes. "I wish I had a *normal* mother."

Children her age have the capacity to say cruel things, so I made light of it. I didn't tell her that normal mothers couldn't afford to take their daughters to Europe. I just laughed and said, "Well, I'm afraid all you have is me. However will you manage?"

WHEN I RETURNED from the trip, I had to admit to Roosevelt, "I don't believe the British system will work for us."

"Why not? It's the dole, isn't it? You know I'm against the dole, Frances. Don't you get any dole in here!"

"It isn't the dole," I explained patiently. "We won't be giving a handout. I want an *insurance* program, as I've told you."

"Then what's wrong with how they do it in England?"

"You won't believe me, but when it comes to unemployment, the Brits keep stacks of handwritten documentation, and an army of little bespectacled old ladies climb ladders to make notes on each record and keep it up to date. If we were to do this, we'd have to get some of the smart gentlemen at IBM to work on an automated recordkeeping system for us."

The image of bespectacled English grandmothers perched atop ladders tickled his sense of humor. And I cursed myself. I should've known better than to paint that colorful picture for Franklin Roosevelt. For years after, he'd bring up "little old ladies on ladders" to argue that social insurance was crazy. But that didn't mean he was hard-hearted to the plight of the poor as the breadlines grew and the economic situation got worse.

He didn't like my suggestion, but he hoped someone would have a better one, so he called a special session of the legislature, where he gravely intoned, "When people who are willing and able to work and support their families cannot find a job, then a civilized people must—not as a matter of charity, but as a matter of social duty—prevent the starvation or dire want of its fellow man."

It was, for him, a moral crusade but also a political one. Especially now that it seemed Hoover was giving up. Thumping his desk, FDR said, "Hoover pretends there's nothing he can do by way of federal action. But the United States Constitution has proved itself the most marvelously elastic compilation of rules of government ever written. Hoover won't even try. He's defeatist. He's quit on Americans."

It might've been an unfair assessment of Hoover, but FDR convinced himself it was true. He thought Herbert Hoover didn't *deserve* to be entrusted with America's future. Of course, it was equally true that Franklin Roosevelt had never given up his dream to be president. Not even now that he was wheelchair bound and diminished in physical strength.

The gleam in his eye told me he was gunning for Hoover's job, and I came to a dim awareness that *I* was the instrument by which he meant to get it.

Chapter Forty-Three

★ ★ ★

New York City
November 1930

Dear Miss Perkins,

I've read in the newspaper that you say girls my age should stay in school, but my family has fallen on such hard times that I haven't had a new winter coat in years and the one I have now is too small and falling to pieces. It's shaping up to be a cold hard winter, and I need to help provide for my family. I need a job, and if you can't help find me one, I'm hoping that, as a lady in government, you might have a friend who is about to buy a new coat. If so, can you plead with her to give me her castoff so I don't freeze to death?

~Miss MW, Binghamton, New York

People had no money to spend, and without money to spend on, say, a coat, there was no one to buy from the coat factory. And if the coat factory didn't need to produce coats, they didn't need to keep employees on the job. Which meant more people couldn't afford coats or anything else. It was a vicious cycle.

Amid growing economic calamity, Roosevelt was reelected to the governorship of New York in a landslide. Which made everyone in the party happy—well, almost everyone.

I ran into Belle Moskowitz in the powder room at the Cosmopolitan, and after a few pleasantries, she said, "Why doesn't Frank want Al Smith's advice, Frances? He didn't mind that Al went out and campaigned for him, but he won't accept help governing when it's offered."

I knew she was still sore that Roosevelt hadn't hired her, and, hoping to smooth things over, I said, "Oh, Roosevelt just wants to be his own man. Al Smith casts a big shadow, you know, and like a child wanting to get out of the shadow of a parent, FDR is charting his own course."

I shouldn't have had to point out that a man like Roosevelt— having been underestimated and cut down in his prime—needed to at least metaphorically stand on his own two feet. But Belle said, "What a shortsighted man *your* governor is."

I felt a chill. *"My* governor?"

"Frances, you have to choose. You can't be with Smith *and* Roosevelt. You've got to say you're with one or the other."

"No, I won't say that, Belle. I'm for Roosevelt because I work for him. I like him. I believe in him. I think he's doing the right thing. He's supporting all the things I care about. I think the world of Al Smith for the same reasons."

I was determined not to get in the middle of a feud but feared it was inevitable when Belle said, "Al is going to run for president again. You'll see. He'll make a great comeback. You don't want to be on the losing side, do you?"

With the memory of burning KKK crosses seared in my brain, I thought it was the worst possible idea for Al Smith to run for the presidency again. I didn't share Belle's optimism about his chances. Moreover, losing the presidency again would shatter Al's already broken heart and might break the nation along with it.

Besides, Al was finally making good money for his family as president of a corporation that was building the Empire State Building. He was still doing good work for the state that he loved. Why would he give that up?

When I paid a call to my old chief at the ribbon cutting of what would be the world's tallest skyscraper, I was reassured to hear him say, "Run for president again? Ha! Who do you think I am, kiddo? William Jennings Bryan?"

I believed it was a time for passing on the baton, though sometimes I grieved over it. Especially when I visited Florence Kelley in Germantown, where she lay gravely ill.

When she saw me in the doorway of her hospital room, she sighed and said, "What a disappointment."

I was pained by the rasp of her words and by her frightfully wasted appearance. "Oh, Mrs. Kelley, I'm so sorry I didn't come sooner."

"That's not what I am disappointed about. You see, Frances, I thought I'd live to be a hundred years old. I made plans for it. I believe that times will be safer for idealism in the future, and I wanted to be here to see it."

"You might!"

"No, my dear. The fact is, I'm dying."

Fighting down panic for this woman who had been a kind of mother to me, I asked, "Is that what your doctor says? I'd like to speak to him."

"I'd rather you just sit with me, Frances."

So I sat. We reminisced about the old days at the Consumers' League. We talked about her frustrations that so many of the battles she'd fought remained unwon. "We still have child labor," she said with a cough. "We still have so much poverty. I've done as much as I could. But now if I'm to leave any legacy at all, I must count on you to carry on the fight without me. Fortunately, you've never failed me. Not even once."

I held her hand, and she gripped mine in return with expectations that I'd struggle the rest of my life to meet.

Florence Kelley died at the age of seventy-two. The papers ran headlines that said she'd been the country's first woman factory inspector. Such a small epitaph for the passing of a giant. It was a profound loss to the country. It was also a profound loss to me. And my voice quavered when I spoke at her memorial service. "There are many women in this audience whose first knowledge of Florence Kelley was when she didn't find it too much trouble to journey in the dead of night to a small New England town where a little handful of college girls studied economic sociology."

I could only put it that way—as if I were speaking about other women—as I told them how she'd taken me, formless in aspiration, and molded me into a woman with definite purpose.

After the funeral, Mary Rumsey insisted on taking me home in her private car. "I'm so sorry, Frances; you look heartbroken."

"I can't talk about it anymore, for it will make me too sad. Can you distract me with frivolous talk?"

"Frivolous talk? I have a talent for that. Shall it be horses, romance, or politics?"

Staring out the window, I said, "You choose."

"How about a little of all three? You know, you're eventually going to have to decide between the men in your life and choose a racehorse to ride to victory. If you continue to flirt with them this way, people will think you're a floozy."

I stiffened, worrying that some vile rumor was passing around regarding my marital fidelity—as it seemed such rumors often attached themselves to women who did unconventional work. "What men?"

"Al Smith and Franklin Roosevelt, of course. They're both running for president—it's obvious to anyone who has eyes—and each will expect your support."

"I couldn't possibly choose," I said, even though, intellectually, it would be an easy choice. Al had already run and lost. The party wanted to win, and Roosevelt was a winner.

Still . . .

Miserably, I said, "The first vote I ever cast was for Al Smith. It still makes me sentimental to think about."

"We all have first loves," Mary said. "But I think you've found your political soulmate with FDR. You *love* working with him."

"I loved working with Al Smith too."

"But did he give you a free hand?" she asked. "Did he let you write his speeches?"

I bit my lip because she already knew the answer to those questions. "I just enjoy the way Roosevelt boils things down to their simplest form. And that he has such preternatural political instincts . . ." Still, I *loved* Al Smith, and I hated to be disloyal. "Well, I won't go to the convention. I'll throw my support behind the nominee, whoever he is. Let the delegates choose."

"Nobody will let you get away with that," Mary said. "Your political paramours are on a collision course, and you cannot put off a choice forever."

Mary's words were, unfortunately, prophetic. For, not long after, Mrs. Moskowitz cornered me to demand that I support Al Smith's fourth bid for the presidential nomination.

"For God's sake, Belle," I sputtered. "Don't let him run."

She narrowed her eyes. "*Et tu*, Frances?"

"I'm saying this for his own good as well as everyone else's. You'd split the Democratic party wide open if you tried to run him again. It'll be unsuccessful. It'll be ruinous to Al. You know he's a man who wears his heart on his sleeve."

Snottily, Belle replied, "You've made your choice, then."

I suppose I had. After all, I'd learned the practical political lessons Al Smith had taught me quite well. "Franklin Roosevelt can *win*."

"From a wheelchair?" Belle sneered. "He can't even limp over the finish line."

That was absolutely the last straw, and I felt my teeth grind. "Oh, Belle, what you don't know is that he'd *crawl* over it, dragging his legs behind him if need be. A year from now, we'll be swearing in a new president—if the nation survives that long—and that will be Franklin Roosevelt."

With that, I walked out.

In fact, I stormed out.

Then I went directly to a telegraph station to send FDR a wire that read, "THIS DAY NEXT YEAR WILL BE INTERESTING."

To which he replied, "I APPROVE YOUR FAITH."

Chapter Forty-Four

New York City
Spring 1932

*T*IME MAGAZINE THOUGHT FDR WASN'T physically fit to serve as president, but Eleanor quipped, "If the infantile paralysis didn't kill him, the presidency won't."

In some ways, this idea that he was too fragile to run played right into FDR's now very strong hands. He'd been doing laps in the pool to build up the muscles of his arms; he'd learned new tricks to balance and stay upright on his braces. Even more impressively, he had the supreme capacity to *hide pain*.

Even if he were in agony, you'd never know it until the cameras were gone or he was out of view. Fortunately, for him, campaigning was the best painkiller. He'd always enjoyed the adulation of a crowd, but it was different now. Campaigning at his side, I saw that it brought him *joy* to be out among people.

And he had a new appreciation for the woman voter too. Just to get my dander up, he'd say, "Frances, we need to make issues simple enough for a woman to understand." Then he'd wink. "Because once women understand it, the men will finally be able to understand it too."

He often sent me ahead of him on the campaign trail as a warm-up act. And one hot sultry night, someone whispered to me at the back of the hall where I was fanning myself, "The governor is running late. Keep the crowd going until he arrives."

I don't remember all I said onstage that night, but I do remember improvising the line, "What the people of the United States want is *security*—security of life, security of opportunity to earn a living, security to plan their lives."

The wild thrilled applause to that line nearly knocked me on my heels. And it didn't stop. I tried to keep speaking but kept getting interrupted by cheering. I'd hit a vein of something in the body politic.

It seemed that I wasn't the only one tired of a thousand little fixes for a larger problem. People were ready for a *big* change. Social insurance could give us the security we needed—not just as individuals, but as a nation—to prosper. I just had to convince Roosevelt of it.

"Do you regret it?" Paul sometimes asked. "Choosing Roosevelt over Smith?"

"Never," I said, for if I had pangs of conscience, they were all destroyed by a speech Al Smith made at the annual Jefferson dinner denouncing FDR. There, he had said,

I will take off my coat and fight to the end against any candidate who persists in any demagogic appeal to the masses of the working people of this country to destroy themselves by setting rich against poor.

He was denouncing us as if we were Bolsheviks. He was denouncing us for pursuing the very policies we'd begun while *he* was in power. I certainly didn't remember any talk about setting the poor against the rich while Al Smith and I were climbing around on fire escapes. But it seemed to me that the once Happy Warrior was now a bitter one, and that made me even more certain of my choice.

MY DOORMAN WAS quarreling with a belligerent reporter who wanted me to comment on Hoover's latest numbers. I had plenty to say that summer, but not to *this* newsman, who had recently violated my express request not to write about my daughter, even going so far as to include the address of her school.

This had agitated Paul beyond reason because there'd been a rash of kidnapping cases—most recently, the abduction and murder of Charles Lindbergh's little boy. Well, now I gave that reporter a piece of my mind, half hoping that Paul would hear us and unleash the dog, as that was no longer an idle threat.

It was otherwise a lovely afternoon; Susanna was spending the day with friends at Coney Island—she'd promised to stay off the rickety thrill rides and stick with sipping sarsaparilla and eating ten-cent hot dogs on the boardwalk. And since we'd have a day alone, Paul and I planned to go to a matinee, just the two of us, for a movie starring Greta Garbo, Joan Crawford, and John Barrymore.

I was relieved when Paul was waiting for me in the foyer with a wide smile. "I have the solution," he said.

I stooped to pet Balto, who gave me a slobbery kiss. "What solution?"

"The solution to the economic depression," Paul said, leading me to his desk, where old actuarial tables were spread out like a fan. "The solution to wiping out poverty in America."

"Well, you certainly have my attention. What's this about?"

"I'm getting to that, but first there's something I must tell you, Frances." He sat, took my hands, pulled them between his knees, and stared earnestly into my eyes. "It's a secret that's been weighing on me for years."

I swallowed nervously. "Oh, dear, this sounds serious . . ."

"I'm afraid it is. In fact, keeping this secret from you has been the cause of many dark moods. I can't tell you what a relief it will be to finally explain myself."

As he was saying that, his hands trembled a little, and I squeezed them in encouragement, even if I dreaded what he might confess.

Paul cleared his throat. "Do you remember when I took a job

with the War Shipping Board? Well, I was never entirely honest with you about my work during the Great War. I couldn't be. It was very secret."

My eyes widened. It should've occurred to me that the government would want my husband's mathematical mind for something vital. "I had no idea. Were you a code breaker?"

"You're not far off," Paul said. "My work involved looking for patterns and predicting outcomes."

I nodded, trying to understand.

"Just the way insurance companies study patterns in behavior," he explained. "We do it to predict how long someone might live in order to decide what their premiums should be."

I nodded again. "What does this have to do—"

"*Probabilities*, my dear . . ." With that, he let go of my hands, gathered up the papers on his desk, and held them against his chest with the tenderness of a father toward a newborn babe. "An economic depression can be predicted, Frances. This one should've been. Certain events make the likelihood of other events more probable. Which means we can predict when this starvation and suffering will finally end—and hasten that outcome."

I inched closer, fascinated. *"Really?"*

His eyes lit with more excitement than I'd seen in years. "I discovered the algorithm years ago, during the war. Unfortunately, I couldn't prove its application until now."

Paul put the papers back down on his desk, spread them out again, and beckoned me into his lap so we could both look at them. "Here, let's do the math together."

I saw that he'd scribbled formulas all over the actuarial tables. I started to process them . . . then I stopped. I stared at all these numbers and equations with a slow dawning horror even as Paul's excitement positively thrummed through him; I could feel his racing pulse against my back. "Do you see, Frances? First, the market crash, 1929. September 1929. That is 91929. Add that together, and what do you get?"

My hands went to my mouth, hoping this was an elaborate prank. I shot out of his lap to look at him, but he didn't crack a smile. He was entirely earnest. He sensed my distress but mistook its origin. "Oh ye of little faith, Frances. Don't worry. It's not as simple as adding numbers. You must run them through a very complicated equation. Do you see here?"

Taking a pencil, he circled a blank space on the page. *A blank space.* Then he circled it more emphatically.

He was circling nothing.

Nothing was there.

"Oh, Paul . . ." I trailed off, not knowing what else to say. "We'd better call the doctor."

"I don't need a doctor! I feel better than I've felt in years. I've finally made good on my promise as a public servant. This formula will save the country from economic ruin."

Dear God, he really believed what he was saying. Gently, I tried to bring him back to reality. "Paul, this doesn't make sense."

"It will. Give it time. I've been working on this algorithm for more than a decade, whereas you've only seen it today for the first time. It's going to take a few days for it to make sense to you, but I have complete faith that my brilliant wife will soon grasp it."

With that, he kissed the top of my head. Then he pulled another chair out for me. "Here, just sit and study it while I break out some bootleg champagne to celebrate."

I stood there dazed, horrified—my limbs so heavy that it took real effort to reach for his arm. I didn't know what to do. All I knew was that whatever was wrong with my husband liquor would only make worse. "Darling, I don't want champagne just now, and surely you shouldn't drink either."

Paul insisted, "It's a special occasion! We ought to celebrate. Please don't be jealous, my darling. I won't claim the credit; I couldn't have done it without you. This discovery belongs to both of us, and you're welcome to all the public applause. Just let us have a little private celebratory toast."

He was all charm. How badly I wished to be swept up into his beautiful delusion. So badly that I was tempted to sit and study the pages on his desk to be *sure* there really wasn't something there. Instead, I said more firmly, "You know you cannot drink, Paul. Not with your condition."

The charm evaporated. "I don't appreciate when you treat me like a child."

"Do you think I appreciate playing the role of your mother?"

"Don't you?" Paul popped the cork and began to pour. "Sometimes I think it's the only reason you married me. To become a mother. You do *love* telling people what to do."

I pinched the bridge of my nose, trying not to rise to this bait, as he continued, "You can't stop yourself with Susie. You scold, and instruct, and inspect, always looking for violations. Never realizing that she hides her tears from you."

My heart clenched. Was that true?

My husband and I had quarreled many times before, as married couples often do. Maybe we quarreled more than most, and sometimes the subject of our quarrels was our daughter. But we'd never tried to be hurtful to one another, and it seemed he was trying to hurt me now.

This isn't Paul, I told myself as he continued to berate me with a very long litany of my faults. Everything from my inability to cook to my lack of warmth. Finally, I broke in to say, "I'll try to be better . . . I'm sure I could use improvement . . . but at the moment—"

Paul threw his glass into the wall across the room, and I jumped at the crash as glass scattered onto the floor.

Balto came running, barking and growling as if he suspected an intruder. And I stood paralyzed, having never seen my husband do such a wild and uncivilized thing before.

Truthfully, Paul seemed rather surprised to have done it too. As he silently stared at the evidence of his own violent temper, I finally found my voice. "What would Susanna think to see you behave like this?"

At that question, Paul turned on his heel, crunching over the glass and slamming into his bedroom, leaving me to clean up the broken mess.

I BROKE THE news to Governor Roosevelt over the telephone. "I simply *cannot* go to the Democratic convention in Chicago for you this summer."

Roosevelt must've heard the strain in my voice, because he didn't even attempt his usual congenial banter. "What's the matter, Frances? This isn't about Al, is it? I know you must feel torn, but—"

"It's my husband. He's . . ." *He's had a psychotic break*, the physician had explained. An explanation I couldn't bear to repeat. "Paul is feeling poorly. Very poorly indeed."

I prayed FDR would not press me for the humiliating details. Details that included my having had to pretend the visiting physician was an official from the Navy sent to confirm Paul's great algorithmic discovery.

Thankfully, FDR was a man who knew, all too well, the indignities of illness. He simply said, "Well, tell Paul I wish him well. Don't worry about Chicago. The best political service you can do for me is to remain a dependable social scientist, and keep Hoover on the run."

Thus, while the great political drama played out in Chicago, a much more tragic battle played itself out in my private life. When it became clear that Paul's break with reality wasn't resolving itself, I asked the physician, "What is the latest treatment?"

"Your husband must be committed to an asylum. Against his will, if need be."

I hugged myself against a shudder, knowing the conditions of most sanitariums to be barbaric. Even if I could get him into one of the better facilities, how could I have my husband carted away like a criminal and locked away? I couldn't possibly. "Surely there is some course of treatment we can provide him at home."

"Mrs. Wilson, I wish I didn't have to tell you this, but with manic-depressive insanity, this is the inevitable progress of his ailment. Many patients in your husband's state have less innocuous delusions. Some become violent."

"Paul would never hurt anyone," I insisted.

"Even so, he may become a grave danger to himself. Some in his condition believe they're angels and try to prove it by stepping in front of oncoming trains."

I turned to the window, fighting back despair, only to have that despair compounded by the sight of a breadline on the street below. "For the moment, at least, Paul's delusions *are* innocuous, aren't they?"

"Yes," the physician agreed. "At least until the manic euphoria wears off. Then he'll plunge into depression."

Depression. How I hated that word! "He's come back from it before."

"Mrs. Wilson, maybe he will come back from it again, but in the meantime, your husband will likely get worse than you've ever seen him before."

Well, I'd just have to take that risk. We had, after all, lived an intermittently normal life since Paul was first hospitalized more than a decade earlier. I'd just find a way to *manage*. I always did.

"WHY DOES DADDY need a secretary?" Susanna asked suspiciously.

"Your father is working on something important and needs help with research." That was the story I'd concocted for Paul to make him accept the help of the nurse I'd hired to watch after him during the day. I hoped Susanna might be fooled by it, too, but that was a vain hope.

Susanna arched a perfectly groomed brow, piercing my attempt to deceive her. She was a teenager now, too old to believe in fairy tales. I'd have to be forthright. "All right, darling. I didn't want to worry you, but your father isn't making sense. The doctor thinks it best that he has a companion look after him."

Susanna arched her other brow. "What if Daddy doesn't want a minder?"

"That doesn't change the reality that he needs one. It's time that we, and everyone else in this country, stop hoping bad things will just get better on their own . . ."

Chapter Forty-Five

New York City
July 1932

ROOSEVELT WASN'T INEVITABLE; IT ONLY seems that way now. Al Smith still had tremendous influence in the party, and he pulled out all the stops to win the nomination. I listened to the balloting on the radio at the office, feeling grateful not to be in Chicago, where Al prevailed upon all his old friends to abandon Roosevelt.

I wouldn't have switched sides, but many did. And in the end, Roosevelt had to break a deadlocked convention by getting the Texas and California delegations to throw him their votes.

I didn't want to know what he'd promised them. It was a narrow win, a very narrow thing indeed. But *Roosevelt* emerged victorious, and my heart soared!

To cement the nomination, FDR flew out to Chicago to give an acceptance speech, which was against all custom. But it was *exciting*, in keeping with the urgency of the moment, and it showed courage, for planes were a rather new technology and still considered quite dangerous.

There in Chicago, as the Democratic nominee for the presidency, he said, "I pledge you, I pledge myself, to a New Deal for the American people."

It was a call to arms. And I felt called.

But I feared that sometime soon Roosevelt would have to battle on without me, because my husband's condition was becoming the fight of my life.

AT HOME, PAUL was sometimes lucid, sometimes not. It was all I could do to shield my daughter from the worst of it. Nevertheless, I had a job to do if I meant to keep my family off the street.

That autumn, I went to Albany to meet with FDR in the informal theater where he liked to take the elevator up to the third floor of the Executive Mansion to watch movies.

He was reading headlines about how Hoover was burning unemployed war veterans out of their ramshackle shelters in the nation's capital. "Appalling," Roosevelt said, for the Army had drawn sabers and fired guns, shooting two veterans dead.

I honestly believe FDR wasn't just upset about it because Hoover was now the only man standing between him and the presidency; he was genuinely *shaken* by the photos. "These are scenes from a nightmare. These veterans fought for their country, and now they're out of work with nowhere else to go, and they're being shot at by their own government. It's a wonder there isn't more resentment and radicalism when people are treated this way."

"What would you have done in his place?" I asked, genuinely curious.

"Well, to begin with, I'd have met with them and sent out sandwiches and coffee. It's the decent thing to do."

Noticing that his advisors had ducked out, leaving us alone together, FDR leaned toward me to discreetly ask, "How is Paul, by the way?"

"That's too long a story for tonight."

"Doing that well, is he? Well, then how are *you*, Frances?"

If I answered that honestly, I might very well unravel at the seams, so I said, "I am just fine."

FDR gave me a sidelong glance. "Yes, I, too, am always just fine."

"It's your good New England Delano blood."

Now his eyes softened in sympathy. "We understand each other, Frances."

I nodded. "Yes. Yes, I think we do."

Then the sympathy melted to mischief. "Going all the way back to our battle for the fifty-four-hour bill. Which I voted for."

"Will you *stop*?" I said with unexpected laughter, just when I thought I couldn't laugh anymore . . .

ON A CRISP autumn afternoon, with the presidential campaign in full swing, I received a call from my husband's nurse. "I'm so sorry, Mrs. Wilson. But I couldn't stop your husband from leaving the house. He's too strong—he pushed past me and out the door—and now I don't know where he is. I've looked everywhere, and he's been gone for hours."

For days now, Paul had been lethargic and quiet. The *tells* of his depression. I'm ashamed to say his low mood had come as nearly a relief after the wild manic delusions; he tended to grow thin and listless in a slump, but he was far more manageable. Or at least I had thought so.

Now he'd gone missing. "What did Mr. Wilson say before he went?"

"He said reporters were following you and Miss Susanna, and the only way to protect you was for him to leave."

This was a new escalation. *Where in the world might Paul go?* I hadn't the faintest idea. We searched Central Park until dark. Then I spent a sleepless night calling old friends Paul might have gone to visit, waking them up from their beds, pleading with them for discretion.

I even had Mary Rumsey go check our old cottage by the sea. Then, first thing in the morning, I went to Paul's place of employment at the insurance company, from which he'd taken temporary leave.

When he wasn't there, on a whim, I decided to try city hall. And that's where I found my husband sitting on the curb.

As I approached, he simply lifted his still-handsome face from his hands.

"Paul," I said softly. "You know you don't work here anymore, don't you?"

"I'm just here to think." He pointed to a spot just behind me, where a would-be assassin had aimed his gun at Mayor Mitchel all those years ago. "I was almost shot there. I *should've* been shot that day. It would've been better for everyone."

"No, my darling," I said, trying to lift him to his feet before city employees began to arrive. "Why don't we go home?"

"That would put you and Susie in danger. They're after me, Frances."

"Who is after you?"

"The Germans," he said, as if it should be perfectly obvious.

Did he think it was still wartime? Maybe that made a certain kind of sense. Even the run-up to war had been a dangerous time in New York, with explosions in the harbor and desperate people out of work, all while he needed to tend a bedbound wife with a high-risk pregnancy. It was the time in Paul's life that he'd felt the most pressure bearing down upon him.

I hadn't even understood the full extent of it, and I began to wonder if such times could leave wounds on the psyche. "They want my algorithm," Paul now groaned. "I can't let them have it, so I destroyed all the notes."

I played along to get him up off the pavement. "Then it's perfectly safe. I'm sure you destroyed every scrap."

His expression crumpled, and he made a keening sound, holding both sides of his head. "But it's in here, Frances. Don't you see? It's in my *head*, and if they catch me, they'll extract it. So, there's still one last thing I have to destroy . . ."

I'll never forget the pain in his voice, so sharp that I felt cut by it. I lowered myself down to sit beside him, and that's when he showed me what he had in his pocket. *Pills.* I didn't know how he got them but felt certain they were enough to kill him if he swallowed them.

I wanted to shake him, but how can you look into the eyes of someone you love, see all that agony, and not want to comfort? "Paul, you mustn't even speak of harming yourself."

"I must protect you. I must protect *everyone*. Only when I'm gone will the secret be safe."

His mind had cunningly contorted itself to convince him suicide would be a selfless, heroic act. And at last, I knew that he was too twisted up now for anything I said to reach him. I couldn't reason with him. I couldn't plead with him, as I used to do, to let our love keep him alive. And I will not recount, or even force myself to remember, all the details of the terrible day I committed my husband to the sanitarium.

This isn't Paul, I said when he accused me of being his jailer.

This isn't Paul, I said of the seething, silent stranger he became.

This isn't Paul, I said when he accused me of being an impersonator, demanding to know what I had done with his *real* wife.

Some part of me wanted to know what he had done with my real husband. I had pity for the poor creature who inhabited him, but my husband seemed to be well and truly gone. And I didn't know when, or if, I'd ever get him back . . .

In the meantime, all I knew is that I'd have to be both mother and father to Susanna. We two would have to build our lives over. I'd have to make sure she was happy in her school, that our home was steady and calm. And I was going to have to find some way to pay for the outrageous expense of my husband's institutionalization.

Others relied on family in times of crisis. I couldn't. My mother and father were gone. Paul's parents too. I had only a sister in Massachusetts with whom I had never been close. Susanna and I would have to rely upon our network of friends here in New York.

Thankfully, I had some very good friends indeed. Some of whom gave generously to keep us afloat. Mary Rumsey insisted upon paying some of my bills, even as I insisted it must be a loan. She also brought a bouquet of flowers to brighten the now seemingly empty house.

Seeing me and Balto curled up miserably in my husband's old armchair, which smelled comfortingly like Paul's pipe smoke, she said, "I know what it's like to mourn a husband, Frances. Paul isn't *gone*, precisely, but you still have a right to mourn. Just don't let Paul's illness corrupt the loving memories that you'll need to sustain you now."

"I'm not mourning," I told her. I wanted to hold on to hope, after all. But I knew that even if Paul got well again, I could never, *ever* rely on it again. Not for the rest of my life.

Mary's words echoed in my mind when I next visited the sanitarium and found a heavily sedated shell of a man who could not open his eyes. I sat beside Paul in wifely devotion, finally allowing myself to grieve the loss of a man I loved. I'd denied it; I'd been angry about it; I'd even tried to bargain with God. Now, in reluctant acceptance, I held my husband in my arms, stroking his hair, and composing a poem I knew he would never read.

Thank you for the years of grace, dear soul, thank you for the days of peace and thank you for the hours of bliss no longer mine.

I always knew that these must end, their span brief—I was not born to constant happiness, and if my heart is wrenched, my spirit low, now that these are gone, I thank you nonetheless that I have known the touch of love, the days of comradeship—the moment, oh so brief, when I was not alone.

And if the pattern of my life is loneliness, then all the more I sing in joy to know the days of comradeship, and by the glow of those beloved days I will warm my heart for all the rest of my long life.

Chapter Forty-Six

Dear Franklin,

I send this Christmas card and incline to prayer when I think of all that the humble and lonely and hurt of this land are expecting of you. Joy in the homes and the laughter of courage hope and happiness on the lips of the working millions is the vision. And you dear friend are perhaps the tool to be used for God's purpose.

- Frances

Franklin Delano Roosevelt had been elected to be the next president of the United States. And he won on the strength of our work together here in New York State. I was so terribly proud, even though, given the sad state of my family, I'd drawn inward.

Oh, I was present at the Biltmore's grand ballroom on election night as streamers fell from the ceiling and hundreds of jubilant Democrats went wild to the tune of "Happy Days Are Here Again." And later, I'd taken the train out to Hyde Park for the late-night celebration.

I felt as if I had to go.

That I had to be there for FDR.

After all, I could still remember the man he used to be—the snooty, unimpressive lawyer who got by on money and good looks—but these political handicaps had long since been washed out of him by the cruelties of life. He'd been faced with his own mortality and forced to reckon with the immense privileges he'd taken for granted. He'd had to learn to swallow his pride and accept help from others, which made him want to help them in return.

Now the American people had chosen Franklin Roosevelt to lead them out of this horrific time. But given the depths of the economic depression, was it even possible that our nation would recover?

I wasn't even sure that *I* would recover. I was still consumed with the depression that had robbed me of my husband. Sometimes, at night, I wandered the house, touching Paul's things, catching glimpses of him as if he were a ghost. There he was rummaging in the closet for his tennis racket. There he was in the kitchen, over the coffeepot where he'd made his special brew. There he was in the armchair, reading, blowing the occasional ring of smoke from his pipe.

I tried to brush it off, as always. Get back up, dust yourself off, start again. I went to church and prayed. I went to work. I ate my meals, juggled my bills, and kept a stiff upper lip for my daughter. Only my loyal little dog knew that I curled up in bed at night with one of Paul's old sweaters, feeling as if absolutely *everything* in my world were coming to an end . . .

At a farewell dinner party for the outgoing governor, Roosevelt managed to steal a quiet moment with me. "It was an awfully nice letter of Christmas greetings you sent me. Did you mean it?"

"Of course I did. And I am praying for you."

"Good, because I'm going to need all the help I can get."

He told me that a friend said if he succeeded at battling the economic crisis, he'd go down as one of the greatest American presidents in history, but if he failed, he'd go down as one of the worst. FDR had snorted and replied, "No. If I fail, I'll be the last."

I agreed with him, and at the enormity of the stakes, both of us sucked in a breath.

Then Roosevelt gave me a tender smile. "Well, this is my final day as governor of the state, so please let me take the opportunity of telling you how grateful I am for the fine work you have done these four years. I know of the difficulties you've met, and the fine way in which you've handled them, and always with your mind set on doing the most good for the greatest number. I know you, too, must have a tremendous feeling of satisfaction at what you have accomplished."

He was thanking me, and I quite nearly teared up. In fact, I had to wave him away with my gloves to keep my emotions under control, or I might've tried to hug him in farewell. I *did* feel a tremendous satisfaction at what we'd done together, even though I wished we could've done so much more. Swallowing down the lump in my throat, I said, "I assure you that it has all, every moment of it, been my very great honor."

I wished to say more, of course. To give him a fond parting line, an echo of words I had spoken to him a decade before. *Good luck in Washington, Mr. Roosevelt. I wish you success.*

But now that he was the president-elect, a flock of people descended upon him for his attention, and I was obliged to fade into wallpaper before I had the chance to say a proper goodbye. I'd let myself be edged out of the inner circle, which was only natural, of course. I was only a state official; in a presidential campaign, there were far more expert persons required, and of course all of them were men.

The financiers wanted their say too. Including Bernard Baruch, the Lone Wolf of Wall Street, who recommended that FDR let the gregarious General "Iron Pants" Hugh Johnson pen his economic speeches for him.

Did I feel a pang at having helped launch FDR into the White House only to be left behind? If I did, that pang was swiftly replaced by the realities of federal politics and of my personal situation. I needed my nice steady job here in New York. I needed to duck my head from public view, make a paycheck, and create some semblance of stability for my daughter, who still sobbed some nights over her father, saying that maybe the doctors made a mistake. Other days she cherished the notion that he'd get better soon, and she wanted to make sure that the house was ready for him.

Because I wanted to believe it, too, I indulged her in this. "Your father *will* need everything to be very comfortable and orderly when he returns."

So together my daughter and I rang in the New Year by tidying up the apartment, and rearranging the furniture, and otherwise making our lives as calm and pleasant as possible. I helped Susanna with her studies at school and filled our free days with church services and book club discussions.

I also defended our privacy with zeal.

Unfortunately, I had become a very public person. But even at the height of sparring with President Hoover, I hadn't received as much press attention as I suddenly got now.

In the summer before Paul's break with reality, my name had been floated in the newspaper as a possibility for the cabinet if Roosevelt were to win the election. But of course, that was idle speculation, and a lifetime ago . . .

Nevertheless, trying to guess whom President-Elect Roosevelt might appoint was one of the newspapermen's favorite games, and I became the subject of press speculation.

Reporters were following me in packs. One of them even cornered me at a fruit stand, thrusting himself between me and the pomegranates. "Miss Perkins, I presume?"

"You do," I said coolly.

"I'm very sorry, but you know publicity is one of the evils one has to stand when one is a celebrity."

A celebrity! That was the very last thing I wanted to be. I

managed to keep my composure when a camera was thrust in my face there on the public street, but I nearly panicked returning home to find reporters loitering in the lobby of my apartment building, sniffing about my mail.

Would they find a bill from the sanitarium, or one of the letters from Paul insisting that he felt perfectly fine? Oh, how I *dreaded* for it to become public knowledge that I'd locked my suffering husband in an institution. It made me feel hunted and very short of temper.

The next day, on the way to one meeting, coming straight from another, I ran into one of the Goldmark sisters at the Cosmopolitan Club. "Frances, these little items in the newspaper are the most exciting thing in the world!"

I should've simply replied that it was flattering. But, at my wit's end, I burst forth with, "I'm not going to be in Roosevelt's cabinet. Please stop talking about it. Stop thinking about it. It's just something that you, as a Consumers' League person, think would be wonderful, but it wouldn't. It hasn't been offered, and I don't believe it will be offered. Even if it were, I couldn't do it. It just isn't possible."

Well, I felt just terrible afterward. I had to send flowers as an apology. And I decided that I had better put an end to the speculation before the reporters hounded me into an asylum next to Paul.

At the risk of being presumptuous, I wrote FDR, saying I hoped he wasn't considering appointing me. I explained that my personal issues would impair my usefulness to him, and that in any case, someone else would be better for the United States of America.

And do you know what that man wrote back?

Just one line.

Have considered your advice and don't agree.

PART II

Chapter Forty-Seven

New York City
February 1933

I LEFT FDR'S HOUSE IN A STUPOR AROUND NINE o'clock in the evening, blinded by snow and his offer to make me the first woman in American history to serve in a presidential cabinet.

I'd tried to decline, only for him to say, *I consider that you have a duty to say yes.*

But was it true?

To sort my thoughts, my New England constitution required a walk in brisk weather, and I found myself, almost as if by instinct, in Central Park, where my family and I had laughingly pelted one another with snowballs in happier times.

Now the old drained-out reservoir was a blight of dirt and ramshackle shelters for desperately poor people, the stink of sweat, urine, and worse heavy in the air. I kept a pocketful of quarters for beggars and gave some away to a shivering homeless woman with two ragamuffins at the knee. "Thank you," she said with a Southern drawl, trying to wipe her dirtied hands onto her knitted scarf as if she weren't worthy to take something from a woman like me, in gloves, pearls, and a fur-trimmed coat.

"There ain't no running water here," she said apologetically. "Only so much you can do to keep clean using buckets of melted snow."

She told me she once had a house with an Armstrong Perc-O-Toaster in the kitchen where she served breakfast on her grandmother's gold-rimmed china, and an RCA radio in the living room where her husband listened to baseball games. But that was before the bank collapsed and her husband abandoned her, taking what little remained of their life savings. Stories like hers were distressingly common. And if it wasn't the banks, it was the drought. Families who'd worked farms for generations were seeing their lands dry up and swallow their futures whole.

As I walked through the park, I gave the rest of my quarters to a pair of gaunt old women wearing once-fashionable hats who had been pawing through garbage cans for a bite to eat. They reminded me of my mother and my grandmother. Women who lived good, respectable lives, who might have, but for a twist of fate, been forced to scavenge through rotting fruit to survive.

It was an utter indictment of this country.

The economy was now on the ragged edge of nothing, the spiral downward and accelerating. Something had to be done, but was I the person to do it? The troubles we faced were the greatest the nation had *ever* faced, and it was pure hubris to think I was any match for them. I was scarcely a match for my own troubles.

Thinking of Paul in the sanitarium and my daughter's fragile peace at home, I found myself in church on my knees until my bishop finally said, "Miss Perkins, I'm afraid we must close the doors."

He'd let me stay far later than he ought to have, because I'd confided in him what I was praying on. Now, he smoothed his purple vestments as he slid into the bench beside me. "What if the nation were at war and faced with a crisis in which you could render service that no one else could render with the same measure of effectiveness?"

"It'd be a much easier decision," I admitted.

"Well, our present crisis is graver than war," he said, and I could not disagree. This economic depression was unlike any in our history, and it was the sort of fire from which the nation would either burn away or be born again from the flames.

The Lord makes nations rise and then fall, builds up some and abandons others. But did God choose the midwife when a great nation must be reborn—and if he did, must she answer the call?

The bishop smiled at me kindly as I stared up at the cross—a reminder of a sacrifice much greater than any I would ever be called upon to make. "Miss Perkins, God has fitted you by natural gifts and by experience for a service few others are competent to render. That service can mean great things for multitudes of distressed and bewildered people whom He wants helped. I really believe that it is God's own call. And if it is, you can't refuse."

MARY RUMSEY STOOD outside my bedroom door, trying to reassure Susanna. "Of course she isn't crying. Never, in more than twenty years, despite every possible calamity, have I known your mother to shed a tear. Frances Perkins does not cry."

On the other side of the door where I'd buried my tears in Balto's rust-colored fur, I now hurriedly dried my eyes to hide the evidence that proved her wrong.

"Frances?" Mary knocked sharply, and Balto barked in answer.

"I'm not feeling well." I sniffed into a kerchief, blowing my nose. "I've come down with a cold. It might be catching, so you'd best not come in." Mary came in anyway, and I smiled weakly, hoping she'd overlook my puffy eyes. "I'm perfectly fine. Just under the weather."

I was forced to bite my lower lip to keep it from trembling on that lie. And I wasn't sure it convinced her, or Susanna, who lingered in the doorway, asking, "Should I get you some tea?"

"Yes," I said. "Thank you. That would be nice. With honey and lemon. Make a big pot."

Susanna padded out to put the kettle on, and our tear-soaked dog reluctantly followed. Only when we were alone did Mary whirl upon me. "Now, what is the matter? Did you speak to Paul?"

"Yes." Not that Paul was in any mental state to give good advice, but I couldn't show him the disrespect of making such a monumental decision without talking to him about it. "Fortunately, he was having one of his good days. He worried he'd have to live in Washington but calmed when I told him if I accepted the job, he'd stay here in New York, and I'd visit every weekend just as he used to do during the war."

Mary blew out a relieved breath. "Then it's settled. Oh, Frances, we should be *celebrating*. What would Mrs. Kelley say if she were here right now and saw you so distressed?"

It was low for her to use the memory of Florence Kelley against me. Just the lowest of the low, for I could almost hear Mrs. Kelley's voice in my mind. *Glory be to God, Frances! How dare you even think you can say no?*

I missed my mentor, who had died believing I could carry on her work. But now I thought aloud, "I'd make a mess of it in federal government. I know who to trust in New York, but I haven't any idea how to *manage* in Washington."

Mary refused to accept that argument. "Miss Jay has agreed to go with you and continue as your secretary. She'll help you navigate things. Frances, if you don't take this appointment, it might be another hundred years before another woman is asked. You've been the first to do so many things so that other women could follow in your footsteps."

It was true that I'd broken many barriers, so I knew it could be done, and that after I'd done it, other women were asked to do things. If I said no, the door might close on other women, but was that reason enough to agree?

"I cannot go just to be a symbol for women. FDR will have a

cabinet full of national figures—powerful and accomplished men who will be vying for his attention—and they will edge me out."

"Oh, men have been trying to edge you out your entire life, and it hasn't worked yet."

"But, Mary," I said, fighting back renewed tears. "I've only now got Paul settled and my life even remotely manageable. I like my church, and my apartment. We have a good cook, a loyal dog, and everything is as nice as it can be. All my hopes left in life are right here. Where would I even live in Washington, without a husband, all by myself?"

Mary briefly narrowed her eyes, then her entire countenance brightened. "I'll go with you. Why not? I have business there with a new magazine venture. In fact, I'd like to buy a national newspaper, so why not live in the nation's capital? I'll find a place we can share. You won't have to do this alone, Frances."

That was a comfort, and even sounded somewhat appealing, but there were still more important things to worry about. "How can I tear Susanna out of her school, where she's doing so well?"

"Let her finish her schooling here in New York," Mary said. "You can have her stay with friends or find a full-time live-in governess. Keep the apartment and spend weekends with her."

"Oh, honestly, Mary, what an absurd arrangement that would be. How can I do the right thing by my daughter from a distance?"

"It's not as if you're shipping her to boarding school—which, I might add, plenty of very good parents do."

I rubbed at my throbbing temples. "Even if I could manage to hire someone to watch over her with a week's notice, it can't be right to leave a girl Susanna's age alone with servants all the time. All my daughter wants in the world is a *normal* mother, and—"

"Then she should've been born to someone else," Mary insisted. "Do you really want Susanna growing up to believe it's *normal* for women to play no part in the highest levels of their own government?"

"Of course not."

"Then look me in the eye and tell me the truth, Frances. Would a man—*any* man—consider turning this opportunity down?"

At that, I burst into tears again, and it was perfectly humiliating. I'd always known that if I let myself cry, I'd fall to pieces. Now here we were. "But I'm not a man," I sobbed.

Mary rubbed my back. "Please calm yourself, my darling friend. I'll help you with everything, Frances. It will all be fine. I promise."

"You can't promise that," I said, helplessly mopping at my eyes. Then came a whispered confession from the hidden depths of me. "I know how they'll treat the first woman cabinet member. I won't be taken as an individual. I'll be a lightning rod simply because I *am* a woman. If ever I do anything the least bit out of step—if I make some error of judgment about my political responsibilities—there will be a terrible public hysteria against me."

There it was. The shameful truth. I was *afraid* to take this job. Before now, I'd been able to call upon reserves of courage, but my tears were the manifestation of a fear I simply couldn't grapple with. Not merely a fear of failure. A fear of leaving behind a terrible legacy in my wake . . .

"Every mistake I make will be used to attack me for getting above my place as a woman. They'll blacken my name and sully all my good work. Why should I open myself up to that? Why should I do it?" I felt my fists ball up as I inhaled. "Well, I won't do it. I don't *have* to do it. I can still call him up."

Mary gave me a little shake. "You have to say yes. I'll murder you if you don't! Do you know what FDR would say if you called him and refused this appointment?"

Of course I did.

Don't be a baby, Frances, he'd say. *It'll be all right . . .*

Well, maybe FDR would be all right. The Roosevelts always were.

But *No good deed goes unpunished* might as well be my family motto. Still, we always did our duty in the end, didn't we?

All those years ago, when I'd so foolishly pleaded with God to make me his instrument, my grandmother said if somebody opens a door for you, if you're quite sure you haven't pulled wires or made arrangements to get that door opened, and if somebody just opens it for you unexpectedly without any connivance on your part, walk right in and do the best you can. For it means that it's the Lord's will . . .

But was this *really* the Lord's will?

I wished for some sort of sign, but I supposed I'd have to work it out myself. Having finally cried myself to exhaustion, I said, "All right. Let me compose myself, and I'll be out for tea."

In the bathroom, I splashed my face, pinched my cheeks, ran a comb through my graying hair, and otherwise put myself back together as best I could so as not to frighten my daughter any more than I'd already frightened her. By the time I finally emerged, the tea was lukewarm, and the dog was wagging his tail at the doorman, who had brought up the mail.

"Something odd came for you," Susanna said, puzzling over a book in a red bow. She set it down near me with a thump. "It came with a card."

I opened the card, which read, *On urgent loan from the senate library by request of Governor Roosevelt. Please return.*

This was bewildering.

What was that man up to now?

I pulled open the ribbon, which revealed a fat, dusty old senate journal. Pursing my lips in irritation, I began flipping pages, but none of them were marked. Then I noticed the year: nineteen twelve.

Oh, he was incorrigible.

I narrowed my eyes, found the right page, and smugly ran my finger down the roll call. Then I blinked with a sharp hyena laugh.

Susanna stared, and Mary asked, "What's so funny?"

In answer, I could do nothing but point at the page, and Mary leaned forward to scrutinize me as if she feared I'd cracked completely. Finally, I managed to get out the words between hiccups of laughter. "He voted for it."

"What on *earth* are you talking about?"

"FDR voted for my fifty-four-hour bill back in 1912!"

I don't know *how* he did it, but his vote was recorded in the affirmative. I know he slipped out of Albany before the roll call, but he must've had someone proxy for him to get his vote into the record once he knew which way the wind was blowing . . .

Which was just like him, really. A wily politician to the end. Well, whatever tricks he'd pulled, he'd stood with me all those years ago. Now I supposed I'd have to stand with him even if I didn't know how I was going to manage. Maybe I could serve a symbolic year and resign. If absolutely necessary, I could serve two. In the scheme of things, that wasn't so very long a time, was it?

Chapter Forty-Eight

Washington, DC
March 4, 1933

S USANNA AND I ARRIVED IN THE NATION'S capital to a scene of perfect bedlam. The outgoing Hoover administration was racing for the trains, while Roosevelt's people were flooding in. Meanwhile, the run on the banks caused financial institutions to collapse; people were literally fainting of hunger in the streets with checks they couldn't cash in their pockets.

A terrible fear gripped the whole country.

In the station, we were jostled in the panicked crush. And with every hotel in the city filled, I was lucky to get a room at the old Willard, which was so old-fashioned that Susanna mocked the ornate floral decor.

She'd enjoyed all the letters, gifts, cards, and congratulatory telegrams, but I don't think it had sunk in for her yet what a monumental change in our lives this was going to be. I told her that I didn't intend to keep the job long and that her life need not be much disrupted, but with every passing moment, I think we both realized this was a lie.

For the inauguration, Susanna dressed in something festive, while I wore an expertly tailored black outfit much more in keeping with the mournful mood. I felt almost as if we were going to a funeral as people filled the streets, grim and apprehensive.

It was nearly impossible to get a taxicab. And when we did, we had a terrible time getting through the traffic. Just blocks from the

Capitol building, we were stopped by police barriers, and Susanna asked, "Are we going to make it?"

I glanced at my watch and groaned. I could already imagine the headlines and attendant gossip if I was late to the inauguration:

Just like a dizzy dame to miss the big day—

—probably off somewhere powdering her nose—

How can we trust such a silly creature with the reins of government?

When FDR announced my appointment, he told the press, *You watch her. She's a brilliant person.*

But I didn't feel brilliant as I ducked under the ropes and broke into a sprint across the dewy lawn, dragging poor Susanna with me. By the time we found the entrance, sweat ran down my neck, my shoes were ruined, and the back of my dress was spattered with mud.

The band was playing "Hail to the Chief" as we searched for seats in the crush of important government officials, world-renowned diplomats, Supreme Court justices, and a quite sour-faced outgoing President Hoover.

Hoover didn't recognize me, and that was probably for the better. For the rest of his life, he'd refuse to shake hands whenever we crossed paths, because he remembered me as the woman who cost him his presidency. But that day, I was filled with unexpected sympathy for him. To leave the presidency under such a pall, with people in very great distress. Industry wasn't even operating. The farm situation was almost beyond description. We'd said that we could fix it, but what if we couldn't?

My hands shook, and I had to clench them to keep them still. Then out came FDR, in a silk top hat and sunny smile. I sucked in a breath, shocked to see him so ebullient on his son's arm. But Roosevelt stood on his own to take the oath of office, seeming to grow taller with each word. "I, Franklin Delano Roosevelt, do solemnly swear that I will faithfully execute the office of President of the

United States, and will, to the best of my ability, preserve, protect, and defend the Constitution of the United States, *so help me God.*"

It was spoken like a holy sacrament. Then Roosevelt was the president. My president.

After strained applause, he began his inaugural remarks. But it didn't sound like the draft of the speech I'd reviewed that morning. I happened to glance over at the speechwriter, who went pale, and I realized that FDR must have changed the speech first thing this morning when he heard about the banks and the dread that had taken hold of an already weary nation.

He's improvising, I thought worriedly. For that is how he sometimes got in trouble. But now, he boldly and confidently said, "*We have nothing to fear but fear itself.*"

With these words, he injected hope directly into our veins. Gasps erupted all around me, and a tingle of electricity passed through the crowd, setting my hair on end. As I swallowed back emotion, I saw people crying. The faces of hard-boiled men were suddenly soaked with tears as our new president encouraged us to remember that people who knew better than we did had built this country, and now we'd simply have to rebuild it.

For me personally, it was like a church revival. As if he'd looked right into my heart and asked, *Come now, do you believe in America?*

And to that unspoken question, I whispered, "I do."

LATER, AT THE White House, I felt dazed by the famous portraits and historic crystal chandeliers. I'd never been to the White House before, and now two military aides escorted me and Susanna to a little red room with a punch bowl filled with slices of frozen banana floating in pink lemonade. I was afraid to enter, protesting, "But it's roped off."

"Yes," the marine said. "For cabinet members only, madam."

He looked at me expectantly, and then it struck me anew that I was soon to be a member of the cabinet. It was, ostensibly, where I belonged. I didn't know how I was ever going to get used to it.

Given the crisis, President Roosevelt wanted us sworn in right away and on the job Monday morning. After the inaugural balls, he expected the next hundred days to be a flurry of activity. I hadn't been warned. I'd been told there'd be time to bring Susanna back to New York and get her situated. I hadn't even packed more than a suit, a plain black dress, and a sequined velvet dress for the inaugural balls.

Well, I'd just have to make do. And though I didn't know it yet, *making do* was about to become a way of life. I soon found myself standing in a circle with other appointees in the oval room with President Roosevelt and a black-robed justice.

"I hope you don't mind being sworn in on my old Dutch Bible," the president said to us. "You won't be able to read a word of it, but it's the holy scriptures, all right."

As the secretary of labor, I had the lowest rank by seniority in the cabinet, so I waited as the others swore first. Roosevelt had chosen some of the men for his cabinet to pacify business interests. Others, to pacify the party's various political wings. And it dawned on me for the first time that I wasn't simply the only woman in the cabinet—I might also be the only member of the cabinet that FDR counted as a *friend*.

When the Bible finally came to me, with my daughter looking on proudly, I lifted my hand, then glanced at the new president, keenly aware of the immense burden he was undertaking, a burden he had asked me to share.

I came to Washington to work for God, FDR, and the millions of forgotten, plain common working men, but not only for them. I came to rebuild this country, brick by brick, on a stronger foundation for all its citizens. To me, that meant some sort of *social security* for our people. But could it be done?

Now FDR smiled at me, and his eyes crinkled as if to ask, yet again, *Come now, Frances, do you believe?*

And my heart again answered, *I do.*

Chapter Forty-Nine

Washington, DC
March 6, 1933

WITH KISSES AND WAVES, I SENT MY daughter off in the custody of family friends to catch the early morning train back to New York so she wouldn't miss school. Then I hurriedly washed out my underthings in the hotel sink and toweled them dry so I'd have something clean to wear to work. Not that I knew how to start . . .

I didn't have any instructions from the president. In fact, I didn't even know where the Department of Labor building *was*. I'd awakened early, assuming someone would send a car, but before I could make inquiries, I was fielding a frantic telephone call from our housekeeper back in New York. "The dog got out and has run away."

Not now, Balto! Of all the times for my mischievous little dog to play tricks on us. If anything happened to that dog, I couldn't bear it, and it would devastate Susanna. "He was wearing his collar, wasn't he?" I decided to make a call to the local ASPCA—or at least have Miss Jay call for me while I finished getting dressed.

As it happens, I needn't have hurried.

By ten in the morning, Balto had been found and returned by a fireman, and I still hadn't heard a peep from the outgoing secretary of labor. Not even a courtesy call.

Unwilling to wait any longer, I opened a telephone book and called to let him know that I'd been sworn in, and that the president wished for me to start right away. "I hoped you might introduce me around the department," I said, and didn't give him an opportunity to refuse.

The Labor Department was presently housed on G Street, not far from the Treasury, and I was surprised to see that it wasn't a proper office at all, but rather an apartment building that had been taken over for government purposes during the war.

I bumbled about asking questions at the front desk until I found an elevator to the suite of rooms where I was to work until they finished construction of the new Labor Department building. I hoped they finished sooner rather than later, because *this* place was dark and dirty, with grimy windows, an old-fashioned spittoon, ash piled in ashtrays, and garbage pails that had gone too long without emptying.

It was also remarkably cluttered for an office that was soon to be vacated. Weren't they packing to go?

Then I remembered that no one expected me to start for another two weeks. Now my first order of business was getting rid of my predecessor. How to do this politely?

Once we'd exchanged pleasantries and he'd introduced me to the staff, I said, "Mr. Secretary, I presume you have a luncheon engagement. If it's all right by you, I'll tell the receptionist to pack your things while you're at lunch."

He looked as though he were going to drop dead with offense that I was evicting him, but off he went.

It was many hours before we had all the books, papers, and knick-knacks ready to be hauled away by truck, but only after the boxes were packed did I stand before the desk that was to be mine.

I traced the edge of the desk with my finger, noticing it was scratched and dented, with an unsightly water stain on the top. It would need to be sanded down, refinished, and polished to be presentable. But in the meantime, I'd just cover the stain with the vase of red roses that had been sent to me by my college friends, along with a nameplate.

FRANCES PERKINS, SECRETARY OF LABOR

It felt strange and surreal to see it engraved there. I felt entirely like an impostor. But this was now my title and calling, and so I would simply have to find a way to do the job anyway. After all, working people had to look to me, and only to me, to solve their problems. There wasn't anybody else in the government who was going to bother about them, or whose duty it was to bother about them.

Where to even start?

The thing I cared most about was implementing a revolutionary plan of social insurance, but Roosevelt still wasn't convinced. And there wasn't time to argue with him about it now anyway. First, I had to contend with a thousand different issues that fell under my purview, from public works projects, to labor disputes, to immigration.

Determined to get started, I rattled a drawer to fill it with pens and paper. It was stuck, and I had to yank hard to get it open. When I did, a creature jumped out at me. I leapt back, thinking it was a mouse, only to realize it was a cockroach, the largest I'd ever seen.

Well, that did it. It wasn't going to be enough to get Hoover's people to vacate the place; we'd have to *literally* sweep them out and scrub it down. I sent Miss Jay out for soap, water, ammonia, and roach paste, and then I personally set about driving the vermin out of my office. I pulled down drapes to be laundered. I took a wet rag and scrubbed dirt off the wall, all the while having a little laugh at myself.

Over the weekend, I'd been made to feel so important, being escorted to roped-off little rooms in the White House, dancing at inaugural balls, and being feted by well-wishers who now supposed me to be quite *a woman of influence.* But here I was on my very first day as secretary of labor, rolling up my sleeves and scrubbing every surface in my office with disinfectant.

"The kind of dirt that's been here, we'll never scrub out," Miss Jay sniffed. But together we washed the windows until they sparkled. Then we swept the floors to catch every crumb and scoured every surface until it was clean enough to eat off of.

I was feeling rather triumphant until we reached the outer office, where the elderly receptionist sat. His desk was absolutely crawling with roaches, and he explained that as a colored man, he had to eat his lunch at his desk every day because the department's cafeteria was "for whites only."

That was an injustice that was going to be remedied immediately if I had anything to say about it. Then I came to the terrifying realization that I had *everything* to say about it. This was my department, and I now answered only to the president himself . . .

Chapter Fifty

★ ★ ★

I ARRIVED EARLY FOR MY FIRST CABINET meeting—and when the gentlemen finally filed in, I made a conscious decision not to interrupt as the president went round the table. I wanted to take the measure of each man, and that was easier to do if I simply listened. So I remained silent, jotting notes.

The secretary of state, Cordell Hull, was a dignified, impeccably dressed Tennessean who sported a beautiful shock of white hair and a black ribbon hanging from his pince-nez glasses. Given the order of seniority, he'd always be first to speak.

As the lowest in seniority, I'd be last to speak, so it was some time before all eyes would turn my way.

I used that time to evaluate my colleagues and decide who might be an ally and who might try to edge me out or stymie my agenda.

Henry Wallace, the solidly Midwestern secretary of agriculture who performed his own experiments on corn, I counted as an ally. I wasn't so sure about the combative secretary of the interior, Harold Ickes, who occasionally cast an irritated glance my way. To appease men like Ickes, I treated the discussion as if I were observing a gentlemen's club, at which a woman's intrusion would be unwelcome. I wanted to give the impression of being a quiet, orderly woman who didn't buzz-buzz all the time. A serious woman who could be trusted.

I think FDR knew what I was up to, because when it was finally my turn to speak, he smiled at me conspiratorially, like an encouraging sibling goading me to jump into the pool for the first time. "Well, Miss Perkins, have you anything to say, anything to contribute? What *have* you been thinking about?"

I'm thinking about social insurance—a means by which we can give the American people lasting security, I thought. But it was best not to say anything radical in the first meeting. "We must tackle unemployment. People are rioting for food, and crime is rising because people need to survive; we need to give them something productive to do and put food in their bellies with a program of public works."

I could've elaborated, explaining the economic principle that when all else fails, the government is the spender of last resort, but I thought it best to keep it short and to the point. I never wanted to give these men an excuse to tune me out, and I sensed a few of them were relieved. Several even spoke in support of my priorities.

After the first cabinet meeting, we were met by a gaggle of reporters outside shouting questions. "Now, Miss Perkins, tell us what happened in the cabinet meeting."

Did they think I'd just fallen off a turnip truck? I might not know how Washington worked yet, but I wasn't about to share the inner workings of the president's cabinet.

"By the way, what do we call you?" another reporter asked.

"My name is Perkins."

"Yes, but how do we address you?"

"Miss Perkins."

"But we say *Mr. Secretary* to the secretary of state, and *Mr. Secretary* to the secretary of the interior. What do we say to the secretary of labor?"

"Miss Perkins is all right with me," I replied, but, sensing this wasn't going to work and noticing that the Speaker of the House happened to be here, I said, "Perhaps we should ask an expert on parliamentary procedure."

The Speaker of the House was a cartoonish creature—a patronizing, puffed-up know-it-all who intoned, "She will be addressed, hereafter, as Madam Secretary."

Madam Secretary.

There it was, spoken like a pronouncement from the heavens. It was the first time I heard the title. And I knew I must somehow embrace it as mine, even though it would give me more trouble than any other in my life.

NOW THAT I had a cockroach-free office, I needed to do something about the rest of the vermin in my department.

Section 24 was the nickname for agents working under a section of the immigration law that empowered the secretary of labor to deport people. A power that'd been sorely abused. New York policemen had long warned about Section 24 agents behaving like gangsters, roughing people up and raiding private homes and dance halls looking for immigrants to blackmail with threats of deportation if they didn't pay protection money. They'd even rounded up thousands of US citizens of Mexican descent and "repatriated" them across the border to "save jobs for white men."

These agents were thugs, plain and simple. Most of them owed their positions to nepotism rather than talent or skill. They had to go. But I was warned by a trusted informant inside the department that if I tried to get rid of them, they'd plant something on me.

Well, I was acquainted with dirty tricks from the rough-and-tumble world of New York politics, but I had naively hoped that I'd find more elevated characters in the nation's capital.

Now I asked, "Did they plant something on my predecessor?"

"They have *something* on him, and that's why he never could touch them no matter what they did."

Well, then I'd have to move quickly. There'd be no time to bring them up on charges, and because this squad was under the civil service, I couldn't just fire them on the spot. But I *could* eliminate the positions altogether, pleading a lack of funds, which was actually true because they'd already stolen all the money in their budget.

Thus, I abolished the whole Section 24 first thing the next morning in a lightning strike that caught the staff by surprise. Once I'd made the announcement, I didn't want to give anyone time to plead their case—and I had more pressing matters to deal with anyway.

For one thing, I had to figure out where I was going to live. I couldn't stay at the Willard; I knew what would be printed about that.

SECRETARY OF LABOR LIVES IN ORNATE LUXURY WHILE STARVING CITIZENS DISMANTLE THEIR HOMES FOR FIREWOOD

Fortunately, Mary found a place for us. "I've taken a house in Georgetown. And before you object, I assure you the house is handsome but modest, and affordable to boot."

Mary had not exaggerated . . . *much*. The brick-fronted row house on O Street found shade beneath mature trees, and the wrought iron gates and the little atrium opened upon exotic decor in the way of batik tapestries and a tropical mural. It was an elegant home, but not extravagant, so I agreed to move in.

With my living arrangements settled, I returned to work. It was nearly eight o'clock—long past office hours—a time I'd found was usually quiet enough for me to get things done without interruption. I smiled at the elevator guard, who was a nice enough fellow but old enough to have fought in the Spanish-American War with Theodore Roosevelt.

When we reached my floor, I heard voices overhead. "Who's still in the office?"

I had the notion that I'd go up and greet them and foster a sense of camaraderie with the hardest-working members of the department. But the guard said, "Oh, it's them fellows from Section 24."

He meant *them fellows* whose jobs I'd just eliminated, and, without thinking too much about it, I said, "Take me right up there."

As soon as I stepped off the elevator, I saw they were working, all right; there was no question about that. Just not for the United States government. The villains had peeled off their coats and rolled up their sleeves to rifle the files—no doubt for the names and addresses of people they'd shaken down for payment.

They were yanking papers out of files, reading them over, and sorting them into piles.

I'd caught them red-handed.

One actually gaped, astonished to see me. The rest turned to stare, and I realized just how outnumbered I was by armed former agents. "Please hold the elevator," I told the stout old guard. If violence erupted, I supposed he wouldn't be much help, but I didn't have anybody else on my side . . .

"What's going on here, gentlemen?" I asked, taking advantage of the element of surprise. "Your duties here have been terminated."

The ringleader was a quick-witted man who replied, "Yes, but the notice was so sudden we didn't have time to get our personal belongings."

Unfortunately for him, he wasn't quick-witted enough. "These files can't be personal," I said with a calmness I didn't feel. "They look like official files belonging to the United States government. Surely anything personal must be in your desks and not in the files."

"Well . . . they're scattered."

I wasn't falling for it. "You're not to take anything out of the files. I suggest you come tomorrow morning, and secretaries can assist you in getting anything that belongs to you. Now I think I'll have to ask you to leave the building."

The air thickened with tension, and several men glared, crossing their arms, knowing that I hadn't the physical power to drag them out against their will. They were probably calculating whether the old guard would be willing to draw his weapon on them before they could get rid of me.

LADY SECRETARY OF LABOR SHOT BY HER EMPLOYEES FIRST WEEK ON THE JOB

Wouldn't that make a delicious headline? I knew I couldn't show fear. Instead, I projected the most placid demeanor possible—that of a weary schoolteacher who has dealt with truant boys many times before. "Gentlemen, you can leave the papers just as they are; the file clerks will sort it out in the morning. Now go."

One by one, the men began to file out. Of course, some probably had secreted away scraps of stolen papers under their coats or in their pockets, but I wasn't about to ask them to let me search. The only thing I insisted upon was the key to the building.

I held out my hand and demanded it.

The ringleader turned it over with such a snarl that a chill swept over me. Even without knowing that some of these men would later go to prison for serious crimes, I decided I'd better have the locks on the building changed.

This job was going to be a little more perilous than I supposed. And from that day on, I carried a copy of my insurance policies and my last will in my handbag so that if anything did happen to me, I wouldn't cause anyone any fuss.

The next morning, a sour-faced and disinterested Miss Jay knocked to say, "There's some man named Franklin on the phone."

I squinted, trying to think. "I don't know any Mr. Franklin. Ask him where he's from, for whom he works, and what he wants."

A few moments later, she came back to say, "He says he's from New York, he works for the United States government, and he wants to know what you're up to over at his Labor Department."

"Oh, Miss Jay, *honestly*!" I said, diving for the telephone, only to find President Roosevelt laughing at his little prank.

While he was in a good mood, I felt as if I better let the president know what I'd done. Fortunately, my brazen behavior gave him a big laugh. "Oh, Frances. I have a flotilla of burly Secret Service agents carrying pistols, but *you're* the one who goes up against the crooks, armed with nothing but a handbag. You're lucky nothing happened. What possessed you to confront men like that?"

I laughed. "Old instincts, even if they're a little rusty."

"Oil them up. We've got a fight ahead of us. And you know I love a good fight."

Chapter Fifty-One

Washington, DC
March 9, 1933

*I know 3 trades. Speak 3 languages. Fought for 3 years. Have
3 children. And no work for 3 months.
    But I only want 1 job.*

                                    –A veteran of the Great War

My first assignment was the Civilian Conservation Corps. It was
FDR's brainchild. We'd done something similar in New York, but
the devil was in the details. So while everyone else in the cabinet was
still nodding in approval of the idea to send unemployed young men
off into the wilderness with axes, I felt unsettled by what felt like a
harebrained plan. "Mr. President, what are they going to do when
they get to the woods?"

"Well, you know," Roosevelt said, hesitating to scratch his chin.
"Do the work that has to be done with trees. We must preserve our
forests. We must build dams to keep the water from running off."

I knew he felt strongly about this but wondered where unemployed men were going to learn forestry and dam building, and if
he'd given any thought to the fact that most of the unemployed were
city folk. "You're just going to take those poor men off the breadlines
and take them up to the Adirondacks and turn them loose? Just because they're unemployed doesn't mean they're natural-born lum-
bermen."

Roosevelt threw the whole thing in my lap. "There's always a way to get through it, so work it out, Frances."

It would be a logistical nightmare—I'd have to coordinate with the Forest Service, and even once I knew what they wanted done, how was I to transport potentially hundreds of thousands of jobless men to the remote wilderness? How would they be paid, fed, and housed?

The rush of questions brought a slick to the back of my neck as I considered telling the president that it wasn't feasible, even though every wise man in his cabinet was afraid to gainsay him. Rarely had I ever been so aware of being the only woman in the room. If I objected, would they think I lacked courage?

All I knew was that we couldn't make a mess of it. And that if we did make a mess of it, Roosevelt would blame me. That's what political underlings were for. Perhaps knowing that gave me a sudden flash of inspiration. "What do you think about this? We've got a big military. It isn't busy. They must have trucks, tents, cots, and blankets. They must have a lot of things we need. Why can't we use the Army?"

Roosevelt's eyes crinkled. "That's a brilliant idea. You see, gentlemen, I told you she was brilliant."

Just like that, my irritation was replaced with a warm feeling of appreciation. I'd pushed FDR's idea and improved it in a way that might help the country.

The president wanted me to have the CCC going full speed by summer. That wasn't much time, but I was now eager to prove to him, to myself, and to the nation that a woman could do the job. That *I* could do the job . . .

ELEANOR ROOSEVELT DECIDED to hold a press conference, and there was no talking her out of it. I worried it would set a terrible precedent for First Ladies that we'd all soon regret. If she made herself too approachable now—even if only to women of the press corps—they'd expect access all the time, until inevitably she'd say the wrong thing and we'd all be savaged for it.

Of course, while I was worrying about Eleanor's press conference, I should've been worrying about my own. I'd invited the ladies of the press to my office too. Of course, unbeknownst to me, Mrs. Roosevelt had received *her* contingent of women writers in the White House with a tin of candied oranges, which she passed around while inviting them to sit casually upon the floor when there weren't enough chairs.

The contrast with my own stiff reception probably couldn't have been more marked. I had them stand uncomfortably around my crowded desk as its two telephones rang off the hook.

My intent was to present myself as a very businesslike woman. But I must've seemed brittle as a pencil and equally liable to snap when a fashionable reporter in animal print pumps asked, "Can you tell us a little about your wardrobe, Miss Perkins?"

"Serviceable," I said. Glancing down at my plain white blouse and black skirt, I wondered, *If I wear the same thing every day, might it stop becoming a matter of comment?*

Another reporter asked what my hobbies were, and, already pining for my life in New York, I replied, "Music, art, sculpture. I no longer play tennis, but I've been known to swing at a golf ball . . ."

I tried to redirect the conversation to governmental news, but they bowled over me. "What do you hate?"

"Distractions," I teased as the phones continued to ring. Then, to keep the mood light, I added, "Noisy things like trains, radios, and *telephones.*"

They laughed, so I tried, again, to talk about work, and some of the reporters scribbled in their notebooks. I thought we might be getting somewhere, but the follow-up questions were awful.

How will you sign your checks without using your married name?

—are we to call you the Madam Secretary or Madam Perkins—

What are your personal plans for an active social life in the capital?

"None," I said as cheerfully as possible. "I shall be very busy with the national crisis. Besides, New Englanders like to keep to themselves."

Then came the question I most dreaded. "Why isn't your husband here in Washington with you?"

"He's ill." My head began to throb, and in a panic, I added, "With the flu."

That was the sort of polite lie I'd told in New York, where no one would inquire further. I might not get away with that here. I was inwardly berating myself when the same reporter pressed, "What does your husband do for a living?"

"Is that important?" I snapped. "Is this quite necessary?"

Except for this one moment, I thought I'd done well in contrast to the First Lady, who had gabbed to reporters about dogs and books and poetry. But while Eleanor had the ladies' press corps literally eating candied fruit from the palm of her hand, I was blasted for my jest about trains, radios, and telephones.

What right does Roosevelt's resentful, impatient, and petulant secretary of labor have to insult three modern industries so crucial to the American economy?

I was in the soup now, and I realized that Eleanor was somehow much better at this than I was.

Chapter Fifty-Two

Washington, DC
April 1933

Dear Miss Perkins,

*Reading about you I've come to understand you are fair and im-
partial. So, I'll have to get a load off my chest about the factory
where I toil. We work ten hours a day in the grime and dirt of a
nation. We handle diseased rags. Tuberculosis roaming loose. We
go home tired, sick, and dirty—disgusted with the world. Tired
on the train going home, sitting at the dinner table, too tired to
even wash ourselves, what for? We're slaves of the Depression! I'm
even tired as I write this letter. I sleep now with a prayer on my
lips, hoping against hope, that you will better our conditions.
Give us a New Deal, Miss Perkins. . . .*

~JG, Brooklyn, New York

On my desk, I already had more than two thousand pleading letters
and plans to solve the financial crisis, submitted by crackpots and
experts alike.

I was beginning to suss out that I was up against entrenched
moneyed interests in the government itself. For starters, the budget
director didn't want to spend any federal money because we were in
the midst of catastrophic deflation. By one school of economic thought,
government spending could make matters worse. That was a defen-
sible position . . .

But it was the wrong one. When a man hasn't a job, he can't

spend, and if no one else is hiring or spending, the government *must*. Especially when people are so needy they'd burn dollar bills just to keep warm.

Unfortunately, the budget director didn't want to have an honest argument about it, he just wanted to shut me out. And he wasn't the only one. I soon heard a rumor about how people outside my department were working on *something big*.

At first, I thought it was all smoke and mirrors, and told the president, "If there *is* a genius plan, they're keeping it absolutely quiet, very secretive. Do you know what they're doing?"

This last question was the right weapon to deploy, because Roosevelt didn't like to think he was out of the loop. "No, I do not. They've kept it from me, too, and I won't tolerate it."

"Well, then, I'd like you to appoint me to be your snoop."

The president was accustomed to relying on women to be his eyes, ears, and legs, so he didn't hesitate. "Yes, you go and tell them I've appointed you to investigate this. I must know, and you're to find out."

I went at it like a bloodhound, wheedling and cajoling my way through everyone in my contact book. Finally, I learned that a meeting had been called—not a cabinet meeting, mind you, but a meeting of Washington insiders—at the State Department, of all places. And it was being headed up by Hugh "Iron Pants" Johnson, the former brigadier general.

He didn't have a reputation for playing nice with others, but I dialed him up to say that the president was sending me over. He tried to put me off, but I told him I was coming whether he liked it or not.

By the time I got there, the meeting had started without me. I introduced myself, took a seat, and quietly listened, realizing that they were cooking up a price-fixing, wage-fixing, and employment-quota scheme. This would violate antitrust laws, and they worried the Supreme Court would come down on them like a ton of bricks. But the square-jawed Johnson was saying, "Well, what difference does it make? Before anyone can get these cases to the Supreme Court, we will have won the victory. Unemployment will be over so fast that nobody will care."

Taken aback by his cavalier attitude about the law, I ought to have concluded that this wasn't a serious enterprise by serious people. This was just another cockamamie scheme like the two thousand others on my desk. After all, who would support this? What department would it fall under, and whose budget would pay for it?

General Johnson didn't have any role in government. Nobody had elected him or appointed him to do anything. That should've been enough for me to dismiss it. However, I'd acquired a sixth sense of political energy and the direction it was flowing . . . and my senses were tingling. Men like General Johnson didn't hole up in the State Department without pay, or stay at pricey hotels on their own dime, if they didn't think they had the support either in Congress or at the White House. And FDR—who had an even better instinct for political energy than I did—was more intrigued than alarmed when I reported back to him.

To my dismay, he wanted me to get these men together, in his office, to hash out a national recovery plan.

I'd been on the job only a month, and already I was being outmaneuvered.

"Frances," Mary warned. "There's tremendous momentum gathering behind Johnson's plan. I'm hearing about it from friends in the Senate. FDR's campaign backers are pressing him on this, and they're some of the most important men in the country."

Mary had excellent connections on the Hill, and if she'd heard this, then there was no doubt the train was leaving the station without me. "You don't think there's any way to derail it?"

She shook her head. "Congress is so desperate they'll sign on to almost any legislation the president wants. You've told me that FDR wants a quick and easy win, and he can get this without friction."

I wanted to flail my arms in frustration. It's true that I hadn't presented Roosevelt with any plans he could enact *without friction*, but Hugh Johnson's scheme was a hundred times more radical than anything I'd suggested.

Yet, the next time I saw the president, General Johnson and his coterie were in the Oval Office, and Roosevelt said, "Keep Miss Perkins informed. She'll cooperate and act as a go-between."

It was only right that some public official be involved, but my hackles went up that FDR promised my cooperation. What's more, he'd reduced me to a liaison on what might be the largest economic undertaking of the administration. I must've looked as appalled as I felt, because the president asked, "You do believe in this, Frances, don't you?"

"Well . . ." What was I to say? I didn't yet have the data, the legal knowledge, or, frankly, the political standing to argue against it. Fine, then. If I couldn't derail the train, then I'd hop aboard and see how far it could carry me. "Yes."

Oh, how I'd live to regret that answer and the insecurity that drove me to it. I didn't want FDR to think that the very first woman ever appointed to a presidential cabinet would be fractious, disagreeable, and unable to work well with others. I certainly didn't want him to think I was the sort to undermine his authority. And, as a matter of personal temperament, I never liked to argue a subject when I had too little knowledge about it.

I'd given a precipitous answer because, surrounded by all these experienced and domineering men, I felt I couldn't properly discuss the legal implications of this plan—or even some of my own plans.

I wasn't a lawyer, but that afternoon I decided I had better get one . . .

"DON'T YOU LIKE the lawyers you've got over at the Department of Labor?" the president asked.

"The ones I inherited are lazy hacks. I can only think they got their degrees from a Cracker Jack box."

Roosevelt said, "Well, all right, let's get some new blood in here."

We asked for recommendations from the renowned legal professor Felix Frankfurter, who told us, "You want Charlie Wyzanski up in Boston. He's a prodigy. Young, ambitious, and principled."

The professor proceeded to tell us a story about this Wyzanski wunderkind that tickled the president, who made me send for the young lawyer to come down from Boston on the train.

The boyish Mr. Wyzanski arrived to meet me at the Willard Hotel wearing an expensive suit and fedora, his dark hair slicked back, his eyes burning with brilliance. If I squinted, I could almost see *Paul* as young man . . . but to think of my husband these days was an agony, so I pushed that thought away.

We exchanged the usual pleasantries, and then I said, "President Roosevelt and I heard a story about you, Mr. Wyzanski. I'm told that as a brand-new hire at your firm, you were assigned to argue against employees who were trying to join a union, and you refused to take the case."

"That's essentially correct, Secretary Perkins," Wyzanski replied. "You have the right of it in concept if not form."

I smirked at the young lawyer's Harvard affectation. "Well, that took *moxie*, Mr. Wyzanski. You could've been fired when millions are out of work. Why did you risk it? Are you a champion of labor unions?"

His smile turned wry. "*Nope.* I just don't like giving the big guy so much power over the little guy."

What an interesting character this young man was proving to be.

"Well, Mr. Wyzanski, I'm told you are the best and the brightest student Professor Frankfurter ever had. An agile thinker. An innovative legal tactician. An untapped genius." Wyzanski didn't shy away from the praise, so I asked, "*Are* you the best and the brightest?"

He looked me right in the eye. "You bet I am."

"Well, then," I said, rising from the table to pull on my gloves. "Come along. We'll talk as we walk."

"We're not having lunch?"

"No time," I said, looping my handbag over my arm. "Why? Are you hungry? I hope you didn't skip breakfast . . ."

"My mother sent me on the train with a tin, but when I got to the station, I saw elderly folks picking through the trash and gave it to them, thinking I'd just grab a bite to eat later."

Mr. Wyzanski looked away at that confession, embarrassed, and I smiled at that little crack in his armor. "Very occasionally it's good for ambitious young men to have a little hunger in the belly. Especially when meeting the president."

At hearing that, the young lawyer stopped dead in the middle of the sidewalk, and his voice rose an octave. "We're going to meet the president?"

I nearly laughed at the way his bravado melted away. "Yes. He's the one who'd have to appoint you, after all, so we'll want to see if he thinks you're right for the job."

"I—I can't meet President Roosevelt. I'm not ready for that."

Resuming my stride, I told him, "None of us ever are."

ON THE SECOND floor of the White House, half the cabinet, General Johnson, and the budget director were huddled in the Oval Office with FDR, who wiggled his cigarette holder between his teeth in greeting.

I saw a bit of shock register on Wyzanski's face. Some Americans didn't know the president was wheelchair-bound, and now the young man couldn't seem to stop himself from stealing glances at the hints of metal leg braces disguised by the president's trousers.

Unfortunately, there was no time for introductions; the president's men were having a spirited debate about Johnson's plan—the supposed magic elixir that would balance the budget and fix the economy without *any* government spending.

I remained skeptical. And, fearing this new program might derail everything I'd come here to accomplish, I felt my little list of priorities burning a hole in my pocket.

But the president thought Johnson's idea was clever, and the meeting went on for hours while young Mr. Wyzanski stood with the other underlings, his back against the wall.

At long last, the conference broke up, and I whispered into the president's ear. "Mr. President, this is Charles Wyzanski Jr., the fellow I want to be solicitor of labor."

"Charlie," FDR said, beckoning Wyzanski. "You're up."

The young man froze as if he couldn't quite believe the president was talking to him, much less bestowing a nickname.

It wasn't the first time I saw someone so awestruck by FDR that they couldn't make their feet move, but the president looked at me as if to ask, *What's the matter with this one?*

Then, all at once, Wyzanski blurted, "Mr. President, I want you to know I voted for Herbert Hoover."

I pinched the bridge of my nose, but Roosevelt burst out laughing. "I don't care, son. You work for me now, so what I want you to do is have on my desk tomorrow morning a draft of a bill carrying out this idea you've just heard discussed."

It was an awfully big job for a young man who up till now had been, by his own admission, writing memoranda on innocuous cases for a law firm. But I was relieved that the president was going to let me keep my thumb on the drafting of this bill by giving the job to my new lawyer.

And as FDR wheeled away, I said, "Congratulations, Mr. Wyzanksi. You're going to be the United States solicitor of labor."

The young lawyer sputtered, "But I haven't agreed."

"There's no point in trying to refuse him. Trust me, I've tried."

"This can't be how things are done in government," Wyzanski said. "Everything is chaos and confusion. When did you even decide I was the right choice?"

I gave him a sly smile. "Not until you told me you gave your breakfast away to someone in need."

TWENTY-FOUR HOURS LATER, Charlie Wyzanski had his draft of what would come to be known as the National Industrial Recovery Act written up, and when I readied to send it over, the young man fretted. "You're not going to edit it?"

"No. It seems to me that you've done the job you were asked to do, and it might even be enacted in much the same form you wrote it."

"Well, it *shouldn't* be," Charlie said. "This is a nutty scheme."

"I'm afraid I agree with you," I said.

"Then why didn't you tell the president?"

"Because I'm not prepared for open warfare on the idea. If I was the lone naysayer in a room full of enthusiastic political players before they'd even fully hashed out their program, I wouldn't have any say over the economic recovery in this nation. If I did that, I might as well hand in my resignation."

Charlie looked as if he was thinking about handing in his . . .

I tried to explain my thinking. "Once I knew the president wanted this bill, I did what I could to make sure we could write it in as fair and sensible a way as possible here in the Department of Labor. If important men are hell-bent on government collusion with private industry, then we need to make sure working people have some rights in this matter too. You see, if we're going to be locked in combat over the direction of economic policy, then we'll have to be clever about it."

Charlie stared. "Is it quite proper for someone who works for President Roosevelt to try to manage him?"

"Oh, everyone *tries*," I said. "But I sometimes succeed."

Chapter Fifty-Three

★ ★ ★

Washington, DC
May 1933

Dear Susanna,

Just a quick note to say how proud I am to hear that you're doing well in your schoolwork. Your art teacher also has many wonderful things to say about some watercolors that you've been painting. I can't wait to see them when I come up from Washington this Saturday. Maybe we can take them to your father, and it might soothe his troubled mind.

~ Your loving mother

Coming down the stairs to dinner in the Georgetown home I now shared with Mary Rumsey, I overheard her talking to the maid about her guest list and I interrupted to say, "You did not *dare* invite Sinclair Lewis to dine."

"Oh, really now," Mary replied. "We're all old friends!"

I sulked at the foot of the landing. "We *were* friends until Red published his ridiculous new novel."

"It's quite good," Mary said, arranging a Chinese vase full of bright orange tulips on the Chippendale entryway table. "You'd know if you read it."

"When would I find time?" I couldn't possibly admit I'd already purchased Red's latest smash hit and that reading it had nearly killed me dead.

"It's a love letter to you," Mary argued.

"Precisely the problem! I cannot have former suitors penning literary love letters to me and publishing them for the world to see." I certainly didn't want Susanna reading it.

But Mary took great amusement from my predicament. "Don't worry. Red tells the newspapers that *Ann Vickers* was inspired by his second wife. Only a few of us could possibly know it's about you."

"Too many people can guess and will naturally assume the scandalous passages are a reflection of my private life." It was just like Red to do something so monumentally indiscreet, to test our friendship this way. I knew it was just his nature, but given the timing of the novel, I was all out of sorts.

"Be reasonable," Mary said. "Red couldn't have known you were going to serve in the president's administration when he wrote that book. Now, don't spoil the occasion, Frances. Besides, cabinet secretaries need to entertain to be successful. Other cabinet secretaries know this."

"Other cabinet secretaries have *wives*," I complained, knowing that bachelorhood had been the ruin of more than one public official.

"Well, I'm a great deal better at entertaining than most wives, so when I say we're having people over for dinner, perhaps you should just nod and say, *Yes, dear*."

I was too exhausted to argue with her. And the dinner was, as it turned out, highly interesting, with a variety of cultured guests, including Sinclair Lewis, who shambled in with all the confidence he'd earned as the first American to win the Nobel Prize in Literature. Even so, the real star of the evening was his second wife, the journalist Dorothy Thompson, bureau chief in Berlin for the *New York Evening Post*.

According to the story he told over dinner, Red had hounded the celebrated foreign correspondent to the altar—literally cornering her on the first night they met, and repeatedly asking her to marry him.

Which sounded terribly familiar . . .

"I asked him *why* I should marry," Dorothy explained while Red gazed adoringly at her statuesque form, too fixated to notice me silently stewing. "He said I should marry him because he wanted us to build a house on a farm in New England, maybe Vermont."

"Why not *Maine*?" I mumbled into my wine, grateful when the conversation moved on to current events.

Dorothy had secured an interview with Adolf Hitler in '31. Back then, she hadn't thought much of him, writing, *He is inconsequent and voluble, ill-poised, insecure. He is the very prototype of the Little Man.*

Now, she insisted, "He's going to start the world war all over again. The maniac told me so himself. At the time, I thought it laughable that he could convince the German people to vote away their own rights and let him do as he pleased. I'm not laughing now."

None of us were. The stories coming out of Germany were awful. Violence, intimidation, and concentration camps filling up with thousands of political opponents. I'd already raised it as an issue in the cabinet, and the president thought he should say something in public against the Nazis, but the secretary of state warned against it, and I hadn't felt it was my place to press the matter.

Now I wasn't so sure.

Dorothy drew out the suspense in her discussion of Germany, leaning forward to get a cigarette from its case. Red lit it for her before she continued, "Hitler is a cut-rate Mussolini. He's fixated on persecuting Jews. I cannot emphasize enough how dangerous it has become."

My appetite fled, and I put down my napkin. "Do you really mean *dangerous*?"

"Quite." Red downed his drink in one swallow. "But Dorothy tells me people everywhere want a dictator these days . . ."

"Really, Red," I said stiffly. "I hope you're not going to repeat that nonsense people spout about how FDR should become dictator."

"Don't worry, sweets. I'm just saying *it could happen here.*"

He studiously avoided my gaze, which meant he knew I was furious with him. He'd written that I—or rather Ann Vickers—had enjoyed the embraces of both women and men, carried on sexual affairs, obtained an abortion, and so on. Also, that she knew *how to create a fortress of social niceties to safeguard true feelings.*

Well, at least the latter was true, so I raised my glass in acknowledgment of his point with a thin smile.

Then Dorothy positively silenced the room with a litany of horrors being perpetrated upon Jewish artists, scientists, authors, and trade unionists. Not even a fork clanked against a plate as she summarized, "German Jews are in a truly hopeless state. Hitler's jackboots are beating them in the streets."

I couldn't convince myself she was telling the truth. Especially when she predicted Hitler would put German women in breeding camps to create some so-called *Aryan* superrace. Perhaps skepticism shone in my eyes, because Dorothy rapped the table, startling me. "I've told my German friends to get out—leave all their belongings behind if necessary and *flee.* I only hope they can find sanctuary here in the United States now that you're in a position to do something about it, Miss Perkins."

WAS I IN a position to do something about it?

When next I went to see FDR at the residence, he raised the subject himself, jesting grimly, "Well, things were starting to get a little dull around here with a mere collapse of the American economic system. We might as well add Europe's problems to the mix." The Nazis were, after all, a distraction we didn't need. But FDR had come into power at the same time as Adolf Hitler, and the rising threat weighed on the president's mind. "What can we do for those poor devils over there?"

Since I'd recently had my new solicitor prepare me for a press conference on the matter, I explained, "By law, I'm allowed to take in just shy of twenty-six thousand German immigrants this year. That's the quota. We're not filling it. Despite all these German Jews trying to come over, and all these open slots for refugees, our consulates aren't granting visas."

I guessed it was because former president Hoover didn't want Jews coming to America. So I suggested the new president call the State Department and tell them to make a change in policy.

Roosevelt winced because he hated having his own fingerprints on controversial decisions. "All right, I guess I'll have to. In the meantime, will you stay for dinner and *the children's hour*?"

That's how he referred to his nightly gatherings where he mixed cocktails for guests while a disapproving Eleanor hosted a tea elsewhere in the residence. No matter which one I chose to attend, it would be better than staying for a *thoroughly* unappetizing dinner cooked up by Mrs. Nesbitt—the White House housekeeper.

FDR joked that Eleanor had hired Mrs. Nesbitt just to punish him. And Mrs. Nesbitt was so horrible a cook that I strongly suspected it wasn't a joke.

As I had no desire to eat liver and beans, I pleaded paperwork and went off for the evening thinking our discussion about Jewish refugees was a settled matter. So I was flummoxed the next day when I got a call from an undersecretary at the State Department.

"Miss Perkins," he said. "You're giving the president bad advice. Let me tell you how we're going to handle immigration in this administration."

I didn't know this man. And despite lingering insecurities, I'd already become so accustomed to taking orders only from the president that I stiffened. "On whose authority are you purporting to *tell* me how we're going to handle immigration?"

He ignored my question. "We won't grant visas to fill those immigration quotas from Germany—"

"Did the president—"

"It will upset the labor unions—"

"Pardon me," I broke in again, sitting very straight. "I'm going to stop you right there. I really must express, in no uncertain terms, that it will be up to the Department of Labor to handle labor unions and other matters under our jurisdiction."

The man snorted. "It's obvious to any nonhysteric, *madam*, that the public won't like what you've proposed to the president. We can't afford to take in a bunch of indigent Jews."

Fortunately, it was in my nature to retreat behind a cool professorial demeanor when upset. "What you may not realize, sir, is that more people are leaving this country right now than are coming to it, which is, economically, a long-term disastrous situation. I also wish to take this opportunity to remind you that the American experiment has repeatedly proved that people fleeing tyranny make grateful citizens—decent, hardworking, and productive. We've reaped tangible benefits by taking in scientists, artists, inventors, and entrepreneurs. And yet even the immigration application of Albert Einstein has faced opposition by your State Department, though any country in the world would be lucky to have him."

The undersecretary wasn't moved an inch—but I'd spelled out my convictions as much for myself as for him, because I realized this was going to be another front on which I'd have to fight.

When I forcefully hung up the telephone, I found my poor, overworked boy solicitor staring at me. "Mr. Wyzanski, I don't need to tell you that Jews are in terrible straits in Hitler's Germany."

He frowned. He was himself Jewish and didn't like to talk about it—he was a good New Englander that way, all buttoned-up. So I simply said, "I need you to find me a legal loophole to get around the State Department."

Charlie tilted his head. "Why doesn't the president just call them back up again and order them to do what he says?"

"Oh, bless your heart . . ." Having the president give an order *was* the obvious solution. Legal and pure. It was also impolitic and betrayed how much Charlie still had to learn. "I know Roosevelt. If he's getting this much resistance privately, he won't want to take the blame for it in public. He'd rather the blame fall on me."

"And you're willing to take it?"

"What else are cabinet officials good for?" I wasn't as sanguine as I pretended. I never wanted immigration in my portfolio, and it was a distraction from absolutely everything else I'd come to do. But lives hung in the balance, so I'd do my duty as I saw it. As my grandmother always said, *When in doubt, do what's right.*

After all, what was the point of keeping America standing if she didn't stand for something?

"Can you find me a legal solution to help refugees fleeing the Nazis?" I asked.

Charlie paused for a disconcerting amount of time. "I'll see what I can do, but don't expect miracles."

I resisted the urge to ruffle his hair. "Oh, I never expect miracles, but I do have *faith*."

Chapter Fifty-Four

★ ★ ★

Washington, DC
May 22, 1933

Mrs. Wilson:

I am a Democrat and a great admirer of FDR. I can't understand, though, why he appointed a woman to hold the office of secretary of labor when it is so decidedly a job for a red-blooded HE-MAN. You are embarrassing the president by continuing in office. Presume he hasn't got the intestinal fortitude to tell you to scram. You are a round plug in a square hole. The laboring class needs someone of high executive ability to represent them at a time like this. A woman's place is in the home with her husband.

~A Detroiter

My home had been without a husband for more than eight months. Paul was still in the asylum, where he now paced by the window. "There's nothing whatsoever wrong with me, Frances. Which you'd know if you visited every weekend, as you promised."

"I'm *so* sorry, darling." I was fending off exhaustion with a cup of coffee that one of the nurses had kindly slipped into my hands. There was, however, nothing to help me fight off the guilt. "I do try to come as often as I can . . ."

I'd taken the overnight train from Washington, on which I'd slept not a wink because I was writing a speech I'd have to give later to the Welfare Council of New York. After which I'd take another overnight train to get back to my office in Washington by morning.

There wouldn't be any time for rest in between, but I *had* promised to visit Paul on the weekends, and I felt terrible about how difficult that promise was proving to keep.

"The doctors haven't any idea why I should remain here," he insisted. "In fact, they're puzzled how I ended up here in the first place. They say I'm a perfectly fit specimen."

None of this was true except for the part about Paul's physical fitness. The facility boasted a tennis court, and he spent a great deal of time working on his serve.

He was still handsome and athletic, evoking memories from younger days. In my mind's eye, I could still see his thick mane of hair blowing in a breeze off the ocean at our shack by the beach, his strong arms cradling Susanna when she was born . . .

Yes, *physically*, he glowed with good health for a man of fifty-seven. Mentally, he wasn't stable at all. And now he literally shook with fury, shouting, "You can't keep me caged like an animal! Do you hear me?"

I'd been shouted at by drunks and malcontents and thugs in the tenement slums. But this was the man with whom I'd pledged my troth, and I could never get used to being shouted at by him. "You're not caged. You're only here to get well. The moment the doctors tell me—"

"I want to go home." Paul's hands balled into fists. "I *insist* you find a way for me to go home now."

But Paul's doctors advised he was still in no condition to leave the asylum . . . unless, of course, I was unable to pay for his medical care. Then, I knew they'd be perfectly willing to kick him out into the street.

Other patients, abandoned by their families, faced eviction from the facility. I knew this because one of Paul's roommates hadn't been able to pay. That poor man had then written his family asking for them to at least help him buy a new pair of boots so he wouldn't have to face a harsh New York winter on the streets barefooted. Instead, they told him they were too broke to help, and that he ought to go south where the weather was mild enough that he could go without shoes if need be. Last we heard, he'd been living a tramp's life, his mental illness quite untreated, and he died hopping a ride underneath a freight train.

I'd work myself to death before I let that happen to Paul. I had taken a life insurance policy to protect my family if *I* should die. But what would happen if age or disability or infirmity prevented me from working? Those were the terrors that kept me awake at night and tormented the sleep of millions of other Americans . . .

"WERE YOU MISQUOTED?" the president barked into the telephone. "Tell me you didn't really say the South is an untapped market for shoes."

I pressed my lips together, guilty as charged.

In my speech before the Welfare Council of New York City, I'd been giving an example of how the United States is a self-sustaining economy with a robust domestic market, which was why we needed to build up purchasing power so that the average citizen could buy goods—like shoes—right here at home. But my remarks landed as a crass joke at the expense of Southerners, and now all of Dixie was writing vitriolic editorials condemning me.

"Should I apologize?" I asked Roosevelt.

He grumbled. "Just let it blow over. If it doesn't, chat with my missus."

He wouldn't have told one of the men in his cabinet to confer with Eleanor, but my gaffe was being exploited as an indictment of women in government. It was also a mistake that alienated the president's Southern allies in Congress and a mistake that was costing me his confidence. So when it didn't blow over, I slunk over to the White House with my tail between my legs to confer with the First Lady, who had an undeniable way with the press.

"Oh, Frances, it's easier for me than it is for you," Eleanor said generously. "I can speak to reporters without intruding on my husband's side of the news, whereas you *make* his side of the news. I'm the sort of woman they're used to—a wife and a hostess—whereas you're doing a job that men have always done. Which means they'll dismiss you if you speak too much like the sort of woman they're used to, and they'll resent you if you speak to them in a just-the-facts fashion like a man."

I sighed. "You've diagnosed the 'damned if you do, damned if you don't' situation precisely. But I ought not let myself off the hook, and the president seems to think you might have some advice for me about this gaffe."

"Well, my best advice is this," she said. "Deny it, dismiss it, or diminish it with laughter. When you know to laugh and to look upon things as too absurd to take seriously, the other person is ashamed to carry through even if he was serious about it." Then Eleanor added, "Also, refreshments help."

"Refreshments?" I didn't like that idea. Journalism was a business, after all. Why should the taxpayer foot the bill for feeding reporters? But I decided, rather grudgingly, that I'd serve ginger ale and Lorna Doone cookies the next time I spoke to the press.

On the way out, Eleanor gave my hand an unexpected squeeze. "Frances, at least you won't have to worry about the ladies of the press corps asking after your husband. When one of them tried to press me on the matter, I let it be known—discreetly—that your husband is in a condition that would be impolite to write about, and they've promised me they'll steer clear of it. I'm sure they know that any of them who doesn't . . . well, they won't be invited to my weekly press conferences ever again."

There were, it seemed, very great advantages to being friendly with the First Lady. And as difficult as it sometimes was to navigate that friendship, I was unutterably grateful for it.

IN ASKING ME to come to Washington with him, Franklin Delano Roosevelt had made me feel that we were a team. He'd convinced me he needed me *especially*. In short, he'd wooed me and won.

But now—perhaps thanks to my inability to generate good press—I was being jilted and pushed to the side.

General Hugh Johnson had laid siege to the White House with this National Industrial Recovery Act scheme—and though I was wedging my priorities into the program, I felt as if my gaffe about Southerners and shoes had allowed the general to chip away at my influence with the president.

"It's best to keep old Iron Pants close, then," Mary advised. "It's what Eleanor does when new interests come into Franklin's life. She keeps an eye on them."

I wasn't sure we were talking about politics anymore, and though we never broached it outright, I'd become aware of the tiniest difference in our thinking about the Roosevelt marriage—namely that Mary was always and forever on Eleanor's side.

"Invite General Johnson for dinner," Mary suggested. "Tell him you're new to the federal government and desperate to pick his big powerful brain. Lay it on thick. Then let me charm him with chicken cutlets and a bat of my long eyelashes."

I laughed, but, as I was learning from Mary, the art to Washington society was becoming accustomed to dining with—and being very pleasant to—people you don't like who are plotting against you or everything you stand for. So I did as Mary advised, and not long af-ter, General Johnson was complimenting Mary's chef and guzzling bourbon at our table.

I'd also invited my new solicitor to dinner—a bit of an apology for working the young bachelor half to death—but I regretted it as Johnson bloviated about his plan to make big Blue Eagle posters that shopkeepers could put up to prove they were cooperating with the government.

"This plan will never pass constitutional muster," Charlie Wy-zanski said, finally losing his patience. "The Supreme Court will strike it down."

Johnson banged his glass of bourbon onto Mary's table. "Listen, young man. This is war! We're in a war against depression and pov-erty, and we've got to do what you do in war. Give orders and make everyone obey."

Charlie's fork clattered on his plate as he glanced at me to see if *he* was the crazy one. He wasn't, but I was glad he simmered down at my warning glance. As far as I could discern, my solicitor wasn't a Demo-crat nor particularly liberal-minded. He also had an air of youthful arrogance that told me he thought himself quite superior in intelli-gence to just about everyone.

And in many respects, he was.

I also knew Charlie Wyzanski regretted taking the job, but to that, I wanted to say, *Welcome to the club.*

Charlie was still stewing when I finally called the *very* drunk gen-eral a taxicab. And I tried to fight down my doubts. *This is the man to whom the president was going to entrust a sweeping economic recovery program?*

I returned from seeing the general off, holding a book Johnson had given me as a parting gift. When I set it on the table, Charlie said, "That's about Mussolini's fascist system."

"Oh, dear." I glanced at the book in dismay. "Exactly the sort of book one does *not* want to receive from a military man."

Mary—who, during dinner parties, confined herself mostly to being a charming hostess—now asked, "You don't think Johnson is a fascist, do you?"

I sputtered a nervous laugh. "The general seems more of a blunderer. I don't think he understands the implications of giving out this book."

"But *I* do," Charlie said. "That man talks like a natural-born dictator, and the president is enabling him."

I couldn't help but defend FDR. "Charlie, you know some people want a dictator like Benito Mussolini in Italy, or Adolf Hitler in Germany. *God forbid.* But President Roosevelt isn't like that."

"Then why does he want to pass a program like this, and why are we helping him do it?"

"Because there are still almost thirteen million people out of work in this country," I said. "I estimate the unemployment rate to be twenty-five percent. Banks have collapsed, farms are failing, and desperate migrants are flooding into the cities for help. Johnson's not wrong to say we're in a war against the Depression; we need to get some public relief, and his way may be the only way to get it."

When I saw that didn't comfort Charlie in the least, I added, "We're also going to get rid of child labor, reduce working hours, and get a public works program out of this. Once we get those through, I'll convince the president to take power out of Johnson's hands so we can get to work on a *sensible* social insurance plan."

That was an awful big promise. I wasn't at all confident I could keep it, and Charlie wasn't fooled. "You're a gambler . . ."

"Yes, and so is the president. He's gambling on me, and I'm gambling on you, and the country is gambling on the lot of us, so we'd best not let them down."

Chapter Fifty-Five

Washington, DC
June 1933

I
N THOSE EARLY DAYS OF THE ADMINISTRA-
tion, I was so busy I sometimes bathed with a sponge at the office bathroom sink and splashed water on my face to stay awake.
My driver—a holdover from the last administration—up and quit on
me, complaining of the long hours to which I was subjecting him.

I worried I was becoming too much like the exploitive industrialists
I'd battled all my life, but even *they* managed to find time for their
families. And I was trying desperately to find time for mine. So, when
school recessed, I insisted Susanna come to Washington for the summer.

At sixteen, my daughter no longer let me twist her hair into cork-
screws named after characters in Peter Pan; she styled her own hair,
which was darkening from honey blond to golden brown, in a
fashion-forward chin-length bob with finger waves. And she had her
father's good looks—a thing that sometimes consoled me and other
times gave me the greatest pain.

Whenever Susanna came to visit, she and Mary's daughter spent a
great deal of time together, playing with the dogs, going to the picture
shows, gossiping, and doing things that normal teenaged girls ought to
do. But I wanted to carve out time for the two of us, so over the summer
I took her to buy paints for her watercolors. We went to church together.
I found time to take her to an afternoon matinee. Then, to help her appreciate why I'd thrown our lives into such turmoil, we volunteered in a
soup kitchen feeding an endless line of homeless people.

After that, I brought her to the office with me. "A bit of a shabby building," I said apologetically. "But at least the cockroaches are gone."

Susanna spun in my swivel chair. "When they finish construction of the new office, will you put unemployed artists to work in decorating it?"

"Oh, I doubt that's possible."

"Why not? You've hired people to plant trees for the Civilian Conservation Corps. I'm sure not everyone we saw at the soup kitchen was fit to work outdoors, but some of them were artists. So why can't you give a starving painter or sculptor a job?"

She had a very good point, and I was impressed with her ability to articulate it. Not that anyone in government was likely to agree. Humoring her, I said, "Darling, that's a good question. Perhaps I'll raise it with the president."

I was surprised to see her sit up straighter. "Promise you will!"

My heart swelled with love to know that my daughter had compassion for those down on their luck. "No promises, but I'll look for an appropriate moment when Roosevelt will be in a mood to hear the suggestion."

That pleased my daughter enormously, and her enthusiasm led her to wonder, "What about public plays? Surely the nation could foster playwrights . . ."

We were, in fact, to attend a play that very evening. I'd already had Miss Jay acquire the tickets. Unfortunately, just before we were set to leave, I was saddled with a stack of documents that needed to be reviewed by morning.

"NOW, DON'T POUT, Susanna," Mary scolded when I dropped my daughter back at our house in Georgetown. "You're a mature young lady now, old enough to appreciate that your mother has to work."

Susanna folded her arms over herself. "She's not even going to stay for dinner?"

"All right, darling," I said. "I'll sit down for a quick dinner at least, but then I really must get back."

We all sat down together for a meal, where Susanna asked, "Isn't it time that I had a coming-out party?"

A part of me wanted to tell her how foolish it was to even *think* about debutante parties while so many girls her age didn't even have a soft pillow upon which to rest their heads at night. But another part of me remembered the point of my taking this job wasn't to make my daughter as miserable as the poorest children in the nation. My job was to try to make sure that the nation's children had as many opportunities as mine did. And if I did my job well, then maybe we could all look forward to better days.

So, as gently as I could, I said, "Maybe next year."

To her credit, my daughter tried to hide her crushing disappointment by biting at the corner of her upper lip. If she'd shouted or slammed about as so many teenaged girls were prone to do, it wouldn't have been so gutting.

How I hated to disappoint her!

Into the awkward silence, Mary made a dramatic sigh. "Well, thank *goodness*, Frances. I was so afraid you'd make poor Susanna go through a dreary makeshift debutante season."

Susanna peered up curiously at Mary, who explained, "It was bad enough last year, when the banks were collapsing and it felt too insensitive to throw a normal coming-out party with ball gowns for my daughter. I had to improvise a barn dance where everyone came in overalls to eat ham, eggs, and applesauce."

That sort of lark was all well and good for the daughter of Mary

Harriman Rumsey, an heiress for whom simpler pleasures were novel. But my daughter dreamed of glitter and glamour, as surely Mary knew, because she added, "The stories I'm hearing have me feeling sorry for this year's debs. The out-of-season dresses, the paltry menus, the sour *mood*; none of this year's crop of girls will be allowed to shine."

"Oh," Susanna said, still worrying at her lip. "I hadn't thought of that. That isn't very nice for them."

Mary nodded. "You're so lucky you're young enough to wait, Susie. Next year everything is going to be so much better."

I thought Mary might be laying it on a bit thick, but she turned Susanna's mood around entirely.

How grateful I was to Mary for this and so many other things. Grateful, too, that my daughter was turning out to be such an interesting person. Yes, Susanna could get caught up in the vain pastimes of youth. She could also be quite lazy at times, sleeping in late. But she was bright, intellectually curious, and sometimes she quite surprised me with her interests.

By way of example, one night that summer, as I was leaving for a function, Susanna said, "Mother, you can't wear that fur stole."

"Oh, dear," I said, having already debated whether I ought to wear jewelry for a change. "Here I thought the mink looked rather elegant with—"

"It's from Leipzig," Susanna broke in. "And given what Hitler is doing, we should boycott German goods. All my friends and I have joined the boycott."

I flushed with pleasure—and surprise—to realize Susanna kept more current on world affairs than I supposed. "Well, that's very high-minded, and I'll quite happily join that boycott."

Of course, I already *owned* the mink, but symbolism mattered. Especially for a public official. And especially for me, given what I hoped to do for Hitler's victims . . .

"EXPLAIN AS IF I were a small child," I said to Charlie when he said he had finally found me the authority I needed to force the State Department to take in refugees fleeing the Nazis in Germany.

"I'll try." Charlie sat back smugly. "Why do American diplomats refuse visas to German refugees?"

"They claim it's because they think refugees will be a drain on our economy."

Charlie nodded. "Now, how do our diplomats form this belief?"

"Well, I don't know. I suppose they must ask questions about financial resources. Ask for references, perhaps, some guarantee from a person that they won't be a burden . . ."

Charlie's coal black eyes lit up. "Exactly. And that guarantee can be in the form of a bond. A little-known fact is that, by law, the secretary of *labor*"—Charlie pointed his pencil at me—"has the legal power to accept that bond and allow the immigrant into the country."

I was giddy at this solution to a knotty problem. "You really *are* a prodigy, aren't you?"

He should've smiled at my praise, but instead, Charlie stared at his feet. "Secretary Perkins, the law is on your side, but the State Department isn't going to like it. Their lawyers are going to want to argue."

"Well, let's get into a room with them and fight it out."

I said this with full confidence in Charlie—a confidence shaken when my young gun showed up to the meeting with the State Department lawyers without even a page of notes.

"Where is your argument?" I hissed in his ear when he sat down at the conference table.

Charlie pointed at his forehead. "Up here."

I'd never been taken seriously without notes, but as I was soon to learn, Charlie Wyzanski *made* people take him seriously. He peppered the State Department lawyers with precedents, rattled off citations and page numbers, then added insult to injury by quoting long legal passages he'd committed to memory. His opponents never stood a chance. He left them absolutely sputtering in defeat, and furious too.

At the end of the legal tussle, one of the State Department lawyers snidely asked, "Say, what kind of name is Wyzanski, anyway?"

Charlie gave an uncharacteristically feral grin. "Bostonian. To be sure, it looked good on the masthead of the *Harvard Law Review*."

The opposing lawyer muttered, "Spoken like one of Frankfurter's hot dogs."

Appalled, I broke in. "Pardon me, what did you just say?"

The State Department lawyer shrugged. "Just clearing my throat."

He must've thought I was a fool. I knew there was ugly gossip of a conspiracy between Justice Brandeis and Professor Frankfurter to surround the presidency with a brain trust of young radical Jewish *hot dogs* who would allegedly subvert President Roosevelt to *the Jewish interest*. I simply never dreamed I'd hear such rot spoken by any member of our own government.

Now I realized that these lawyers resented Charlie Wyzanski for more than just being young or right on the law. They resented him for being a Jew. Worse, he knew it, too, and I saw him shrink a little inside himself. My solicitor hadn't developed the emotional calluses of age, and in an effort to spare him—and soothe tempers—I suggested we let the attorney general make the final decision.

Later that day, I went to see Charlie in his office on the eighth floor. He wasn't expecting me, and I found him staring out the window, puffing on a pipe, which he hurriedly tried to put out when he saw me in the doorway.

"Oh, it's perfectly all right," I said, waving him back into his seat. "My husband smokes a pipe. I'm accustomed to it. I find the scent comforting."

Charlie raised an eyebrow, perhaps because it was the first time I'd ever mentioned my husband to him. It was a bit of an offering. An opening for him to share something personal if he wished to. But he remained disconcertingly silent.

"Are you all right after what happened with those lawyers today?" I asked.

"I'm just fine." He gave me a warning look, one I understood perfectly well. "Why wouldn't I be?"

He was bottled up tight as a cork, but I tried again. "I'd like to talk about how you're getting on at the department. I know it must be quite different than what you were used to at a law firm."

"Are you firing me, Miss Perkins?"

"Heavens, no! It's simply that employers should care about the concerns of their employees. So do you have any . . . concerns?"

"Only that I feel like I've been in a madhouse ever since the day I arrived."

I sympathized. "Yes, well, the whole world has gone mad . . ."

He heaved a heavy sigh. "Every day since I took this job, I've been trying my hardest to pretend I'm not terrified that I'm too young, too inexperienced, and too outmatched." It was a painful admission, I knew, but one that was, perhaps, less painful than the one that kept him from looking me in the eye. "The country is in trouble, and it deserves better than to have its future in my untested hands."

I went quiet because I could all too plainly identify with those feelings . . .

Charlie put his hands on his desk as if bracing for what he said next. "After today, I see that I'm more of a hindrance than a help. So, I'm tendering my resignation."

"Oh, no," I said. "Please don't be rash."

He rubbed his brow. "Miss Perkins, I'm conservative by nature. I'm not sure I agree with these programs, and—"

"I know you're not a party man, Mr. Wyzanski," I interrupted, perching unbidden at the edge of his desk. "When you first heard of the New Deal, you probably laughed. But the notion must've touched something in you. Otherwise, why pack up your life to work for me?"

"It was a good opportunity. Anybody would take it."

That wasn't entirely true, and we both knew it. Though the job paid well, it was largely thankless and exhausting. Worse, every man who had ever worked for me took ribbing about it. "But why did *you* take the job?"

Charlie looked away. "You'd laugh."

"I won't."

"Maybe you won't laugh, but you *should* laugh. I took the job because my Polish grandfather came here with nothing. Couldn't even read or write. America took him in anyway, and because of that, his grandson got to study at Harvard and be offered a position to work for the president of the United States."

This was, I realized, the most he had confided in me about absolutely anything, so I trod gently. "You want to serve your country."

"Isn't that a laugh?" Charlie waved a hand, as if disgusted with himself for trite sentimentality. "Well, nobody thought I was serving my country today. Everybody in that room saw me as a Jew arguing to save other Jews, not as a government lawyer arguing for the best interests of the United States."

"You're wrong. I saw you as the *only* government lawyer in the room arguing for the best interests of the United States. Did you never think that maybe today, in that room, under these circumstances, the United States of America needed a Jewish solicitor?

Someone who understood that refugees often prove to be crucial assets to this country? Someone who wouldn't be blind to it simply because these refugees are Jews?"

Charlie only rubbed his face, but I'd given him something to think about, anyway.

I glanced at my watch. "Now I must pick up my daughter and take her shopping for a new butterfly-skirted frock. But I'll leave you with this. Our work here is changing lives. Your work today might even *save* lives. You must give that more thought before you resign. I'd like you to stay."

He gave a noncommittal grunt.

But Charlie Wyzanski was in the office again bright and early the next morning.

Chapter Fifty-Six

★ ★ ★

Washington, DC
June 1933

W
E BROKE THROUGH THAT FIRST HUN-
dred days with a feeling of triumph. I'd gotten the
Civilian Conservation Corps staffed and running,
and it was a wonderful shot in the arm for the country's morale—
giving young Americans a sense of purpose and pride.

We'd also passed more than seventy laws. Laws to help farmers,
modernize food production, and keep people in their homes. We'd
allocated money to build roads, bridges, and vital national infra-
structure. We'd started dams that would provide electricity to remote
areas. We'd regulated working conditions, raised wages, and, at long
last, prohibited child labor everywhere in the country.

But the sheer avalanche of programs had gotten me off course
from what I most wanted to do. We needed a long-lasting solution,
and that, I believed, was social insurance. Particularly for the elderly,
whose suffering was illustrated for me in letter after letter sent by
anxious Americans.

Just four months ago, the president had called my idea crazy. But
a lot had changed since then, and I decided it was time to reassert
myself.

I found FDR working on his next radio address from bed. He
received me in the bedroom wearing an old gray sweater to keep his
shoulders warm, while spectacles balanced on his stuffy nose.

He had a cold; still, he was in relatively good spirits, and I was happy to report, "We're seeing improvement in the economic numbers."

"Good," he said, reaching for a glass of water and some aspirin on his nightstand, by which he kept the latest detective novel to help him fall asleep. "It means the New Deal is working."

Of course, at that point, *the New Deal* was becoming synonymous with General Johnson's National Recovery Administration and its Blue Eagle. Some companies flew the eagle because they were patriotic and wanted to do their part. Others put the Blue Eagle in their window for fear of someone vandalizing their shop if they didn't. That's how high emotions were running, and the president didn't discourage it.

Blowing his nose, he said, "We're going to have some parades to celebrate the Blue Eagle and the end of the Depression."

"Mr. President, I think celebrating the end of the Depression is wildly premature. This country won't be on firm footing for some time, and certainly not until we get some form of social insurance."

"I knew you'd nag me about that," he said.

"And I knew you wanted me to."

The president smirked at me over the top of his spectacles. "Well, you've convinced me that we need unemployment insurance. But I'm not convinced a social insurance program can work for the aged and disabled and orphans and others. And people aren't going to like how it sounds."

"Oh, I don't know. People want security. In their personal lives and in their society. They want *social security*. You might remember that when I talked about it in those terms on the campaign trail, they went wild."

He rubbed at his chin thoughtfully.

Sensing I had the advantage, I pressed, "You know we're going to have to do something for the elderly in this country, and it might as well be under a program that alleviates *many* problems at once. It's probably our only chance in twenty-five years to get a bill like this!"

"They're going to say it's socialism," he said.

"Well, it isn't." I should know, because my Socialist friends all condemned the idea as a ploy to prop up a failing capitalist system.

Roosevelt shook his head. "I dunno, Frances. It still sounds crazy to me. I'll need more time to think."

"Of course," I said, snapping my portfolio shut. "On the other hand, you were rather quick off the mark in embracing Hugh Johnson's plan . . ."

That made FDR laugh. "Oh, don't brood, Frances. I let you have your way, didn't I?"

He was referring, I supposed, to the fact that I got him to pry the Blue Eagle's talons off the money for the public works programs.

General Johnson hasn't the temperament to handle all that money, I'd argued.

My judgment had been validated by Hugh's recent altercation at a public hearing, where he'd nearly come to fisticuffs with a critic. But I suspected I'd make an enemy for life if the general ever realized it was me who persuaded the president to let someone else administer the money.

Now FDR grinned. "You must've handled him with a velvet glove, Frances, because do you know what Hugh told me? He says you're the best *man* in the cabinet!"

"A laugh riot," I said sarcastically. "But it's Mary Rumsey who has a way with him. She gets him talking about horses and newspapers over one of her now-famous Sunday night dinners, and he's putty in her hands."

"Well, that's interesting," the president said. "Very interesting . . ."

I didn't know what he found so interesting about it until I came home one night to find Mary sipping from a wineglass smiling like the cat who ate the canary. "Out with it," I said, throwing myself down onto the sofa and putting my feet up next to hers on the ottoman. "You're wearing your favorite red striped dress and acting strangely. Did you buy another newspaper?"

"No, I lost my bid to buy the *Washington Post*," she said. "But Hugh Johnson is going to appoint me as chairwoman of the Consumer Advisory Board, and the president has agreed."

"Dear God. That might be my fault. I think something I said may've made FDR think it was a good idea to throw you into the arena with old Iron Pants."

She laughed. "I think it might just be a good idea, in truth. It's certainly a way for me to keep an eye on the rogue general. I can be your spy behind enemy lines."

I smirked, amused. "Was I naive never to realize national politics could be so cloak-and-dagger?"

"Probably, but I'm partially aghast, of course. I've never had a position in government, and I don't know that I have the qualifications. But women do most of the shopping in this country, so I feel as if it's only right that a woman represent consumers, and since I love to shop, it might as well be me."

"Honestly, Mary, I don't know anyone who would do better at that particular job." In this position, her connections were the best qualification she could have. And like me, Mary never stopped until she got her way.

But *she* managed it all with a sweet smile.

"I think it will be fun!" she cried. "And it means I'll be staying in Washington, so we're likely to end up like an old married couple."

She rubbed her toes against mine, and we both laughed, for we knew plenty of women in romantic friendships, so-called Boston marriages, and even women in sexual relationships with each other. Not only academic women, radicals, and reformers—even well-heeled second wives at fox hunts, society mavens at the bridge table, and filthy-rich garden party widows like Mary.

Perhaps my life would've been easier if I'd married a railroad heiress, I mused. But I'd said my vows to Paul Caldwell Wilson, which now left me suspended between grief, hope, and regret.

AT SUMMER'S END, as we packed Susanna's bags to return to New York for her last year of high school, I promised, "I'll be up to see you next weekend."

Oh, how I hated to part with her!

"And we'll go together to see your father," I said, praying it would be one of Paul's good days and that he wouldn't disturb Susanna with his shouting. "What sort of treat shall we bring him?"

My daughter was busy musing this point, poised atop her half-packed suitcase, when the telephone rang.

"Frances," Mary said, poking her head into the room. "The president wants to see you—it's an emergency."

Well, I kissed my daughter's forehead, grabbed my jacket, and dashed through mud puddles to get to the White House in a hurry, having no idea what it might be about.

In the Oval Office, the president rolled toward me, his face wan. "They're up in arms in New York."

"About what?" Panting, I expected other cabinet officers had been summoned too. But we were alone . . .

"They're mad at Hugh Johnson," the president told me. "There's a rumor that he's sleeping with his secretary, Miss Robinson."

I stared in complete exasperation.

I'd held my peace when the president recently credited the economic turnaround to Johnson without mentioning the hundreds of thousands of Americans I'd helped put to work planting trees, building dams, and working on soil conservation. I didn't complain when he sent me out to champion Johnson's NRA and its Blue Eagle posters. I kept quiet about my fears that a great deal of the NRA was proving to be a boondoggle. And I'd even kept quiet about the reports that Hugh Johnson was a fall-down drunk.

So why on earth would the president try to draw me into this?

I didn't think it was true that General Johnson was sleeping with his secretary. But Roosevelt certainly couldn't throw stones at a man having an affair. Which made me ask, "Is this not a rather *private* matter?"

"I should think so! But tomorrow is the big 'end of the Depression' celebration in New York City. The party higher-ups won't tolerate Hugh's secretary being part of the Blue Eagle parade; they think she's his mistress and won't have her there."

How this was an *emergency*, I couldn't guess. The solution seemed simple enough. "Tell him not to take her."

"What if he needs her?"

I took a breath. "He can keep her away from the parade and the viewing stand. If he needs her, he can call her at the office." Then, because I couldn't quite fathom that FDR was going to continue to let his presidency be endangered by this man, I said, "The most important thing she does is to keep Hugh Johnson from drinking. You know that, don't you?"

Roosevelt looked up with big eyes. "Does he drink too much?"

I wasn't buying his innocent act. "You must've heard it by now. Johnson's alcoholism is the worst-kept secret in Washington."

The president scowled. "Well, I'll deal with it later. In the meantime, Frances, tell that girl not to go."

"Mr. President, what a job to give me!"

It certainly wasn't to be found in any known job description for a cabinet officer to have to tell another man's secretary that she couldn't go to a parade because all of New York City suspected she was a whore.

"Besides," I said, looking up at the clock, "I'm sure they're already boarding the plane."

Roosevelt waved a hand to shoo me. "Take a White House car, Frances, and get there. Don't follow any speed limits. Just head them off. Get that girl off the plane."

This was utter madness. "If that isn't the craziest thing. And dirty too. Why don't you send one of the others?"

"Because you're a woman. You'll know how to say it."

I snorted. "That's how much you know about women, Mr. President. It'll be much worse, and more humiliating, coming from me or any other woman. Just call Miss Robinson yourself. If you tell her to get off the plane, she'll respect your authority."

He cringed away from the confrontation. "It has to be you, Frances, and that's an order."

Coward, I thought. *Low-down yellow-bellied coward.*

Oh, the look I gave him.

Still, he was already calling for a car to be brought round, so I went out to the airport, sirens screaming all the way.

Secretly, I hoped the plane would leave and I'd be excused from this unseemly duty. Alas, the plane had been delayed on the tarmac. I made some pretext and got the girl aside and made sure Miss Robinson knew how mortified I was to be sent on this errand. She was very decent about it all, and I felt just terrible. It was all so very unfair . . .

Her reputation was in tatters, and after this, I didn't know if the girl would ever be able to show her face again. Had I done the right thing getting her off that plane or made matters worse?

Later that night, at home, I stood in front of my bedroom mirror, staring at myself, feeling quite ill-used. I understood there was at least a *little* comedy to the situation, but I also took it quite hard.

Mary passed by my door and noticed me standing still with my head bowed. "Frances, are you all right?"

"It's only that I've already stumbled so badly in the job that the president has relegated me to errand girl. What am I *doing* here in Washington playing at *Madam Secretary*? It's pointless. I should resign and go home with my daughter on the next train."

Mary sighed and leaned against the door. "You think the president has lost confidence in you, but I think it's the opposite. He always turns to you when he finds himself in a ridiculous corner that he doesn't know his way out of."

I wasn't mollified. "Well, that better be the last dirty thing FDR *ever* asks of me."

To which she just laughed and laughed.

IN LATE NOVEMBER, the president sent me off to the Midwest on a different sort of errand. I was to give speeches touting the beneficent Blue Eagle. I was to tell the country that the NRA had worked beyond my wildest expectations, putting four million people back to work and reducing unemployment. All of which I believed to be true.

There were a great many wonderful things in the NRA. But I also thought it a temporary fix, that the moment the country's greedy industrialists recovered from their shock of having broken the economic system by bleeding it dry, they'd go right back to trying to suck the marrow from the decomposing bones of the nation's corpse.

We were still in the clutches of the economic depression, and the evidence was everywhere obvious to the eye. Not only to be seen on the gaunt faces of the hungry—but even in the parched land itself. My train passed mile after mile of desiccated and exhausted farmland, some of it ravaged by the recent dust storm—one of the worst in the country's history. It had scoured once-fertile topsoil right off overworked fields.

Everything out here in the middle of the country was now covered in a layer of dirt; I could taste the dust in the air—a lingering earthy bitterness at the back of my tongue. A taste that told me that American crops would fail again, and we'd all go a little hungrier. Some of us more than others . . .

Staring out the train window, I saw children of the heartland just as malnourished as any I ever studied in Hell's Kitchen all those years ago. Little boys huddling together on front porches, barefooted and listless. A dirt-smudged sharecropper's daughter wearing nothing more than a flour sack to protect her against a cold wind as she tried to collect a few precious eggs from skinny chickens in the yard. Farmers in denim overalls trying to dig their plows out of what looked to be a dune of sand.

And this was only Missouri; the storm had hit much worse in places like Kansas and Oklahoma.

After all the time I'd spent in the tenements of big cities like Chicago, Philadelphia, and New York, one might think I'd become calloused to the sight of hopeless faces. But this kind of poverty was new in America, with once stable and prosperous families now living right out of their motorcars by the side of the road with laundry flapping out the windows. Their vacant stares betrayed complete shock at having learned they could work hard all their lives, save their pennies, go to church, do right by their family, and still end up with nothing but sand slipping through their fingers . . .

I ought to have looked away from the windows and concentrated on the papers in my lap, reviewing my speech for St. Louis. But when the train slowed, I bore unwelcome witness to the drama playing out in a family who had packed everything they owned into the back of a truck—little children clinging to mattresses and an old stove—leaving behind a frail old grandmother on a rocking chair at a now-empty farmhouse.

The old woman raised her kerchief in farewell, and then, as they drove away, she cried into it so violently that I felt the pain in my own chest.

Had they abandoned her? Why couldn't she go with them? I couldn't help but imagine what my own grandmother would've done if the old Perkins place in Maine had been reduced to a roofless shack, dirt and dust covering everything in her once-spotless summer kitchen, the meadows stripped bare of wildflowers and grass, the gravestones of her ancestors buried under sand, and the river dried up to mud. Why, she might've sent her family away for greener pastures while settling in her rocking chair to die of a broken heart.

And thinking of her, I knew that even if Roosevelt sent me out in the night to pull girls off planes, my role at his side wasn't *pointless*. I believed a robust social insurance program could help these people, and I had a duty to use my position in the cabinet to bring it about. Yes, it's true I was on my back foot. I'd made gaffes with the press, and I'd let Hugh Johnson push me out of policy decisions while the president relegated me to madcap errands and New Deal cheerleading.

Well, that somehow had to change, I decided.

I was just going to have to find a way to battle my way back to the front. I was going to stay and fight for my ideas and for my fellow Americans—every last one.

Chapter Fifty-Seven

★ ★ ★

Washington, DC
December 1933

M Y CHAUFFEUR WAS WAITING FOR ME
when I returned from my journey, and he had a letter
from Mary Rumsey. *Do not go to the house. Come directly to the National Theatre. Ask for me. Very important.*

Well, this was all very mysterious, wasn't it?

The play had already started by the time I got there, but the usher took me down to Mary's seat, and she whispered, "I'm giving a theater party for Miss Robinson. But I told everybody that this party is for you."

"I haven't even changed from my trip!"

"Well, maybe freshen up in the restroom," Mary said. "These women only accepted the invitation on your account."

I soon realized that Mary had used her particularly influential position as a socialite extraordinaire to invite every important woman in Washington to this party, where they would be forced to see, and be seen with, Miss Robinson. This was Mary's bright idea to blunt the gossip about the affair with Hugh Johnson. Her way of quieting it, showing that respectable women of good position not only gave parties for Miss Robinson but went to parties with her.

I was touched by the gesture because I knew Mary had done it for my sake. So I happily played along, and I'll never forget how we laughed that night because it was absolute social *warfare* but all so *proper*.

Mary was so smart and quick about social things, which is why I didn't fight her *too* hard on New Year's Eve when she informed me of what she'd arranged for me in keeping with the expected tradition that cabinet officers' wives would host receptions to celebrate the New Year.

"I realize it's a time-honored tradition," I said. "But I rather thought that since I haven't a wife, I might be excused."

"No, Frances, you most certainly won't be excused. I've already heard complaints from the ladies of Washington that you don't leave—or even *have*—calling cards."

"Oh, for heaven's sake!"

Mary shrugged. "You must be more social. All work and no play makes Frances a dull girl."

Sullenly, I said, "Decorating a tea table so strangers can tromp through my home isn't my idea of *play*."

"Which is why I've reserved the Sulgrave Club! Three other cabinet wives have agreed to join you so that you may all receive guests under the artistry of friezes and French windows without raising any inquiries about your husband or living arrangements."

I stared at Mary, absolutely overwhelmed by her thoughtfulness. And she looked pleased with herself. "You can't think of a single complaint against my plan, can you?"

"Only that I cannot afford—"

"Don't be silly! I'm taking the expense entirely upon myself. Because if I didn't take burdens off your shoulders, you'd never have *any* fun." Mary gestured with her chin to the two glasses and bottle of champagne awaiting us. "Despite the miserable times we're living through, we're surviving as two women alone in the world. We must celebrate that and snatch joy where we can."

"You're right," I said, startling a little as she popped the cork early. "I do, after all, have many things to be grateful for."

"Yes, you do." Mary poured. "Let's toast them. What are we most grateful for?"

"Well, our children, of course," I said, for Susanna was growing into an impressive young woman, and Mary's children were thriving.

"To our children," Mary agreed, clinking her glass against mine. "Now let's toast to your first published book! To *People at Work*. May it become a bestseller."

I groaned, because *People at Work* was not so much a *book* as a compilation of articles I'd written and speeches I'd made. The project hadn't been my idea in the first place, and, worse, the publisher's tight deadline forced me to hastily quilt these pieces together between giving speeches and mediating labor negotiations. "I believe the book will flop and be panned by reviewers."

"It won't," Mary said. "But even if it does, I'll buy as many copies as you'll let me. I am, after all, your greatest fan."

Her words warmed my heart. "The feeling is mutual, and we can toast to that. To our friendship."

She clinked her glass against mine a second time, then took a big gulp. "I do adore you, Frances, even though you show no interest in my farms, horses, and fox hunts."

I smirked. "Because fox hunts are barbaric."

"Spoken like a woman who has never had her hens slaughtered by a fox. Now, what else can we toast? And don't say we ought to be grateful to have food on the table while the country starves. It's too maudlin for a toast."

But I *was* grateful for that, especially after what I'd seen in the heartland. "Well, what do *you* want to toast?"

"How about good press coverage?" Mary asked. "After years in the society pages, I'm finally being treated like a woman with a brain. And the media has been praising you too."

I stared at the rim of my glass. "They only praise my work ethic. They say I'm *efficient*."

"Pshaw! They also call you the Ann Vickers of the New Deal."

I pulled my glass back. "Oh, I refuse to toast to that. I still want to wring Red's scrawny neck for writing that novel."

Mary smirked, leaning back on one elbow. "What do you suppose the great Sinclair Lewis is up to tonight?"

Given that Red had been doing his level best to be the *bad boy* of literary circles, I guessed, "Probably running down the hallway of some European hotel in his pajamas, drunk and raving about *his* latest reviews, which will all be better than mine."

Mary giggled like a girl. "Why don't we call him?"

I raised my eyebrow at her giggle. And because I was still a frugal Yankee at heart, I asked, "Call overseas? Are you tipsy already?"

"I might be," she admitted, draining her champagne and pouring more. "I can't seem to hold my liquor ever since *the change of life* came upon me."

"An unlucky symptom."

She sighed. "Oh, trust me, there are worse symptoms, but I'm too delicate to detail them . . ."

"Delicate? And here they used to call you the American Diana," I teased. "For me it was mostly swollen ankles and hot flashes during a campaign. And I couldn't even complain, because my candidate was dragging around heavy leg braces. It was all very ghastly and inconvenient."

As I stared down resentfully at my still stubbornly puffy ankles, she gave a whimper in sympathy. "At least now we're free of that *other* inconvenience."

I lifted my glass to that. "Our sole compensation for the indignities of menopause."

"Tell me, Frances. Are we supposed to feel like shriveled-up old prunes now? Because I have more zest for life than ever."

"Me too. Maybe it's the urgency of reaching a certain age. If we don't keep chasing the future, we'll think too much about the past."

At that, Mary glanced fondly over at the photograph she kept of her late husband. "Thinking about the past isn't all bad. Do you ever wonder what your life might have been like if you accepted Red's marriage proposal?"

I sank back into the sofa cushions, feeling a little tipsy myself. "Do I wonder what my life might have been like if I said yes to the undignified fool yelling below my window?"

Mary grinned. "In hindsight, don't you think it was rather romantic? No one bellows beneath our windows anymore . . ."

"Thank heavens," I said.

"But don't you wonder?"

"Never." I *had* mused about how much easier my life might have been if I'd married a railroad heiress, but there wasn't any part of me that regretted saying no to Sinclair Lewis. I wouldn't have Susanna. I wouldn't even have the wistful memories of the happy times with Paul. And most importantly: "If I'd married Red, I'd likely be in jail now for his murder."

Mary snorted her champagne and pointed to one of Agatha Christie's novels on the bookshelf. "Miss Perkins in the parlor with a penknife?"

I smirked. "You jest, but with the way he philanders, I'm sure one of his wives is going to do him in . . . and that he'd deserve it."

That was indiscreet of me to say about Red, and I regretted saying it, but, draped over the chair, Mary graciously changed the subject. "All right, one more round. What else shall we toast?"

"How about *absolute* legal victory? The Justice Department says my solicitor is right. I can legally accept persecuted refugees from Nazi Germany, and there's nothing the State Department can do to stop me."

I thought Mary would mock me for ending our fun with a mention of work, but she quite enthusiastically cried, "Well done! I'm happy to learn that your young Mr. Wyzanski is as much of a genius as he thinks he is . . ."

WITH THE COMING of spring, I'd been a cabinet secretary for a year, and I was still trying to convince Roosevelt, and the country— and even myself—that he hadn't made a mistake in appointing me. Now, after watching me engage in a terrific fight with Hugh Johnson, the president fisted his hair.

"Frances, between you and Hugh, I don't know if I'm coming or going. You tell me not to give this speech. Then Hugh hammers at me that I've *got* to give this speech."

"Which one of us has better political sense?"

I tried not to hold my breath while he considered his answer.

Roosevelt finally sighed. "All right. Look over the speech and cross out what you don't like."

I edited the offensive passages.

FDR liked my changes.

Hugh Johnson did not. But I was starting to make the president see that he'd been wrong to make the New Deal synonymous with the Blue Eagle. And FDR surprised the general by saying, "I'm sorry, Hugh, but I'm going with Frances on this."

The morning of the speech, I relaxed until I heard Roosevelt read the part I'd taken out. The part that made him sound like a dictator giving commands. And I sat bolt upright in the silence as people in the audience gave one another shocked and wary looks . . .

Loyally, I clapped to help fill the room with something other than consternation. But it was no use. Already, I could see people were angry—and while they might not have the nerve to attack the president, they were going to tear the rest of us to shreds.

Oh, the *look* I shot General Johnson across the auditorium. I almost took a perverse satisfaction in his misery the rest of the afternoon as speaker after speaker protested the excesses of the NRA. "You know what businessmen want? We want you New Dealers to leave us alone!"

Back at the White House, the president was grim, and, seemingly unable to meet my gaze, he muttered, "Hugh stapled it back into the speech."

"You didn't have to read it," I pointed out. But that wasn't fair. The president assumed that when someone handed him a speech, it was the one he'd agreed to. He could be halfway into a sentence before he caught something amiss. And because of the man involved, it was impossible to know whether Hugh had *intentionally* tricked the president or if it was a liquor-laced misunderstanding.

Now, sheepishly, the president said, "Frances, surely you don't read *every* speech that's put into your hands ahead of time."

"I do. In the car or backstage. I'm a suspicious woman."

Roosevelt moped a little. "Well, there's one thing this incident makes plain."

"What's that?"

"We can't run on the Blue Eagle in the next election. People are starting to turn against it. And if we lose the midterms, then we won't be able to accomplish anything else."

"That's right," I said, resisting the urge to cross my arms in a pose of *I told you so* because I hadn't, in fact, told him so when I should have. Back when it might've mattered.

Now Roosevelt took a deep breath and fixed me with those inscrutable blue-gray eyes. "All right. I'm ready to hear you out; tell me more about this old-age insurance plan of yours."

Fighting down the urge to cheer, I pulled a chair beside him and said, "I thought you'd never ask . . ."

Chapter Fifty-Eight

★ ★ ★

Washington, DC
May 1934

B ONNIE AND CLYDE WERE ROBBING STORES and gas stations. Pretty Boy Floyd was breaking into banks and allegedly setting fire to people's mortgages. John Dillinger and his gang were in shoot-outs with FBI agents. And it was all my fault . . .

Or so said the letters to the editor in the newspaper that blamed my allegedly lax policy on immigration.

As far as I knew, Bonnie and Clyde, Pretty Boy Floyd, and John Dillinger weren't immigrants—and immigration was at a virtual standstill anyway—but my efforts to rescue Jewish refugees had been leaked by the State Department, and I was in a blue funk about the bad press.

Especially now when I was just winning Roosevelt over to my way of thinking.

Immigration cases made up only the smallest part of our work at the Department of Labor but always got me beat up in the papers. And they riled up the nativists against me too.

Recently a group called Friends of New Germany held a pro-Hitler event at Madison Square Garden. Anti-fascist organizations tried to rush the hall and ended up in a melee with police, and the bomb squad had to be called in, but in the end, the rally went off in the swastika-laden hall, where I was denounced *personally* as an enemy in front of a pro-Nazi crowd, twenty thousand strong.

Thankfully, the president said I ought to wear *that* as a badge of honor.

THAT SPRING, ROOSEVELT was all grins under his white brimmed hat, greeting guests as if the USS *Indianapolis* was his very own pleasure yacht.

For the first time in decades, the American fleet was sailing into New York Harbor as a show of readiness against the growing threat overseas, and the president had invited my daughter and me to join him in reviewing the fleet.

"I told you that you should've worn white," Susanna whispered, eying the First Lady in her white turban and light billowy dress. "Now you're going to overheat . . ."

"Don't be silly," I whispered back, grateful for my daughter's company. "I'm a New Englander. I have frost in my blood. Besides, I don't own anything white."

"You would if you let me pick something for you."

I couldn't argue against my daughter's sense of style—after all, Susanna drew the eye of everyone aboard in her smart skirt suit, with her sleek curls pinned beneath a coordinating straw cloche hat. She was a veritable fashion plate with a strong personality, and I took pride in that. It was simply that the beautiful clothes she wore were entirely impractical for *me*. If I should accidentally spill coffee during a tense negotiation, I'd be left looking disheveled. And even if none of that were true: "You don't upset anybody in a simple well-tailored black dress."

Susanna rolled her eyes. "Especially not *your* black dresses, which look like they were designed by the Bureau of Standards." She'd read *that* in the papers and must've known it wasn't nice, because she said,

"Sorry. I'll make it up to you by not complaining about your heavy pocketbook. What do you have in there, anyway?"

"It serves as briefcase and impromptu garment bag, carrying every conceivable thing I might need when at the beck and call of the president, who has a habit of sending me places on a moment's notice."

Today Roosevelt seemed relaxed and happy, propped up at the rail of the ship with his braces locked in place. As soon as he caught sight of us, he hailed Susanna and me to his side.

"Welcome aboard, ladies," Roosevelt said, basking in maritime glory. I think no president has ever loved the Navy half so much, and he reached up as if to pat the big gun overhead like a favorite toy. "Fine day to be underway, isn't it?"

"You're in a good mood," I said as we sidled up to him.

"I'm always in a good mood on the ocean . . . Is this little Susie Wilson all grown up?"

Susanna blushed furiously at the president's attention. And I was delighted that he took a real interest in her. FDR asked about her schooling. Then: "So what do you think of your mother's work?"

"I think it very good so far," Susanna said. "Though I keep asking why there can't be public works programs for artists too."

I startled at her boldness. Susanna had pleaded with me to take this up with the president, and I hadn't found the right moment, but now she argued the idea herself. "The nation needs trees planted, but don't we also deserve to beautify our cities with murals and sculptures in the public parks?"

"Why not?" the president said. "Artists are human beings; they need to live. Surely there's some public place where paintings are wanted."

I knew he didn't appreciate artwork himself—unless it was a picture of a ship—but he wasn't just saying this to be polite. With the encouragement of other people who had the same idea, he'd later implement this plan. But at the time, I was ever so grateful for the way he made Susanna glow with the feeling of being *heard* and included.

And I was so *absolutely* proud of her for mounting her own crusade. Proud, too, of the way she looked at me—as if maybe she might even *look up to me*, which was among the most precious consolations of my life.

When my daughter went off to sit with the president's youngest son, the president told me, "Susie's a smart one, like her mother."

While I tried not to preen like a peacock, FDR told me a little about his forthcoming summer vacation to the Virgin Islands, Panama, Haiti, and Hawaii. He'd be the first president to pass through the Panama Canal. Or to visit the naval base in Pearl Harbor. And now the president said, "I'm told you're becoming quite the world traveler yourself, Frances. How many speeches have you made this year?"

"Nearly a hundred," I said.

"I hear in Alabama they presented you with a bouquet of flowers *in a shoebox*!"

The president laughed, but the most I could manage was a smile. Everywhere in the South, people still made cracks about not wearing shoes. Some even organized barefooted protests against me. "When am I going to live down that ill-considered remark? I fear it's going to be on my tombstone."

The president grinned. "Oh, I'm sure you'll give them something else to write about before you die."

I was certainly trying.

In a list of the president's most trusted advisors, I'd now been ranked fourth. Some were even saying I was so influential that if I were a man, I might *be* president. Of course, I didn't feel influential, because despite everything, the president was still letting General Johnson run the show.

A matter I couldn't help but needle him on when he asked, "How is the automobile strike going?"

"Oh, isn't the general handling it?"

FDR laughed. *"Meow, meow . . ."*

I pressed my lips together, not sure if he knew Johnson had just been checked into Walter Reed to dry out—too delicate an issue to broach aboard a warship swarming with reporters.

The president mistook my silence for peevishness. "Well, all right, Frances. You win."

"Do I want to know what prize?"

FDR laughed at my cheek. "I'm giving you the go-ahead for your social security program. Unemployment, old-age pensions, help for widows and children and the disabled—health insurance too. Put it all in and see how far you can take it."

I absolutely gawped at him. "You mean it?"

He nodded. "You've nagged me into it. Are you happy now?"

"Positively *over the moon.*"

"I want a bill as soon as possible," Roosevelt said.

I really was giddy. The only trouble was that we'd exhausted Congress. "I'm not sure they've got it in them to do the grueling work necessary for a bill like this until after summer."

"All right, then get a committee going to draft it for them," FDR said. "Come January, this social security idea is the first thing on the agenda. Which means, Frances, I need to see a plan by Christmas."

Now I felt the first flicker of panic. This would be a gargantuan legal undertaking. "Since there may be constitutional issues, perhaps the attorney general should chair the committee."

"No, no. You care about this thing, Frances. You believe in it. You'll put your back into it more than anyone else. You'll see that something comes of it without delay. We must have a program by next winter. We must get it started now, or it will never start."

This was such a tremendous show of faith that I forgave him everything that came before. And as we watched the parade of naval ships pass by into the harbor to the cheers of the onlookers onshore, for the first time since I'd sworn my oath, I felt the salty sea-spray fizzle of *confidence* in my veins.

NOW THAT I had Roosevelt's approval, I wanted to put all my focus on a social security plan. But in June, a longshoremen's strike in San Francisco took a bloody turn—the police having shot three men dead. The governor of California wanted the federal government's help in getting the ports open, and the president wanted me to take charge.

"Now, about this San Francisco situation," FDR told us in the cabinet meeting. "In case it becomes more serious, I want it clearly understood that the secretary of labor is boss. Follow her lead."

Roosevelt had never been so explicit before in giving me authority, though I supposed he might not have needed to even say that any of the other cabinet officials were in command of their own portfolios.

It wouldn't be the vice president who would serve as acting president in Roosevelt's absence but the secretary of state, Cordell Hull, with whom I had a cordial relationship. But not long after the president's departure, he called to say, "We need to talk about this strike."

I tried to reassure Secretary Hull. "Yes, it's very unfortunate, but we think it will soon be over."

"I am afraid you're mistaken," Hull said. "I've been talking to the attorney general, and we think it's very serious. And as acting president, I think I should take some severe and drastic steps."

My mind spun, wondering what he could possibly mean by *severe*. I'd already threatened to invoke federal arbitration. What could be more drastic? Fearing he might mean the use of military force, I grabbed my gloves. "I'll be right over."

I found the secretary of state and the attorney general in the law library and started talking even before I was fully into the room. "I assure you, gentlemen, this strike will be over very shortly. We're making progress."

Hull said, "I don't think progress is possible."

I knew that neither of these gentlemen had ever been nearer a strike than you can get by reading the newspaper over the breakfast table. "Well, my people tell me—"

"I don't care about your people," countered the attorney general. "My US attorneys in San Francisco say you've let things get out of control."

Was it a coincidence that the moment the president was out of town, the men in the cabinet began treating me like I was a cream puff they could tread on underfoot? Well, I couldn't let them get away with it. "Now, I suppose your US attorneys are well-to-do gentlemen who have offices in the central part of San Francisco. I doubt they are closely in touch with bakery wagon drivers, or streetcar operators, or printers, or longshoremen on strike. But I am in touch with precisely those people, so you'd better hear me out."

Secretary Hull said, "The police are not able to keep streetcars running. I'm sending in federal troops to break this up."

The hell he was.

Somehow I managed to keep my cool. Quietly, very quietly, I

asked, "How would they break it up, Mr. Secretary? You mean force men to get on the bakery wagons, force them to drive them?"

"Yes, or drive with armed guards so that if any group of bakery wagon drivers attempts to stop them, they can be . . ."

"Shot?" I asked. "You're willing to *shoot* people when this could be resolved in a day or so?"

I didn't let either of them answer.

"Let me predict what will happen," I said, leaning both hands on the table. "Sending in federal troops will create the most terrible resentment, and the rest of the trade unions will join the strike. What's more, San Francisco doesn't take things lying down. They'll gather to hoot and jeer and throw things at the soldiers. Then you know what will happen: The soldiers will fire. The mob will attack. And all because we called out the military against American citizens who haven't done anything except inconvenience the community. They haven't committed murder. They haven't rioted . . ."

I could see my argument wasn't swaying them, so I said, "What a mess for the president to return to! Think of the reaction to the Hoover administration sending the military to shoot at protesting veterans. People will never forgive him for it. So, I think it quite unwise to begin the Roosevelt administration by shooting working people!"

"Madam Secretary," said Hull. "I am resolved to send in troops."

Which meant I had only one card left to play. "Then as a matter of record, I *insist* you get the president's authorization."

I had no idea what I was going to do if he refused. Cordell Hull had the authority, but the president had explicitly said that on labor matters, Hull ought to follow my lead. If he refused, all I could think was to rush to the phones and call the rest of the cabinet together to fight it out . . .

Fortunately, Secretary Hull said, "Well, all right, it'll take us a few hours to make arrangements, but I'll send a wireless through the naval communications system to get final approval from President Roosevelt."

I wandered out of that meeting convinced I was going to have to stoop to something low.

While the two men conferred, I had myself patched through to naval communications. To the sailor who answered, I said, "This is Miss Perkins, the secretary of labor, and I'm going to ask something quite unusual. It's extremely important that I get a rush message through to the president. Now, I know the secretary of state is also going to send a message, and I believe it's about the San Francisco strike, which the president put in my charge. So it's extremely important that President Roosevelt get my message before he gets the secretary of state's message. Would you and your mates be willing to make sure of it?"

I expected the sailor on the other end to panic, to call his superior officer. To tell me I had some nerve. Instead, he gave a jolly laugh. "You got it, Madam Secretary."

In my message, I told FDR that I thought sending in troops would be a disaster. That the secretary of state didn't properly understand the situation. That I was sure I could bring it to a peaceful close with more time. But that *if* he was going to authorize federal troops to fire on American citizens, he'd better come back to Washington right away.

Then I went back to my office, too nervous to drink the cold cup of coffee that Miss Jay left on my desk. Truthfully, I wasn't sure how I was going to get through the day. Cordell Hull was more experienced than I was. And even if he weren't, most people would defer to him over me. Most people would think that, as a woman, I was simply too soft and fearful to resort to bloodshed when it was warranted.

But Franklin Delano Roosevelt wasn't like most people.

The president's reply was everything I'd hoped for. He authorized me to keep negotiating. And he wasn't cutting his trip short either—an implicit message to everyone that he trusted my judgment.

Thankfully, I earned that trust.

Two days later, I got the longshoremen and their employers to submit to arbitration without another shot being fired.

Chapter Fifty-Nine

Washington, DC
August 1934

FLUSH WITH VICTORY, I GREETED ROOSEVELT upon his return. "Welcome back, Mr. President," I said to a tanned FDR, who looked thoroughly rested and refreshed. "I see your Pacific cruise agreed with you."

"Take a look at this," he said, showing me photographs of his being presented with a flower garland by the Hawaiians. "Isn't that something?"

I nodded appreciatively. "It looks like paradise. I wish you could've stayed longer, but people have missed your fireside chats."

"Oh, yes, everyone's frantic to see Papa home again," he said. "But relaxation is important, Frances. It clears the mind. You ought to try it sometime . . ."

It'd been two years since Paul's manic-depressive breakdown, two years during which I'd not stopped to catch my breath, much less clear my mind. "I don't dare."

"Oh, I don't suppose the whole country will collapse without you."

I laughed darkly, because during the longshoremen's strike, it had seemed like it might. "Well, I haven't wanted to ask, but I'd love some time off to spend with my daughter before she starts at Bryn Mawr."

"Susie can't be old enough for college!"

"She's nearly eighteen," I said, wilting with dismay, for it seemed as if time was running out before she'd be on her own, and I could barely stand the thought.

"Take next week off," the president said. "You've earned it."

A week's vacation? I wasn't sure I'd know what to do with myself. Still, I jumped at the chance. "Thank you, Mr. President."

He put a hand on mine. "Frances, I know the boys got in your way while I was gone, but you handled yourself."

What I'd done was potentially subvert the chain of command and put some sailors in a terrible spot. But Roosevelt spoke so approvingly that I glowed with pleasure. "Well, I didn't want you to come home to a bigger mess than you've already got on your hands."

He grimaced. "Hugh Johnson?"

Feeling emboldened, I said, "How long are you going to let this go on?"

As Mary had told me, *Hugh is wrecking himself, wrecking the New Deal, and might wreck the president if someone doesn't stop him.* If the drinking, the gossip about his secretary, and his meddling with the president's speeches weren't bad enough, the drunken general had now gotten into a row with our biggest ally in the Senate.

And when I shared this with Roosevelt, he asked, "Do you think we have to get rid of Hugh?"

I took a deep breath, then made my riskiest move yet. "Yes, I think you do have to get rid of him, although I don't like to say so."

The president hung his head. "I just don't know how to do it without hurting the man terribly."

Despite everything, Hugh Johnson was a patriot. He'd worked himself nearly to death trying to make the Blue Eagle a big success for the country. He didn't deserve to be humiliated, so I said, "Maybe a soft landing could be found—some position that would allow him to save face . . ."

The president agreed. "I'll send him to Europe on a fact-finding mission."

That was an excellent idea. But, fearing a meeting between Hugh and Il Duce would spawn a thousand disastrous comparisons, I said, "Just don't let him get anywhere near Italy."

Roosevelt gave a hoot of laughter, then sent me on my way.

Well, that was that. What a relief. Straightaway, I called up Susanna to ask, "How would you like to get away from the summer heat and take a little trip up to the White Mountains? I thought we'd take in the scenic beauty together, just you and me."

My daughter actually gasped with excitement, and I found myself grinning from ear to ear.

Since Susanna was currently staying with friends in Cooperstown, I said, "I'll drive up on Friday to pick you up. Then we'll be off."

My position had robbed us of much precious time, and I desperately wanted to make it up to her. To give her some happy memories to compensate for the roller coaster of her father's condition, which so often seemed to improve only to deteriorate dramatically again.

That night, as I was packing to go—half-distracted anticipating the feel of crisp mountain air in my lungs—I got a call from the president. "Hugh refused the appointment to Europe, but do you know how I found out? Over the ticker tape!"

I was flabbergasted. "I thought he'd take the soft landing when offered."

Miserably, the president said, "I suppose I've just got to fire him outright."

I decided to push my luck. "*Tomorrow*, I should think. Delaying will mean more speculation in the papers." I didn't envy the president this sorry duty, but nobody else could do this for him. "Good luck," I said, zipping my suitcase.

"Bon voyage," FDR replied.

LESS THAN AN hour later, the telephone was ringing again. This time it was an operator asking if I'd accept a call from my daughter. "Hello, darling," I asked, straining to hear her voice over the crackling line. Glancing at my watch, I worried at the late hour. "Is something the matter?"

"Nothing terrible," Susanna finally said, apologizing for the cost of a long-distance call. "It's only that I can't sleep."

It seemed as if everyone I knew was having trouble sleeping that summer; the heat was unbearable. "I'm sorry, dear. Why don't you open the window and let the night breeze in?"

"I already have," she said as wearily as if she'd already tossed and turned for hours. "But it's still *so* hot, and I'm too excited about our trip tomorrow."

I smiled, sitting up in bed, wrapping the telephone cord around my fingers. "Did Miss Jay let you know that she booked the Mount Washington Hotel for us?"

"She *informed* me. Very brusquely."

I gave a knowing little snort. "Well, I'd worry for Miss Jay's health if she was anything other than brusque."

"She's not coming with us, is she?"

"No, darling. Just you and me. I promise."

"And you're not bringing work?"

"Not a single slip of paper," I vowed, eager to escape the tall pile of reading on my bedside table, and the even taller stacks of files waiting for me at the office. "I hope to do nothing but eat and sleep and hike and fish."

"I doubt the fishing will be as good as in Maine," Susanna replied, for we both had an incurable bias in favor of our annual summers at the old Perkins place. But I'd let my sister and her family have it this summer and didn't want to share.

"Well, there'll be other things to do than fish. I'm told the resort even has its own cog railway to take us to the top of the mountain, where the views are said to be astonishing."

"Miss Jay read me the brochure," Susanna said dryly. "It has a dance hall, a theater, precious artwork, *and* an indoor swimming pool. I want to do and see everything!"

"Then you'd better sleep, or you'll be too tired to enjoy it."

"It's just that my mind keeps *whirring . . .*"

I frowned to hear it, remembering Paul's sleepless nights and what they had presaged in terms of his mental illness. I had to remind myself that Susanna was merely an excited girl, staying with friends and trying to sleep in a strange bed. It need be no more complicated than that.

I slid back onto the pillows of my own bed. "Why not tell me what's whirring in your mind?"

I thought she might have a case of the nerves about enrolling at Bryn Mawr. Or maybe she'd confide in me about a romantic crush. But she said, "I hate the swimsuit you picked for me. It makes me look like a little girl."

"Is that all?" I asked, blowing out a relieved breath. "We shall splurge and buy you a new one at the resort. *If* you promise to try to get a good night's sleep."

I could almost see her grin. "Something sporty and fashionable, with sandals, a new straw hat, and sunglasses?"

I laughed. "Yes. I give in. You're a tough and opportunistic negotiator. You might do well trying to settle labor strikes someday."

Susanna groaned. "Oh, I never want to do *anything* like that."

Tentatively, I asked, "What is it that you want to do?"

She paused, as if this were still a very strange question to ask a young woman. "I suppose I'd like to get married one day. I don't know. I like fashion. I like to paint. Did you know *you* wanted to become a government official when you were my age?"

Thinking back, I couldn't have even conceived of it. "I only knew that I wanted to get an education and to do something to serve the Lord with the talents He gave me."

"How odd that He gave you a talent for labor negotiations," Susanna teased. "It would bore *me* out of my senses."

Truthfully, I also found labor negotiations to be terribly tedious— but I'd never admit it. "Well then! Perhaps if I tell you about the longshoremen's strike, it might put you to sleep."

"I'd rather count sheep," she said with a welcome little yawn.

Now I was yawning, too, imagining my Susanna curled up, her hand cradling the phone to her ear; I could almost smell the familiar scent of her hair . . .

We exchanged a few more sleepy words. Then the operator cut in. In farewell, I reminded her that in just a few hours, we'd be off together for a mother-and-daughter adventure. With that happy thought, I drifted to sleep, dreaming of mountain trails and the making of fond mother-and-daughter memories.

THE NEXT MORNING, with my suitcase by the door, I was finishing my coffee when I nearly spit it out upon the early edition of the newspaper.

PRESIDENT TELLS JOHNSON
HE MUST STAY ON THE JOB

That was the headline, written in bold ink. And I felt a sudden flush of fury at FDR. *Why* had he said he was going to fire Johnson if he didn't want him gone?

If he'd disagreed with me, he could've said so. Instead, he'd sent me on a vacation where, no doubt, he hoped I'd be too busy to realize he'd decided to ignore my advice again.

I will not telephone, I told myself. *I will not show any interest. I don't care what happens. I'm going to Cooperstown to pick up my daughter.*

I was washing my hands of this.

Grabbing my suitcase, I got in the car, and off I went. The chauffeur drove most of the day, and we arrived just before supper, around five o'clock. But the moment we pulled into the drive, Susanna and everyone else in the house came rushing out. "Come quickly! Washington has been calling you all day long. It's the president's office. It's very, very important."

"So *important*," Susanna muttered bitterly.

I went inside and dropped my bag. "Can I please get a glass of cold water?" It'd been a hot day and a hot drive, and I wanted to freshen up, but I was ushered to the phone.

FDR's secretary answered. "The president says you must be here tomorrow morning at the White House at ten o'clock."

My stomach dropped out. "I talked to him only yesterday, and he said it was all right for me to go away for a week. What in the world does he want me for?"

"Haven't you seen the morning papers? Figure it out."

I clenched my teeth and hung up the phone. *Figure it out?* That was curt and disrespectful . . .

Well, I'd swung my ax for Hugh Johnson's head and missed. If he knew, he'd swing back. The most logical explanation for calling me back to Washington in a curt and disrespectful way was that *I* was about to be fired . . .

I'd seen it speculated about in the papers—that FDR wanted to be rid of me but didn't have the nerve. Maybe I should've seen the signs. I'd certainly made no friends at the State Department while advocating for Jewish refugees. I'd irritated the attorney general during the longshoremen's strike. Maybe Johnson had convinced the president I had to go.

Well, I wasn't going to break my promise to my daughter and rush back to Washington just for *that*. Franklin Delano Roosevelt knew how to use a telephone if he wanted to get rid of me. In fact, he wouldn't have to lift a finger to dial. I was ready to write up my resignation letter on the spot . . .

Or so I told myself as Susanna lingered in the doorway in saddle shoes and a new seersucker skirt, her eyes red-rimmed and angry. "Here's a glass of water before you go."

She knew I *would* go. No matter how furious I was about it, I was the first female cabinet member and had to maintain the dignity of that office; if the president summoned me—and he was *always* summoning me—I'd have to go.

My throat tightened as I took the drink from her. "I'm so sorry, darling. We'll plan another trip. We'll go to the Brick House in Maine."

Susanna only nodded, silently and sullenly.

I'd gotten her hopes up. And that made me even angrier at Franklin Delano Roosevelt. I was practically cursing his name as I washed my face and changed into a fresh set of travel clothes. Then I kissed Susanna's forehead and held her face in my hands. "I'll make it up to you. I'm leaving a little check for you to buy that new swimming suit."

"Sure." The sadness in her lowered eyes was an arrow to my heart.

I was always leaving her, it seemed, and I hated myself for it!

It was a miserable trip back to Washington, and by the time I got to the White House, I was as foul-tempered as I'd ever been in my life. "For heaven's sake, what *is* this?" I asked the president's secretary.

"I gave up a trip with my daughter, which the president himself told me to take."

The secretary replied, "I can only tell you that he's also asked to see Johnson and his number two."

Well, this was appalling. Was I about to be replaced by Johnson's underling? I wouldn't have thought the president had it in him to humiliate me in such a way . . .

Just then, Johnson marched in, red-faced and vacant-eyed, the way he usually looked when he was fresh off a bender. Seeing me, his nostrils flared . . .

Wordlessly, I followed the general into the Blue Room and found the president with his back to the windows, looking very grave. It was our habit to break tension with some sort of joke, but I was so mad I only bitterly quipped, "Well, Mr. President, I have had a beautiful one-hour vacation with my daughter in Cooperstown."

He didn't crack a smile. "Sit down."

The three of us sat.

Me, Johnson, and his number two. Once we were seated like three schoolchildren called to the principal's office, I braced myself. But the president didn't pay any attention to me. Instead, he said, "General Johnson, I think we've been misunderstanding each other. I asked you to go on a mission to Europe. But you refused."

I found myself looking at my altogether too-sensible shoes. *Dear God*, the president wasn't firing me. He was firing Hugh Johnson after all. Now the president made that explicit. "I think you should resign at once, Hugh. Frankly, you've become a problem. I can't discuss it further, but I think you should resign immediately."

Oh, no, this was just terrible. Dreadfully awkward. I'd have wished myself out of existence to avoid being in this room. Then the president rapped the table to make us all look up. "You understood what I said, didn't you, Miss Perkins?"

"Yes, sir," I murmured.

Johnson turned purple. "Very well, Mr. President, I'm a good soldier. I do what I'm asked to do by my commander in chief. Unless there's something more . . ."

"Nothing more, General," said FDR.

Then Johnson strode out.

I figured he'd run straight out to the press, so I made ready to follow and stop him if I could, when the president called after me. "Wait a minute, Frances, I want to speak to you."

FDR now looked like a wreck. Wiping his brow, he groaned. "Gee, that was awful. Just *awful*. Thanks for coming."

I sputtered, wondering if I ought to remind him, again, that he'd ruined my vacation with my daughter. Instead, I settled on asking, "Why in the world did you send for me?"

"I had to have witnesses," the president explained. "I already fired him once, but he was so drunk he went out to the press and told them I asked him to stay on with his boots nailed to the floor. This time I had to have witnesses, and I didn't know anybody else I could safely have. Johnson trusts you."

"Not after today, he won't," I said. "He'll never trust me again."

"Why not? You won't tell the world about this. I expect that he'll be confused again by tonight and not know whether he's been told to stay or go."

Sometimes the president could be so worldly and clever, and other times as innocent as a child. But he was also filled with compassion—genuine compassion. "Hugh has a disease," he said. "He'll be at the bottom of a bottle by night's end, but he will believe you when you tell him what I really said, Frances. You can soothe him. He's awfully upset, and I feel terrible for him."

"I won't be able to soothe him," I said. "And Mary won't be able to do it either. He's going to believe I'm a backstabber who engineered his downfall and wanted to be here to see it through. He's not likely ever to speak a civil word to me again."

And it's true; Hugh Johnson never did.

But I suspected the real reason the president called me back was that he needed me to put steel in his spine, because he said, "I just needed you here, Frances. I *needed* you."

I stared at him where he sat in that wheelchair, his hands calloused from pushing at the rims. His hair still a little damp from the swimming pool he'd had installed at the White House so he could try to keep the rest of his body from withering like his legs. So that he could get some relief from the constant pain. He pushed himself every day—and not just for his own ego but for the nation.

Knowing all that tamped down my anger at how hard he was pushing me.

His voice was hoarse when he said, "With Johnson gone, I'm going to need you now more than ever. If we want to win the midterm elections, you're going to have to get out there and be the voice of the New Deal."

I nearly said that I didn't care if we won the midterm elections. Unfortunately, these midterm elections were, paradoxically, more important to *me* than they were to FDR, because no matter what else happened, Franklin Delano Roosevelt would still go down in history as the president of a great nation.

But if we lost, all the sacrifices my family had made would be for naught. We didn't yet have a social security program, and if we didn't win these midterms, we never would. So instead of planning another vacation, I hit the campaign trail.

Chapter Sixty

* * *

Brunswick, Maine
September 3, 1934

WHY WAS I CHOKING ON SMOKE AND THE scent of burning rubber? My thoughts were jumbled. And the remains of my breakfast rose like gorge as I heard Miss Jay moan in pain next to me. My elbow was somehow wedged in her back, and I faintly tasted blood in my mouth.

Hers? Mine? I couldn't tell. She shouted something, but the sound cracked against my already-throbbing temples.

I've always hated shouting, I thought.

My sister's tantrums. Paul's raised voice when he couldn't control himself. It wasn't his fault, but it made me simmer sometimes, quietly resentful that he couldn't be a dependable husband and father. *Poor Susanna.* How thin she'd looked when we'd waved goodbye. I was always leaving her. Why was I always waving goodbye?

The speech, I thought. *I'm going to be late . . .*

I groaned as cold water rose higher around me, and something hissed beyond my vision. Then, through the broken window, I glimpsed my driver's legs bespattered in mud. "Miss Perkins, are you hurt?"

Reality rushed back. Now I remembered that I'd been on my way from Maine to Boston to give a speech for Labor Day. I also remembered how my driver had swerved to avoid hitting a car ahead of us. The screech of the tires and our screams. The flash of blue sky, brown earth, then blue sky again in the window as we tumbled end over end.

The car had come down in a ditch. Miss Jay and I had landed hard together, arms and legs akimbo. I didn't know how long we'd been lying here, muddy water leaking in one window and smoke in the other.

I tried to push myself upright. Pain shot through both my arms as I moved, forcing me to make a hiss of my own.

"Help Miss Jay," I finally called out. "Can you pull her out?"

"I'll try," said the driver, reaching in.

"Just hurry up about it," snapped Miss Jay. Then, trembling, she let the driver help her crawl out of the wreckage. I followed carefully, climbing over glass and rent metal and her abandoned shoe. By the time I clawed my way onto the grassy embankment, a crowd had formed on the roadside above, and Good Samaritans were hastening to help.

"Are you hurt?" I kept asking Miss Jay.

"Are you hurt?" I kept asking the driver.

They kept asking me the same. None of us were sure. As we stared at the wreckage of the automobile, it was a wonder we were alive. Someone fished our luggage out of the ditch while someone else agreed to take us to the nearest inn to clean up while the town doctor was summoned.

After poking and prodding us and bandaging our little cuts and scrapes, the physician said, "Well, none of you seem badly hurt, but I recommend a visit to the hospital just the same."

Oh, how tempting it was to go to a hospital and climb between crisp sheets and be taken care of. Miss Jay limped to the phone. "I'll ring up Boston and tell them to call off the speech."

I started to nod because I ached from head to toe. But I *couldn't* cancel the speech. It was Labor Day, and I was the secretary of labor. I needed to report to an anxious country that five million people had now been put back to work and that payrolls were up sixty-three percent since the low point of the Depression. I had to tell them that there was hope and that I had a plan . . .

"Don't cancel," I rasped. "I'm all right. I'll just be late."

A WEEK LATER, all my cuts and scrapes had healed, and I only felt a little banged up. "Can you come to the wedding?" Mary asked. "My son is going to set tongues wagging. Imagine: the grandson of a railroad baron marrying the washerwoman's daughter. It's a new world, Frances. What do you think of my boy's wonderful audacity?"

"I'd think it even more wonderful if he hadn't set a wedding date during the weekend of the AFL's convention."

"Drat! That's right. Very inconsiderate of him not to consider the labor unions and the midterm elections when planning connubial bliss," she teased. "Well, then, you and I are destined to be passing ships in the night. When you get back, hopefully we can go for a picnic at my farm."

"I'd love to," I said, bolstered by the notion.

In the meantime, I was determined to embrace Mary's cheerful mindset and see my daughter off to college properly. I'd hoped, of course, that Susanna would choose to attend my beloved Mount Holyoke. But Bryn Mawr was closer and certainly had its charms. So we took the train up to Philadelphia bright and early and ate lunch at the college's cottage tearoom, where Dutch toast was a specialty.

Despite the vapid chatter of stylish students wearing peaked hats and trading cigarettes, I thought my daughter would get a very fine education here.

"The Dutch toast is very good with cinnamon on top," I said to my daughter. For years now, I'd taken to eating sparsely because public officials who overindulged while the rest of the country went hungry could only court resentment. But this was a special occasion. "At least try the bacon; it's extra crispy, the way you like."

"I'm too nervous to eat," Susanna said.

Well, it was normal to be nervous for the first day of college, I decided. It might take some adjusting, but I'd taken Susanna to Europe, introduced her to world leaders, and let her take part in dinner parties with famous authors and philosophers and businessmen. She already had a depth of experience that few of her classmates could match. I'd seen to that, and I could at least take pride in that aspect of my parenting.

After an expensive trip to the bookstore, we found Susanna's room, unpacked her bags, and started to put things away. "You know your father wishes he could be here with us today. He would be if he could be."

"Is he *ever* coming home?" she asked.

It was the most painful of questions. And I wished I had a better answer. "I hope so. There's been talk of releasing him into a boardinghouse with supervision, but as of late, he is feeling terribly down . . ."

"He doesn't seem any different to me."

That was because I never let her see her father when he was at his worst. I only let her visit when Paul was having a good day. To reassure her, I said, "Well, his doctors say there may be some promising new treatments on the horizon, and—"

"I wish I could take Balto with me to college," Susanna interrupted abruptly. Strange behavior on her part. Plainly, the subject of her father was too painful to discuss. Should I be irritated or grateful?

"Alas, that's not allowed, darling. Balto will just have to come live with me and Mary in Washington."

Susanna sighed, staring at herself in the mirror. "Did you see those girls in the tearoom? They all looked so sleek and sophisticated."

"Most are older than you," I pointed out.

"Thinner too."

"Goodness. You're looking *too* thin these days. And you didn't eat more than a bite of lunch."

She shrugged. "It tasted off to me. But you'd eat sawdust if it got you through to your next appointment."

That wasn't as much of a lie as I wished it were. "I don't have to worry about you, do I? You must promise that you'll start your days at Bryn Mawr with some sort of nourishing breakfast. Some milk, some—"

"I'm not a child, Mother."

I swallowed, the enormity of seeing her off to college hitting me anew. "Well, that's true, but you're still *my* child, and I'm afraid being meddlesome is an imperative of motherhood."

"Mary is more of a mother to me than you are."

My heart! If she'd aimed to wound me, her arrow hit its mark. I had to fold my arms over my chest as if to stanch the bleeding.

Susanna had been stewing ever since our interrupted vacation over the summer. And now she said, "I bet you forgot about my coming-out party. Mary is planning it for me at the Rainbow Room. Did you know?"

"I didn't forget, and yes, I know Mary's *servants* are planning your coming-out party at the Rainbow Room because I can't afford to. Which is terribly generous of her."

"It's going to be in December, just before Christmas," Susanna said, then asked sarcastically, "Do you think you'll be able to make it?"

"*Susanna,*" I said, a warning in my voice, as there were limits to how far I'd allow disrespect.

Then we were both quiet for a time, stuffing clothes into closets and pulling sheets tight on the bed. All the while, I was remembering making up her crib when she was a baby, the warmth of her on my chest when she slept, her joy at seeing sunspots in my grandmother's summer kitchen, and the way she crawled to me to share her excitement.

I remembered, too, brushing her hair and reading her to sleep, her little girl's fingers curled in my firm hand. How I longed for the closeness and intimacy of those days; how I feared my daughter and I might never be close again . . .

So for the rest of the afternoon, I kept up a steady stream of sweet and silly chatter in the hopes we might both take from this day the happy new memories I was so desperate to make.

Chapter Sixty-One

★ ★ ★

Dallas, Texas
October 1934

Dear Paul,
You must try for calm and peace and constructive, easy, relaxed
living. You'll soon do it, my dear love, and be reunited with us.
~ Your loving wife

These days, I was always traveling somewhere for the president, as if
on the run from my own troubles. While my committee worked on
getting a social security bill drafted, I rushed from state to state, city
to city, even politely smiling through gritted teeth as a Texan choral
group greeted me by singing "All God's Chillun Got Shoes."

If we want a social security plan, you'll have to get out there and rally
the voters, the president had told me, because we both knew the midterm elections were going to decide the fate of the country.

And the things I saw on the campaign trail only stiffened my
spine. I could never forget that old grandmother in Missouri sitting
in her rocking chair while her family drove off and left her behind.
But the specter of unemployment—of starvation, of hunger, of the
wandering boys, of the broken homes, of the families separated while
somebody went out to look for work—stalked *everywhere*.

The unpaid rent, the eviction notices, the furniture and bedding
on the sidewalk, the old lady weeping over it, the children crying, the
father out looking for a truck to move their belongings to his sister's

flat or some relative's already overcrowded tenement, or just sitting there bewilderedly waiting for some charity officer to come and move him somewhere.

All of it made me flare with a righteous anger that our Republican opponents didn't seem to believe a government of the people, by the people, and for the people ought to do anything about it.

They deserved to lose the election even more than we deserved to win it.

I'd just arrived at a hotel and was removing my hat—a new one given to me by the hatters' union, with bows and a silver buckle, one side of the brim turned up and the other down, to remind me of the ups and downs of the New Deal—when I got a call from Mary. "Frances, you might want to come home . . ."

Worried, I nearly crumpled the hat in my hands. "Is it Paul?"

"It's Susanna. She's developed a serious case of whooping cough."

My heart clutched. I'd just left Susanna at Bryn Mawr a few weeks before. I knew illness could come on suddenly, but a mother never ceased to blame herself for missing the signs.

"It's serious enough that Bryn Mawr intends to quarantine her for three weeks," Mary continued. "But Susie's feeling so miserable, I think we might rather have her at home with us."

"I'll take the next train back," I said.

Before I could hang up, Mary added, "I don't want you to be shocked when you see her. Susie's quite *thin*. The school nurse says she's been subjecting herself to some manner of extreme diet."

Now I felt almost sick with guilt. Wasn't I the woman who'd done her master's thesis on child malnutrition? I'd noticed that my daughter looked terribly thin, and yet I'd left her there at college . . .

By the time I got back to our townhome in Georgetown, a gaunt Susanna was sleeping in a big feather bed upstairs. And to calm me,

Mary said, "Her cough is easing. I got her to eat a little soup. And don't worry about your speech tomorrow; Eleanor is taking it over, and she says you're not to argue."

I was being thoroughly *managed*, but for once in my life, I didn't mind, because between Mary Rumsey and Eleanor Roosevelt, I couldn't be in better hands. Now, if only I could manage my daughter half so well . . .

AT FIRST, SUSANNA was weak as a lamb, too beset by a brutal cough to refuse tea and soup. Now that she was recovering strength, she declared, "Mother, I'm never going to fit into my clothes if I keep eating like this."

"Then we'll have your dresses let out," I said, holding a spoon to her lips with determination. "You mustn't refuse food when so many children in this country are starving."

"Let them have it," she whispered, turning away.

The physician had said that whooping cough could sometimes cause a lack of appetite, but I knew this had been going on since before she got sick. And her moods—oh, how they swung.

In the other room, the telephone was ringing again. I knew these were calls from my office—urgent business, mostly from the committee I had formed on social security, which couldn't agree on anything. Balto echoed my annoyance with the occasional bark at the ringing telephone, but I refused to answer until I understood what truly afflicted my daughter.

"I understand you're interested in beauty and fashion, darling," I said gently. "And I hate to sound like my mother, but it *can* be taken to the point of vanity, which is a sin."

My daughter dared to roll her eyes, which made me happier than it should have because it was the most spirit she'd shown in days.

"You realize that you can't go back to college until you're well, and you won't get better unless you eat."

Cautiously, Susanna peered up at me from beneath her lashes. "What if I don't want to go back?"

I nearly dropped the spoon. "Why wouldn't you want to go back?"

"I'm so *lonely* at college," she admitted. "I don't have any friends at all."

"Oh, but it takes time to make friends in a new place, darling. I didn't know anybody when I started at Mount Holyoke, but I was elected class president in my senior year."

"I'm nothing like you," Susanna said, staring down at her hands.

"Are you *quite* sure about that?" I brushed damp strands of hair from her brow. "Because you seem to be every bit as stubborn as I was at your age. But, of course, you're much prettier than I ever was and more charming when you *want* to be. So I know you'll make friends eventually. You're a very well-informed and interesting young lady."

Softening, Susanna murmured, "You're the only one who thinks so."

"Now, that's not true. The president himself was in your thrall on the ship the day of the naval inspections."

She allowed a hint of a smile at the memory. She even let me spoon the rest of the soup into her mouth. But then she was beset with another coughing jag so intense it nearly made her vomit.

Oh, my poor, poor girl.

She'd become literally sick with loneliness. *My fault. All my fault.* With her father in an asylum and me in the president's cabinet, had she been lost in the shuffle the way I feared she would be?

In the hours that followed, I sat near her bed, watching her sleep, until Mary pulled me aside to whisper, "Frances, she's very well cared for; you needn't play nurse."

"I'm her mother."

"You're also a cabinet secretary," Mary replied. "*I* can get her soup. But the phone is ringing off the hook because the election is almost here, and the president needs you."

Well, at the moment I simply didn't care.

After all, it wasn't only Susanna's physical needs I was tending to. Something afflicted her mind, and I was terrified that it might be the same thing that afflicted her father. But, of course, I couldn't bear to even speak that fear. "A child wants to feel loved and cared for by her own mother. It's perfectly natural."

Mary replied, "You *do* love and care for her. Intensely. But even if you didn't, plenty of children grow up perfectly normal having been paid much less attention than you pay Susanna. Look at *you*. You've never even spoken of your own mother as being affectionate, much less attentive."

"My grandmother was."

"Your grandmother, who lived to so old an age that if she were still alive now, she might be picking through garbage cans for her meals . . ."

"That's simply horrid of you," I said in answer to this transparent manipulation. "Beneath you entirely. I suspect Eleanor or the president put you up to saying something like that."

She didn't deny it.

Though the First Lady had been gracious in taking over some of my speeches, I could virtually *feel* the impatience radiating from the White House. And Mary could too. "What if I sit with Susanna for a little while so you can get some rest or answer your phone calls?"

"I'm precisely where I want to be."

"Just go for an hour or two," Mary said sweetly. She even batted her eyelashes at me.

"*Just* an hour," I said, finally relenting.

When I returned, my daughter was propped up, waiting with a suspiciously agreeable expression on her face. "Mary says the president's party always loses in the midterms. Is it true?"

"Just in every election since the Civil War," I chirped, as if that knowledge didn't terrify me.

Susanna hugged her pillow. "And what will happen if you lose the midterms?"

Oh, I will only have wasted two years of our lives, I thought. *And the New Deal will probably go down in flames.*

The stakes in these midterms were incredibly high. Perhaps the highest of any election in my lifetime. But I patted her knee and said, "That's not for you to worry about."

"I *do* worry about it," Susanna murmured, her lower lip quavering. "I know your work is important. It's just that sometimes I wish someone else could do it."

"Oh, my darling." I sat beside her on the bed and gathered her in my arms. "I'm sure someone else can." As much as I liked to flatter myself that Roosevelt depended upon me, the truth was that Harold Ickes, Harry Hopkins, and Henry Wallace were all extremely able lieutenants and ardent New Dealers. "The president is just going to rely on others until you're well. In the meantime, I intend to just be a *normal* mother and nag at you to eat your breakfast, lunch, and dinner."

A small smirk played upon my daughter's lips. "I don't think you know how to be a *normal* mother."

I laughed because it was probably true. And if I'd tried to deny it, it probably would've angered her. But, perhaps seeing that I was vulnerable, too, Susanna sighed. "If I promise to eat every bowl of soup put before me, will you stop hovering and go make the speeches the president wants you to make?"

I was deeply moved to know that my daughter—as needy and

troubled and resentful as she might be—was trying very hard to be grown-up now. "You don't really want me to go, do you?"

"I do," Susanna finally said. "Really, I do."

"What on *earth* did Mary say to you?"

"That's our secret," Susanna said smugly. "But I want to live in a country where young people like me have a future. So, you must go."

My heart swelled with gratitude. But even with her blessing, it was hard to leave. It helped to remember that I was doing it for other girls her age, just starting out in life, without prospects. And that I was doing it for Susanna too. Because even with the advantages I'd given her, she could find herself in terrible straits if fate took a dark turn.

TUESDAY, I CAMPAIGNED for the Democrats in Ohio, where I ran into an old classmate whose husband had fallen on hard times. She'd come to see me wearing a threadbare coat, and when I saw her shiver, she tried to excuse it by saying, "I had far too many cups of coffee this morning."

I bet coffee is all you've had for days, I thought, insisting on buying her lunch.

Wednesday, I campaigned in Indiana, where a man in the crowd started bawling right out there in the open as he told me he'd take any work at all. He'd offered to paint fences, pick up trash, or mow what grass there was left, but nobody would hire a man over forty-five.

Thursday, I visited both Missouri and Minnesota, where homeless men slept on sacks of scratch seed in the park, and a mother begged for shoes for her children. The town's factory owners were Republican, but the mother and every man sleeping in the park said they'd vote Democrat.

Friday, I crisscrossed Iowa, where, to combat falling prices that caused foreclosures, misguided and desperate farmers had dumped milk into the parched ground. They wanted farm relief. And they wanted a sense of social security. If anything, some felt Roosevelt had been too timid.

Saturday, I stumped in South Dakota, which had been hit hard by the bank collapses, the crop failures, the storms, and a swarm of grasshoppers. One self-reliant man confessed to me that he'd bought insurance to protect his family from calamity but lost it when he couldn't afford to pay the premiums. And I assured him that a social security plan would help.

Sunday, I stormed Nebraska, where little children lay dying of dust pneumonia, and people in every town spent what money they had left on masks instead of food.

At each stop, I told them we'd help if they sent Roosevelt supporters to Congress. "You've got to pull the lever for the Democrats."

In short, I made a whirlwind trip to rally the faithful. Meanwhile, the president tried to rally *my* spirits. A newspaper photographer at some campaign function had caught me in a pose that looked almost coquettish, and FDR clipped the picture and sent it to me with a little note that read, *After all these years of trusting you, I believed that I could let you go to Chicago without a chaperone. You really must not let the cameramen catch you when you are so truly coy!*

It was cheeky flirtation that meant nothing but always tickled my funny bone. Now—with the blur of flashbulbs, podiums, and chicken dinners behind me—I rushed back to New York to cast my own vote, bright and early Tuesday morning.

The crowds on Election Day looked good, the weather was wonderful, and I hoped for a good off-year vote. Some were predicting that we might just beat the historical odds and have a Democratic victory, but it turned out to be quite a bit better than that . . .

"A landslide," Roosevelt crowed when I got back to the White House. "We've got two-thirds of Congress now!"

The president's mood was buoyant. He'd worked hard for this victory, spending so much time on a train and in a car that if you'd asked him, he'd have been able to name every county in America and who the party leader was there. Now our victorious allies in Congress were planning a week of jubilation, and I felt satisfied from the top of my weary head to my aching toes.

As I shared a celebratory cocktail with the president, I said, "Do you know what this means? Republicans can no longer claim Americans haven't had a chance to weigh in. The voters *want* us to press forward with a social security plan."

"And we *will*," the president vowed. "Frances, you do whatever it takes to get your committee to agree on a plan by Christmas."

Chapter Sixty-Two

Washington, DC
November 16, 1934

La la, Madam! Your actions thunder so loud they drown out your denials of communism. Senate and House would serve well their country to impeach FDR and you.
~Anonymous postcard

On the heels of political victory, the first ten refugees I helped flee Hitler's Germany had just arrived in New York—Jewish lads between eleven and fourteen. All downtrodden, hungry, and traumatized.

At least we've saved these boys from the Nazis, I thought.

I couldn't imagine the sight of persecuted children would arouse anything but pity in the hardest of human hearts, but in that I was wrong. Almost immediately, angry nativist groups bayed for my blood because—with the help of the German Jewish Children's Aid society—I'd cleared the way to get two hundred and fifty more Jewish children out of Nazi Germany and into the United States.

My detractors said I only did it because I was myself a secret Jew. And a Russian Red communist too. As evidence, they pointed to my supposedly gentle treatment of communists they claimed had infiltrated the American labor movement.

They even said I ought to be impeached.

Of course, everyone in the office dismissed the criticism. Laughed at it, even.

Just bigots whining about so-called undesirables in our midst—

—can't impeach her, anyhow—

Miss Perkins doesn't even have a parking ticket to her name.

My enemies had been waiting in vain for years to see me compromise myself in money matters, or love, or some other way, and now I resolved anew that I would never give them the satisfaction.

Still, it was the first time I heard of anybody wanting to impeach me, and I was less sanguine about it than everyone else in the office. A constant tension took up residence in my neck, and I began to worry they weren't going to only blacken my name but derail social security too.

"I don't see why anyone should be so angry about these Jewish children," I said at the breakfast table. "Not one—not one!—will end up on the public dole."

"You know why," Mary said with a heavy sigh.

And Susanna took an angry bite out of her buttered crumpet. "They're just plain prejudiced."

I was glad both for my daughter's righteous anger and for the color in her cheeks. If things kept on this way, she'd soon be fully recovered and able to return to Bryn Mawr. So I enjoyed watching her eat in this rare moment of domestic tranquility. For nothing in my work life was tranquil at all.

The president's Christmas deadline for a social security plan was coming swiftly upon me, and my committee still could not agree. A federal system or a state system? Should everyone get benefits or just the needy? Flat rate or tiered? Which plan would pass constitutional muster? Round and round the arguments went.

I was beginning to fear we'd spend ten years studying the problem and issue a report nobody would read.

Not that the president made it any easier . . .

THAT MAN. OH, that man!

"Now, don't do anything rash, Frances," Mary warned as I hurriedly changed clothes from the outfit I'd worn to a conference of policy experts that FDR had thrown into chaos.

"Did you hear Roosevelt's speech?"

"I heard," she said with a knowing groan. "But he's the president, Frances; he's allowed to change his mind."

"No, he's not," I insisted, having spent the afternoon being *heckled* by reporters. "Not about social security."

FDR liked to joke that a conservative was a man with two perfectly good legs who has somehow never learned to walk forward. But he was going around in circles, and I wanted to throttle him.

Putting on one shoe while gesturing with the other, I said, "He sent me all over the country stumping for a social insurance plan, and now he doesn't want it? If he's changed his mind, then I'm going to march over there and change it back again, or he can find a new secretary of labor."

"*Frances*, I'm not letting you leave the house until you promise you'll try to be diplomatic."

I promised just to get out the door, and by the time I got to the White House, I'd worked out something calm, sensible, and diplomatic to say. But the moment Roosevelt rolled into the room, I cried, "Mr. President, you have me at the end of my rope!"

That man actually had the audacity to grin. "Well, I always say, if you've reached the end of your rope, tie a knot and hold on."

Wringing my hands, I asked, "What could you have been thinking? We ran and won on social security. Now you're getting cold feet?"

The president tugged his chin in the way he always did when he was up to something. "Who says I'm getting cold feet? I never said I was ruling it out."

"That's not what the papers will say about your speech. You're going to make voters howl."

A sly grin slipped past his hand. "Maybe I want them to howl."

I stared at him. Then stared at him some more.

Oh, this was FDR at his most cagey. He wanted the citizenry to send a flood of angry letters. He wanted the phones in Congress to be ringing off the hook with a demand for social security so they couldn't backtrack on their election promises to support our plan . . .

Whatever that plan ended up being.

Roosevelt was *brilliant* when it came to politics—but I still wanted to wring his neck. "Well, you could've warned me what you were up to."

His eyes flashed with mirth. "Oh, Frances, when it comes to politics, I don't even let my right hand know what my left hand is doing."

He was altogether too proud of his deviousness, so I decided to lance a vulnerable spot. "The risk of your gambit is that you're going to look like a swishy feather duster if you keep going back and forth on social security."

He frowned in a way that told me he knew about his old nickname but was going to let my insubordination go unpunished for the moment. "Well, then go out there and say I'm not going back and forth on anything."

He could've corrected the record himself if he wanted to. Instead, he was going to trot me out there to argue with the press. And I was going to do it, because I'd become a good soldier.

"DON'T FORGET ABOUT the tea party this afternoon," Mary said, packing for a jaunt to the countryside, where she'd be doing something horsey about which I'd paid too little attention.

"Oh, this tea party I won't forget," I promised.

I generally ducked out of Washington parties—especially those held in the middle of a workweek. But this one was to be hosted by the wife of a Supreme Court justice, and that wasn't an invitation one could turn down.

"Don't wear black," Mary advised.

"I like to wear black," I said.

"Because you like to remind men of their mothers," she said. "But today you'll be with ladies; borrow my cobalt blue jacket upstairs— the one with the fur collar."

I feared that jacket would be too tight, but at long last I'd learned not to argue with Mary about such things.

I arrived at Justice Stone's household as late as politeness would allow but was still obliged to chitchat about trivial matters with a crowd of Washington ladies over black tea.

Accepting an irritating number of compliments on Mary's blue jacket, I took a sugar biscuit, which was so dry I feared breaking a tooth. Stifling a cough, I slipped back to the dining room to dispose of the biscuit somehow and refill my cup. It was there, by the napkins and tea cart, that I spied Justice Stone. He still had a coat over one burly arm as if he'd just returned from the court, hoping to grab a quick cup of tea and disappear into the recesses of the house.

I should've let him go unmolested, but some powerful instinct took hold of me, and I cleared my throat to make my presence known. "Why, Mr. Justice. What a delight to see you."

"Oh, dear," he said, plate in hand. "I was hoping to snatch a bit of cake to go with my tea without my wife seeing and scolding me about my waistline."

I looked over my shoulder, then back at him conspiratorially. "I certainly won't tell. If she comes in, I'll say the cake is mine."

He laughed at that, and now that we had rapport, he asked, "Tell me, Secretary Perkins, how are you getting on?"

He asked it the way one asks about someone who has been given a fatal diagnosis and is putting up a brave but futile fight. I imagine he'd been reading all the outcry against me in the newspapers and suspected a woman wouldn't be able to hold up under all the public criticism much longer.

"I'm perfectly all right," I said, then changed my mind. For once, it might be better for a man to see me as a damsel in distress. "Well, truthfully, I am having big troubles, Mr. Justice."

"Yes, yes, I've heard."

I looked up at him wide-eyed and then made a wild roll of the dice. "I'm especially vexed when it comes to the Social Security Act, which I'm working on. The committee is deadlocked. I can't get them to agree to a plan."

To try to get him to opine on the matter was, I admit, the longest of long shots. I wasn't even sure it was strictly proper, but I was desperate, so I rambled on, "We're not quite sure, you know, what will be the wise method of establishing this law. It's a very difficult constitutional problem . . ."

He chuckled, seeing through me. "Yes, that *is* a difficult problem. How will you solve it?"

As always, I tried to brazen it out. "Well, I don't know. Perhaps you can give me a clue!"

It was perfectly deniable; he could've laughed it off. Instead, he glanced over his shoulder to make sure no one was listening, then leaned near my ear to whisper, "The taxing power, my dear. You can do anything under the taxing power."

EUREKA! I NEVER confessed to the committee how I'd come to this decision, but I was adamant. "The whole program must rest on the authority of Congress to tax for the general welfare."

We were working over the weekend, and the argument continued to go round. Then Miss Jay shuffled in with an expression on her face that was sour even by her standards. "Madam Secretary, Miss Wilson is on the telephone."

My daughter so rarely telephoned me at the office that I picked up the receiver immediately, not even waiting for privacy.

Susanna's voice was strained when she said, "There's been an accident. Several riders were hurt at a fox hunt, and Mary took the worst of it. She's at the Emergency Hospital in Washington."

So it was that I abandoned the committee abruptly, rushing to the hospital, where I found my daughter outside Mary's room, visibly trembling.

"Her horse rolled over on her," Susanna said.

We went in together, and oh, the relief to see Mary's eyes flutter open. Her cheek was scraped bloody, and she breathed shallow breaths in obvious pain. I took her hand tenderly. "Oh, my poor Mary. I'm so sorry this happened to you."

Somehow Mary cracked a pained smile and rasped, "It's what I get for riding sidesaddle."

"Mrs. Rumsey's condition is satisfactory," the doctor reported. "Unfortunately, her leg and collarbone are broken, and she possibly has a hip fracture to boot."

It was a horrific array of injuries. The doctor explained that she'd be confined to the hospital for weeks if not months. And Mary groaned at this unwelcome news. "I can't lie in bed for *months*."

"You haven't any other choice," I said.

"I'll die of boredom," Mary whispered on a pained puff of air.

"I'll visit," I promised. "I'll keep you entertained."

I was as good as my word, in and out of Mary's hospital room every spare moment. And by Friday, Mary was propped up on pillows, joking with her children and welcoming guests—even the First Lady.

From the hospital room doorway, Eleanor shook her head in amazement. "Here you are, trussed up like a turkey in that hospital bed, and yet you're still playing hostess! I told Franklin that nothing can kill Mary Rumsey."

"Certainly not a horse," Mary replied gaily.

But she was very tired, and once Mary drifted off, the First Lady turned her attention to me. "Have you decided what you're going to wear to my costume ball?"

The Washington press corps was hosting its annual dinner at the Gridiron Club, yet again excluding all women—even female reporters. In retaliation, the First Lady was hosting a competing event to make them sorry. And knowing that I didn't want to go, she said, "Frances, you must help me deliver a comeuppance. You *especially* cannot let this insult to women pass."

"Why me especially?" There was, after all, a smattering of other women in government now. Caroline O'Day was in Congress. Josephine Roche was now assistant secretary of the Treasury. "Surely another lady can carry the mantle for all womanhood for one night."

"Every other member of the cabinet was invited to the Gridiron dinner," Eleanor said. "You alone were excluded, and not one of the gentlemen in the cabinet declined the invitation in solidarity."

"Oh, really, I couldn't care less—if I attended, the press would only roast me and the New Deal, and I'd be expected to sit there and grin about it."

"They'll roast you anyway," she said. "Behind your back. And do I need to mention that you could do better with the press?"

I'd recently been described in the newspaper as a frosty schoolmarm who refused to suffer foolish questions, all of which might be true. And now Eleanor said, "Reporters need to see we're just ordinary people."

She was herself anything but ordinary. Many people believed she had an ungainly appearance, and her enemies said her "horse teeth" were worsening with age. But Eleanor had learned to be enormously charming by way of a disarming tendency to share her thoughts and feelings. She didn't mind being vulnerable even to strangers.

And they loved her for it.

I thought I'd managed to beat down my instinctive New England horror at this, but the prospect of a costume ball stirred up discomfort all over again. And she could see it. "Show these reporters that you're human," she advised. "That you can let your hair down on occasion."

"Why must it be *this* occasion? Whatever I wear to a costume ball will be ridiculed. It will seem as if I'm frolicking while working people suffer. I think this the worst possible idea. What are *you* going as?"

"A European peasant girl," Eleanor replied.

I shook my head, wondering how she dared risk the comparison to Marie Antoinette, playing at peasantry. Then again, the press corps liked Eleanor because she wasn't in a position of formal power or authority. They'd probably let her get away with it. They wouldn't make allowances for me. "I couldn't possibly attend; I can't miss visiting hours at the hospital."

Eleanor scowled ferociously. "I already know the hospital makes exceptions for you. So come to the masquerade, wear a costume, and please don't make me bother Mary about this; she needs to spend her energy getting well, not trying to talk sense into you."

It was cunning of her to threaten to drag Mary into this quarrel. Sometimes it occurred to me that Eleanor and Franklin Roosevelt were more alike than they were different, and this was one of those times. Weakening, I asked, "*If* I came to your costume ball, would you mind terribly if I brought Susanna?"

Eleanor smiled in victory, pulling gloves on as she prepared to leave. "*When* you come, of course you must bring your daughter. The girl deserves some cheer. Now, please give my love to Mary when she wakes."

About an hour later, a nurse came with medications. Mary managed to swallow them all down, then noticed me working in the chair next to her bed and gave a wistful smile. "Frances, darling. You're still here . . ."

"Where else would I be?"

"At this hour?" Mary asked. "I should think you'd be home in bed, getting some well-earned rest."

"I find it more restful to keep my eye on you. The last time I left you to your own devices, you let a horse roll on top of you."

She wheezed out a laugh. "You're not devising a plan to regulate fox hunts, are you?"

"I might; they're barbaric, as I've told you before."

"You're right. I shall give them up. You've reformed me."

"Reform *is* my speciality."

"Was the First Lady here?" Mary asked.

"Yes, don't you remember? We all had a lovely conversation before you drifted to sleep."

Mary sighed, then reached for me with one of her bruised hands. "Life is full of surprises, isn't it? I always supposed it would be my husband who would dote on me in old age."

I took her hand and protested, "You're not old; you're younger than I am."

Certainly, I didn't think of myself as elderly. But of course, there was a hue and cry against civil servants serving past the age of forty. And in the rest of the country, the aged who couldn't work were helpless, and the able-bodied were being squeezed out of employment.

"You know what I mean, Frances. My accident has forced me to do a great deal of thinking, and I want to say something serious now . . . These years since my husband's death have been a little empty. I was making the best of it; really, I was. But this past year and a half of living with you has been exhilarating. I feel guilty for saying so, because I know how difficult it's been for you, but I'm so grateful to you for this time we've had and all the excitement of doing important things together."

I gave her hand a warm but tender squeeze. "I'm the one who should be thanking you. I could never have taken this job if it weren't for you. I've leaned on you terribly hard for help with Susanna and everything else—even to give me a roof over my head. You've eased my struggles, but you've also magnified the joys."

How lovely her smile was at hearing that. "We've leaned on *each other*, I assure you. Isn't it a great comfort to know that we'll always have each other? We won't end up wandering about in aged confusion, so terribly lost and alone in the world."

I nodded, vowing, "You'll never get rid of me."

"Fortunately, we *do* get on rather well. Give us another few years together, and I believe we shall conquer the world."

"I'll settle for conquering poverty in America."

Mary sniffed with mock disdain. "That's the problem with you, Frances. You always think so small . . ."

Chapter Sixty-Three

Washington, DC
December 1934

MRS. ROOSEVELT'S *WOMEN'S ONLY* MAS-
querade ball was already proving to be the social sensation of the season. More than five hundred women
were in attendance, dressed in elaborate costumes as queens, founding mothers, movie stars, and more.

It was the first masquerade ball to be held in the White House in
nearly a century, and, having fully recovered from whooping cough,
Susanna was terribly excited to come along.

Greeting us in the East Room, the First Lady clapped with delight at my daughter's costume. "Don't you look lovely, Miss Masked
Ballerina!"

Then Eleanor turned her gaze to my costume with considerably
less approval. "Oh, Frances, really. A cap and gown and not even a
mask? That's hardly in the spirit of masquerade."

"But frugal," I said, as I'd been awarded several honorary degrees
in the past few years, so I had the cap and gown handy. "I've come as
a member of the president's fabled brain trust."

Eleanor chuckled ruefully. "That's not going to win you any
points with the press."

"It's not going to lose me any either," I replied. "If a photo is
printed, at least it won't be something silly for people to mock."

With an exasperated sigh, Eleanor straightened the white kerchief atop her head. "Have it your way." Then she disappeared into the crowd.

She'd planned a costume parade and contest, but refreshments were kept simple—the most novel being fresh peanuts.

It was, I admit, a jolly time. Despite all my grouching beforehand, I quite enjoyed myself. I chatted with ladies dressed as Spanish dancers carrying castanets, Dutch girls in wooden shoes, and even audacious movie stars like Mae West.

Susanna and I left the party *certain* that Mrs. Roosevelt had utterly eclipsed the chauvinistic Gridiron dinner, and we couldn't wait to tell Mary. But in the hospital room, my daughter was suddenly struck with just how difficult a recovery Mary still had ahead of her. Susanna's coming-out party was only two weeks away, and she said, "I think we should cancel. It wouldn't be right if Mary couldn't attend."

"Oh, you mustn't cancel," Mary insisted. "The show must go on. Besides, I'm getting better every day. Look at me wiggling all my fingers and toes. In two weeks, I'll insist they discharge me in a wheelchair if need be, so I won't miss your big day."

A WEEK LATER, I paid my daily call to the hospital, keen to ask Mary what she thought about the radio speech I gave. And I found her ashen-faced brother, Averell Harriman, outside her door.

Through the window to her room, I saw that Mary—who had been bright-eyed, rosy-cheeked, and filled with mirth only a few days ago—now looked pale and clammy.

"What's happening?" I asked, then turned to the doctor. "Was it a blood transfusion? Are you sure you gave her the right blood?"

"Quite sure," the surgeon said. "We think it's pneumonia."

Pneumonia. Dreaded pneumonia. I'd long known it for a vulture of a disease, preying on those in a weakened state. Now, sitting beside Mary, I realized that she needed to cough—to clear her lungs. But it was agony for her because of her broken ribs. Her breathing was labored as she blinked in and out of awareness, whispering only a few words, none of them terribly lucid.

Nothing can kill Mary Rumsey, Eleanor had said.

I clung to that, repeating it to myself like a prayer, grasping Mary's hand as if *I* were the drowning woman. How desperately I wanted to blow my own breath into her lungs.

Yet Susanna and I could only join Mary's weepy family in sitting vigil, hour after hour.

Mary's gasping battle went on into the night.

She just needs to get through this, I thought. But each pained lift of her chest became shallower until, finally, at nearly eleven in the evening, there was the most terrible silence.

"She's gone," someone whispered.

And I sat in numb horror. I wanted to reach into the bed and shake Mary's frail and limp body. Surely some mistake had been made. I simply refused to believe this was happening. It was too sudden, too shocking, too surreal to be anything but a terrible dream. Mary couldn't be gone. I simply had to wake myself up from this nightmare.

But try as I might, digging my nails into my palms to keep from sobbing, I finally began to accept that Mary's death was a cruel reality from which neither she, nor I, would ever awaken.

RICHEST WOMAN IN WASHINGTON DEAD

That was the headline. And oh, how it embittered me. As if Mary Harriman Rumsey had done nothing and been nothing more in her life than *rich*. She was so much more than that . . .

Surveying the crowd gathered for Mary's funeral service, I saw diplomats and millionaires grieving alongside girls barely making wage. I saw a vast sea of people whose lives Mary touched through a lifetime of generosity.

And the pain of losing her left me in such a stupor that I could barely speak to anyone who attempted to console me. Other than polite exchanges, I focused my mind on the details—the large spray of flowers sent by Sinclair Lewis, the fine purple velvet drape over her casket, the music that accompanied her on the way out of the church. It was all tasteful, and I hoped it would meet with Mary's approval . . .

When the pallbearers carried Mary away, the First Lady and I walked closest to the casket by previous arrangement. But after the service, only I would accompany my poor deceased friend and her family to her final burial ground in New York.

Perhaps regretting that she couldn't go on that last sad journey, Eleanor reached for my hand. And for once, I let her take it without hesitation, knowing we'd be bound forever by this mutual grief.

For nearly twenty-five years of my life, Mary Rumsey had been my touchstone. She wasn't my first or only cherished friend but my dearest. I knew her before my husband. Before my daughter. Before Franklin Roosevelt.

In some sense, I knew her before I knew myself.

Mary had recently been more of a partner to me than Paul. And without her, I somehow felt a stranger in my own skin. Before she died, she'd asked, *Isn't it a great comfort to know that we'll always have each other?*

Now that comfort had been obliterated.

I didn't know how there could be life after Mary here in Washington, where we'd lived together for nearly two of the most difficult years of my life. Mary had played the role of hostess, advisor, friend, guardian, and even substitute parent to my child. Now what would I do without her?

I was still wondering this when it began to snow, and Averell approached. "Frances, I'm so terribly sorry, but I must speak to you about the house . . ."

I braced against the chill winter wind. "The house?"

Averell's gaze was steady. "With Mary gone, it won't make sense for her estate to keep paying the lease."

"No, I suppose it wouldn't."

He winced. "Perhaps I could sign it over to you and you can find another roommate."

He was right to guess I wouldn't be able to pay the lease on my own. Between my husband's hospital bills, my daughter's college tuition, and the apartment in New York, I'd depleted my savings. Now, a painful lump rose in my throat, over which I managed to utter, "Oh, no, I couldn't imagine living there with anyone else."

It wasn't a lie; the expense aside, I'd resent someone else coming down the same staircase Mary bounded down each morning. Even now, when I closed my eyes, I could *see* her reading the newspaper in the living room, fingers twirled thoughtfully in her polka-dot scarf. I could smell her perfume and feel the warmth of her feet propped up next to mine by the fire . . .

No, I would not do it.

That decision made, I stood arrow straight as Mary's steel casket was lowered into the earth next to her father, the railroad tycoon who had worked his way up from errand boy to titan of American industry. With his money and indulgence, Mary might've done anything with her life—or nothing. Instead, she'd chosen to do *everything* with gusto.

I didn't cry, but my daughter was more like her father, capable of letting herself show great emotion. And I embraced her, stroking her hair, wishing I could think of words to comfort her.

Together we took handfuls of wet earth to drop onto Mary's grave. I clutched mine so tightly that the soil became a heavy ball, and when I let go, chunks of it fell onto the casket with hollow thumps that echoed the now seemingly hollow beat of my heart.

Chapter Sixty-Four

New York City
December 1934

THE NEXT NIGHT WAS SUSANNA'S DEBUT; Mary's death had come so suddenly that there wasn't time to cancel. And now I didn't seem to have the strength in my hands to help zip up Susanna's dress for her party. It took three tries, while my daughter's mood swung wildly from grief to a spark of excitement about coming out into society.

"Mary said the show must go on," I reminded her, though I couldn't make myself believe it. In the Rainbow Room that night, my own mood swung between love for my daughter and the notion that when the band struck up, we'd all be dancing on Mary's grave.

Hearing people laugh seemed a cruel affront, an insulting reminder that the world carried on. Still, I tried to grin and bear it as guests congratulated and complimented me.

You must be so proud!

—so pretty, and a college girl, too—

A real credit to you, Frances.

I did take pride in Susanna. There she was, in her beautiful gossamer gown, looking for all the world like a redeeming angel. Thankfully, as the evening wore on, Susanna lost herself to the merriment, which meant I could slink away to splash some water on my face in the powder room.

There I ran into Congresswoman O'Day, who took me by the arm. "How are you holding up, Madam Secretary?"

I smiled weakly. "As well as can be expected . . ."

"Here, drink this," she said, pressing a glass into my hand. "It'll help."

It was only a cocktail, not nearly strong enough, but I downed it anyway. "I'm afraid it's going to be a grim Christmas."

"*Another* grim Christmas," she said. "For the country, I mean. But at least you've given them hope for a better year ahead. People are counting on us to deliver. So you must let me know if there's anything I can do to help with the social security plan. If you need me to make phone calls, or even provide a quiet place to lay your head, my house is your house. And I'm going to do all I can to shepherd your bill through Congress."

I thanked her profusely, not daring to confide that there was no bill yet. And that there might never be one. Or how much I dreaded returning to Washington without Susanna, who would be going back to Bryn Mawr.

Nevertheless, I was on the train the next morning, en route to a very dark and empty house from which I was soon to be evicted.

On the foyer table, I found a notice that payment on utilities had been stopped.

No one could say Averell Harriman was inefficient . . .

All the Christmas decorations were gone. Only a trail of pine needles remained where our tree had been, as if Ebenezer Scrooge had passed through and snatched it on his way. Despite the cold, the front door was ajar and the hall crowded with boxes—most of Mary's things already packed up. The servants were gone, too, and I was almost thankful for that, for it left me with the privacy to wander from room to room, consumed with memories.

Mary at the dining room table, twisting her pearls at any particularly concerning headline. Mary by the old stuck window, wrestling it open herself to fend off summer heat. Mary arranging flowers on the entryway table while we bickered about Red being invited to dinner . . .

That's when the grief *fully* took hold of me.

I sank down there, on the stairs, holding my head in my hands, fighting back the sobs that were dammed up behind my cold shock.

I was nearly fifty-five years old. My best-beloved friend was dead. My husband was in an asylum. And I'd just launched my sometimes-troubled daughter into the world as a grown woman. I was feeling miserably sorry for myself.

And terribly, terribly alone.

Which is why I was so startled by the knock on the half-opened door. I looked up to see my young solicitor and suffered a pang of guilt, for Charlie Wyzanski had probably been sent to remind me that I had thus far failed to produce the social security plan the president wanted—and it was nearly Christmas.

I hastily cleared my throat. "Something wrong at the office?"

"Always," Charlie replied, stamping the snow off his feet. "And hello to you too. I just wanted . . ." He held out a tin. "Well, I just wanted to give you this. Rugelach. From my mother. We serve them during Rosh Hashanah to usher in a sweeter new year, but I thought they might not be amiss this Christmas."

"Well, that's very thoughtful."

He dug his hands deep into his pockets. "I'm awful sorry about Mrs. Rumsey."

"Thank you. Yes. We all are."

He glanced at the remaining furniture draped in sheets. "Where are you going to go now?"

I pried the lid off the tin of cookies. "I'm going home." *There*. I said aloud what I'd been thinking, which freed me to say more. "I'm going to resign and return to New York. I never wanted this job. People don't think I'm good at it. And without Mary, I can't do it."

His eyes narrowed and his voice took on an edge. "Well, in that case, I'm leaving too."

I glanced up in dismay. "Oh, no. It's different for you. You have a brilliant career ahead of you in government." I savored a bite of cookie. "My compliments to your mother, by the way."

I patted the stair beside me, inviting him to sit and share them with me. He sat and took one. "I'll be sure to tell her you liked them in my next letter."

"You don't call?"

"Letters keep us from arguing. My mother expects them every day, but I don't write as frequently as all that."

It was absolutely the most Charlie Wyzanski had ever shared with me about his personal life. "My mother was the same. What do you write to her about?"

"Mostly I complain about the work you pile on me and your pie-in-the-sky ideas."

We both laughed. Then, fondly, I said, "I threw you right into the deep end of the pool, didn't I?"

"I didn't think much of your methods at first," he admitted. "Now I can't imagine staying if you go."

A bit of cookie stuck in my throat. It took a moment to swallow it down with my emotions. "Oh, my dear boy. I simply must change your mind. We can't both leave; the department can't lose its gray matter."

He shook his head. "Your successor will want someone better and more experienced anyway."

"More experienced, maybe," I admitted. "Not better. There's no one who understands what we've done, and what we have yet to do, better than you."

"*You* do," he said, letting me stew in the unspoken accusation of abandonment.

He didn't have to say it outright. I read it in the slump of his shoulders and his hangdog expression. And all at once, I felt as if I were drowning in guilt and couldn't stay afloat. "My leaving isn't a whim. I'm dealing with altogether too much in my private life. To begin with, my husband is very ill."

"I know," Charlie said.

"No, you don't," I murmured. "I tell people he has the flu, or somehow or other indicate that he's an invalid, but Paul isn't sick the way people think. Physically, he's strong as a bull. It's his mind. Or rather his mood . . . he suffers from an up-and-down disease."

"Manic-depressive insanity." Charlie stared at his polished oxfords. "Unfortunately, I know all about it."

I sucked in a breath, terribly embarrassed. "I've spent so long trying to keep it a secret . . ."

"I'm sorry. I overheard Miss Jay negotiating your medical bills." The next words he spoke sounded as if he had to pry them out from between his own teeth. "My father had it. We had to have him committed."

His father had died just that past summer. Charlie had gone home to Boston for the funeral, and I'd sent a wreath. I hadn't any idea of what the man suffered. "Oh, Charlie, I wish I'd known."

He shrugged. "It wouldn't have been any better if you'd known. It might've been a good deal worse."

I sighed deeply. "What a terrible illness. There isn't any wound to dress. There isn't any broken bone to set. You can't see what's wrong, and it makes one feel so—"

"Helpless," Charlie finished for me.

"Then you, of all people, must understand how hard it is to leave my own husband under the care of doctors. I visit him when I can, but I keep thinking that maybe he'd get better if I were back in New York. Maybe he could come home again."

"Or maybe you'd go crazy yourself trying to cure something that can't be cured."

I hugged the tin. "It isn't only Paul that I'm worried about. It's Susanna too." I didn't want to tell him about her struggles with extreme diets, so I said, "She's going through a very troubled time."

Charlie shrugged. "She's a teenager."

"Yes, but I know mental illnesses can be hereditary. There's a strain of madness in my family, too, and she is near to the age her father was when he first exhibited signs of the illness. Which is even more reason I ought to resign and spend more time with her."

"You can't move into her dorm room, can you? Besides, if it's hereditary, there's nothing you or anybody else can do." Charlie turned his head away, but not before I glimpsed the ticking clock the young man guarded just behind his eyes. For the first time, I saw terror that his father's illness might one day snuff his genius right out. And now I knew the reason for Charlie Wyzanski's burning ambition. He feared he was in a race against his own brilliant mind.

Dear God, he reminded me of Paul in that moment. Hadn't he always? I had the strangest thought that if our son had lived, he would have turned out just like Charlie . . .

We both lapsed into a somber silence, and I knew we'd take this conversation to the grave. "New Englanders don't talk about things like this, do we?"

Charlie grimaced. "No, we don't."

"In private matters, we don't like to cause a fuss."

"No, we don't." He seemed to warm to the subject. "We don't complain about the weather either."

I laughed a little, in spite of myself.

Charlie wiped crumbs from his tie. "You know what else New Englanders don't do? We don't quit."

At those words, I felt a rush of heat up the back of my neck. "Oh, you don't dare call it *quitting* when I've just explained—"

"If you resign now, no one else will make social security a reality. Not even the president. Not without you."

"Well, I'm flattered you think so, but no one is indispensable in a democracy. There's always someone else who can move the work forward."

"Sure," Charlie said. "Someone else might do it someday. Maybe in a generation. Maybe in twenty years or fifty years or eighty years." I squeezed my eyes shut as if to deny his words, but he kept talking. "Miss Perkins, sometimes there's a man—or a woman—who is made for a moment. I happen to think you were made for this one."

His words touched my heart but also threw me into utter despair. "Even if that were true, I can't get it done. The president needs the plan on his desk by Christmas. I'm not even going to have a home, or electricity, by tomorrow."

Charlie tapped his watch. "We've still got twenty-four hours."

I didn't know what to think of this earnest young person who apparently believed in me. Was I like him when I was his age? Not as brilliant, but perhaps as confident in my judgment of people. I wondered if Florence Kelley felt about me the way I was coming to feel about Charlie. So in the end, I decided to let him be right about me . . .

Social security was the trusty parasol with which I hoped to fend off American poverty. If I'd been born to do anything, it was this. "All right. Bring me the telephone and let's see what we can get."

Charlie summoned his assistant, the even younger Thomas Eliot. And I summoned the whole committee. I didn't give anybody the opportunity to grouse about ruining their holiday. Instead, I slammed a big bottle of hard liquor on the dining room table, poured each of us a glass, and said we weren't leaving until it was finished.

Thus, the Social Security Act was hammered out at Mary Rumsey's table, with her belongings boxed up in the corners and the electricity set to be cut by morning. We decided on a plan around two or three o'clock in the morning.

Now we had to get it through Congress.

Chapter Sixty-Five

★ ✶ ★

Washington, DC
January 1935

I T WAS HARD TO BELIEVE THAT ONLY A YEAR ago, Mary and I were clinking champagne glasses and laughing late into the night. Now she was dead and buried, and my social security plan was dying of a thousand cuts in Congress too.

It's communism, that's what it is!

—unconstitutional and written by Jews—

Taxes are already too high!

Though we'd campaigned on a social security plan during the midterms and won on the strength of that promise, Congress didn't want it. To be more exact, their financial backers didn't want it. Big business had already conspired to kill any meaningful change behind a big Blue Eagle; when that didn't work, they lined up against my reforms. And they were winning . . .

By March, no lesser authority than the *New York Times* ran the headline saying,

HOPES ARE FADING FOR SECURITY BILL

For once, the newspapers were being too kind. Hopes weren't just fading. They'd evaporated. Social Security was dead in the water, and a petition was being circulated for my ouster, calling me *the Most Dangerous Woman in America*.

Which prompted a sympathy call from an old friend . . .

"Hey, sweets," Red joshed. "I hear you've still got some job with the government . . ."

I hit back with, "And I hear you're still trying to write a good book."

"Touché! So, listen, I happen to be passing through to meet with my publisher. Let me take you to lunch."

I glanced at my watch. "I'm afraid I can't. I'm going to visit with Paul and then catch a train back to Washington."

"C'mon, France, I know you're in need of a little consoling, courtesy of the Lewis Comforting Corporation, Ltd. Besides, you've *got* to forgive me for *Ann Vickers* sometime."

"Oh, I've already forgiven you," I admitted. "I didn't have any choice. These days I simply haven't the energy to spare in holding a grudge."

"That's good to hear, I think," he said, a hint of mischief in his tone. "Because you might not like your role in my new book."

"Oh, Red," I said, dismayed. "Can't you find someone else to write about? You know I'm under fire. My reputation cannot take any more gossip."

"Don't worry. It won't be that kind of book. I'm thinking of writing a novel about the rise of American fascism. I want it to be a real kick in the pants for all those complacent fools who keep bleating, *It can't happen here.*"

"I'm afraid to ask, but where would I fit in?"

"I think that in the book, you're going to be defeated on the ballot for the presidential nomination in '36."

I strangled the telephone cord. *Dear God, had alcoholism robbed him of every crumb of good sense?* "That's worse! You'd be making a mockery of my—"

"To the contrary, this book is going to be deadly serious. Long ago, I promised that if you found a way to change the world, I'd write about you. Well, you found a way, but now you're floundering, with the president's reelection at stake. You need my help."

"I really don't. *Please* tell me there's a way of talking you out of this."

"Now, now, as a government official, you'd never try to stifle the rights of the free press, would you?"

"You might be surprised," I grumbled, thinking of a recent altercation with a photographer who took my picture without permission.

"I know you're having a hard time of it, France. But just indulge my brilliance and promise you'll still like me when all is said and done."

"When did I ever say I liked you?"

He laughed. "Say we'll still be friends."

"All right." I sagged in defeat. "As it happens, I'm running short on friends in this world . . ."

"Well, no matter what happens, you'll always have this ugly, scrawny redhead in your corner."

THE RUMOR IN Washington, *again*, was that Roosevelt was going to fire me. And when I next visited the White House, I sincerely hoped he would. I found the president working on his stamp collection, sitting with his withered legs on a curved chair to get some relief from the aches and pains.

He gave me a toothy smile, lifting his magnifying glass to examine a stamp he held up with tweezers. "Are you settling into your new place, Frances?"

"Yes, thank you, Mr. President. Congresswoman O'Day is a pleasant roommate."

"I meant your new office."

The construction of the new Department of Labor building was nearly complete. Its majestic white columns mounted the new Federal Triangle complex like a temple to human toil, and I was its high priestess. At least for now. So I said, "I like it so much that I spend most of my time there. As you've no doubt heard, there's a shower . . ."

Roosevelt grinned. "I read something in the papers about how you're refusing to share your bathroom with your solicitor."

I scowled with renewed affront. "The architect who planned the building never considered that a woman might be showering in that bathroom and it ought not to be shared with men."

"Oh, Charlie Wyzanski seems like a nice young fellow," the president said, poking fun. "You don't trust your protégé to knock before he enters?"

I trusted Charlie a great deal but stoutly insisted, "In absolutely no circumstance would I risk an employee coming across my underthings."

This sort of primness always made the president laugh—and now he laughed until he was red in the face. Slapping his knee, he said, "I hear you even made the architect brick up the adjoining door!"

I hugged myself against his mockery. "Yes, and the architect no doubt leaked the story to the press, who have been painting me ever since as a prissy duchess who pampers herself with taxpayer-funded bath salts."

Roosevelt dabbed his eyes, which still danced with merriment. "Do you prefer violet-scented salts or lemon verbena?"

Ignoring his mischief, I tried to get to the point of why I'd been summoned. "I'm hearing Social Security is stalled on the Hill. I suppose you have bad news for me."

"None that you haven't heard already. No, I called you here because my missus tells me you've declared war on the American press."

"They declared war on me first."

All the sniping little stories about how I allegedly backstabbed General Hugh Johnson—*Just like a woman.*

How my salary was too high—*It's not like she's a husband with a family to support.*

How I shouldn't charge speaking fees—*The average woman usually needs no inducement to talk!*

It had all made me very cross.

"Frances." The president now said my name with an edge to his usual conviviality. "You've been quite unlike yourself these past few months. You're lashing out."

"Why shouldn't I? I stand accountable to the public for my work, not my bath salts."

He waved off this complaint. "Oh, you're not angry about a few nasty stories. You've been snapping at student groups, confronting photographers . . ."

I couldn't deny any of it. He probably didn't even know that I stopped serving ginger ale and Lorna Doones at press conferences. Let the jackals buy their own butter cookies!

Now the president eyed me with concern. "Eleanor thinks the rumor that you're a secret Jew is eating you up."

I snorted. "If I were Jewish, I would be proud to say so. No, the people behind that rumor are just angry that I managed to save a handful of children from concentration camps. It's too pathetic and transparent a smear for it to bother me."

Or so I told myself each night.

"But you *are* angry, Frances," he said, putting me under his magnifying glass. "It's simmering behind your eyes."

"Oh? What do I have to be angry about?"

I could think of a dozen things, but he said, "Mary Rumsey."

I winced at her name, as it still felt like too fresh an open wound. "Her death was an accident. There's no one to blame."

"Not even God?" he asked softly.

Despite the gentleness of his tone, his words struck me with the force of heresy. One cannot be angry with God, after all. It would be childish. Is that the kind of woman he thought I was?

Roosevelt indulged my silence with the knowing patience of a wise father. "Everyone gets angry at God at one point or another . . ."

For the first time in my life, I couldn't meet his eyes. I walked to the window and stared out at the lawn.

"It's natural to be angry with God," he continued, speaking to my back. "Unfortunately, it doesn't do anybody any good, so we lash out at everyone else instead."

I glanced over my shoulder at him, remembering that he was a man of great pride. Being cut down in the prime of his life—deprived of the power to walk—must've seemed like the cruelest injustice from the Almighty.

Maybe he'd raised his fists at the sky.

Maybe he'd cursed at God.

Yet, as far as I knew, he hadn't taken it out on anybody else. He'd found a way to become better from the loss. A better man, a better leader, and even a better friend. And now he was also trying to be a better child of God. "Have you been to church?" he asked.

Still hugging my arms around my middle, I admitted, "I don't think I could find the words to pray just now."

"God already knows the words in your heart."

Well, I certainly hoped not. In the name of a supposedly merciful God, I'd spent my career remedying the senseless suffering of strangers while the lives of my nearest and dearest were cruelly afflicted and extinguished. I could see no reason for Paul's illness or Mary's death. No purpose. No divine plan. And if I were to pray to God, I might damn well demand an explanation . . .

FDR gently suggested, "If you can't pray about Mary, then just pray about something. Anything. Talk to God about how to move forward with strong and active faith to revolutionize the country with the Social Security Act."

Maybe I would. After all, God only knew how the bill would ever get passed. *It will take a miracle*, I thought.

And in the end, a miracle is what we got . . .

Chapter Sixty-Six

★ ★ ★

Washington, DC
Spring 1935

Dear Miss Perkins,
President Roosevelt gave us great hope but was it only a feint,
with the promised helping hand snatched away at the last mo-
ment? Congress is putting the selfish interests in this country over
the common people. If we cannot get your modest Social Security
plan passed, then the federal government should just tax the rich
and redistribute the wealth.
Sincerely,
Mrs. PQ, Ypsilanti, Michigan

Letters and telephone calls rained down on the nation's capital from
furious Americans. After five years of the worst economic calamity to
ever befall the United States, their savings and patience had run out.

The elderly were reliable voters and they *demanded* old-age pensions. Moreover, they no longer cared much about which plan got it
for them, whether it was Roosevelt's Social Security or Dr. Townsend's
proposal that elderly Americans receive two hundred dollars a month
from the government. Or maybe Huey Long's Share Our Wealth
program, an attack mounting on Roosevelt's political left flank down
in Baton Rouge.

I thought neither of those two other plans was sensible, but the
ideas spread like wildfire, spawning clubs with millions of members.

Which put the fear of God into the nation's elite class.

Speaking on the telephone with another businessman who suddenly wanted to throw his support behind Social Security, Roosevelt crowed, "Oh, now *my* plan doesn't look so radical, does it?" The president let me listen as he continued, "If we don't lend a hand to millions of folks out there who've lost everything, they'll be sitting ducks for nationalist demagogues. Just look at what happened in Italy and Germany. It's going to come to blows one day. We've got to give our people a reason to believe in our democratic system so they'll stand up for it. If we want to keep our American way of life alive and well, we need to give our folks some security and a democracy worth fighting for."

It was the first time I heard Roosevelt make that explicit. The first time I knew he was casting a wary eye over the sea in anticipation of a titanic clash of ideas. Maybe even another world war . . .

And from that day forth, I'd see the preparation for it in every move we made.

WITH THE PUBLIC at our backs, the Social Security Act sailed through the House but hit roadblocks in the Senate. I'd been back and forth to the Capitol at least a dozen times during the wrangling. And as they stripped out health care and disabilities while granting all manner of exemptions, I told myself, *Just remember the canneries.* I was still willing to take half a loaf and come back for the rest later. I was ready to compromise nearly *anything* to get the thing started. Even so, nothing quite prepared me for what the president had to say in the Oval Office.

"They're going to pass your plan in the Senate," he said, his tone oddly subdued for such good news. "But you aren't going to like their terms, Frances."

I already didn't like that I was hearing about these terms from the president himself and not from one of the members of Congress with whom I'd been working so closely. "What do they want to take out of the bill now?"

"You," Roosevelt said.

I sat, folding my gloves in my lap. "*Me?*"

"Congress doesn't want you to have anything to do with Social Security," Roosevelt explained. "They've agreed to establish a board only if they can remove all authority over it from you."

I tilted my head in complete confusion. "I don't understand. How can—"

"It's petty malice," Roosevelt said, his expression softening. "They want to punish you, and that's all there is to it."

Stung, I asked, "But why? If they like my plan—"

"Frances, it's no secret that you've made enemies in Congress. They don't like that you're a woman, they don't like when you advocate for black workers, they don't like what you said about Southerners and shoes, and at least one senator is hopping mad that Miss Jay was rude to him when he came to see you."

My hands went to my cheeks in dismay. "Miss Jay is rude to *everyone*, but I can have her apologize and—"

"It won't help. The plain truth is that, well, you've become a lightning rod."

His tone let me know that he'd made a decision and that I had to accept it. So I took a deep breath, reminding myself that I'd always known the day might come when he'd sacrifice me for politics; he'd be a fool not to, and he wasn't a fool. The country couldn't afford for him to put loyalty or friendship or my personal pride before their interests. He really would have to fire me, and if I meant to keep my dignity, I wouldn't make it hard on him.

But oh, how it stung!

Squaring my shoulders, I said, "Well, you must accept the deal, of course. If getting rid of me is what it takes to get social security through, then it's a small price to pay. They needn't go through the humiliating shenanigans of stripping away my authority. I'll write up my letter of resignation by morning."

Roosevelt frowned. "Now, why would you give them the satisfaction?"

Because this is a slap in the face, I thought. How could I carry on as secretary of labor while having the program I championed stripped away? "If it makes you feel better to send me off on some European trip—"

"I'm not getting rid of you, Frances."

"Well, you *should*," I said as my hands tightened in my lap. "I never meant to become a lightning rod."

"The hell you didn't. You've been a lightning rod since the day we met. Did you think I didn't know who you were when I hired you?"

We both smiled a little at that.

Finally, I asked, "But how could I continue on with any political effectiveness?"

"You'll find a way to stand your ground and turn it all around on them to get what you want. Just like you always do." Then, more emphatically, Roosevelt said, "Haven't I told you how much I appreciate all you've accomplished? Maybe the country doesn't know what you've done, but *I do*."

His expression was free of guile. He meant it. His praise was an unexpected kindness, which always made me emotional, and my voice rasped as I told him, "Thank you, Mr. President, but you have to think about your reelection campaign, and if I've become this unpopular, I don't want to be a drag on the ticket. This is the easiest time for me to go. You have a friendly Congress willing to confirm anyone you want to replace me."

"I don't want anyone else." He patted my hand. "You mustn't

worry about this thing with the Social Security Board. You won't really be cut out. I'll appoint anyone you want. Give me a list."

He wanted me to take this like a good soldier. But I was so tired of marching. "The truth is, Mr. President, I want to go. I've wanted to go home since Mary died. Before that, even. I haven't a lease anymore, and I've already started sending my belongings back to New York. I want to be a good wife and mother more than—"

"Frances, how can you be so selfish?"

I startled. "*Selfish?*"

He pointed a finger right at me. "You heard me. You know I've got Huey Long populist demagogues rising to the left of me. And I've got greedy Wall Street on the right, plotting a coup. Because heaven forbid anybody in this country tries to make life just a little more decent for everybody."

I tried to get in a word, but he wouldn't let me.

"No, Frances. You're the one who nagged me into this. You shoved a list under my nose. Well, you can't just start a thing and skip off into the sunset. You have to see it through. Once the bill passes, the social security system will have to be set up, and it will have to be defended in the courts."

I wilted at the thought that the Supreme Court might strike down the law. But the president sat ramrod straight in determination. "If the courts strike it down, we'll have to start again from a different angle. We've got to use the momentum to our advantage. Do you understand?"

"*Like suffrajitsu,*" I murmured to myself.

Then Roosevelt's steely eyes pinned me in place. "Whatever you think, Frances, I didn't make a mistake when I appointed you. You've got to stick with me. You know better than anyone how much the people of this country need help."

I did know it—from painful personal experience, too, thanks to my family's fragile financial house of cards. Yet most of the country was in *much* worse straits . . .

"Well, I'll think about staying, Mr. President. But let's not consider this matter sewn up."

Chapter Sixty-Seven

Washington, DC
Summer 1935

I MADE MY PEACE WITH THE COMPROMISES needed to pass the Social Security Act, and it cleared the hurdle in the Senate in the middle of June. Then it went to the conference committee while I fought the urge to bite my nails to the quick until I got word it was headed for final passage.

It wasn't everything I wanted. I could rattle off a thousand objections to the law as written, but it was a start. And the president was euphoric. FDR had said, *No government can or should solve all the problems of every citizen, but we'll help to cushion the blows of life from cradle to grave.*

That was his own succinct way of expressing our vision for Americans who, by making monetary contributions throughout their lives, would be entitled to the benefits that would guard against future economic depressions. And, freed from the worst terrors of injury, sickness, poverty, and agedness, they could turn their attentions to invention, entrepreneurship, and public service.

It would make us a stronger nation.

A more competitive nation.

A nation with a bright and secure future.

That was our dream. A lovely dream that we were manifesting into being. And despite all the sacrifices, I knew it was a moment to celebrate. With his staff gathered and his drink cart at the ready, Roosevelt shouted, "Have a cocktail, Frances! I'm feeling so good I may just be brave enough to fire Mrs. Nesbitt so we can get a decent meal around here."

Every bit as elated, I said, "I *will* have a cocktail, Mr. President, and you can make it a double."

"That's the spirit," he said.

We were all over the moon. Once the bill was signed, a *million* suffering Americans were going to get help right away. And millions upon millions, generation after generation, would know an American existence no longer dependent entirely upon the cruel and fickle whims of fortune.

Eyes twinkling with triumph, FDR handed me one of his special martinis. "Frances, when I sign this bill into law, I want you standing behind me smelling of lavender or lemon verbena or whatever you use in your bath."

Everyone laughed, and I took it in good humor. "I'll be there, Mr. President. Freshly bathed and wearing my tricorn hat."

Because Social Security might not be as bold as some of the things they tried in Europe, but here in America it was nothing short of revolutionary.

NOW, WHERE IS my hat?

On the day of the signing, I was running late—my hands shaking and my stomach roiling with upset—for I'd been awakened by a call from my husband's sanitarium, telling me that Paul had gone missing. On this day of all days . . .

Of course, my first instinct was to hop on the morning train to New York City and lead the search. But if I wasn't standing behind the president when he signed the Social Security Act, the press would demand to know why. And if they went sniffing, it would all come out.

All of it.

Eleanor's long-ago warning to lady reporters had helped to shield me for a time, but if given the chance, every newspaper in the country would dissect Paul's psychosis and vivisect my marriage. They'd humiliate my husband. They'd shame me and embarrass my daughter while she was still struggling to find a place for herself in the world. All this to say nothing of stealing attention from the president's signature act.

I *had* to be at the signing, but how was I to pretend all was well with cameras in the room? If only Mary were here, she'd know what to do. About all of it. But I was now very much *on my own.*

When I finally found my hat—which I'd somehow overlooked in exactly the place it should be—I didn't have time to pin it. I'd have to do it in the car. Then, as soon as I got to the front door, I had to turn around for the pens I'd promised to bring to the ceremony.

The president wanted to give them out as tokens of thanks, and I'd chosen them specially, knowing what cherished keepsakes they'd be. Clutching them to my heart, I told my driver, "Just this once, you're going to have to run a red light or two."

We sped to the White House, and I raced into the crowded Cabinet Room. I normally prided myself on being unflappable, but I felt like a nervous wreck, mopping sweat off the back of my neck, wilting under the swampy August heat and the floodlights of the press all gathered there.

Then the president wheeled in, balmy and cool, wearing a summer suit of ivory linen. He beamed, motioning me to the front. "Come stand over my shoulder while I sign, Miss Perkins."

"Thank you, Mr. President," I said, knowing what an honor it was to be asked. And a thumb in the eye of my enemies in Congress too. So there I stood between Roosevelt and the fireplace, over which a portrait of Thomas Jefferson presided.

FDR didn't normally belabor the signing of bills—but Social

Security was special. This time he practiced, getting the various copies of the bill in order.

As he did this, I caught glimpses of myself in the reflection of the desk, which had been polished to a mirror finish. How strained I looked. I couldn't do anything about the circles under my eyes, but I breathed deeply, willing myself to calm. I just had to get through this ceremony, then I could slip out, hop on a train, and look for Paul.

I imagined all the possible ways in which tragedy might yet befall the father of my child while the clock on the mantel ticked down just behind me and Franklin Delano Roosevelt signed into law the most important legislation of my life, his presidency, and the century.

The president gave the first pen to Senator Wagner. Another went to Congressman Lewis in the House, and so on. Meanwhile, I was so preoccupied wondering where Paul might've gone—and what he might have done to himself—that I allowed someone else to jostle forward and get the last pen.

Until that moment, I hadn't realized how much I'd wanted one, but now I felt the loss of it as a keen physical pain. I had to scold myself. It was only a memento, whereas the achievement it represented was, hopefully, eternal. Besides, I had much more important things to worry about than a pen.

FDR looked at the cameras and spoke directly to the American people. "Today, a hope of many years' standing is in large part fulfilled." He wanted the citizenry to understand that "if, as our Constitution tells us, our Federal government was established among other things 'to promote the general welfare,' it is our plain duty to provide for that security upon which our welfare depends."

The Social Security Act was, he said, the *cornerstone* of the New Deal. Flashbulbs popped around the room and pen snatchers glad-handed with the president, and though I was eager to get away, he called me to heel.

"Frances! Come with me into the Oval."

It was a command, so I followed him as he wheeled himself out, nattering on about how he was going to have the rose garden redesigned. As if I cared!

Only once we were out of earshot of the others did he ask, "Is something wrong?"

I didn't want to spoil the day, so I tried to make light of it. "Oh, just some family high jinks. My husband has gone missing, you see, and I'm going to have to rush back to New York to find him. It's happened before and everything turned out all right. A little marital game . . ."

FDR played along. "We all have our unorthodox conjugal amusements . . ." Then his eyes softened. "No doubt Paul is chafing under supervision. I understand it. I've been known to escape my Secret Service agents from time to time. It isn't easy for a man to lose his independence, you know."

I sucked in a breath, having never thought of mental illness as a different kind of handicap. Instead, I'd come to think of Paul as more of a needy child than a husband. Sometimes I'd even let myself get resentful. Now, with FDR's words, I felt chastened, more sympathetic and understanding. "You're right. I must remember Paul's situation must be even more frustrating for him than it is for me."

The president nodded. "I'm not the man Eleanor married anymore either, and she's had to put up with an awful lot. I imagine you have too."

Truthfully, I wasn't sure how much Eleanor put up with; she'd long since abandoned the wifely duties of day-to-day living. Yet FDR always spoke of her with unshakable gratitude for all they still shared. And I needed to learn to follow his example. "Mr. President, do you think I could slip out without being noticed by the press?"

He peeked out and nodded. "But before you do, at least take one breath to savor the moment. Did you get a pen from the signing?"

"No, I didn't," I said, with a little shrug, as if it didn't matter. "The pen snatchers got them all, but it's all right."

Seemingly horrified, he fumbled in his jacket. "Well, then you must have mine."

Bracing against just how much I wanted that pen, I said, "Oh, no, I couldn't."

He knew I couldn't. It would be the most churlish thing in the world for me to take it from him. But he insisted. "No one deserves it more than you. Take it with my most heartfelt thanks and appreciation."

I shook my head, afraid to speak for fear I might *blubber*. I even backed away, but he stopped me by reaching for my hand, pressing the pen into my palm, and gently closing each finger over it.

"Don't argue with your president," he said.

Then our aging hands—which had achieved something together both historic and magnificent—clasped in intimate but pure communion.

"Frances, this is just the foundation. Stick with me and help me build on it."

I looked up to see tears—actual tears—glistening in his eyes.

"I need you," he said. "Really, it's personal, I suppose. I know who you are, what you are, and what you'll do, what you won't do. You know me. You see lots of things that most people don't see. You keep me guarded against a lot of things that no new man walking in here would even think to protect me from."

This tearful personal plea was meant to be the coup de grace. For there is no feeling on earth like being understood, seen, and valued by someone who has a great and terrible job to do, and who must do it, even if it kills him. And I began to wonder if I could ever leave Franklin Roosevelt if he wouldn't let me go.

Chapter Sixty-Eight

New York City
August 14, 1935

FROM A BOOTH IN THE RESTAURANT, PAUL sheepishly folded a cloth napkin in his lap. "I just wanted some egg foo yong. Then I realized I didn't have any money . . ."

The Chinatown restaurateurs on Mott Street had been kind enough to let him use their telephone to ring up our apartment building on Madison Avenue, and the doorman got hold of me straightaway. Now I felt more relieved than I could express to find my husband safe and sound.

Sliding into the booth beside him, I tried to keep my voice steady. "Darling, don't you realize what a fright you've given me?"

"I'm sorry," Paul said. "It was a beautiful day, and I wanted a walk down Fifth Avenue—remember when we used to take Susie in her baby carriage?"

"Yes, I remember."

He ran his hands through that thick mane of hair that I liked so much, even now that it was turning snowy white. "Well, I got lost. Then it started getting dark, and I was so confused and hungry . . ."

"That must've been terrible. That's why you must stay at the facility until you're not so confused."

His gaze dropped to his hands as if he, too, feared that day would never come. "I know I have to go back, but can we have dinner together first?"

I was surprised to find myself considering it. He seemed calm enough now, but at any moment he could shout or cause a scene. It was risky, but I was still a bit of a gambler. "Well, I think that's a marvelous idea. It's been ages since I've had egg foo yong."

We used chopsticks that night, and toasted one another, pretending our egg rolls were champagne glasses. Glancing up at the silken hangings, Paul suddenly said, "I think we once ate here at this very restaurant with Sinclair Lewis to celebrate the publication of one of his books."

"You're right. Red's first book, in fact." I smiled at the memory.

Paul smiled, too, but his was tinged with that old wry amusement. "You know, I hated him in those days. Him and his cleverness. It was always so easy for him to make you laugh, whereas I had to work at it."

I reached for Paul's fingers. "Darling, it was easy for Red to make me laugh because I didn't care if he thought I was a silly woman, whereas I wanted you to take me seriously."

Paul chuckled. "Of course, now I'm remembering how much you disliked Franklin Roosevelt in those days, and all the terrible things you said about him. My, how things change . . ."

I laughed, sipping oyster soup from my spoon. "Oh, I stand by what I said. Roosevelt was terrible back then. Thankfully, things change, and people do too."

"Everyone but you," Paul said.

"Goodness, I hope that's not true. I like to think I'm still learning and growing."

In fact, I believed I was learning and growing in that very moment.

Ours was such a troubled marriage, but I was learning to accept the blessings of good times between the bad. Learning to cherish the moments of Paul's lucidity. To salvage *something*, even if it could never be everything I wanted. So, taking a deep breath, I asked, "Do you want to know what I did today, Paul?"

"I very much want to know."

I told him about the signing of the Social Security Act. I explained how the system would work; how it was based, in tiny part anyway, on many discussions we'd once had. And my husband positively beamed when I said, "If it hadn't been for you, Paul, waxing poetic about the brilliance of insurance, I don't know that I would've clung to the idea, or been able to convince the president."

"Thank you for saying that, Frances." His smile turned wistful. "It makes me feel as if I did at least one or two things right in my life . . . that it hasn't all been madness."

"Oh, *Paul*," I said, laying my hand atop his.

"No, no, don't pity me. I pity *you*. That of all the women in the world to be saddled with a madman for a husband, it should be someone as sensible and sane as you."

"Sensible and sane?" I gave a little snort and shook my head. "Well, I see I have you fooled. Really, when I think about it, Paul, marrying you and starting a family was one of the only sensible and sane things I've *ever* done. I think I've been a little mad my whole life long."

After all, I'd fashioned myself, almost from the start of my life, as a crusader. I'd decided as a young woman in a country that denied me the right to vote that I had the duty, and the capacity, to make a better nation.

That was as much madness as it was hubris.

"Certainly there's nothing sensible or sane about what I have been doing for the past two and a half years."

No entirely sane person would willingly subject themselves to the strain, sacrifices, slander, and smears of public office. Even less sane to do it as the first woman in such a role. Yet Roosevelt had me considering staying on, because I'd formed a determination to end poverty in America as we knew it. Now I was on the cusp of doing it. So maybe a spark of madness was what it took to accomplish anything truly revolutionary in this world.

OF COURSE, AMERICAN poverty was not obliterated with the stroke of Roosevelt's pen that summer. To begin with, the new Social Security Board had to be appointed, funded, and staffed as a separate agency.

The first public assistance checks wouldn't go out until early in the next year, and payroll taxes to fund the program wouldn't be collected for another two years. The states would have to create their federally compliant programs, and the Social Security Act itself would have to survive the scrutiny of a hostile Supreme Court.

That's why I braced myself in November when Charlie Wyzanski came into the office, freshly barbered, smelling minty like Aqua Velva. Given the way he paced between my desk and the American flag in the corner, I sensed he had bad news. And the taste of my morning coffee went stale in my mouth. "Is there a challenge to the Social Security Act in the courts yet?"

Charlie scratched the back of his neck and hesitated before answering. "Well, I've heard there's a machine company in Alabama that—"

"Never mind," I interrupted. "I can't bear to hear the details."

The legal wrangling was now out of my hands. It'd be up to the Justice Department to defend the Social Security Act in court. Until then, we'd have to live in a state of nervous suspense.

With a brief sympathetic smile, Charlie finally said, "Miss Perkins, I'm sorry to have to give you this . . ."

He pulled an envelope from his inner jacket pocket, and my heart stopped as I realized it must be a resignation letter, no doubt written by hand in his cramped script. "Oh, Charlie, don't you dare. What happened to our solidarity of last Christmas when we said we wouldn't quit?"

As the room filled with the sound of Miss Jay's clacking type-writer in the outer room, Charlie cleared his throat. "I'm not quitting in the way you think. When you first took me for a raw recruit, I—well, I didn't realize that you'd open my eyes to a great many things—most importantly, to a moral obligation . . ."

I realized that this was a farewell speech—and in a desperate gambit to fend it off, I said, "If your own judgment tells you that you must go, then of course I'll assent and be grateful for all that you have done. But, Charlie, you've become like a stout walking stick for me. I should find it very difficult—if not *disastrous*—to lose you as an advisor, thinker, and counselor."

His gaze softened as he reassured me, "Miss Perkins, you could never lose me as that. It's only that someone competent must defend our New Deal legislation at the Supreme Court. And I believe it should be me. I've decided to go to work for the Department of Justice."

I wanted to protest—even to beg him to stay—but I could see from the ambition still burning in his coal black eyes that his mind was made up.

A profound sense of sadness washed over me to know I'd no longer have a real confidant in the office just next to mine. That this young man, who had become like a son to me, would no longer be fighting at my side. But he wasn't leaving the fight, which he made clear when he added, "I hope you won't think me too arrogant, but the plain truth is, I don't trust anybody else to defend our work and your legacy."

As his words sank in, I melted in bittersweet gratitude. "Truth-fully, my dear boy, I'm not sure I trust anyone else to do it either."

In fact, I was deeply moved that he believed I might have a good legacy to defend. Would it be one shaped by my own hands and heart? Perhaps. At least in part. But I knew that, in time, when I was finally too old to brandish my parasol for another battle, my legacy would be shaped by those who came after me. And as I watched Charlie walk away, his shoulders squared for the fight ahead, I felt hope for the future.

Glancing down at my desk, I realized that I was finally becoming accustomed to what I saw on the nameplate there.

FRANCES PERKINS, SECRETARY OF LABOR

For nearly three years now, the title had sat uneasily upon my shoulders—I'd wanted to cast it off at the soonest opportunity. But now it finally felt like mine, and I decided I might just keep it a little while longer.

Epilogue

Ithaca, New York
March 1963

I T'S ANOTHER SNOWY MORNING, AND I HAVE another list in my pocket.

Nothing so grand, this time, as a program to transform America. These are just bullet points written in print large enough for me to read now that my eyesight is fading. A list of things I wish to say at a speech I've been invited to give for the fiftieth anniversary celebration of the Department of Labor.

In truth, I was both surprised and delighted to receive an invitation to speak. After all, it's been decades since I was anyone of importance.

Thirty years have passed since Franklin Delano Roosevelt first asked me to be his secretary of labor. Thirty years, and a world transformed . . .

In this time, I've seen another world war, the dropping of the atom bomb, and astronauts orbiting earth. All of which is to say nothing of the rise of Elvis Presley and the appearance of the miniskirt . . .

But I have also seen the world transformed by the lasting achievements that Franklin Roosevelt brought about with my help. I still remember with complete clarity that snowy evening I went to meet FDR with a list of ambitious goals in my pocket . . .

Where have all the days gone?

My grandmother always said that in America, one must be

prepared to go up suddenly or come down suddenly, and one has to do either with grace. As it happens, there wasn't anywhere to go but down from Roosevelt's cabinet—in which it was my honor to serve for an unprecedented twelve long years.

FDR always found some reason to reject my resignation, flattering me, bullying me, and even tearfully pleading with me not to leave him in the midst of a fight with Hitler. In the end, of course, Roosevelt was the one who left *me*, dying suddenly of a brain hemorrhage just before we won the Second World War . . .

That was nearly twenty years ago, and a grieving country learned to move on. So did I, eventually. Now I eke out a living in academia, writing the occasional book. And my name—if mentioned in the press at all—pops up in New Deal retrospectives or trivia questions.

On good days, I like to think I've faded away as gracefully as the ink of old headlines. But on bad days, I feel like I've been clipped out and tossed into an old forgotten trunk in the national attic. So I'm flattered someone in Washington has thought to take me out of mothball storage, dust me off, and put me to good use again for the department's anniversary.

I'm excited at the coming dawn, and despite my creaky old bones, I'm up and dressed before the alarm clock goes off so I can make the bus, because I no longer have a driver or a car—and, with my vision impairment, I wouldn't trust myself to drive it if I did.

As I make my way down the stairs at Telluride House here at Cornell University, where I live in a little yellow room at the top of the stairs as a visiting professor, one of my students cries out, "Miss Perkins! Let me take your arm; the street is covered with ice."

I straighten my proud New England spine against the implication that I'm too old to contend with *winter*. But at more than eighty years of age, I dare not break a hip, and, discretion being the better part of valor, I beckon him with a sly smile. "Yes, do take my arm, young man. I wouldn't want you to slip and fall."

He startles at my deadpan humor, then laughs, looping his arm in mine and relieving me of my overnight bag. "Where are you off to so early?"

"To make a few remarks in Washington," I say cheerily as snow-flakes melt on my cheeks. "And after that, a stint on the *Today* show. Can you imagine the shock people will feel waking up in the morning and turning on their television screens to learn that damned old lady in the tricorn hat is still alive?"

My student isn't sure whether he should laugh. After all, the younger generation doesn't know what to make of me. The boys at Telluride House consider me a bit of a den mother, instinctively minding their manners and straightening their ties. Fortunately, I'm too hard of hearing for the antics of rowdy college boys to bother my peace, but I've still managed to overhear the occasional fragment of gossip.

How can she be a miss *if she was married?*
—has a grandchild, even—
You know, she was a wild-eyed radical in her day.

I suppose they cannot be blamed for their confusion, since a whole cottage industry of myths, malicious rumors, and controversies has been stoked about me over the years. And, as a prerogative of old age, I occasionally make myself quite difficult.

No, I won't take off my hat for faculty pictures. What do you mean I'll look more natural? Nonsense. I was born with my hat.

Nevertheless, my lecture courses—Politics and Conscience, The Prevention of Poverty, and US Labor History—are popular, and I am a patient teacher. Even when presented, as I was yesterday, with an earnest young man in the front row who interrupted me to say, "But in the United States, we have *always* had Social Security."

To which I had to bite the inside of my lip to keep from saying, *Oh, bless your heart . . .*

I must continually remind myself that my students came of age in the economic boom that followed the Second World War. They've never known the breadlines, the dust bowl, or a government indifferent to their safety, survival, or stability.

Social Security—which was expanded again and again to cover more Americans of every race and creed—is now so much a part of American psychology that I truly believe no politician, political party, or political group can possibly destroy it and maintain a democratic system. I suppose I should also be grateful that the reforms I fought for are bricks so firmly embedded in the edifice of our national life that Americans now take them for granted.

I buy a newspaper at the bus station, settle into my seat on the bus, and, after reading the headlines, squint at the obituary page in fear of learning that someone else I know will have died. As it turns out, to get old is to get very busy with funerals of friends and loved ones. Alas, I have outlived most of mine . . .

My grandmother. My parents. Florence Kelley. Mary Rumsey. Al Smith. Franklin Roosevelt. Sinclair Lewis. My husband too. All of them with the angels now. Just this past November, I saw Eleanor lowered into the grave next to Franklin, reunited with him for eternity under a slab of white marble that says not a word about who they were or what they did.

I suppose it doesn't need to, for I like to think that their names and deeds will echo for eternity.

At Eleanor's funeral, standing in the rose garden at Hyde Park again after so many years, I had a very distinct memory of Franklin pointing out the spot where he wanted to be buried. *Oh, Frances, everyone should make plans for the end. Or they'll do the damnedest things to you.*

I've decided to heed his advice. Not that I plan to die anytime soon—my grandmother lived nearly a century, and I believe I'm still spry enough to outrun the Grim Reaper—but I should like to arrange everything properly.

I've already chosen a service for my funeral, after which I'll be buried next to my husband in Maine.

I still sigh with a pang when I think of Paul.

In the last year of his life before the stroke that killed him, I brought him home to live with me. He wasn't so confused as he had once been; he wasn't ill, but he wasn't *well* either. He depended upon me completely—fearing for me to leave him. Yet that time together was a blessing, and I still carry with me the happier memories of days when youth, health, hope, and success all seemed to give promise of a long and interesting life together.

Now that Paul is gone, my main worry is how to provide for Susanna. As she came into adulthood, she suffered the same kind of breakdowns that afflicted her father. Fortunately, medical science has made great strides in developing treatments, so the tragedy has not repeated itself exactly, but depression and anxiety have robbed my daughter of all stability in life.

Her first marriage ended in adultery and alcoholism, leaving her without the means to support herself. Her second husband, my grandson's father, is a talented but struggling artist with limited resources. So, to ensure that they have a roof over their heads, I have them live in my apartment on Madison Avenue, where I visit as often as possible.

Of course, Susanna and I do quarrel when I visit.

Our relationship has not been easy over the years, as she is financially dependent upon me while holding me to blame for much of what ails her. And, truthfully, I am not always as patient with her illness as I should be. Certainly not as patient as Franklin Roosevelt taught me that I ought to be.

Once, during a particularly vicious argument, Susanna told me the only thing that was ever wrong with her father was that he stayed married to me, and that the only thing that was ever wrong with her was that I am her mother. It was the disease talking, but the hurtful words lodged like splinters deep under my skin where I can never seem to fully pluck them out. Sometimes I wonder if she is right. Did I sacrifice my family on the altar of public service?

If I did, all I can hope for now is that the sacrifice was worth it . . .

It's probably true that I failed my daughter in some respects as a mother, but at least I excel as a grandmother—I'm more patient and playful, letting Susanna's boy eat arrowroot cookies in bed while I read to him from Beatrix Potter. On long summers and school breaks, I relish time with little Tomlin, catching glimpses of Paul and me reflected in his eyes, which always fills my heart with joy. So, despite the inevitable strife with my daughter, I look forward to visiting my family on my return trip from Washington.

I ARRIVE IN Union Station without anyone shouting questions at me or even recognizing me when I step down from the train, and it feels almost like I'm getting away with something. It's rather *fun* to be without official duties or any heavy responsibilities to the nation, just another shrunken little old lady jostling with other passengers to hail a taxicab on the corner . . .

I make sure to get to the Sheraton early because I want to go over my notes. These days, with my bad eyes, I must do my best to memorize speeches because I can't count on being able to read them in the dim light of a banquet or lecture hall. Reviewing my speech—adding a word in the margin, scratching out lines that don't work as well as I hoped—I'm filled with memories, good and bad.

As the crowd begins to assemble at the tables, I see a few old friends and acquaintances, and I'm very glad to find that I haven't outlived them all.

Charlie Wyzanski is there, too, looking marvelously distinguished in middle age. It was Charlie who successfully defended the Social Security Act before the high court, and I give him credit for rescuing the New Deal. As reward, Roosevelt appointed him to the federal bench back in '41, where he's been serving as a champion of civil liberties ever since.

He has also remained a close confidant and dear, dear friend. So now, as he kisses both my cheeks, I say, "I was hoping to see you, Judge Wyzanski."

He reflexively adjusts his bow tie and asks after my family. Then I ask after his.

"Gisela sends her warmest regards," he says of his lovely, public-spirited Jewish bride—a refugee of Hitler's Germany. "Can you believe my son is in college and my daughter isn't far behind?"

"They grow too fast, don't they?" I ask, still remembering writing a note of congratulations upon the birth of Charlie's namesake. "I want to hear all about your family. We must catch up after the speech, so don't try to sneak out."

"I wouldn't dream of it," Charlie says.

In the meantime, waiters shuffle in and out, pouring coffee into gold-rimmed cups or filling our tulip water glasses, and I make polite chitchat with the other former secretaries of labor on the stage as we become dimly aware of a commotion at the back of the hall.

Then, to the surprise of all, the band strikes up a hastily arranged "Hail to the Chief."

Of course, I can never hear that song without expecting to see Franklin Delano Roosevelt. To me, no matter how many presidents have had that song played for their entrance, there is only one chief.

And oh, how I miss his sparkling eyes and the optimism I always saw shining in them.

But now America has a new president for a new generation. And through the fishnet veil of my caplet, I see John Fitzgerald Kennedy striding up in a tuxedo and gleaming white smile.

As the men on the stage jostle to greet him, the young president cuts his way through with hasty handshakes, trailing the scent of Jockey Club cologne, stopping only when he reaches me.

"Miss Perkins," Kennedy says, reaching for my hand and giving it a warm but gentle squeeze, as if he were afraid to break my aged bones.

"Why, Mr. President, what a nice surprise."

Kennedy isn't due to speak until later this evening, in the other banquet hall, and the waiters are scrambling to find him a chair, so I ask, "Has there been a change in the program?"

"No, there's no change in program," he says in that prominent Boston accent. "I came early because I wanted to hear your opening remarks."

It is a charming lie. And surely it must be a lie, because the president of the United States is far too busy to come listen to the reminiscences of an old lady. Especially *this* president, who has only recently averted nuclear Armageddon during the Cuban missile crisis.

But the boyish Kennedy seems quite earnest, motioning for his chair to be placed next to mine. "Jackie insisted I invite you to join her at a luncheon tomorrow. That is, if your busy schedule will permit. I told her there's no woman in America who has done more to earn a quiet retirement, yet here you are still hard at work, teaching classes, giving speeches and the like."

I'm every bit as flattered as he intends me to be. "One likes to keep busy, even at my age. And of course, I'd be delighted to attend Mrs. Kennedy's luncheon."

It is, after all, not my first encounter with the Kennedy family; I met Jacqueline when she was campaigning for her husband. I wanted Lyndon Baines Johnson for the nomination, but Kennedy has grown on me—especially since he's proposed a Medicare program to expand and supplement Social Security.

Now he tilts his thick head of auburn hair toward me to whisper, "I enjoyed reading your book about President Roosevelt. It was enlightening to see him through a woman's eye."

He means *The Roosevelt I Knew,* which I wrote and published in the year after FDR's death. It was a number one bestseller then, and remained so for two months, but it's been a long time since anyone mentioned it to me. "I'm flattered you found a copy and read it, sir."

"It ought to be required reading," Kennedy replies. "Personally, I'm as interested in what you left out as what you put in it. You were with him from the start, and I'm sure you know some juicy secrets from those days . . ."

"If I did, I'd take those secrets to the grave." I make a gesture as if to zip my lips.

He chuckles appreciatively. "Will you be publishing another book soon?"

"I hope so. I'm writing about Al Smith just now. You'd have liked him. He was a good Catholic, like you . . ."

We both smile with gratitude that America is finally enlightened enough to allow a man to say his beads in the White House. But Kennedy's comments take on a more pointed tone. "I rather hoped you were going to say that you were writing your own memoirs."

I trace my collar, a little aghast. "Oh, I'll never do that. I've left an oral history at Columbia University, and that will have to suffice."

"Surely you're tempted to tell more than the official version."

I laugh. "Only to the imaginary but appreciative audience in my head. They can't argue with my version of events, you see . . ."

Kennedy grins. "But you're a living legend, madam. If you don't write your own story, someone else will."

I shudder at the very idea. "I mean to make it difficult for them. Perhaps I'll burn all my papers."

I'm teasing, but the young president reels back. "Have you no sense of history, madam?"

"Absolutely none," I say.

Then we both laugh, because after all, we're gathered to talk about history.

While Kennedy drinks his coffee, I share stories from the old days, and he's especially amused to hear that my desk was infested with cockroaches—the size of which I demonstrate to him with my fingers, which gets a big laugh. Then I tell him, "Of course, back then, I thought I'd be the first in a long line of women in the cabinet, but there has only been one other, and that was during the Eisenhower administration."

"Regrettably true." Kennedy looks as abashed as a schoolboy at the implied criticism.

I know that schoolboy look, because FDR had the same one and I never let him get away with it either, so I dare to ask, "You've made efforts on behalf of other groups facing discrimination, Mr. President, but what have you done for women?"

Giving a dazzling smile as he fiddles with his white linen napkin, he says, "Well, I'm sure we haven't done enough. I think we ought to do better than we're doing for women, and I'm glad you reminded me of it."

He's humoring me as one humors old ladies. Kennedy is smooth and handsome and charming. What's more, he *knows* he's smooth, handsome, and charming. I bet he's gotten by, all his life, on those looks and that charm, just like FDR did before polio.

But Jack Kennedy is no FDR . . .

Nevertheless, when I rise to the podium to make my opening remarks, I feel the young president's attention is riveted upon me as I talk about our struggles during the Great Depression. I want these government workers to understand that what they do—and what they have done—is vital to the health of the nation.

When I'm finished, the president stands and leads the ovation. Then Kennedy is asked to make some impromptu remarks of his own, and he begins by saying, "I know that those who work for the federal government are frequently unsung and usually not spoken of in the admiring terms which I think they deserve. But I think it is appropriate on this fiftieth anniversary that we pay tribute to them."

That gets the expected round of applause. Then Kennedy continues. "The programs which Miss Perkins put forward when she became secretary of labor—things which we now take for granted in both political parties—were regarded as revolutionary thirty years ago. And Miss Perkins—who looks so quiet and peaceful and sweet—was also one of the most controversial, dangerous figures that roamed the United States in the 1930s."

The crowd laughs, and even I can laugh, despite the lingering pain of those slanders.

"We don't have child labor today," he continues. "But it was a hard fight getting rid of it. We don't have people working twelve hours a day. We don't have women exploited in the factories. All these things, however, took years of effort. But this gives us hope that some of the things which may be suggested today, which may be regarded as controversial, will be accepted as part of the ordinary life of Americans in ten or twenty years. That's what progress is. And everything we do now should be with that shadow of our very difficult past in our minds and the hope we may meet our task as our predecessors met theirs."

On this last note, he looks pointedly at me. And I hold my breath.

Everyone in the room seems to know he's offering tribute not only to the department but to me in particular, and the applause grows louder in volume. Then louder still.

It isn't right to single me out this way! Not with other former secretaries sitting on the dais. He's making a fuss, and it's so unseemly that my cheeks burn, forcing me to stare down at my withered old hands . . .

. . . but it is deeply gratifying too.

I finally look back up to catch the keen expression of President Kennedy as he claps for me from the podium. And I take in the smile of Judge Wyzanski, mind still sharp as ever. In the crowd, shining behind brow-line and tea-shade glasses, are the eager eyes of the women who now work in roles of importance at the Department of Labor. I feel, in their eyes, in this room, and in the nation itself, an eagerness to carry the work forward.

I often say that as secretary of labor, I came to Washington to work for God, FDR, and my country. Now maybe I can rest easy in the knowledge that a new generation has taken up the cause.

So I hope it shall always be. For we are only day laborers in the vineyard of the Lord, to lay our course of bricks in shoring up the republic.

I did my part.

The American experiment goes on, and our democracy isn't done. In fact, the battle for democracy is never done. And ours is worth *fighting* for.

Frances Perkins was the longest-serving secretary of labor in United States history, a member of President Roosevelt's cabinet during all four unprecedented terms in office. She was, for all intents and purposes, the architect and driving force behind much of the New Deal—an expansive set of programs that helped lift America out of the Great Depression, prepared the country to win the Second World War, and enabled at least eighty years of relative peace and prosperity. As has been noted by others, she is the most consequential cabinet officer since Alexander Hamilton. In short, there is no American life in nearly a century that has not been touched by Frances Perkins and her service to the country. And I believe every town in the nation should have a street named for her.

Yet most Americans don't remember her name. This, despite several excellent biographies that have been written about her. Frances Perkins also left behind a sweeping public record for scholars and researchers.

She did not, however, leave behind much of a record of her *private* life and the struggles she faced while transforming the country. And because of it, biographers have mostly shied away from exploring her fortitude and personal tragedies.

Fortunately, as has frequently been observed, novelists can go where historians rightly fear to tread. And it was my honor to ferret out clues, reconstruct hazy instances, and speculate about the inner workings of her heart and mind.

Frances was a trailblazer for women. And her well-founded fears about what might happen to her if she put herself forward as the first female cabinet secretary all came true. She faced constant misogyny, and her battle inside FDR's cabinet on behalf of Jewish refugees earned her the enmity of American Nazis, who eventually financed a humiliating, but failed, effort to impeach her.

Frances was an easy target for her enemies during her lifetime because she rarely let the public see any humanizing glimpses into her life. Americans hadn't the faintest idea the kinds of sacrifices Frances Perkins made for the country while her husband, and eventually her daughter, both succumbed to severe mental illness.

Fortunately, Frances was an even more religious woman than I have portrayed in the book, and her deep faith gave her solace in times of crisis. By the time she was drafting the Social Security Act, she sought out periodic refuge and silence in All Saints convent in Catonsville, Maryland, not far from where I live.

She also found solace and comfort in friends and colleagues. She continued to trust in and rely upon Charles Wyzanski Jr., who became one of the most respected jurists in American history. Yet his proudest work, he said, was with Miss Perkins, and in finding and defending the legal rationale to admit refugees fleeing the Nazis.

In recounting their remarkable two years together at the Department of Labor, he said, "I never met a person who equaled her firm adherence to principle. One of the noblest, strongest characters I have ever encountered. In courage, none exceeded her."

Her courage certainly stood out to me while writing this book. I didn't need to embellish her fending off pimps with a parasol. She had no fear of confronting bosses, factory owners, dynamite-wielding strikers, and corrupt immigration officers. In fact, there were more examples of her raw physical and moral courage than I had room for—including her steadiness during a failed attempt on her life by a knife-wielding maniac.

But as in every historical novel, liberties must be taken to create a coherent narrative—and I would now like to explain my choices and changes.

To begin with, whenever possible, I have incorporated lines from historical records into letters, inner monologue, or dialogue. A case in point is the exchange between Frances and Kennedy about women's rights, which derives from a question he was asked by a female reporter in a press conference. And as with all my novels, the craziest parts are true. For example, Frances Perkins and Sinclair Lewis did chase down a couple they noticed on the ferry, worrying for the girl's reputation, only to be embarrassed to learn they were married. Frances Perkins really was a personal witness to the Triangle shirtwaist factory fire. She really did get into a car crash and walk away to give a speech on Labor Day. And her husband really did run away from his caregivers the day Social Security was signed into law.

As it happens, Frances met many of the most important people in her life when she first came to New York City. When Frances met Eleanor Roosevelt we don't know, but she detailed *precisely* when she met Franklin Roosevelt at that tea dance, and how little she thought of him.

Whether Sinclair Lewis offered feedback on Frances's short stories I was unable to discover, but he did get her to read and offer critiques of *his* stories during that time of their lives, and perhaps long after. What's more, references to Frances Perkins really are sprinkled in several of his books. Frances did credit Lewis's second wife, Dorothy Thomas, with warning her about Hitler's unhinged plans, though records show she was already well aware. And Frances really was personally denounced by American Nazis at their Madison Square Garden rally, albeit in a later year than I mentioned.

Of course, there were even more amazing things I had to leave out. I was faced with an *astronomical* number of people Frances either befriended, worked with, or went to battle against. She knew everyone from political figures like Winston Churchill, to activists like Upton Sinclair and Rose Schneiderman, to wealthy industrialists like Alfred P. Sloan.

To keep the book from becoming a Who's Who of twentieth-century America, I decided to combine historical personages, limit mentions, or even omit people who were important to Frances, such as the humorous and loyal Henry Bruère, upon whom Frances leaned so much during her husband's illness, and Mary Dewson, who pushed for Frances to get the job as labor secretary. I didn't dwell on the socialist leader Joe Cohen, in whom Frances appears to have had her first serious romantic interest. I even left out Margaret Poole, one of Frances's closest and most generous friends. And I couldn't linger on the tremendous accomplishments and influence of her closest colleagues in FDR's cabinet, including Harry Hopkins, Henry Wallace, or Harold Ickes, the last of whom she first met on that snowy night in February when FDR asked her to be his secretary of labor.

I only brushed over the extended family of the Roosevelts, which included FDR's closest friend and advisor, Louis Howe. I also left out bodyguards like Earl Miller, confidants like Daisy Suckley, mistresses like Lucy Mercer, and secretaries like Grace Tully.

When it came to matters in Frances Perkins's life that were unknowable, I either avoided them, supplied my best guess, or allowed ambiguity to reign. For example, we don't know exactly *why* she changed her name from Fannie Coralie Perkins to Frances Perkins, and I have not dwelled much upon that decision. Nor have I spent much time wondering why she spelled it "Fanny" in her letters, or how she managed to get her date of birth wrong on official records.

I also sidestepped arguments with her parents about politics and her wish to convert to Catholicism. (Frances eventually became Episcopalian, which she jested was "halfway to Catholic," and I think she would be gratified to know that she has since been recognized as a saint in the liturgical calendar of the Episcopal Church, and her feast day is celebrated on May 13 of each year.)

Additionally, to keep the focus on Frances rather than FDR, I left out the scandal he was involved in as assistant secretary of the Navy. And though Frances Perkins was keenly interested in the welfare of Black Americans—continuing to examine her own internalized biases the rest of her life—I did not expand upon this because her accomplishments in this area were modest.

Finally, Perkins spent much of her term in office negotiating strikes and labor disagreements. She found these negotiations to be extremely tedious. I *also* found them to be tedious, so I didn't explore them. However, I regretted to leave out two incidents.

The first involved her commandeering of a post office so she could talk to union officials without the interference of hostile local law enforcement and company officials. The second involved her cursing out multimillionaire Alfred Sloane when he went back on his word and torpedoed a negotiation.

Frances had an excellent and colorful memory, but occasionally she was vague, mistaken, or putting a certain *spin* on the facts.

For example, the Triangle shirtwaist factory fire left a powerful impression on Perkins, and she credited it with a change of her life's mission. But the facts tell a slightly different story. The truth is that Frances Perkins was already working on issues of fire safety. In fact, she'd been investigating a similar fire in New Jersey. It's more likely the Triangle shirtwaist fire erased any doubts she might have been having about whether she should continue in her career.

In the wake of the fire, Frances also claimed officials tried to suppress her, going so far even as to demand her employer shut her up. She does not, however, recount a personal confrontation, so I was forced to fictionalize one.

Then there was the desperate phone call she received on the day of her wedding, where she refused to speak on behalf of a man who was going to prison. In her telling of the story, she claimed the man sentenced was the principal proprietor of the Triangle Waist Company.

However, it seems the proprietors of that company were acquitted of manslaughter, so I do not know to whom she was referring. What does seem clear, however, is that she was traumatized by this phone call. And so I wanted to include it in the book despite any inconsistencies in her memory.

Frances also recalled meeting up with the Rumseys in Paris either "before or after the war," but that doesn't seem likely given the historical time line, and I was unable to find any immigration records to confirm it.

For the sake of brevity, I compressed time lines, combined historical instances, and simplified her story. For example, the process by which the United States got a social insurance program is vastly more complex than outlined here, complete with academic rivalries, political skullduggery, and meetings of chance with Supreme Court justices.

Frances got help not only from Justice Stone at a tea party, but also from Justice Brandeis with his daughter as intermediary. Both justices quietly advised ways to make the bill pass constitutional muster.

Though Charlie Wyzanski was Madam Secretary's right-hand man, it was his underling, Tom Eliot, who did most of the drafting of the Social Security Act. Which is to say, many, *many* other hands went into making this program possible. But Frances Perkins was its moving spirit from the moment she accepted the job as secretary of labor, and decided she would, indeed, be the president's conscience and nag him into it. In fact, Wyzanski said she all but *forced* Roosevelt to have a social security program.

I've also simplified some of her other battles.

For example, Perkins had far more complicated feelings for Hugh Johnson than presented. She considered him an eccentric genius and liked him personally. However, the moment she sensed he was a danger, she began using her influence to undermine Johnson's authority. It was one of the most serious internal battles of FDR's first administration, and it was a battle Frances Perkins won.

I was also sorry to have to condense the political warfare behind the scenes between Frances Perkins's Labor Department and Cordell Hull's State Department, against whom she fought a mostly lonely battle inside the administration on behalf of Jewish refugees. Even when supported by Secretaries Morgenthau and Ickes, she took the brunt of the criticism for it.

She also fought the secretary of state on another front, doing the nation a great service by preventing the calling out of federal troops against the longshoremen strikers in San Francisco. But she paid dearly for it, and given the time line of this novel, I was obliged to omit the scandal resulting from her treatment of longshoreman labor leader Harry Bridges, which would ultimately haunt her career.

AUTHOR'S NOTE

There were, however, other matters about which I was perfectly happy to speculate and expand.

For example, I have no direct proof of where Paul Wilson was on the day of the assassination attempt against Mayor Mitchel or that it took place on the exact day Frances miscarried. But it is probable that Paul was nearby during the shooting, so I combined the events.

I also could find no evidence confirming that either Frances Perkins or Mary Rumsey marched with women in 1915, but I find it impossible to think otherwise, and if Mary did, she'd have been on horseback. Additionally, Mary joined Frances's maternity organization in 1925, but I have her involved much earlier, as she may well have been.

Unsure when Frances Perkins met "Miss Jay," I decided to have them meet upon Frances's ascension to the Industrial Commission in 1919. I was also unable to definitively uncover a gravesite or obituary for Miss Jay, so I do not know if she was still alive at the time of the epilogue.

According to Perkins's biographer, Kirstin Downey, Frances never told anyone how she met her husband—not even her daughter. In fact, in her oral history, Frances implies she doesn't *remember* when she met him. I find that scarcely credible coming from a woman who left us vivid recollections of even trivial details about everyone from presidents and prime ministers to secretaries and taxi drivers in France.

More likely, Frances considered the meeting of Paul to be an intensely intimate matter so she wouldn't be goaded into talking about it for any reason; and, like so many other things in her personal life that she wished to keep quiet, she did a remarkable job covering her tracks.

I was left to reconstruct how and where she might have met Paul, but Frances mentions that he must have helped put in a good word for her in Albany, so I had Mary play matchmaker, enlisting him to play the role of tour guide at the Albany state capitol in the place of Joseph O. Hammitt, the lobbyist for the Citizens Union. I also have Paul standing in for Mr. Hammitt in giving her the pep talk about what compromises she should accept in Albany.

While Frances downplayed her romance to her feminist friends, saying that she married Paul Wilson because she liked him and thought she ought to get marriage over with, their love letters tell a much different story. Their correspondence—some of which I have excerpted in this novel—is tender and poignant, painting a clear picture of a persistent friendship that blossomed into passionate love.

During an early, troubled time in their marriage, Frances wrote asking Paul to let her go, claiming that she was "something of a fool" and "an easy-going tender hearted woman who made some rotted blunders." Her implication was that the marriage was a blunder and that she was at fault for it. But she changed her mind after the birth of Susanna, and we can surmise her renewed joy in marriage from a few scraps of poems that she left behind, including one entitled "The Holy Trinity," in which she cherished the loving union of a mother, father, and child.

For those who argue that Frances Perkins never had a happy marriage, Frances was giving speeches at luncheons extolling the virtues of her husband and her happy private life as late as 1929. And when her husband was institutionalized, Frances wrote that tender poem about how Paul was the only person to ever make her feel as if she weren't alone.

This despite his disorder.

Still, Paul's descent into mental illness must have been acutely painful for her, and destructive to the marriage.

Of course, thanks to Frances, the actual manifestations of Paul Caldwell Wilson's mental illness are lost to history. It was an ailment not well understood at the time. But the approximate dates of Paul's worst episodes weren't difficult to pinpoint, and so I dramatized them. And given the few clues Frances leaves behind, they may have been very dramatic indeed.

As for the manifestations of Susanna's illness, I consulted Susanna's son, Tomlin Perkins Coggeshall, who lives with his husband in upstate New York and is active in preserving his grandmother's legacy. He recalled to me that Susanna's illness often manifested in a fear of being alone and that she sometimes spoke of how she shouldn't have been born. So I was guided by his words, as well as the record of what may have been a college eating disorder, in portraying her illness as it started coming to the surface.

There is no doubt that the legacy of Frances Perkins has been shaped, in part, by those who have embraced her as a member of the LGBTQ community. A prevalent belief is that Frances Perkins was bisexual and that Mary Rumsey was her romantic partner. In writing this book, I looked forward to exploring that possibility.

Therefore, I was surprised to learn that surviving letters evidence only what Frances's biographer calls "an intimate friendship" between the two women, whose relationship went back nearly twenty-five years. And when Frances's grandson shared with me his own reason for doubt about this speculation regarding his grandmother's sexuality, it fueled my own.

To be sure, there is circumstantial evidence for a romantic relationship, which I've included in the novel so the reader can draw their own conclusions about Mary and Frances: Mary's monetary generosity to Frances, their shared interests, the way she opened her home to Frances around the time she was first having marriage troubles with Paul, the shared living arrangements in Washington, Mary's veritable adoption of Susanna, and Frances's role in Mary's funeral.

It's entirely possible that Frances had romantic feelings for women in general and Mary in particular; certainly, many of their friends were lesbians, and the idea wouldn't have shocked them. But what seemed far less likely to me is that Frances Perkins—a highly religious married woman who took a dim view of marital infidelity—would have engaged in *any* sexual or romantic activity that might have exposed her to censure when she was under acute public scrutiny. And I hesitated to vividly portray something I had doubts about if it wasn't going to illuminate her character as I understood it.

In short, Frances once said she'd never give her enemies the satisfaction of seeing her compromise herself in matters of money, love, or some other way. And for purposes of this novel, I decided to believe her.

Finally, we come to the outright liberties I took with the book.

There is no clear-cut incident in Frances's life that obviously led to the distance she put between herself and her parents. But Frances says that she and her parents didn't see eye to eye on the plight of the poor. And Frances's leave-taking from home coincided closely with the actual historical accident in which one of the girls Frances was working with lost her hand, leaving young Frances to agitate to get compensation. This had to be traumatic for Frances and everyone in her family, so it was a ready catalyst, ripe for fictionalization.

Similarly, I needed an antagonist for Frances when she arrived in New York, and Miss May Mathews was handy. I unabashedly ascribed to Miss Mathews some opinions about social work that were expressed at the founding of Hartley House, but that she herself may not have subscribed to. She was, in fact, close to Frances in age, had a similar educational background, and probably shared much the same outlook.

Then I had to deal with the avalanche of introductions in 1910, when Frances Perkins seems to have met most of the important people in her life. For example, Frances said she met Mary Harriman Rumsey shortly after the latter's marriage to Charles Cary Rumsey in May of 1910, so Mary was likely on her honeymoon when Frances first met Franklin Delano Roosevelt. But I didn't want to add more characters to the story, so I let Mary make the introduction. Also, in the autumn of 1910, Sinclair Lewis moved to New York City, but Frances left no record of their meeting in Greenwich Village, so I decided to make him show up a little earlier so they could share a writing circle. And I was equally cavalier about his political opinions prior to 1933.

As for the early political opinions of Frances Perkins, she had many socialist friends, including her mentor, Florence Kelley, and her flirtation with Socialism continued until at least 1912 before giving way to progressive values espoused by Edward T. Devine.

Frances Perkins had a strong and fruitful relationship with Mr. Devine, who was ultimately a mentor to her, as well as an instructor. I made their relationship slightly contentious without doing violence to the facts—which are that he did turn her away when she first applied for a job, and she was also hopping mad when his organization turned down a starving child for relief, driving her to seek help from *The* McManus.

Frances Perkins recounted that she told Al Smith about the dynamite in Rome, New York, *years* after she settled the strike, and he reproached her for this. But I had her confess right away so that we could see their relationship develop.

She invariably called Al Smith "Governor Smith" and he invariably called her "Miss Perkins." She was equally formal with Charles Wyzanski and others. However, this formality could seem overly stilted to a modern reader, so I frequently departed from it.

Paul Caldwell Wilson and Franklin Delano Roosevelt were both struck with serious ailments at almost the exact same time, and very likely were treated at the same hospital, but the meeting between Frances and Eleanor was my own invention.

I also implied that Frances saw Roosevelt more than once during his polio illness from 1921 to 1924, but in fact she said that she saw him only once.

Though Frances herself in her oral history said that she was in New York when she heard the convention through a loudspeaker of a neighbor, the PBS special *Summoned* claimed she heard it in Maine, through the tree line. That seemed to me a more likely way for her to feel a religious epiphany of Franklin Roosevelt calling to her, so I went with it.

Frances said Belle Moskowitz was "snotty," dismissive, and insulting of FDR. She never said, however, that Belle was prejudiced against Roosevelt's disability. Nevertheless, I inferred it.

Frances Perkins was so skeptical of FDR's claim that he had voted for her fifty-four-hour bill that she eventually went looking in the old Senate records to find proof. I decided to have FDR send her the journal on loan as a grand gesture, both for brevity and humor.

Frances obliquely gave Susanna credit for "nagging" her into convincing Roosevelt to provide a public works program for artists. There was, of course, much more to the creation of the program than that, but I had Susanna broach the subject with Roosevelt because Susanna's interest gave Frances a sense of pride, and they bonded over the issue.

Judge Wyzanski's family and contemporaries describe him as

being extremely confident in his intellectual abilities, but the historical Wyzanski may not have been as cocky during interactions with Frances Perkins as I have presented in this novel. Moreover, Wyzanski recounted in his memoirs that Frances confided in him her marital troubles, yet his family doubts he would have confided his secrets in return. Even so, it seemed inconceivably cruel to let her discuss Paul's mental illness without him sharing that he knew precisely what she was struggling with. So I let them have a conversation they would take to the grave.

In her own book, *The Roosevelt I Knew*, Frances Perkins recalled that the president interrupted the signing ceremony of the Social Security Act to ask, "Frances, where is your pen?" And when she said, "I haven't got one," he commanded his secretary to get him a "first-class pen for Frances." Then he thanked her publicly and effusively.

I chose to dramatize this differently because of the way the news reporters described there being "pen snatchers" at the ceremony, and I wanted Frances and Franklin to share a private and profound moment.

Finally, Frances Perkins and Mary Rumsey adopted puppies together when they lived in Washington, which leads me to believe that Balto must have died at some point. But I chose not to include that in the novel because in my point of view, beloved dogs should live forever.

As should the spirit, patriotism, and legacy of Frances Perkins.

For more information, please visit StephanieDray.com.

ACKNOWLEDGMENTS

Historical fiction is always, in some way, a collaboration between the author, historical sources, and all the helpers she finds along the way. For this book, I had many helpers.

First and foremost, I am indebted to my superheroine of an agent, Kevan Lyon, and to my incredibly talented editor, Amanda Bergeron, whose feedback and suggestions always make my work better—and in this case, helped give it a shape that I couldn't have carved it into by myself. Thanks, too, to Sareer Khader for keeping the chaos at bay. To Lindsey Tulloch, for whom there are not enough fruit baskets or thank-you gifts in the world. Emily Osborne, for the active and powerful cover design, not to mention her patience with all my suggestions. Jin Yu, for her marketing genius and love of mythology. Loren Jaggers, for publicity expertise and good taste in mugs. Hillary Tacuri and Tara O'Connor, both of whom I'm getting to work with for the first time. And to the rest of the Berkley team, including Ivan Held, Claire Zion, Craig Burke, Jean-Marie Hudson, Christine Ball, and Anthony Romondo, for working so hard on my books and making the experience fun to boot. Can't wait to do it again, folks!

I am also enormously grateful for the following people, who were generous with their time and information: Tomlin Perkins Coggeshall for sharing his memories and insights about his grandmother. John Coggeshall for anecdotes about Frances, and Sylvia Chanler for connecting us. Charles Wyzanski, Anita Wyzanski Robby, and David Rintells—all family members of Judge Wyzanski, all of whom answered many questions and offered a fresh perspective. (I still think Judge Wyzanski needs a book of his own!) Ann Beaudry and Sarah Peskin from the Frances Perkins Center, the latter of whom served as a consultant on this book. Mark Sarney from the Social Security Administration for research advice. Rosalie Chanler for her memories of Daisy Suckley. Derek Baxter for sending me photos from the Department of Labor building. And Stephen Wyckoff for details about the Navy. In crafting this narrative, I drew inspiration from a collection of illuminating biographies, including *The Woman Behind the New Deal: The Life of Frances Perkins, FDR'S Secretary of Labor and His Moral Conscience* by Kirstin Downey, *Madam Secretary Frances Perkins* by George W. Martin, *The Courage to Meddle: The Belief of Frances Perkins* by Tom Levitt, *That Woman in FDR's Cabinet* by Lillian Holmen Mohr, and *Frances Perkins: A Member of the Cabinet* by Bill Severn. Credit also goes to Frances for her own book *The Roosevelt I Knew.*

Needless to say, despite all the help I received, any mistakes in this book are mine alone.

As far as critiques go, I am particularly indebted to Sheila Accongio, Lea Nolan, Stephanie Thornton, Michelle Moran, and Kate Quinn for reading early drafts of this book. Some of them even had to host an intervention to get me to delete an entire time line and point of view from the book.

I'd also like to thank Angie McCain, Martha Jane Swift, and other members of my Drayvanian reader group for giving feedback on early drafts and snippets. Veronica Zarate, Amara Borst, and Lisa Christi, for keeping the gears grinding when I was buried in the manuscript. Liz Von Klemperer, who made the trip to Columbia University to take photographs so that I could pluck out historical letters from Frances Perkins's papers to use in the manuscript.

A special shout-out must go to my readers, who review my books and recommend them for book clubs, and to my favorite bloggers and booksellers, like Lauren Margolin, Ashley Hasty, Jan Boston, Debbie Scheller, and Gary Parkes, who do so much for word of mouth. And to my agency sisters, the Lyonesses, whose talent, professionalism, and support humble me.

I also want to give heartfelt thanks to my family for their steadfast encouragement, and most importantly, my husband, who gives me so much love and support that it lifts me up like the proverbial wind beneath my wings.